AFTER CAMUS

Max Baer and the Star of David is a strange and strangely beautiful tale that conjures up a golden era of boxing in the way A. J. Liebling did in *The Sweet Science*. I was enchanted from start to finish, and when I closed the book I thought "Damn, this dude can write!"

—Gary Shteyngart, *New York Times* best-selling author of *Our Country Friends*

Neugeboren presents a meditation on life, love, art and family relationships that's reminiscent of the best of John Updike.

—Kirkus Review for *The Other Side of the World*

Jay Neugeboren traverses the Hitlerian tightrope with all the skill and formal daring that have made him one of our foremost writers of literary fiction and masterful nonfiction. This new book [*1940*] is, at once, a beautifully realized work of imagined history, a rich and varied character study, and a subtly layered novel of ideas, all wrapped in a propulsively readable story.

—Tim Ruten, *Los Angeles Times* for *1940*

Neugeboren's *1940* is a taut, nuanced, beautifully written novel that captures an anxious and uncertain time in ways that a straight rendering of facts and dates could never achieve. He casts a spell on the first page of his novel that never goes away.

—Peter Quinn, *Commonweal*

Also by Jay Neugeboren

Novels

Big Man
Listen Ruben Fontanez
Sam's Legacy
An Orphan's Tale
The Stolen Jew
Before My Life Began
Poli: A Mexican Boy in Early Texas
1940
The Other Side of the World
The American Sun & Wind Moving Picture Company
Max Baer and the Star of David

Stories

Corky's Brother
Don't Worry About the Kids
News from the New American Diaspora
You Are My Heart

Non-Fiction

Parentheses: An Autobiographical Journey
The Story of STORY Magazine (as editor)
Imagining Robert: My Brother, Madness, and Survival
Transforming Madness: New Lives for People Living with Mental Illness
Open Heart: A Patient's Story of Life-Saving Medicine and Life-Giving Friendship
The Hillside Diary and Other Writings (as editor)
The Diagnostic Manual of Mishegas (with Michael Friedman & Lloyd Sederer)

AFTER CAMUS

A NOVEL

JAY NEUGEBOREN

LAKE DALLAS, TEXAS

FIRST EDITION

This is a work of fiction, and is not intended to resemble anyone living or dead. Portions of this novel have appeared, in different form, in *Black Clock*, *TriQuarterly*, *Columbia*, and *Ploughshares*.

Requests for permission to reprint or reuse material
from this work should be sent to:

Permissions
Madville Publishing
PO Box 358
Lake Dallas, TX 75065

Cover Design: Kimberly Davis
The village in the photo is Eze,
on the Côte d'Azur near Nice.

ISBN: 978-1-956440-73-7 paperback,
978-1-956440-74-4 ebook

Library of Congress Control Number: 2023945351

For Tiffany Cui Ying Peng

One

He had had another good meeting with Micheline Rozan in the late afternoon, and so they were closer, Camus believed, to convincing André Malraux, France's Minister of Cultural Affairs, to provide government financing for a repertory theatre that would initiate and produce new works. Earlier in the day—welcome news—de Gaulle had for the first time declared himself and France (and for de Gaulle, as always, the two were one) in favor of self-determination for Algeria. Although de Gaulle's announcement would doubtless incite acts of violence from the right, Camus found it cause for optimism. For himself—thus his break with Sartre and others on the left—he hoped his native Algeria would not become an independent nation, but would, instead—a rare point of agreement with de Gaulle—remain part of France as a fully equal and independent *départment*.

And so, on this crisp, clear autumn day—September 14, 1959, three-and-a-half months before he would, at the age of 46, die in an automobile accident—Camus had taken himself to the Café de Flore, on Saint-Germain-des-Prés, a bistro where he had spent many happy hours with friends, and where—thus its special place in his heart—he had had the good fortune to meet several women with whom he had had pleasurable liaisons.

1

When he arrived, a young woman was sitting by herself at a table to the far side of the bar, and when he nodded to her, she inclined her head slightly. Her hair up in a chignon, she had the long, slender neck and erect carriage of a ballet dancer. Two of Camus' friends, Léon Bukzin and Guillaume Wiser, both Jews who had survived the war, and both men with whom he had worked on the underground newspaper, *Combat,* during the war, were sitting at their usual table, by a window that looked out on Rue Saint Benoit.

He joined them. They drank, they talked, and they found themselves in agreement that the right, feeling betrayed by de Gaulle's policy shift, would surely commit acts of sabotage, and might even attempt assassination. Still, like Camus, his friends welcomed de Gaulle's declaration, if with more wariness than Camus did—they declared him an innocent—while noting de Gaulle's shrewdness, as ever, in figuring out which side of history to be on, and in daring to begin a process that would lead, they hoped—though who could know the price—to full independence for Algeria.

Camus ordered a second *pastis,* and a coffee, and kept his eye on the young woman. Whenever he had looked her way, she had met his gaze. When he turned toward her now, however, she was removing small bandages from each of her feet. When she was done applying new bandages, he asked a waiter to invite her to have a drink with him. Several minutes later, she slipped a book into a green cloth bag, and left her table.

"You're Albert Camus, the writer," she said, extending her hand.

"I am," he said, shaking her hand, "but I trust you won't hold that against me."

"You're an exceptionally good writer even though you've won a Nobel Prize," she said.

She set her cloth bag on the floor, seated herself across from him, shook the hands of Camus' two friends, then turned toward him again. "I value your novels and stories enormously—more, in truth, than your philosophical musings," she said, "though the latter have their merits and, at times, their practical uses."

"Your French is impeccable," Camus said, "though—forgive me if I am wrong—I sense you are not French."

"I am American," she said. "Tolle Anne Riordan. I'm pleased you find my French worthy of praise, but I also notice that in flattering me you deflect praise of *your* writing, and I wonder why. Is there anything more important to you than your writing?"

Camus hesitated briefly. Then: "Your smile," he said, and when he did, his two friends rose, shook hands with Camus and with Tolle, and made their farewells.

"You are a dancer," he said a moment later.

"I am a dancer."

"And you are here because—?"

"I am here because I know this is a bistro you favor," she said, and added quickly, "and I am here—in Paris—because I'm preparing a ballet about Vaslav Nijinsky."

Camus tapped the end of a cigarette on the table, lit it. "Why Paris?" he asked. "Nijinsky was a Russian, and I believe he spent the better part of his life in Switzerland—in a lunatic asylum there."

"But he's buried here," Tolle said. "Also, through my mother, I've had introductions to people in Paris who have been assisting me in arranging to bring the ballet I've been working on to performance."

"Ah, then your mother is French," Camus said, "which explains your proficiency with our language. I thought at first that you might be Swiss or, perhaps, Belgian."

"My mother is American. She danced with *Le Ballet de l'Opéra de Paris*, after which she became a student, here in Paris, of Merce Cunningham. She was a member of his dance company for several years before I was born, though the ballet I have in mind, unlike Cunningham's creations, where music and dance were intentionally *not* coordinated, will be conventional with respect to these elements."

"I see," Camus said. "But wasn't Stravinsky friends with—not Nijinsky, but with the man with whom Nijinsky was associated? The name escapes me for the moment…"

3

"Diaghilev," she said. "Yes. But Diaghilev destroyed Nijinsky. Nor was Stravinsky much kinder to him"

"Strange I should forget his name," Camus said. "I read Nijinsky's diary when it first appeared—this was before the war—and I can still recall how profoundly he hated Diaghilev, a man who was also his lover, yes?"

"Perhaps," Tolle said. "Diaghilev wanted Nijinsky to find him other young boys. And he preyed on him financially."

"A drink while we continue our conversation?" Camus said.

"We can drink, yes, and we can continue our conversation," she said, "and in that way I can tell you about the story I have in mind for the ballet. I think you'll find it of more than passing interest, and then…"

She hesitated. Camus offered her a cigarette, leaned toward her, touched her hand with his.

"And then?" he asked.

"And then, if you like, you may accompany me to the cemetery to visit Nijinsky's grave."

Camus laughed, withdrew his hand. "I fear you are far too romantic for me," he said.

"Not at all," she said. "Not at all. But I do hope we will visit his grave together. That would please me."

Camus raised his glass. "To Nijinsky, who brings us together," he said.

Tolle touched her glass to his. "So," she said. "From what I have heard, for Albert Camus to spend a night with a woman, or to have an affair, is not so different from what is happening in this moment. Having a drink with a woman, that is, is not so different for Albert Camus than sleeping with a woman. Is that a fair asssessment?"

"I am an unreliable source of information," he said. "But tell me—your seeming self-assurance—does it come from your mother? Has her career been your inspiration?"

"By all accounts, my mother had undeniable talent," Tolle said, "but she chose to leave her dance career behind early in her marriage to my father in order to help him in his business ventures."

4

"Which were?"

She laughed. "More like *ad*-ventures than ventures," she said. "He fancied himself a sportsman—a term he used to define himself, though not in the sense that, say, Turgenev used it. My father is a man who loves, above all, to shine among other men. His great passion is for horse-racing, and so he has attempted to raise thoroughbreds, if on a remarkably inefficient scale, and here I deflect the inevitable question—Native Dancer was *not* one of his horses, since, as he would joke, in his stable his wife fulfilled that role."

"How crude," Camus said.

"Perhaps."

"Perhaps?"

"Whatever their deficiencies of character, my parents have given me at least two gifts I use without apology: a love for dance, and a sense of entitlement."

"The latter appears to be in abundance today," Camus said.

"And my parents' wherewithal—their money—most of which comes from my mother's family, and a significant portion of which became mine when I turned twenty-one a year and a half ago—enables me to do pretty much what I want, and what I want to do—one of my two current passions—is to create and produce a ballet about Nijinsky," Tolle said. "Nor is this a childlike chimera— I'm the founder and director of a small dance company in New York City. "

"And your other passion?"

"You."

"Are you usually successful in realizing your passions?"

"*Usually?*" She laughed in a way that made her suddenly seem to him who she was: a very young woman less than half his age who was delighted to find herself flirting with a famous writer she claimed to adore. "No," she said. "At the moment, however, my hopes are high."

"Ah," Camus said. "Thank you. For there we have one of the unarticulated adages by which I have tried to live: to keep my expectations low, but my hopes high."

*

In the morning, they stopped for coffee and *tartines* at a café near her hotel in the Marais, then took the Métro to Place de Clichy and walked to the Montmartre cemetery. She did not take his arm, and they did not hold hands. Before they had risen from bed, however, she had examined the tubercular scars on his chest, tracing them with her tongue and fingers while, intermittently, talking about Nijinsky's madness and noting—what caused Camus to pull away from her—the fact that after Nijinksy died, a medical examiner, in hopes of discovering the secret of Nijinsky's legendary leaping ability, had cut open Nijinsky's feet to see if the bones or formations within were different from those of ordinary men.

Above Nijinsky's grave, seated on a slab of tombstone, was a statue of Nijinsky dressed as the puppet Petrushka. Camus had not seen the gravesite before, and Tolle explained that after the Second World War, Nijinsky's wife Romola took Nijinsky with her to London, where, in 1950, he died and was buried. Three years later she had his body disinterred and brought to the Montmartre cemetery.

Camus said that he remembered, in 1946 or 1947, touring the grounds of a German lunatic asylum that was situated across a river from the Swiss asylum in Kreuzlingen where, he was told, Nijinsky had lived. There had been a sculpture on the grounds of the German asylum, he recalled—thin tomb-like stones tumbling one upon the other like a line of dominoes, the sculpture memorializing some six hundred individuals defined as 'mental defectives' who, in 1938, were taken from the asylum, gassed, and cremated. Had Nijinksy been in the German asylum, and not on the other side of the river, he would have died with them.

Although there were no films of his dancing extant, Tolle said, Nijinsky was nevertheless generally considered the greatest dancer of the century. She knew, too, that Nijinksy had scandalized Paris by miming masturbation with a scarf during performances of *L'après-midi d'un faune,* and that his psychiatrist in Switzerland had been the famous Bleuler, an admirer of Freud and the man who invented the term "schizophrenia."

Camus touched Nijinsky's stone cheek with the back of his hand, ran a finger over several folds of the ruffled clown collar.

"For a while," Camus said, "I envied Nijinsky his madness."

"Never envy someone's madness," Tolle said.

"Of course not, but—" Camus began.

"Madness is godawful, terrifying, and distinctly painful," Tolle said, cutting him off.

"I was only telling you of my—what shall we call it?—of my reaction to the little I know about Nijinsky."

He reached for her hand, but she refused to take it. Instead, she turned and faced him.

"Aren't you the man who declared that the *only* meaningful question in life is suicide—whether or not life is worth living?" she said. "*Aren't you?* Answer me. Please answer me, or…"

Trembling, she turned away from him. Camus put his arms around her, drew her to him, and she did not resist.

"What I envied, " Camus said softly, "was his ability to divest himself of reason."

He took her hand, and walked with her, away from Nijinsky's grave. "When I read his diary, I recall being taken with his remark about desiring the death of his mind, and also with his disliking Hamlet because Hamlet *reasoned.*" Camus closed his eyes and recited Nijinsky's words: "'I am a philosopher who does not reason—a philosopher who *feels*—'" Camus said "—or words to that effect. I recall copying the line into my journal at the time, and so…"

"And so—?" she asked.

"And so we return to beginnings," Camus said. "To your remark about finding my philosophical musings of less value than my stories, an assessment with which I often agree."

"I have spent time," Tolle stated, "not in lunatic asylums, but in places that are referred to as residential treatment facilities."

"We have a saying in French," Camus said. "If you're poor, you're crazy—if you're rich, you're eccentric."

"We have a similar saying in the States," Tolle said.

She stood still for a moment, then lifted his hand—the hand she had rejected moments before—and kissed its palm.

"My favorite dancer in the States, Allegra Kent—" she said "—we're the same age, and were friends for a while—studied with Nijinsky's sister, Bronislava."

"And you?"

"I'm an excellent and well-trained dancer," Tolle said, "but I'm not Allegra. Allegra's exceptional—*beyond* exceptional. Balanchine took her into his company when she was fifteen. She became a principal dancer three years later."

"Did Nijinsky's sister—Bronislava—ever talk with your friend about her brother?"

"Yes," Tolle said, "and thanks to Allegra, I've corresponded with Bronislava—she lives in Los Angeles—and she has encouraged me in my desire to choreograph a ballet about him, which is something she says *she* never had the courage to do."

"Yet you do."

"It's hardly courage that inspires me," Tolle said. "It's more the sadness of his life."

"Like your own sadness?"

"There is sadness, yes," Tolle said, "and also, in my occasional desire to take leave of this world, a form of madness that, I trust, will not return."

"We hope not," Camus said. "But if—"

"My favorite of all of Nijinsky's lines—" she said "—I've found no way to transform it into choreography yet—is when he declared of his doctors, 'They want to examine my brain, but I want to examine their minds.'"

"A suggestion then," Camus said. "Perhaps you might use his words as an epigraph—in program notes for your ballet."

"Perhaps," she said. "But to return to *your* musings: You often agree with me about your writing because—?"

"Because—no secret to anyone who knows me—my great struggle has been the struggle with—or rather, *against*—reason," he said. "Reason keeps me a prisoner—keeps my *imagination* a prisoner, to be more precise—and despite a certain pride I take in my novels and stories—in my craft—they all seem terribly *restrained* to me—*contained* might be a better word—as if they're the result of homework assignments: Write a novel about modern alienation! Write an allegory about colonialism involving an epidemic or plague! Write a novel about chance and necessity, and how…"

She put a finger to his lips. "Shh," she said. "Enough. I'm leaving Paris in two days, and after that, until we meet again, you will have all the time in the world to write new stories—to think about reason and unreason—but while I have you, I want us to know one another in as many ways as possible, and also—beginnings, yes?—I want to tell you a story about Nijinsky you may *not* know—the story that inspired my desire to create the ballet."

"'While you have me,'" Camus repeated. "I like that. A pleasant and quite *reasonable* prospect."

They wandered the cemetery, pointing out to one another the graves of artists, composers, actors, writers—Zola, Berlioz, Degas, Delibes, Viardot, Dumas fils, Gautier. She told Camus more of what she knew about Nijinsky—of how he had believed not that he *was* a genius, but that he was possessed *by* genius. Nijinsky saw his art as holy, and after the first World War, his sense of being possessed reached alarming proportions. He believed God was in him—a fire in his head—and that he was a god-like saviour who would redeem others. He believed he was the spirit in the flesh and the flesh in the spirit, the wounded bull and God in the bull, and the tree and roots of Leo Tolstoy himself. At the same time, he became wildly labile in his moods, and often violent to his wife Romola. He professed to love all mankind while fearing to be with others—taking himself on long solitary walks, locking himself in rooms where he drew macabre Goyaesque drawings. And he withdrew into long periods of nearly total silence.

In 1919, Romola consulted with Bleuler, who declared Nijinsky incurably insane. She took him to see Jung, and tried to get Freud to see him, but Freud declined, saying that he could be of no help to schizophrenics. And so, for four years he was a patient in the Kreuzlingen Asylum.

For the next quarter century, he was in and out of asylums and psychiatric hospitals. Notwithstanding his well-known homosexuality, he had two daughters with Romola—Kyra, born in 1914, and Tamara, born in 1920. By 1923, however, he was by all accounts a broken man: fearful, weak, mute. At the start of World War Two, Romola brought him back to Kreutzlingen, but soon after she took him out again and they traveled together to her native Hungary, near the Austrian border, where they lived all through the years of World War Two.

"He only danced again once," Tolle said, "and that was in 1945, after Hungary was liberated by the Russian Army. Romola took him outside so he could be part of the celebration, and they came upon an encampment of Russian soldiers who were playing folk tunes on a balalaika and other instruments. It was the first time in many years he had seen or met with any of his countrymen. The Russian soldiers were peasants for the most part, but in uniform. Several of them had heard of Nijinsky, and some were aware that he had once been famous.

"Also, for the first time in years, people did not stare at him or shrink from him because he was a madman," Tolle continued. "The Russian soldiers spoke to him in the same way they would have spoken to anyone. At first, Romola wrote, she felt compelled to warn them to keep away. 'Leave Vaslav alone—don't talk to him, please. He might become annoyed and impatient! He is frightened!' But the soldiers laughed. 'He won't be afraid of us,' they said. 'Let him to do what he wants.' And then Nijinsky came to life as he had not for nearly thirty years. He drank with the soldiers, and he laughed with them, and he suddenly began speaking again. It was as if he had never *been* mute, she wrote, after which, for the first time in decades, he danced—with the soldiers—and he astonished them with his skills."

*

They had lunch in a restaurant across from the Canal Saint Martin, and after lunch Camus purchased a round-trip train ticket that would take him to his home in Lourmarin and, the first week of the new year, back to Paris.

"Your wife and children—twins, yes?—live in Lourmarin," Tolle said when, in her hotel room several hours later, they woke from a nap. "Your second wife, I believe."

"My second wife, yes," Camus said. "I confess to being married, although I'm not a fanatic about it."

"Your wife tolerates your liaisons?"

"We are like brother and sister," Camus said.

"Like brother and sister?" Tolle said. "Perhaps. But I don't believe—not even in the fantasies you've set down about Don Juan—I've ever come across an enthusiasm for incest in any of your writings."

"Not yet," he said. "But who knows? You've inspired me in many ways, you know—you and Nijinsky."

"We share you?"

"Like brother and sister," Camus said.

"I confess you've inspired me too," she said. "I thought it might happen—that if we went to the cemetery together, I would see the way."

"The way?"

"*A* way, rather—a way to make the ballet work—a way to structure it, to make use of the story that gave it life."

They slept again, and when they woke, Camus talked about the urge—a craving like hunger, he said—to return to Lourmarin so that he could get back to work on his novel. It was the first of his novels that was consciously autobiographical—a story based largely on his childhood in Algeria: about his father, a winery worker who died in the first battle of the Marne; about his mother, who was illiterate, mute, partially deaf, and had worked in a munitions factory and as a cleaning woman;

11

about his older brother Lucien, with whom he was close; about his schooling, and about friends he grew up with and their importance in his life.

His primary reason for wanting to complete this novel, however, was so that he could be *done-with-it-and-move-on-to-the-next*: to a novel where he could divest himself of reason and let his imagination take flight. He was tired, he said—exhausted, depleted—from being forever reasonable, rational, accommodating. What he wanted, in his work as well as his life—but in the work above all—was to feel the right to be outrageous, and so he was thinking of basing a character on Nijinsky in order, psychologically and emotionally, to *inhabit* madness for a while. He was thinking, too, of giving Nijinsky a gifted and inordinately mature and precocious young friend who, though suicidal, survived by caring for and nurturing Nijinsky.

"My parents often said that I was never really a child—" Tolle said "—that when I was born, I was already an adult, that I was—your very words—strangely mature and precocious."

"I did not say 'strangely,'" Camus said. "I said 'inordinately'—*inordinately* mature and precocious, though perhaps a more exact word would have been *naturally* precocious and mature ..."

"*Pre*-ternaturally might be more apt," Tolle said. "But I *was* suicidal, if in a decidedly rational way. As, I would guess, you might be, or have been."

"No," he said.

"Never?"

"Although, as you know, I've considered the matter at some length in my writings, strange as it seems—even to me—I have never myself seriously considered ending my life," he said. "I have, however, often considered the absence of this feeling—this *omission*, shall we call it?—a weakness—a tragic flaw, perhaps, that is responsible for diminishing the texture—the specific gravity—of my writing."

"And you never considered suicide because—?"

He shrugged and, as if stating a simple and obvious fact, replied: "Because I have always loved life too much."

12

"I took one pill less than was necessary for an overdose," Tolle said, "and as soon as I'd swallowed the pills, I telephoned my mother and informed her of what I'd done. I walked in front of streetcars several times—this was in Boston, where my father was born, and where most of his family still lives—but I always gauged distances and speeds meticulously so that by the time, braking for me, a streetcar's wheels were shrieking on metal, I would have arrived safely on the other side of the tracks. Had I miscalculated by a half-second or half-inch, you and I would not be here together today."

"But you didn't."

"No. I did other things, though. I had an affair with my father's brother, a married man who was a charming and notorious rake. I stole documents from his desk and was able to do serious damage to his reputation and finances."

"And to his marriage?"

"His wife and I were good friends, before and after," Tolle said. "Very French, don't you think? She even sent me a thank you note. But before I thank *you*—and I will, and you will not stop me from doing so—you should know that when aroused or betrayed, I can be more than mischievous. I intend to be a significant part of your life, you see. I am loyal, tenacious, and ruthlessly persistent. I know where you live. I know your habits. I have means. I hope to make the two of us supremely happy—and happily productive—but if you tire of me, I will be relentless in my pursuit of other forms of gratification."

"You are an unusually intense and passionate young woman, and for that I am grateful."

"So far," she said.

She got out of bed, and sat in an armchair by one of the room's two windows.

"Now, when we cannot touch each other," she said, "I will explicate my text and explain the basis for my gratitude."

"Please."

"I had, shortly before my twenty-first birthday, and after a stay of three months in a residential facility, made definitive plans for

13

leaving this world. I did so not because I was deeply depressed or wildy enraged—or *de*-ranged—but for an opposite reason: because I felt particularly clear-headed and content—supremely confident about my dancing and my choreographic skills, though I had not put them to use for a while, and I also felt rather ecstatic—grandiose?—about a feeling that was with me increasingly each day: that I could accomplish anything I set my mind to."

"I understand," Camus said. "When the writing goes well, it is a feeling with which I am familiar. It is—"

"It was a feeling that had been with me increasingly each day: that I could accomplish anything I set my mind to," she said again. "And so, on the night before I planned to do the deed, I did what, for a while, I'd been doing most nights before sleep: I read some of your writings. And this time I sensed something I had not sensed before, though it had always, I soon realized, been at the heart of what drew me to you, and to your writing. This time—I was re-reading the essays in *Sisyphus*, beginning with your famous remarks about suicide—I thought I could understand exactly what you were trying to tell me. I could hear your voice, in fact, as if it were talking directly to me—it was not unlike what I've discovered it to be, a fact that does not surprise me—and what I heard you say was that precisely *because* life is absurd, it has meaning.

"And so, the next morning, I put aside my plans and, like Nijinsky, I danced again."

"And then—?"

"And *now*," she corrected. "And now I am here, and we are together, and we will be together again when you return to Paris."

Camus' time in Lourmarin went well and quickly. He completed a draft of the new novel, *Le Premier Homme*, and was pleased with it. He enjoyed being with his wife and children, and he enjoyed the quiet life of a village where he did not, as in Paris, have to deal with the inconveniences of celebrity. He wrote Tolle that he missed her, but that for

14

him the best work conditions had always been those of the monastic life: solitude and frugality. Frugality, however, went against his nature, so that while he was working and, thus, being frugal, he often felt as if he were doing violence, albeit *necessary* violence, to an essential part of himself.

She wrote that her own work was going well—would he be embarrassed to find himself, as dancer, on a stage with Nijinsky?—and that it was not at all surprising to her that a writer whose first book was about Saint Augustine would choose a monastic life. Still, she suggested that, like Saint Augustine, he balance the frugality of monastic life with pleasure, and that if he needed a guide to that life—to sybaritic indulgence—she was prepared to make certain unspecified sacrifices.

He wrote that in a quiet unlit room of his mind he had begun planning his next novel, and that he was eager to be with her again so that she might provide him with the inspiration and—more important—the *un*-reason that could make the book possible. Although he would forgo certain pleasures yet a while longer, the work itself seemed—like his time with her—a lightning bolt to the heart, if a fleeting one, and was followed by more blind work and, as ever, by constant doubt.

He reported that negotiations with Malraux for the new repertory theatre were going well, and that his adaptation of Dostoevsky's *The Possessed,* after six hundred peformances at the Antoine Theatre in Paris—a play that, he noted, despite the recognition given him by Alfred Nobel, had previously been refused by a dozen theatres—was on tour, and was being well received. He was also talking again with the actor and director Jean-Louis Barrault about a possible new collaboration.

She offered to meet him at the train station in Paris when he returned in January, and he accepted the offer. Her friendship had become, he wrote, of immeasurable importance to him, for, as he had confided in his journal on the day her most recent letter arrived, what made the world bearable for him were feelings engendered by those elements that joined us to others.

Friendships helped us through life, he explained, because they

15

presupposed more of the same—a future—and because they made us sense that our only true task was to *have* friendships with others. And yet, on those days when we became aware that this was, perhaps, not our only task, and above all when we realized that it was only our will that kept others attached to us, for if we stopped writing or talking, if we cut ourselves off from others, we realized how swiftly the others melted away. People were always ready and able to be interested in *something else*, so that when we came to understand how contingent and accidental everything in what we called love or friendship was, the world went back to darkness, and returned us to that great cold from which human tenderness had for a moment rescued us.

At Christmas, on the first page of the manuscript for *Le Premier Homme*, he set down a dedication to his mother: "To you, who can never read this book." That same week he sent playful, affectionate letters to three women with whom he had been involved before he met Tolle, each of whom he promised to see when he returned to Paris: Mi, a young Danish painter he had met at the Café de Flore; Catherine Sellers, an avant-garde actress and theatre director whose husband had played the part of the protagonist in the stage adaptation of Camus' novel, *The Fall*; and Maria Caesares, also an actress—star of Jean Cocteau's *Orpheus*—with whom he had had an ongoing relationship since 1944.

He had also decided not to take the train to Paris but, instead, to drive there with his editor and publisher, Michel Gallimard, and with Michel's wife, Janine, and their daughter, Anne. In his last letter to Tolle, he explained that he had bowed to Michel's insistence, would be arriving in Paris by car, and would call her soon after he arrived.

On January 2, Camus drove his wife Francine and their twins, Jean and Catherine, to the Avignon station, from which the three of them would take the train to Paris. On January 3, Camus and the Gallimard family, along with their dog, Floc, drove to Macon, where they spent the night at the Chapon Fin Hotel. The next day, they drove north to Paris along Nationale 5. During the drive, Janine would later write, she inquired about Camus' friendships with women, and Camus declared that he believed he had made all his women happy, even those he had loved simultaneously.

Twenty-four kilometers outside Sens, the Facel-Vega Michel Gallimard was driving swerved off the road, slammed into a plane tree, bounced off another, and shattered. Camus was thrust backwards through the rear window. His skull fractured and his neck broken, he died instantly. Janine and Anne, though thrown from the car, were unharmed. Michel Gallimard was taken to a local hospital and died five days later. The dog was never found. Camus had often remarked to friends that nothing was more scandalous than the death of a child, and nothing more absurd—*une mort imbécile*—than to die in a car accident.

Tolle Anne Riordan's ballet, *Camus Visits Nijinksy's Grave*, had its premiere performance one year later, on January 4, 1961, at the *Théatre de la Danse Nationale*, in Paris, and its American premier three months after that, on April 4, 1961, at the New York City Center for Dance.

TWO

November 17, 2004

The President
The White House
1600 Pennsylvania Avenue N. W.
Washington, D. C. 20025

Dear Mr. President:

I am a physician trained in infectious disease, presently the Director of AIDS programs, both for treatment and research, at the Kings County Hospital and Medical School in Brooklyn, New York. On September 11, 2001, I was in Cape Town, South Africa, where I was working with indigenous health care workers to establish treatment programs for people suffering from HIV/AIDS. And on that day and the days that followed, while I watched replays of the event on TV, I found myself thinking thoughts that seemed, even as they occurred to me, politically incorrect.

As we know, some three thousand men, women, and children perished in the World Trade Center on September 11, and I do not wish or intend to diminish these deaths. But I did, on that day, find *myself thinking not so much about the three thousand who died in the Twin Towers, but about the fact that in South Africa alone, where I was—some five to seven million men, women, and children would die within the next decade, and of the fact that they do not need to die.*

Some basic data: In the two dozen years since the first reported case of AIDS (1981), more than 500,000 Americans have died from this disease. Yet last year alone, over three million people beyond our nation's borders died of AIDS, more than 500,000 of whom were children.

Since 1981, AIDS has killed more than 20 million people. More than 40 million people in the world now live with HIV/AIDS, at least 25 million of them in sub-Saharan Africa, over two million of them children. At least eight million people are in immediate need of antiretroviral treatment, treatment without which they will all die, yet only a few thousand, given present conditions and policies, will ever receive this life-saving treatment. By the year 2005, the UN Global AIDS Program estimates some 89 million individuals in Africa alone may be infected with HIV. And of the more than 25 million in sub-Saharan Africa who are now infected, one out of every six is a child, and only one out of twenty of these children is currently receiving antiretroviral treatment. At the same time, AIDS has made orphans of more than 15 million children.

So why do I write to you today? I write because you are President of the richest nation in the world: rich in money, expertise, technology, and—equally important—rich in human beings who know how to utilize this wealth in productive ways. I write because you are my President and because you have wherewithal and power I do not have.

Once upon a time every patient I saw who was infected with HIV/AIDS died. This is no longer so. We now have knowledge, medications, and programs that can extend life for these people almost indefinitely. We can, in addition, not only tend to those afflicted, but can take preventive measures capable of reversing the course of this, the most devastating plague in human history. We have the ability, in short, to save millions of lives.

We have the means, sir, and yet we spend vast amounts of our resources and money on tanks, bombs, guns, and rockets. We spend billions of dollars—more than 200 billion so far in Iraq alone—to destroy life, and to prepare for and become involved in wars and adventures that bring profit to few and misery to many, and that do not leave us any safer than we were before we expended these resources. At the same time—and I write here specifically about help for those suffering from and condemned to certain death by HIV/AIDS—we spend what are, by comparison, miniscule amounts to save life, and we even, according to my newspaper this morning, now threaten to withdraw these miniscule amounts from the PEPFAR initiative (President's Emergency Plan for AIDS Relief) you announced at your State of the Union address nearly two years ago—a welcome start, but a mere drop in the bucket of need—and so, by sins of omission—by not using resources which are capable of saving lives—we murder hundreds of thousands of human beings each month, and millions each year.

I do not minimize the deaths in Afghanistan and Iraq of our own soldiers (nearly 2000 so far), and of soldiers and civilians in those two nations (is anyone keeping count?), but I must point to the fact that, like those who died in the World Trade Center on 9/11, American military deaths are, statistically speaking, small potatoes. Every month more than 240,000 people die of HIV/AIDS, and our response to this fact has been disgraceful and shameful in the extreme.

In the name of freedom and democracy, and to rid the world of a single tyrant—in Iraq today and in who-knows-where tomorrow—we are expending vast amounts of our human and natural capital. Why not use these resources to help rid the world of disease? Why not send battalions of skilled men and women into those nations living with this plague and its dreadful, daily issue? Why not use our resources to develop ongoing programs that would have a real chance to help people enjoy freedom not only from illness, suffering, and death, but from poverty, illiteracy, and ignorance? Why not, in these ways, restore America's good name in the minds and hearts of the world?

If I have a life preserver yet stand by and watch a neighbor drown—if I do not throw the life preserver to that neighbor—I have killed that person. This is what we, as Americans, are doing. This is what you are doing.

You are, Mr. President, a murderer.

Yours in shame,
Saul Allen Davidoff, M.D.

Three

Often, when he doubted his love for her—or, more exactly, his capacity *for* love—or wondered why and how they had stayed with each other for more than forty years in a time when most people they knew—friends, relatives, colleagues—had divorced and moved on to new couplings and marriages—he would go back to the beginning. *This is how we met*, he'd say to himself, and by telling himself the story again, no matter how many times he did, and no matter his knowledge that the effect of doing so was transient, he would for a brief while be reassured. But reassured about what? That they had been truly, deeply in love once upon a time? That they had not erred in marrying, or in having children, or in remaining married? That she did still love him and was devoted to him no matter the ways, they had, through the years, distanced themselves from one another?

More likely, he mused—they were driving south along a country road in France on a clear, unseasonably warm early February morning—Tolle had insisted they not take autoroutes, that they wind their way down from Paris at a leisurely pace—by conjuring up the first time they met, he was able to feel again what he rarely did of late: some genuine affection for her, for the young man he had once been, and for the man he had become.

He saw himself standing across the street from the Metropolitan

Museum of Art on Veterans Day, 1965. The air was crisp, the sky blue and cloudless, the crowd of anti-war protesters, among whom he stood, animated and happy. How, on such a day, standing side by side with people of like mind and heart, could one believe anything was amiss with the world, or that whatever was amiss could not, with good will and hard work, be set right. Across the street, crowds that lined the sidewalk behind police barricades with *their* banners, posters, and flags—in support of the war in Vietnam—seemed equally happy, so that the chants each side launched into the air seemed little more than friendly cheers for rival football teams.

Tolle, in the front row of protesters, wore a pale V-neck lavender sweater, a purple paisley scarf knotted loosely around her neck. Her wheat-colored hair, shoulder-length, was, in the autumn sunlight, laced with threads of gold, and she appeared to him to have stepped straight out of a Saks Fifth Avenue advertisement so as to take her place—out of place—among those whose fashions seemed, for the most part, to have been purchased from clothing racks in Salvation Army thrift stores.

She seemed the kind of woman—beautiful, cool, poised—who had always had the power to intimidate him: a woman who, he assumed, went to debutante balls with self-assured men destined to become diplomats, to run Fortune 500 companies, to own yachts, and—always, always—to sweat less than he did. He imagined she read Jane Austen, vacationed in Monaco, had lunch at the Plaza. What, then, was she doing in the front line of anti-war protesters? And what could a young woman like her ever want with an intense, curly-headed Jewish boy from Brooklyn?

Still, when she turned and looked his way, and when she smiled at him—a quizzical glance, as in: *We've met before, yes?*—he gained the courage he needed, pushed through the crowd, and made his way to her side.

He began talking at once—about the rally, about the weather, about the war, about the organization she was with (she held a placard that identified her as a member of the Committee for a SANE Nuclear Policy)—about whatever came to mind, and she responded

23

easily. Encouraged, and eager to impress, he alluded to the fact that he had rearranged his schedule at Columbia-Presbyterian Hospital, where he was doing a residency in infectious disease, in order to be at the rally, and also that he was a member of The Resistance and, although above draft age, was intending soon, in a public ceremony, to burn his draft card with those of draft age. When chants from both sides of the street grew louder, she tugged on her right ear with thumb and forefinger to indicate that it was difficult to hear him. Her pale hazel-green eyes, above ruddy high-colored cheeks, seemed almost translucent, and—what he had not expected—warm and inviting.

He looked to the right—uptown, to where she pointed—and saw a military band approaching, its music—Sousa's familiar "Stars and Stripes Forever"—blasting away. Behind the band, a phalanx of soldiers in camouflage khakis, rifles to their shoulders, marched in lock-step, policemen on motorcycles cruising slowly at their sides.

Closer to him, she asked his name.

"Saul," he said. "Saul Davidoff."

She shook his hand. "I'm glad to meet you, Saul Davidoff—but would you excuse me, please?" she said, and turned away, slipped under the wooden barricade, walked out onto Fifth Avenue and, along with about twenty others, sat down in the middle of the street, directly in the path of the oncoming parade.

Within seconds, police were there, confiscating the banner she and others had unfurled (END THE WAR NOW! BRING OUR BOYS HOME!), and dragging the protesters away. It was only when he saw her being led to a police van—she did not, like most of the protesters, trained, he assumed, in tactics of passive resistance, go limp, but instead, her hand in the hand of a tall, handsome policeman, walked up three steps and into the van as if she were being helped into a Hansom cab—that it occurred to him that once again, no matter his professed opposition to the war, his inertia had carried the day: he had *not* gone into the street with her and the others—had chosen by his immobility *not* to act. What was worse, and what seemed, in the moment, infinitely more important, he did not know her name.

So he asked around and found out which station house the protesters were being taken to, and after that, which courthouse for arraignment, and at seven-thirty that evening, when she was released on her own recognizance pending a hearing—her organization had posted bail—he was waiting for her.

"I was hoping you'd be here," she said to him at once. She took the single yellow rose he held out to her, inhaled its fragrance, kissed him on the cheek. Then: "Are you hungry?" she asked. "I'm positively ravenous."

She took his hand in hers, and began telling him about what had happened in the half-dozen hours since her arrest—the judge, she suspected, from his manner, was as opposed to the war as they were; the policeman who led her into the van had asked for her phone number; and—best news of all—she had been placed in a holding cell with Grace Paley, one of her *very* favorite writers—and while she and Saul talked, and while they made their way to Chinatown, where in a small restaurant that specialized in dumplings, they continued to talk—more easily than he had dreamt would be possible—and where, when they traded basic biographical information, he found out, to his astonishment, that she was Jewish.

Astonished as well as disappointed, he realized, for he had, in the hours that had passed since her arrest, been imagining a romance that, no matter the banality of the fantasy—'Poor Jewish Boy Wins Heart of Wealthy Sophisticated *Shiksa'*—he thought of as magical—as giving life to the bright, happy flame of his desire, and of—a word he hoped, if he had the courage, later on, to tell her *about* his imaginings, she would find wonderfully old-fashioned—his *ardor*.

She reached across the table, touched his hand.

"You're surprised, aren't you?"

"Yes."

"You're not the first, of course. I'm rarely taken for Jewish." She tapped on her nose. "Which is due mostly to the small, slender promintory I inherited from my father. Irish father. Jewish mother."

"Jewish mother. Jewish father," Saul said, and tapped on his nose. "Jewish son."

25

"My mother's nose may actually be a tad *smaller* than mine," she said, "for when she was a young woman, she had reconstructive facial surgery that, her parents believed, would serve to disguise her tell-tale Jewish origins. The surgical techniques at the time, however, were not especially sophisticated, and the nose-bob was botched—it's unbelievably tiny *and* a bit lopsided—and has always embarrassed her. *Par contraste*, my father's nose, which was once pure Irish pug, has become increasingly larger due to a lifetime of fidelity to maintaining traditions that derive from *his* origins."

"He drinks."

"He drinks *a lot*—more than ever, I assume," Tolle said. "I don't see them much—I'll explain why at some point, though not now, all right?—but both he and my mother have never, in *my* experience, thought of themselves as either Irish or Jewish, but as—as what?—as *patricians*, I suppose. My father used to raise horses, though in an extremely haphazard and unprofitable way. It was a trade his father and ancestors had plied in Ireland, or so he claimed. And what he loved about raising horses was that it allowed him to hobnob with high-born sovereigns of thoroughbred racing. 'Breeding is all,' he liked to say, and my mother would concur. 'Breeding is all,' they always told me."

"Isn't it?" Saul said.

She blinked. "Are you *serious*?"

"Just look at *you*, for example," Saul said. "Mendelian Math: Irish father plus Jewish mother equals an exceptionally beautiful woman with an attractive, slender nose."

"Please," she said, without smiling. "Now my mother, who likes to think of herself as to the manner born—or, more exactly, to the *manor* born—m-a-n-o-r—has been involved in the world of ballet. She chairs an organization that raises funds for ballet schools in and around the Boston area, and she comes to this vocation honestly. She was—before marriage, and before *my* arrival—a talented dancer who performed with major national and international companies."

"And you?"

"I was a dancer too," she said.

"And—?"

"I just *said* that I was a dancer too," she said. "Did you not *hear* me? Were you not *listening*?"

"When the policeman was leading you toward the police van, and when you glanced behind—at me, I thought—"

"Yes."

"—when you glanced behind at me, I noticed that you limped slightly. Is that why—?"

"I'm sorry I snapped at you," she said. "That was ill-bred of me. You're a very *observant* young man, Saul Davidoff."

"I couldn't help but be observant because I couldn't stop looking at you," Saul said. "*Staring* at you, really—"

"I could answer your question in the affirmative, of course—that an accident and subsequent surgeries did necessitate my giving up performing," she said. "The truth, however, is that if not for the accident, I would have found—or, rather, that I already *had* found—another reason to leave my career in dance behind."

"Because?"

"Because," she said.

"You were telling me about your mother," he said.

"My mother, yes," she said. "Thank you. My mother was a highly acclaimed dancer, it seems—I never saw her dance professionally, but—*telle mère, telle fille?*—she too, as I said, gave up her career early on."

"For marriage to your father and his career."

"And for me."

"Because she became pregnant with you?"

"That was the occasion, I suppose," Tolle said. "The *proximate* cause."

"But dancers can continue after pregnancy," Saul said. "I read an article recently about one of the principal dancers in the New York City ballet—"

"Allegra Kent."

"Yes—Allegra Kent," he said, "and the article said she's taken time out from her career to have *two* children, yet continues to perform."

"Allegra's remarkable," Tolle said, and leaned forward, beckoned him to come closer. "And do you know what else?" she whispered.

"What else?"

27

"She's Jewish too."

"So?"

"Allegra's a friend," Tolle said.

"Did you perform together in the same company—is that how you met?"

"Correct that," Tolle said quickly. "She *was* a friend. Like my mother, Allegra had facial reconstructive surgery forced on her because of *her* mother's aversion to being Jewish, surgery that *dis*-figured her. Also—Allegra's mother changed her name, just as mine did. Her mother was Shirley Weissman. Her father was Harry Herschel Cohen. Allegra's given name was Iris Cohen."

"And you?"

"Rebecca Anne Riordan."

"But that's a *beautiful* name!"

"My mother saw no reason to change Riordan to anything else," she said, "and I've come to like Tolle—to like *being* Tolle. It's a Swedish name, and an unusual one—often a man's name, yet rare even as that. Tolle Anne Riordan—I like the sound, the cadence: *Tol*-le *Anne Rior*-dan." She touched her nose. "Fortunately, my parents were not as ambitious on my behalf as Allegra's parents were, and did not try to redesign my face. Nor was I as gifted as Allegra was."

"You're being modest," Saul asked. "Surely you—"

"Please do not compare me to Allegra."

"But you were the one who—"

"Allegra was fierce," Tolle said.

"So are you," Saul said.

"At times, yes," Tolle said. "But not about dance. I was never, as a dancer, talented *or* ambitious in the way Allegra was. She wanted nothing else in life *but* to dance. Her work ethic was—still is—ruthlessly demanding."

"And you—?"

"I want other things."

"Such as—"

"If I tell you, will you stop asking questions?"

"Yes."

"I want to help end the war."

"I know *that*. It's how and why we met—but what else?" he asked, and without waiting for a reply, continued: "Ah—I know! You want to get married and have two-point-three children."

"Exactly," Tolle said.

"And also—the dream instilled in most Jewish girls—to become a doctor's wife."

"Of course."

"Hey—I was just joking," Saul said. "You seem too—"

"Unconventional?"

"Unconventional yes, but—more important—too independent," Saul said. "You seem like a woman who's always known what she wants, and has never cared about what others wanted her to be."

"Even as a child, I've been told I was remarkably mature and self-confident," Tolle said. "I have also had what others consider—and I agree—a curiously *un*-conventionial life, and so I've decided it's time for me to discover what it's like to have a conventional life."

"Because?"

"Because I do," she said. "I believe in Yeats' theory of masks, you see—that's William Butler Yeats—"

"I know who Yeats is," Saul said.

"My apologies—I didn't mean to be condescending," Tolle said. "What Yeats believed is that we are born with and/or develop an innate identity, and that we don a mask of an opposite identity—or alternative identity—and out of the the conflict, or synthesis, we forge a true or tru-*er* self. That's an oversimplified explanation of a complex set of beliefs, but—"

"—but I get the idea," Saul said, "and that, in this new and conventional life, you want to have children."

"I want to have children."

"More than one?"

"I was, in effect, an only child through most of my growing up, and would not want a child of mine to be lonely, resentful, and angry

29

the way I was—" Tolle said "—and also—do not interrupt, please—the way I still am at times."

"You said 'yes' to wanting to be married."

"Correct that," Tolle said. "Marriage is posssible but not necessary."

"Do you want your children to be sired by the same man, or—?"

"*Sired?!*" she laughed. "I like that, Saul Davidoff!" She hesitated, sat back. "Is it a position you're thinking of applying for?"

"Of course."

"And your stud fee?" she said, and as soon as she did, she covered her mouth to stifle a giggle. "My goodness, but you seem to have a way with me of—of what—?"

"Of inspiring you?"

"Perhaps," she said. "But before you ply me with yet another inspiring question, will you answer a question I have for *you*?"

"Of course."

"Why do you make me smile—and you do, although I've kept my *outward* smiles to a minimum," she said. "And a second, more telling question—why am I *telling* you so much about myself?"

"Because you *want* to?"

"But *why*?" she said.

"Because—perhaps—you *like* me?" Saul said. "Because—"

"Stop," she said. "Please let's agree to avoid the adolescent *boy-girl* I-like-you-do-you-like-me-too nonsense, which can devolve quickly into the I-like-you-*more*-than-you-like-me twaddle. I do like you, obviously, or I wouldn't be here, although I don't quite know why, or *understand* why—"

"Do you have to understand *why* you like someone?"

"I asked you not to interrupt," she said. "It's an unattractive habit. And listen to me, please, because I'm trying to tell you something, Saul Davidoff."

"Okay."

"I like saying your name, by the way—"

"Because it's Russian?"

"Because what I'm trying to tell you—what I am *now* telling you, or, more exactly, am about to tell you—is that this is new."

"*What's* new?"

"You," she said. "You're my age, I believe."

"I'm twenty-seven," Saul said.

"Correct," Tolle said. "The men I've been attracted to since I came of age—and before that too—have usually been older men. I've rarely if ever found men my own age interesting or attractive."

"I'll be old some day."

"You're not *listening*," she said. "And you're trying to be clever when cleverness is—"

"Redundant?"

"Redundant—yes. Thank you," Tolle said. "What I'm attempting to say is that this is different—what's happening today is *different*—"

"How so?"

"You're fishing," she said, then suddenly smiled in the somewhat perplexed but friendly way she had smiled at him the first time, at the Veterans Day Parade. "But that's all right," she said. "I don't especially care for the adolescent boy-girl romantic stuff, and I don't care for the way you insist on leavening awkward moments with humor, but I do admit to finding your attempts to lighten me up agreeable, and—"

She stopped. He waited for her to finish the sentence, and when, after several seconds, she did not, he inclined his head towards her in a questioning way.

"*And*—?" he asked.

"And yes, it's good of you—shrewd, actually—not to provide me with words for feelings I'm obviously reluctant to express—words for what *you* imagine *I* might be thinking—and thereby, thank you, to push me to take responsibility for what I say," she said. "So all right. What's new is that I found you attractive when I saw you looking at me, that I liked the fact that you pursued me, that—to my surprise—I found myself wanting to encourage you to do so, that I like talking with you, that I like the intelligence and *curiosity* I can see in your eyes, that I feel I can tell you anything—well, *almost* anything—and that you'll probably understand me, and—"

"Probably?"

She stared at him for a few seconds, then tapped on the side her head with two fingers.

"I have an idea," she said.

"Yes?"

"Would you like to walk me home?"

As soon she closed the door behind them—she lived in Greenwich Village, on Cornelia Street, in a second floor apartment located above an Italian restaurant—he pushed her against the door and kissed her. She returned his kiss, open-mouthed, started to undo the lower buttons on his shirt, and while continuing to kiss him, to pull him with her into another room.

"Here," she said, pushing him down on her bed, and lying on top of him.

"Where?" he asked.

"Here," she said again, taking his hand and placing it between her legs.

"And where else?" he asked.

"Wherever," she said. "As in real estate, location is everything."

"Location … location … location … " he said.

"Oh yes," she said a short while later. "Indeed! So I'm wondering, Doctor Saul Davidoff: Were you, perhaps, a realtor before you became a physician?"

"It's how I worked my way through medical school," he said.

"You must have been very proficient at anatomy *and* sales," she said, and she bent down, kissed him hungrily.

"I think I do like you, Saul Davidoff," she said a few moments later.

"That's excellent news," Saul said.

"Well, you seem to like me too, though I appreciate your not rushing to *say* that you do," she said. "Which means that in addition to being observant, you're a good listener."

"Sometimes," he said. "But at the risk of irritating you, I'm going to ask yet another question."

"You're an exceptionally good kisser," she said as she unbuckled his belt, then traced the curve of his mouth with the tip of an index finger. "But now—your question?"

"In the newly launched conventional life you've undertaken, " he asked, "have I been chosen be an accomplice in your desire to have children?"

"Probably," she said.

"*Probably*?!" he said, and when he did, they both laughed, and began kissing again, but more slowly than he believed possible given the wild craving he had to be inside her, and what seemed her desire to have him there. Without talking, they undressed each other, folding each item of clothing they removed and setting it on the floor beside the bed before removing the next item.

It was only later, when he rose from the bed to go to the bathroom, and she told him where the light switch was so that he wouldn't crash into things, that he saw the posters on the wall—one for the Parisian premiere of *Camus Visits Nijinksy's Grave*, and one for the New York City premiere.

Four

When she opened her eyes, she saw that it was a few minutes past four, and that Saul was sleeping soundly. She kissed him on each side of his spine—his angel's wings—and was aware again, admiringly so, of how beautiful—how lean and strong, like a dancer's—his body was. Had this been what she'd noticed—and without realizing she had—that had drawn her to him? Through the years, she'd had a fair number of lovers, and many of them, dancers especially, had been expert in the use of their bodies and in their attentions to hers, yet none of them—not even those with whom she'd had extended relationships that allowed making love to become increasingly adventurous and pleasurable—had given her the deep gratification she'd experienced with Saul.

Though memory, she reminded herself at once, could play tricks, and she recalled that she'd often felt, after the first time she slept with a man, that *that* night of love had been more gratifying and powerful than any previous night of love. Still, she was aware that the pleasures she'd experienced—the sheer excitement and intensity followed by an ongoing stream of gentle, bliss-filled waves—though still with her, were now accompanied by something very calm and sweet, and that this too was new.

Saul was on his side, turned away from her, and she moved closer, spooned him with her body. She kissed his neck, licked the dry, salty sweat from his shoulders, and when she did, he took one of her hands, placed it against his stomach, and pressed back against her so that within a few seconds, she found herself becoming excited again.

It was, she decided, what she thought of as a rare—and *balanced*—combination of passion and familiarity that was the surprise. He had remarked on the latter—on how *familiar* being with her seemed—as if they were, perhaps, a brother and sister who'd been apart for a long time, and were now, *sans inceste,* rooming together for a night.

Pourquoi sans inceste? she had joked, and they had, in French—she was pleased to discover that his French was excellent—bantered back and forth for a while until, with her hand, she brought him off for a third time, and he fell asleep. Although she usually hated it when, after making love, men would comment on how good it—or she—had been, when Saul said what other men said—how it seemed impossible that this was the *first* time they'd ever made love, how their bodies seemed to *know* each other in ways that were familiar in an almost—his word—*preternatural* way, instead of being put off by what he said, she'd found herself responding with a simple "Yes."

Before this, and after the second time they made love—his resilience for a man nearly a decade out of his teens astonished her—he had asked her to please turn over so that he could massage her back. She'd done what he asked and, as she drifted into a delicious post-coital sleep, she recalled thinking: this is what women who want to be loved often do for the men they hope will love them. What she also recalled thinking, but chose not to tell him, was that what she wanted, at least in the moment, was not so much a conventional life as an *ordinary* life—that she wanted more of what she was already allowing herself to feel: the sense that he would care for her and, yes, even *take* care of her—protect and provide in traditional ways because it occurred to her that she might feel safe with him in a way that, though *un*familiar, was, of a sudden, allied with an overpowering desire to be kind to *him.* She also reasoned that although for most women such feelings would have been *ordinary*—as predictable as they were conventional—for Tolle Anne Riordan they were decidedly *un*conventional.

Her thoughts turned to Camus, as they often did after—and some-times during—the act of love, and although she tried now to recall what *their* lovemaking had been like, and although she could recall, almost verbatim, many of their conversations, she could not conjure up any specific memories of what they had done with one another *physically*, of what she had felt while they made love, or what she had felt after-wards. She was also aware that Saul reminded her of Camus in that, like Camus, he could be surprisingly boyish. Although, like Camus, Saul was a capable, strong, and considerate lover, he too was able to allow the boy he once was, still alive within the man he'd become, to show himself forth and delight in the act of love, and—fore and aft, she thought, smiling—in their playful teasing and conversations.

After Saul had seen the posters, he had asked if her ballet had been literally *about* Albert Camus.

"In part, yes," she said. "In fact, it came about—or rather, it came *together* as a ballet because of Camus."

"You *knew* him?" he asked.

"I knew him," she replied.

"But that's incredible," he said, "I mean, I can't believe it, since it's the same for me—"

"You've created a ballet with Camus in it?" she asked.

"Of course not—" he laughed "—and I want to hear more about the ballet, and about what Camus was like, because though I never had the good fortune to meet him, it was the same for me—it was *because* of Camus that my own career, at least in part—like your ballet—came about."

He talked for a while and explained that his father's father, an immigrant who had been a piece-goods finisher in New York City's garment center—a man who died before he was born—had been a casualty of the Spanish flu pandemic that had swept the world in 1918, killing more than fifty million people. And his father, shortly after completing his medical studies at Downstate Medical Center in Brooklyn—Kings County Hospital—had, in September 1942, enlisted in the Army Medical Corps, had been sent to the Medical Field Service

School in Carlisle, Pennsylvania for special training, had contracted polio there, and had spent the rest of his life in wheelchairs. Although Kings County Hospital gave his father a series of administrative positions, he never again *practiced* medicine in the way he'd hoped to practice it, had become severely depressed, and had died of complications of pneumonia in 1962 at the age of 57.

It was only when Saul read—and was inspired by—Camus' *The Plague*, however, that he made the decision to specialize—to do his residency—in infectious disease. Once he'd done so, it seemed obvious to him, given his family's sad history, that the decision had always been there waiting—the soil in which Camus' novel, seed-like, had found a home. And so he had committed himself to a medical career in which he would treat individuals affected by diseases such as polio and influenza, and—the future, of course, remained, of necessity, vague and unplanned—to do what he could to prevent the spread of those diseases that cut down millions of lives around the globe: tuberculosis, cholera, measles, smallpox, pertussis, malaria.

"I read *The Plague* again this past summer," Saul said "and I also read a biography of Camus, and what I've decided to do when I complete my residency this spring is to travel through France, and perhaps North Africa if I have time: to Mondovi, where Camus was born—and to visit as many of the places where Camus lived as I can."

"And the place where he died?"

"Yes," Saul said. "Of course. And I thought what I'd do—a way, perhaps, and I hope it doesn't sound too corny—of honoring Camus, and of thanking him—would be to take copies of *The Plague* with me, in English and in French, and to read a chapter each night before I go to sleep."

"You're very romantic, aren't you," Tolle said.

"How can you tell?" he asked, smiling.

"By the tender yet passionate way you have of kissing," she said.

She kissed him, a long and lingering kiss, and then: "But I think it only fair to tell you that I am decidedly *un*-romantic."

"Despite what you just said, and the way you—"

37

"Shh," she said, placing a finger against his lips. "I can, from time to time, I'm pleased to report, be carried away—transported—if not by what most people think of as romance, then by what I've come to think of as a healthy indulgence in sybaritic pleasures."

"That's excellent news," he said. "But you shouldn't worry about not being very romantic. I have more than enough romance to serve both of us."

"I'll tell you more about my ballet by and by," she said, "and about the role Camus played in its creation—the influence he had *on* it— but for now what I'm wondering is this: if and when you make this journey—this *pilgrimmage?*—would you be willing to take a somewhat un-romantic traveling companion with you?"

Five

When they were no more than two hours from their destination—Spéracèdes, a village in the South of France four miles west of Grasse—they stopped for coffee in a small restaurant near Castellane. The previous afternoon they had turned off Nationale 95, the old *Route Napoléon*, and meandered through villages that seemed little changed since they had first passed this way twenty-eight years before. Sitting on the restaurant's terrace, and looking out at the Lac de Castillon, its surface a beautifully rippled azure blue, Saul realized again, as he had the instant their plane had landed in Paris the day before, just how relieved he was to be far from the hospital, and from the latest AIDS political storm, one that had burst forth in early February when a research foundation on whose board of directors he served had released information, at his urging, about a nasty new strain of the AIDS virus, one that was proving resistant to all known antiretroviral therapies.

The accusations that followed upon the announcement of this virulent strain of the virus had been predictable: scientists and physicians accusing him and his foundation of being alarmist and self-promoting, and gay activists asserting that the announcement was merely another pretext for demonizing gay men as crazed drug addicts wantonly spreading a killer disease. The truth, which he did not state publicly, though he longed to do so, was that because of the new antiretroviral medications, gay men were once again, as in the eighties, fucking like bunnies. Some of his own patients, juiced up on Viagra and metham- phetamines—crystal meth—had been boasting to him that, with the Internet as the favored go-between, they frequently scored twenty or more sexual partners in a single weekend.

Their behavior had infuriated him, and he had found himself dis- liking these patients with such force—actually *despising* them—that he'd come, and not for the first time, to doubt his ability, or right, to be their doctor, and the kind of doctor he's prided himself on being. The truth too, which he'd made little effort to hide from himself *or* from Tolle, was that he had lost heart for the struggle—had lost the passion that had driven him for most of the previous twenty-five years when, working eighty, ninety, and a hundred or more hours a week, he had seen every single one of his patients die.

During the early years of the AIDS epidemic, he had sometimes reacted to the dread realities of his life by seeing himself as Holden Caulfield, but a Holden Caulfield who had metamorphosed from a neurotic preppie into a mature, heroic physician. With the years, how- ever, instead of imagining he was, like Holden, saving children—catch- ing them before they tumbled lemming-like over a cliff—he'd come to picture himself sitting behind a desk in a long, dark tunnel, a syringe in one hand, a jar of pills in the other, and on the desk in front of him, piled high, boxes of condoms and packages of sterilized needles that— his sole job—he was to dispense to those men and women who, gravely infected with HIV were, like grotesque figures in a Hieronymous Bosch painting, limping, lurching, and crawling their way towards him.

Ever since the pandemic had erupted in the early eighties, his time—and life—had not been his own. Every time he opened a door, or picked up the phone, or checked his e-mail, or got on or off an elevator, someone had been there—to consult, to complain, to tell him he was wanted somewhere else for someone in need, in pain, in extre- mis. Other than several vacations he and Tolle had taken in the years before the outbreak of the pandemic—and before their children, Julia and Sam, were born—he could not, in fact, recall the last time he and Tolle had been away together, just the two of them, for more than two consecutive days.

From 1982 on, and from a distinctly low-key medical career—he had been Chief of Infectious Disease at Kings County Hospital, and Professor of Infectious Disease in its medical school at a time when infectious disease was among the least desirable—the least *sexy*—of specialties, he had found himself at the center of discoveries, controversies, and grueling work schedules that accompanied the efflorescence of this new plague. Inertia again, he thought, as in: I was chosen *for* the work—a man who *happened to be* an expert in infectious disease, and *happened to be* working with drug addicts and gay men in a densely populated urban area afflicted with poverty and, thus, with a large and fast-growing population of HIV-infected individuals.

With the advent of effective antiretroviral medications, however, things had changed, and for the second year in a row, he had not lost a single patient. Yet it was as if this good news—this *better* news—was itself the cause of his fatigue, or, what was probably more accurate, was allowing him to acknowledge the bone-weary exhaustion that had accumulated in him through the years. So that when Tolle reacted to the news he brought home of the latest crisis in his life as spokesperson for his AIDS foundation, and director of AIDS treatment and research at Kings County, by suggesting they go to France for a well-deserved getaway, he had offered only token resistance.

Before he'd met Tolle, he recalled, he had set to heart a passage from *The Plague*'s penultimate paragraphs that he recited to her on their first night together—a passage he would later type out, frame, and hang on the wall in his Kings County office:

> ...*Doctor Rieux resolved to compile this chronicle, so that he should not be one of those who hold their peace but should bear witness in favor of those plague-stricken people; so that some memorial of the injustice and outrage done them might endure; and to state quite simply what we learn in time of pestilence: that there were*

more things to admire in men than to despise.

Nonetheless, he knew that the tale he had to tell could not be one of a final victory. It could be only the record of what had had to be done, and what assuredly would have to be done again in the never ending fight against terror and its relentless onslaughts, despite their personal afflictions, by all who, while unable to be saints but refusing to bow down to pestilences, strive their utmost to be healers.

He recalled, too, that Tolle had found his identification with Camus' Doctor Rieux as sentimental as his identification with Holden Caulfield had been silly, since both Holden and Doctor Rieux were, in her opinion, decidedly implausible creations. Yet even Doctor Rieux, while practicing medicine during an imaginary plague in what she considered was one of Camus' least convincing inventions, had at times been consumed with despair and self-doubt. While admiring of the work Saul did, Tolle liked to remind him that he was just a man doing the best he could in a difficult and *very real* situation. Although the work he did was, of course, laudable, in addition to being a renowned AIDS doctor, he was also a man with a family that occasionally needed him as much as his patients did, and if he did not take better care of himself—she continued to worry about the possibility, which he acknowledged was real, that he could, no matter how careful, be lethally infected—he would be of use to no one: neither to her, his children, *or* his patients.

He couldn't disagree, and since, with the emergence of the antiretroviral therapies, he was also compelled to agree that he was no longer indispensable or irreplaceable in the way he'd been in the early years of the epidemic—younger doctors, nurses, and staff members were taking over, and doing so efficiently—perhaps, he mused, the time had come for him to do what, shortly before he agreed to leave Paris, and his editorial work at Gallimard, Camus had decided to do: to live the life of a normal man. "The only effort of my life," Camus had written in a passage Saul came across in one of Camus' journals during the same week he had written his letter to the President, "the rest having been given to me (except for wealth, to which I am indifferent): to live the life of a normal man. I didn't want to be a man of the abyss."

And believing he was a normal man who *could* rise from the abyss he had labored in for more than two decades, Saul had begun to feel free *to act* on matters that enraged him instead of merely *re*-acting to them. So that when he read an item in the *New York Times* about federal budget cuts for AIDS treatment and research, he had not hesitated—had told his secretary to hold all calls, had gone into his office and written a letter to President Bush, and had walked out of the hospital and put the letter in a mailbox. And when, ten days after he'd sent the letter, the Dean of the medical school invited him for lunch, Saul immediately guessed what the occasion was, and even considered, in a flush of pride that made him feel almost giddy, the possibility that he had, perhaps, written the letter *in order* for it to make its way to the Dean, and produce what he foresaw would be a predictable and, yes, a longed-for outcome.

After telling Saul he was in receipt of a copy of a letter Saul had sent to the President of the United States, the Dean expressed his admiration for the truly important work Saul had accomplished, and sympathy for the heartbreaking frustrations he had endured during his years at Kings County. The hospital and medical school, the Dean assured him, valued Saul's contributions, and appreciated the terrible pressures under which he had been working for more than two decades. Those pressures, the Dean went on, had doubtless contributed to Saul's lapse of judgment, not in composing the letter—the Dean shared Saul's outrage—but in sending it off, and in doing so without consulting others, and on hospital stationery. Saul was, the Dean suggested—and how not, given his career?—doubtless suffering from a kind of battle-fatigue—from burn-out. Therefore, the Dean believed, Saul would benefit from some well-earned time off, and to that end he had been authorized to propose that Saul consider taking a mini-sabbatical of four months, at full salary, a sabbatical that Saul could prolong if he wished. The Dean did not mention retirement, but the suggestion was clearly there.

43

Tolle's reaction to Saul's account of his conversation with the Dean was to insist that he accept the offer, and that they return to France for an extended period of time. And if he didn't, she added—though without referring to the obvious: that their marriage was pretty well burned-out too—she would go by herself. We've been deprived too long, she said, and so, earlier that day, before he met with the Dean, she had begun making inquiries, and the good news was that the house they had rented for their first stay in France, and on subsequent visits, was available. She had forwarded a deposit for a three-month stay with the option of renewing for an additional three months. With or without him, she declared, she was going.

The house had been situated on a quiet road a few hundred yards from the center of Spéracèdes, a village situated in the first range of the Maritime Alps, and from the house they had been able to see, some seven hundred feet directly above them, Cabris, a *village perché* where Camus had lived for a year while recovering from the debilitating effects of tuberculosis. At 1800 feet above sea level, and with magnificent views of the Mediterranean, Cabris had been a favorite residence of Camus' friend André Gide, and the home in which Camus had lived, *Les Audides*—a vacation house a short walk from the village center, and belonged to Pierre and Elisabeth Herbart (Gide had had a daughter with Elisabeth)—was a simple two-story Provençal–style house surrounded by terraced fields covered with olive trees and cypress.

Saul's schedules—between the completion of his residency at Columbia-Presbyterian Hospital and his first day as a physician and faculty member at Kings County Hospital—had left him with only seventeen days of leave, and, in typical bureaucratic fashion, had not been finalized until two days before his leave could begin, so that they had arrived in the South of France the first time, two months after they had met—had flown to Nice, where they rented a car—without having booked a place to stay. They took a small room in a hotel in the center of Cabris, above *Le Petit Prince*, a restaurant villagers claimed was owned by Saint-Exupéry's mother, and had tried for several days to find larger, more comfortable accomodations. Then—their good fortune—at lunch in *Le Petit Prince* on their third afternoon in Cabris, an American painter, Jerry Ravitch, hearing them talking in English, had come to their table and introduced himself, and when they told him why they'd come to Cabris—rarely a destination for tourists, especially American tourists, Jerry noted—and of their frustrations in finding the kind of place they'd hoped to find. He told them they had met the right man since he knew of a very pleasant house in the village below—where he lived and worked—that was available.

The house, like most houses in the region, had a name, *La Farigoulette,* and Saul and Tolle fell in love with it, and with the village of Spéracèdes, as easily and happily as they had fallen in love with each other. Set into a hillside and, like Camus' house, with splendid views of the Mediteranean, Spéracèdes was a village of some four hundred people where each morning in the village square's stone fountains women washed their clothes; where the village's butcher had his own flock of sheep that a shepherd led through town several times a week; where old men sat outside the village's lone bistro, drinking and playing cards; where the village gave homes, rent-free, to the local doctor as well as to the teacher of the village's one-room elementary school; and a village remarkably peaceful because, Jerry informed them, the *Guide Michelin* considered it so nondescript—*sans distinction*—that it advised readers and travelers to bypass it.

Set among terraced olive groves, and with stone walls more than two feet thick, *La Farigoulette* was situated on an unpaved road that led to the village's cemetery, about two hundred yards from the village center. According to the house's owner, Clément Merle, who also owned one of the village's two épiceries, and who had been born and raised in the house, it was at least four hundred years old. Its three rooms, each about twelve by fifteen feet, were stacked one upon the other on three floors, the bottom floor opening onto a small garden that contained a single mimosa tree along with strawberries, parsley, coriander, basil, and—the source of the house's name—an abundance of thyme. From their bedroom on the third floor—a room with floor-to-ceiling glass doors that opened onto a narrow balcony with a wrought-iron balustrade—they had spectacular views: to the east, of St. Cassien Lake and Estérel Mountains, and, directly south, beyond a deep green valley covered with broom, cypress, olive, and mimosa trees, of the Mediterranean. Early on a clear morning, Monsieur Merle promised, and after a fierce north wind—the *mistral*—blew through, they would also be able to see the island of Corsica, which lay one hundred and fifty miles out to sea.

They had assumed this was a practical joke villagers enjoyed playing on tourists (*Vous n'avez pas encore vu la Corse?*), but five days after they settled in, there was a loud banging on their shutters one morning before sunrise, and when they went out onto their balcony, Monsieur Merle was standing below, smiling broadly and pointing to where, to their amazement, they saw the mountains of Corsica rising from the sea as if from an island no more than three or four miles from shore.

They had stayed on the balcony, huddled together for warmth—the air was fresh, cool, and exhilarating, as if, Tolle said, angels had vacuumed it clean during the night—until, the sun rising and heating the honey-blue sea, the island, like a desert mirage, faded and disappeared.

They had returned to Spéracèdes three times in the years before Julia and Sam were born, and had stayed in *La Farigoulette* each time—had been able to arrange their vacation time according to its availability—and, in addition to walking the mile or so up to Cabris most days to visit *Les Audides*, they had adopted the custom of leaving Spéracèdes two or three times a week and sometimes staying away overnight in order to search out another city, town, or village where Camus had spent time: Grasse, Avignon, Lourmarin, Sens, Isle-sur-la-Sourge, Chambon-sur-Lignon, Saint-Étienne, Saint-Brieuc. They would start out after breakfast, arrive at their primary destination within a few hours, wander the village's streets, enjoy a leisurely lunch, and after lunch would adjourn to a local hotel where they would make love.

They would do the same in villages that they happened upon and, by doing so, made their own—villages that Camus might have known, but were not mentioned either in the biography of Camus Saul had read, or in Camus' journals: Sisteron, Draguignan, Digne, Rousillon, Gap, Mons, Ys, Apt—each name still, nearly thirty years later, having the power to evoke specific memories. In Digne, Saul recalled, in the *Hotel de Ville*, the wallpaper had been composed of faded red and green chevrons like those on Chevrolets; in Rousillon, they had, within less than a minute of entering their room, and with most of their clothes on, made love standing up, his back against the door, her legs clasped around his thighs; in Lourmarin—where Camus had been living at the time of his death—they had talked for the first time about getting married; in Apt, on a noisy, broken-springed bed, he had—another first— entered her from behind; and on a broiling August day in Entrevaux, in a room with a huge chestnut armoire, one whose doors were faced with narrow gilded mirrors covered with colored streaks that, in memory, appeared to be dried blood stains, he had, after making love, and on sweat-drenched sheets, fallen into the blackest post-coital sleep he had ever experienced.

When he awoke, he recalled, Tolle had been sitting up, her back against the wall—there was no headboard—with a dazed expression on her face. He had caressed her legs, and asked a question he had asked on their first night together: Was he correct in assuming that the scars—two small half-inch scars on her right knee, a longer scar of three to four inches below the knee, and a long scar over the outer edge of her ankle—were related to why she had stopped dancing.

"Later," she said, and had added, with a smile: "But I haven't stopped dancing. I do still dance, though I no longer consider myself a dancer."

When, in Entrevaux, he asked the question again, she had shaken her head from side to side to clear it of distractions, had kissed the top of his head, and said it was no big deal, that the scars were the result of surgery following injuries that had occurred while riding one of her father's horses. She had taken a narrow trail that ran alongside a dry riverbed—the trail pocked with rather large rocks and stones that rose from soft clay-like earth—and while pushing her horse to go faster than she knew was good for either of them—her father had cautioned her never to ride this trail, and this was, given how eager she was to oppose any rule her father imposed, doubtless the reason she'd decided to take the trail—they had come, too quickly, to a high stone wall that curled around a sharp curve, and the horse, to avoid a long trench-like furrow to their left, had suddenly veered to the right, crashed into the wall, and in so doing had crushed her right leg against it, then dragged and pounded the leg against the wall for perhaps another fifty or sixty feet.

This had happened in Hadley, Massachusetts, where her father owned a run-down farm and a ragged assortment of racehorses, the majority of them well past their prime. He raced them mostly in county fairs and, using forged Jockey Club registrations, and reworking the horses's lip tattoos, or making them illegible, he would pass the males off as able-bodied thoroughbred studs. The horse she had ridden that day, Blue Jade—her favorite because of the way, when she approached him, he clicked his teeth together, as if sending her a Morse code greeting—though eight years old, would, when juiced up on a cocktail of steroids, anti-inflammatories, and other performance-enhancing, pain-killing drugs, still race three or four times a season, and regularly finish in-the-money.

Her father, no surprise, had been as cruel to her as he was to the horses—many of which he bought for less than two hundred dollars and raced until they broke a leg, foot, or ankle, or became ill and useless, and had blamed her for ruining a horse that still had good years left in him, and would now have to be sent, like other broken-down nags he'd owned, to a knackery.

Her mother, after excoriating her father for treating both horse and daughter with his typical cold-heartedness, had put Tolle in a car—laid her down across the back seat—and driven directly to Massachusetts General Hospital in Boston, two hours away, where X-rays showed a broken ankle and a tibial plateau fracture of the knee. Surgeons operated on her that day, after which, despite exhaustive and exhausting months of rehabilitation, Tolle was left with the mild limp Saul had noticed on the day they first met.

By continuing to do exercises that, of necessity, put no weight on leg or ankle, she explained, she'd been able to regain a high percentage of flexibility and motion in both ankle and knee—enough to allow her to *teach* dancing, but not enough for her to ever again dance professionally. Nor had she ever again ridden a horse.

Thirteen months after the accident, her father's drunkenness and ongoing harshness to horses, daughter, and wife, along with her mother's return to her role as her father's defender and, what was new, her frequent tirades against Tolle for having willfully—and spitefully—ruined the dancing career she had, at great personal sacrifice, prepared Tolle for—Tolle had decided to divorce her parents.

"Divorce your *parents*?" Saul asked.

"By the time I'd recovered physically and emotionally, the latter helped along by my first long stretch of psychotherapy—I'd moved back to New York City, where I'd been living before the accident, and had taken a teaching position at the Stamford City Ballet School—I came to the conclusion there was no reason to ever see them again," Tolle said. "I ran the idea past my therapist, and though I think he secretly thought it a splendid idea—he neither approved nor disapproved, but—what was crucial—neither did he caution me against the decision. And he actually laughed when I first presented the idea to him, and commented—I was on the couch three times a week, and he was rigorously non-directive, so this was a rare event—that this was definitely a novel way to resolve a parent-child conflict.

"I consulted with a young rabbi I knew who was delighted by the idea —he was a balletomane and a friend of Allegra's mother—and drove up to Hadley with him and two friends, the three of them to serve as witnesses. It was a spectacular day in early June, and we timed our trip so that we arrived shortly before six o'clock, when I knew my parents would be on their porch, getting sloshed before dinner. I walked up to them, and said, 'I divorce you' three times. 'I divorce you. I divorce you. I divorce you.' Then I turned around, got back in the car, drove back to New York, and never saw them again."

That difference had been there from the start, Saul knew, and he had remarked on it during their first hours together in Tolle's

Greenwich Village apartment: that when she knew what she wanted to do, she could make decisions in a seemingly uncomplicated manner, and with a self-assurance that seemed forever to elude him, whereas he always felt as if major choices in his life—his having had the courage to start a conversation with her being a rare exception—were, somehow, always being made for him.

Now, when it occurred to him that on their way to Spéracèdes, they could, by making a small detour, pass through Entrevaux, he let a hand rest on her lap, and told her that if he seemed distracted it was because he'd been musing on times gone by—on the day they'd first met, on their first sojourn in France, on French villages they'd visited, and the memories coming in a rush, he'd been recalling an especially sublime afternoon they'd spent once upon a time in Entrevaux and he wondered if she recalled the afternoon he was referring to.

She said she did.

"Perhaps we can go there again," he said.

"If you wish."

"I was also wondering if you still miss the dancing."

"No," she said quickly. "Of course not."

"I remember you telling me—this was on our very first night together—that your dancer friend, Allegra Kent, considered dance to be an antidote to life."

"She was wrong," Tolle said.

"How so?"

"There is no antidote to life," Tolle said and, lifting his hand from her lap, she stood. "I think we should move on so we can arrive in Spéracèdes before dark and have time to settle in. Unless you've stopped here in order—was that the impetus for remembering Entrevaux?—to talk about divorce."

"In fact, I *was* remembering the story you told me of how you divorced your parents," he said. "But why would you think I'd want to talk about divorce? The idea of our divorcing has never occurred to me, not even when—"

"*Never?*" she said. "Not even once?"

"Although I know you don't like to have the obvious put into words—*spoken* words—I wanted to tell you how truly happy I am that we're here again," he said. "And—sit, please—I wanted to talk with you about something else."

"About—?"

"About the children," he said. "But also—and while I have your attention—I wanted to thank you for insisting we come back here together. I *am* aware of how hard—"

"Please," she said. "Enough."

"I do still love you, you know," he said.

"Spoken words," she said.

"And when I touch you," he said, "or merely look at you, as now, I still desire you."

"As much as you did, say, in Entrevaux?"

"Probably," he said.

"*Probably?*" she said.

"Probably," he said again, and smiled a half-smile to let her know he was teasing her.

"All right," she said. "What about Sam and Julia?"

Six

When you died, did I die too?

Camus, sitting next to Saul, cocked his head to the side and looked at her with a mix of skepticism and affection, and when he did she was aware again of how much, at the beginning, and again now, Saul could remind her of him.

Although I still look like an aging version of the woman whose younger incarnation was the woman you knew, I often think that woman is no longer here, and has not been here since you died. I had a great deal of admiration for her, and she has shown up now and then through the years. I do admit to missing her enormously at times—but never enough, clearly, to have done much about it.

So that Saul would think she shared his concern about Julia—he was worried because Julia had, five or six weeks before, taken up with a guy Saul said was like the others: an untrustworthy, manipulative drifter—she asked questions: Was the guy an alcoholic? Was he doing drugs? Was he abusive? Was he gainfully employed? Was he *clean*?

Saul was declaring that he would, when next he saw Julia—whether she was still with the same guy, or had moved on to the next—say something to her: something direct and blunt that from Julia's point of view would doubtless be perceived as judgmental and disapproving.

But he thought it was time he stopped being the all-loving father who accepted Julia for everything and anything she did.

"Blunt *and* direct?" Tolle asked.

Saul ignored her question, and started on one of his familiar riffs about his affinities with Camus, of how, from *their* very first day together—he and Tolle, not he and Camus—when he had watched her walk out onto Fifth Avenue he'd noted that too often he'd been a man more of reflection than of action, and he recalled that Camus had been plagued by a similar thought: by the oscillation in his life between the love of philosophy and the desire to effect *actual* change in the world.

"But you *have* effected change," Tolle said.

"I think more about the changes I've *not* been able to make—" Saul said "—the lives I've *not* been able to save. And I think of how I probably do judge Julia more harshly than is good for either of us, and—"

"You're a good father and an honorable man," Tolle said.

Saul shrugged her words away, words she had used so often they'd become pale and perfunctory, and it occurred to her, and not for the first time—could she tell him this, or would it encourage that part of him she had little desire to encourage?—that at his core, Saul was a man who, like Camus, was a moralist of a fairly pedestrian kind—that he valued loyalty, honesty, courage, hard work, and, above all, a sense of fair play. He felt most comfortable, as Camus had, among those whose origins, like his own, lay in poor or modest circumstances. Just as Camus, when a young man, had had an inordinate passion for soccer and the friends he played the game with, so in the lower middle-class Brooklyn of his childhood, Saul had had a similar passion for sports—baseball, basketball, football—and for the childhood friends with whom he played these games.

But why did I lie to him? Why, after all the years gone by, can't I tell him the truth about the accident—that I was not alone on the trail, that my father had come up alongside me, whipping his horse and lashing out at mine, forcing my horse into the stone wall, and that when I was on the ground—him hovering above me and telling me he had warned me, hadn't he? He?—he had stroked my forehead with a tenderness he rarely showed, and told me he loved me for being headstrong—that he loved me because he could not break me the way he'd broken we-knew-who—and had kissed my forehead, my cheeks, and—was I dreaming? semi-conscious?—had probed my bleeding mouth with his tongue, the sick son of a bitch.

Camus showed neither shock nor disapproval. Instead, he cast a somewhat indifferent glance toward her, then turned his attention to Saul as if Saul were a disconsolate teammate and Camus was, by turning away from Tolle and toward Saul, urging *her* to be kind to him.

But I'm protecting him, can't you see? I'm protecting him by lying to him. It's what I believe—that you lie to the people you love—for if he knew what truly happened, of what use now would it be to him? It would only confuse him...

Camus arched his eyebrows, as if to say: Confuse *him*?

Saul was saying that although he knew he'd made life-saving differences in the lives of many patients, by dwelling more often on those for whom he had *not* made a difference, he was also, he liked to think— flattered himself *by* thinking—like Camus, who had intervened privately to save the lives of many individuals, especially Algerians facing imprisonment and/or execution during the French-Algerian war, but who often despaired concerning the larger political situation. Generally—another affinity?—Camus had preferred not to make public utterances or gestures and, most notably—what caused the rupture in his friendship with Sartre—believed Algeria should remain part of France—a *département*—and that the French who had been there for several generations, as Camus' family had, should stay on as French-Algerian citizens.

What confuses me is time. What confuses me is being in France again and realizing that I'm three times the age I was when you and I met, and nearly twenty years older than you were when you died. I'm grateful for your presence, but I'm wondering: Have you returned now because you believe this time I'm going to stay indefinitely? Are you hoping, as you once said you were (though your words pleased, of course I didn't believe you), that this time I will not be returning to the States?

Camus lit a cigarette, offered her one.

What confuses me is that, yes, I do miss the dancing even though I'm at an age when women no longer dance in professional ballet companies. Other than Margot Fonteyn who, I believe, still performed with Nureyev when she was sixty, and Allegra, who danced once a year, on and off, well into her fifties, most of us are done by our late thirties. After that we can teach young women and, in classes with them, or with other dancers past their prime, we can use ballet the way—what?—the way women our age swim, or play doubles-tennis, or go to exercise classes.

With his eyes, Camus invited her to tell him more.

What confuses me is that the truth is we are here because of you—that we've returned in order to visit, again, places where you lived so that—Saul's hope, though my idea because I thought it would give him hope—our adventure might restore him and—perhaps, perhaps—restore our marriage (renew it?) and enable us to get along for the duration. Although I have withheld things—stories—from him (even as a young woman, you may recall, I've always believed, as the French do, that deception is the secret of marriage), there's nobody who knows me as well as Saul does. We've shared a history: our families, our children, our illnesses, our careers, the deaths of siblings (his brother, my sister), the deaths of our parents. Four decades, Albert. Four decades!

Saul had stopped talking about Julia, said he'd also been worrying about Sam—about Sam's immaturity, and inability to settle on a career path—and had segued from talking about Sam's meanderings to talking about the path *they* might take: about how, after they'd spent some time in Spéracèdes, they might want to begin traveling, perhaps visiting places where Camus had lived they hadn't been to on previous visits, or re-visiting places they'd visited before.

"Whenever," Tolle said, and aware that Saul might find her response dismissive—which it was—she took his hand in hers. "But why so intent on planning our stay, Saul? We'll be here for at least three months. Why not just let things happen? Why can't we be wherever we are without thinking of where we *might* be?"

"I agree," Saul said. "In truth, you seemed so distracted I was just making conversation. I thought talking about the children might have upset you."

"Can we just enjoy the view, please?" she said. "As for Julia, let's face it—she's been down this road before. She'll tire of the guy in a month or so, and go on to another."

"And if she continues in her patterns?" he said. "Can you imagine her going on the way she has through her thirties, forties, fifties—?"

"And *sixties*—?" Tolle laughed. "Like us?"

"Like *us*?" Saul said.

"Look," Tolle said. "I see no point in imagining what might be. Julia's Julia. I don't imagine her being anyone else."

Like Saul, Tolle knew, Camus had believed he truly loved his wife, his children, and the homes in which they'd lived, though he'd never felt *at* home in any of them. His only true home, he'd once said to her, was the French language. Was it one of the last things—the *very* last thing—he said to her? They had been in her hotel room—her two suitcases, packed, were by the door—and he'd been talking about how happy he was at the prospect of seeing his children again, and about wishing she could meet them some day, then had shrugged, lit a cigarette, told her how much he wished he could undo the fact of not being able to be in two places at once, and had immediately fantasized *being able* to be in two places at once—conjuring up a series of possibilities and combinations that would, as farce, go beyond anything in *La Ronde* or the many books and movies that had played with the idea that A loves B loves C loves A....

Although it's true we're here because of you, I console myself with the thought that at least we didn't meet or marry *because of you, even if our love for you was a large part of what drew us together, and—perhaps, perhaps—kept us together. After your death, I was convinced I would never love again. Having had my fondest dream come true—what could ever compare?*

Camus drew in on his cigarette, and looked at her in a way calculated to remind her that *he* was in no way responsible for *her* choices.

I agree—of course, of course—and admit, now and again, to having foisted my vow never-to-love-again on you. Though falling in love with Saul—which I did, though not in the way I fell in love with you (that began long before you and I met)—was, if not a dream come true, quite real and wonderful. And how clever of you, I sometimes thought, to have died so soon after we met so that the love could never devolve into the quotidian vagaries, betrayals, resentments, and ennui that seem to plague all love between human beings, and that, given your proclivity for sexual dalliances (and my own), would surely, with time and distance, have done us in.

After you (and before too, Saul was the only man I met who seemed— intellectually, sensually—to be my equal, and not—don't look at me that way—in a brotherly-sisterly way. Which reminds me. There's something else I've been wanting to tell you, which is that I've often thought of us—you, me, and Saul—as a ménage à trois in which one of our trio—you!—is a ghost. It's a notion I've been toying with as the basis for a story or, perhaps, a novel.

Did I tell you I'm writing again?

Camus tossed his cigarette over the wall of the terrace.

Saul was paying the bill, saying that it was probably a good idea, as Tolle had suggested, not to stop in Entrevaux, but to push on to Spéracèdes and settle in. She took out her compact, redid her lipstick, and when she looked up, Camus was gone. She looked past the place where he'd been sitting—to the lake, its surface now grey, calm, metallic—and she wondered if by talking about writing she had hurt him— had, perhaps, *wanted* to hurt him.

After she returned to the States, she'd sent him several of her short stories, had written that when she was a student at Bennington College she had taken a writing workshop with the novelist and short story writer Bernard Malamud. Malamud had encouraged her, and had done something he rarely did with students—had told her it was his opinion that she had the talent to become a writer especially since, as he sensed was true from the assiduousness with which she revised her stories, she possessed a work ethic commensurate with her talent.

Camus had written back that he knew some of Malamud's

work—had enjoyed several of his short stories, though in translation—and that, more important, he had been totally delighted—*vachement impressioné*—by the stories *she* had sent. He found them marvelously clear, inventive, and—their great virtue—ingeniously weird. Therefore, he wrote, he had the distinct honor of informing her—and *avec l'expression de mes sentiments les plus distingués*, he'd added—that he joined Monsieur Malamud in encouraging her.

It had not occurred to her, however—not consciously, at any rate—that telling Camus she was writing again—the cause of his abrupt departure?— might make him think of all the stories, essays, and books he had *not* written in the years that were stolen from him. And of what use would it be for him now, she realized, to tell him that once he was gone, and once she had seen the ballet about him and Nijinsky into production in Paris and New York, she could not recall ever again having had a desire to compose stories or to choreograph ballets until the moment, a mere three weeks ago, she had begun making plans to return to France.

Still, had he stayed a while longer she would have explained that she was not writing because of him, or for him, or out of any impulse, need, or reason other than the desire to be lost in an imaginary world she could—*in words on a page*—bring into being. She thought, too, that he would have smiled at the notion that in a *ménage à trois* where one of the parties was a ghost—thus her notion for a story that would, at least in the intimations she had of it, be decidedly whimsical—more farce than melodrama (like his suggestion of a story in which the protagonist could be in two places at once?)—the ghost would, in Stendahlian terms, be the perfect unattainable love-object.

Then, too, she had cast Camus in this role before, for just as, in *Petrushka*, the three marionettes—the Moor, the Ballerina, and Petrushka—are brought to life by the Magician, so in her ballet, the statue of Petrushka and the dead Nijinsky are brought to life by a magician—by Albert Camus, the maker of stories. The magician, however—Camus—falls in love not with Petrushka (who has fallen in love with Nijinsky), but with a young ballerina who daily places flowers on Nijinsky's grave. Only after Nijinsky is cured of his melancholy and madness, and dances again, is he free to return to his tomb, where Petrushka, once more a statue, will again watch over him. And once this happens, and only after the young ballerina has danced with each of her three men—Petrushka, Nijinsky, and Camus—is she shut, for a moment, of her own melancholy. In a final *pas de deux* Camus and the young ballerina dance, and do so without ever touching, after which the young ballerina watches Camus die a fiery death, then rise to the heavens where, as a ghost, he will watch over *her* forever. Consumed by grief, the young ballerina does a series of six *chaînés*, after which exhausted, she falls asleep on Nijinsky's tomb, her head against Petrushka's shoulder.

Sentimental stuff, of course. For precocious and sophisticated— mature?—as I may have seemed, I was nevertheless a very young woman who was still very much in love. I worked and worked, and the work— creating the ballet, seeing it into production—kept me going. That and the sense that to be in love with a ghost was not unlike being a character in a story you might have written had you been able to create a Tolle Anne Riordan who shared a body and history with a young woman others recognized as Tolle Anne Riordan, yet was—your invention—another being entirely. And I do recall wondering, as now, if you would have approved of what I'd made of you as ghost, as dancer, as magician, as lover. I knew I'd pleased you when you were a man, but would I have pleased you when— my invention—you were a ghost?

Once the ballets had been performed, however, what else was there for me to do except to join you? Kind as ever, you appeared, and cautioned me against doing what I was determined to do—you reminded me that I had told you of the attempts I'd already made (you did caution me; you never told me not to do it)—and the impulse, for that is what it always was for me—more sudden impulse than ongoing desire—I did decide that life was, to use your words, worth the pain—vaut la peine—of being lived. At the time I told myself, and in a way I thought of as quintessentially French, that my decision was—one of your favorite phrases—provisoire-définitif.

The impulse to take leave of this world, helped along by being on the couch three times a week, remained dormant for a while, but when it returned, and you chose to stay away, Saul, his timing impeccable, showed up. Had he not, I might have joined you back then. Now that I'm here again, however—to linger a while this time?—and endowed by the years with more clarity and less sentimentality, as well as a good deal less sentiment—perhaps it's time.

Seven

Saul parked the car in a garage under a Monoprix store near the center of town, then made his way down toward the marketplace. The streets were crowded: women mostly, in pairs, and arm in arm. He descended slowly, glancing into windows of shops—olive oil and olive wood products, hardware, eyeglasses, perfumes, lingerie, auto supplies—and into open doorways that revealed courtyards, fountains, laundry hanging between buildings. He loved the curved stairways, the chipped stucco walls, the hard unevenness of stone under his feet, the sound of the French language in his ears.

It was the first time he had been in Grasse since before the children were born, and when he arrived at the lower part of town—La Place Aux Aires—he was pleased to find that the marketplace was essentially as he remembered it: long rows of vendors, their fruits vegetables, fish, meats, cheeses, linens, soaps, and spices on display, the vendors shouting the praises of their products: *poison frais…! légumes directmenet du jardin…! bon prix…! bon marché…! bon marché…!*

Her laptop computer on a small wrought-iron table, Tolle had been working in the garden when he left, and when he kissed her goodbye—on the top of her head, so as not to distract her—she had turned to him quickly, had pulled him down and pressed her mouth hungrily against his.

61

The warmth of the sun, on his back and shoulders now that he had passed into the open air of the marketplace, reminded him of the warmth and strength of her hand, and with it of the acute feeling of tenderness he had, in that moment, felt toward her. He thought also of their lovemaking—slower than usual—the afternoon before, their third day in Spéracèdes, after which, at dusk, they had, from their balcony, watched lights come on across the valley below and in Cannes. It was as if, these first days back, they were determined to recreate sensations like those they had known their first time here. He experienced a sudden desire to turn around, to tell Tolle he didn't want to be in the marketplace—not the first time he returned, at any rate—without her. Would she put aside her writing, and return with him? Would she take his hand and lead him through...?

But why the unexpected flood of feeling now, he wondered. Why this distinctly unfamiliar urge to open his heart to her: to talk with her about his needs and his fears—about all he felt he had not said, or done, or achieved? Was it his age, and—what he had not told her—the occasional shortness of breath he'd been experiencing lately? In three months he would be sixty-eight years old. Still, he reasoned, if he lost ten or twelve pounds—if he went back to jogging, swimming, and tennis, and if he ate more sensibly, he was confident he'd be fine. Though he wondered too: if he left the world now, would she miss him?

Doubtless, he thought, she would grieve for a while. Doubtless she would talk with Sam and Julia about what a good and admirable man he was. Surely she would emphasize what Sam and Julia already knew: that he was highly esteemed by others, especially those in the world of AIDS with whom he'd worked. Most likely, though, she would be relieved. The truth, he knew, was that he was a good and admirable man mostly—only?—when he was with his patients, one-on-one, or mentoring his medical students.

At breakfast, he and Tolle had talked about dinner: fish with fennel, if fennel was available; fresh vegetables—whatever looked good; perhaps some couscous; fruit and cheese—he'd buy the fish first, ask the man from whom he bought the cheese which one went best with it. A bottle each of red and white wine. He stared at the riot of color that lay before him, but remained momentarily incapable of moving forward. Was it the letter, he wondered, and the confusion he felt for not having told Tolle about it? And what if Fiona kept her word, and actually tracked him down and showed up?

He started on his round of the stalls, made his purchases—bread, *paté*, olives, olive oil, tomatoes, fennel, peppers, squash. He bought fish, cheese, wine. When, his *panier* heavy with goods, he was ready to start the climb back to the center of town, he found that he was feeling faint. The rich mix of fragrances, from the market and the restaurants that lined the sides of the market—spices, grilled sausage, simmering garlic—was thick and heady. Some of the stalls were closing—the open market ended at noon—the merchants packing up, putting their boxes and cartons into cars and small trucks. He thought of buying flowers but, looking around and seeing none, reminded himself that flowers had always been sold in La Place Aux Herbes, a market located in a part of the city that lay below La Place Aux Aires.

His shirt sticking to the small of his back, he walked in the shade of the arcade that bordered the open market, took a seat in the first café he came to, and asked for a *pastis*, after which he ordered *la formule*: melon with cured ham, followed by a *pavé* of grilled rumpsteak with *pommes frites*, and a *crème caramel*. He took out Fiona's letter, placed it to the left side of his plate.

He ate slowly, and when he was done with his steak and potatoes, he ordered coffee. The coffee was rich and black, and he found himself craving a cigarette. He asked the waiter if there was a *tabac* nearby, patted his pockets to indicate he had no more—"*Je n'en ai plus*"—and the waiter returned a minute later with a pack of Gitanes ('*Fumer Tue*' in bold letters on the pack's front), tapped out a single cigarette, and lit it for him.

Saul drew in on the cigarette, imagined his thoughts, like fumes, floating upwards and dissolving in the balm of day. He put on aviator-style sunglasses he had purchased from a street vendor in Brooklyn. Who *was* this man, he imagined people asking. An expatriate writer

63

livng in a villa on the Cote d'Azur? A CIA operative posing as a retired businessman? A gay man sentenced to death, T-cells nearing zero and spending his last days in the place he loved most in the world? An aging actor who had appeared in several of Jean Cocteau's movies—a man who had been friends with Jean Gabin and Jeanne Moreau, and with Cocteau's lover, the actor Jean Marais...?

Yes, he decided. That was who he was. Although they had never seen him—a slim, handsome young man they regularly saw in the village performed Marais's errands for him—Marais had been living in Spéracèdes when Saul and Tolle had first stayed there. Nor had they ever seen Picasso, who lived a few miles away in Mougins, though they had twice parked nearby and walked around the walls of his estate, hoping to catch a glimpse of him.

Graham Greene and Françoise Sagan had been living nearby that year, in Cap d'Antibes, where Somerset Maugham had lived, and John Collier—a friend of Jerry Ravitch—lived a mile or so below Spéracèdes, in Peymeinade. At Jerry's suggestion, Tolle telephoned Collier, told him of her admiration for his short stories, and Collier had invited her and Saul to several of his Sunday afternoon gatherings, these attended mostly by American expatriate screenwriters, many of whom had been blacklisted during the McCarthy era.

James Baldwin had been living in Saint Paul de Vence, Harvey Swados in Cagnes, James Salter in a house outside of Grasse that Robert Penn Warren had lived in before him, and one of Tolle's teachers at Bennington, Nicholas Delbanco, with whom Saul suspected she'd had a fling, had lived in Grasse, and had written a novel, *Grasse, 3/23/66*, to prove it.

Was Jean Marais still alive? Saul doubted it. But he did not doubt that Marais could, despite his fame, have lived on in Spéracèdes forever without having anyone from the village, much less a tourist, bother him, just as Saul could sit at this café all day without anyone bothering him. And if he sat at the café long enough, would Fiona come by?

He stubbed out his cigarette, asked the waiter for another. He had heard stories of husbands or wives who said they were going to the corner to get a pack of cigarettes and would be back in a few minutes, but who never returned and were never found. He drank the last of his coffee—the bitter grounds tasted sublime, and would serve to mask the cigarette taste—took off his sunglasses, opened Fiona's letter.

Dear Saul,

So here I am, and I know you're thrilled to hear from me. But don't break out the champagne just yet, okay? The news isn't all good.

And here it is: I was diagnosed with ovarian cancer about a year and a half ago. From what I know of these matters—I started out in internal medicine, remember, so I've witnessed in other women what lies ahead for me—I probably have four or five months left. As often happens with this stupid disease, there were no symptoms until it was too late. I had some lower abdominal bloating, my periods lasted a bit longer than usual, and there was minor inter-menstrual bleeding. I felt full all the time, but figured—you know me—that I probably needed to go on a diet again. (I'm nothing, you used to tell me—a compliment, right?—if not a woman of appetites.) When the symptoms persisted, I went to see my gynecologist, who felt a mass. We did an ultrasound, and then a CT scan to see if the beast had spread. None of the news was good. The tumor was epithelial, no surprise, but had extended to the uterus and other pelvic tissues. Implants on the peritoneal surface, as expected, were confirmed.

We tried the usual and the extraordinary: a debulking—don't you love the word?—to get rid of as much of the tumor as we could, and then for five or six months, the standard first line chemotherapy—a carboplatin, platinum, and taxane compound, and when that didn't take, our second line stuff—"salvage" is the operative term (though, forgive inadvertent pun, there was no surgery from this point on)—doxil, another taxane compound, and a few investigational drugs that are in phase II studies and whose names I won't recount here. All this (more on request) to assure you that I haven't been playing the martyr: I really did want to live.

So why the letter now, and why the unnecessarily detailed clinical report that delays its reason?

Here we go:

I'm writing to you because, quite simply, you're the kindest man

I've ever known, and because I'd dearly love to spend a portion of the time I have left with you.

I'm in dire need, that is, of a huge dose of your tenderness.

FYI: my medical team have been champs—hard working, resourceful, honest—and I take their word when they say they don't have a lot left to offer me. When the first and second line drugs fail and we're looking at third line drugs or experimental programs, we know there's no cure. And—at least as important for me—there's No Control. Though nobody has good numbers on this stuff, and though my doctors hedge on the time frame, we do know the score, right?

So I've made an executive decision: I know where you are and how to get to you, and I intend to visit you and to spirit you away with me, and should you try to escape, you can be certain I'll hunt you down mercilessly. I am, as you used to remind me too many times, nothing if not spunky, gritty, determined, persistent: a scrapper, a fighter, a worker, blah blah blah.

But maybe not. Maybe, mailed or unmailed, writing this letter will suffice to calm the roiling waters of my soul. The best course might be/have been simply to show up on your doorstep, but before that's possible, I do need to attend to some basics—matters financial and familial: wills, disposition of worldly goods, disposition of usable body parts, etc.

I took leave from the hospital six weeks ago, and that leave has now been extended infinitely. The hospital has been as kind as a hospital can be. I'll put in a few hours a week on a consulting basis for a handful of patients I've been working with, none of whom, thanks to the magic of antiretrovirals, are in extremis the way I am—and isn't it amazing, Saul, what we've lived to see since the days when I was a resident and you and I were attending more funerals each month than....

Okay. Stop. Let's ease up on the nostalgia. There will, I trust—I know—be time for that when we're together. Or maybe not: why, especially now, stay locked in the past by rehearsing what was— what we've already experienced and what we know we experienced?

Which brings us to the essential question: Did I ever stop loving you? No. Did I love others while I kept on loving you? Yes. I was with one man—not a doctor—for four years, and we even lived together for two of those years, but he was—imagine!—younger than I *was, and he wanted a family, and by the time I met him, I didn't. (And need I dwell on the ironies replete in this happenstance? The child you and I didn't have—who would be college-age now—the children I thought I wanted back then, and then the opportunity, rejected, when—*my decision—*I decided no.)*

And, since we're talking irony, let's not fail to mention the fact that women who've been pregnant are alleged to have a 50% decreased risk for developing ovarian cancer, and that oral contraceptives, my life companion, are also alleged to decrease the risk. Once again—a theme I borrow from your med school lectures—let attention be directed in these medical matters to the fact of how-little-we-truly-know.

The long and short then: I will see you soon. Ready or not, here I come.

Love
F.

What he felt, strangely, was envy. How wonderful to know the day of one's death, and to possess the freedom such knowledge could bring. He wondered, though: did the increase of affection he'd been feeling toward Tolle of late derive from the prospect of being with Fiona again? But Fiona *dying*? Fiona *dead*? She was, at most, in her early forties, perhaps ten years older than Julia....

He imagined telling Fiona that instead of replying to her letter he had written a letter to the President in which letter he called the President a murderer. That her letter had been the inspiration for the letter to the President would doubtless delight her, and when he pictured her breaking into a broad smile, he smiled too. He signalled the waiter for the check and, looking past the waiter, was aware that a woman, a cup of coffee at her lips, was looking at him.

He paid the check, walked to her table.

"You're Katherine Turetzky, aren't you?" he said.

"*Grey* Turetzky, actually," she said. "Katherine is my middle name."

"Grey?"

"My parents were related to Zane Grey—a great uncle on my mother's side of the family," she said. "Like Mister Grey, I was born in Zanesville, Ohio. But consider this. They could have named me Zane—which surely, beginning in grade school, would have devolved into 'Zaney,' don't you think?"

"Probably."

"Katherine will do, however," she stated. Then: "You're American, of course, and you seem, to judge from the way you were smiling, a happy man today."

"May I sit?" he asked.

She gestured with a hand, indicating that he could.

"My wife and I saw you perform at the Brooklyn Academy of Music three or four years ago," he said. "You played the Schubert B flat trio, my wife's favorite, and you wore a lovely burgundy gown, trimmed with black lace that Tolle—my wife—commented on. We were planning to go to your concert tomorrow night—we saw the *affiche* in Grasse—but first, please, what *happened*? Why the Turetzky *Duo* instead of Trio?"

He was aware that he was talking very quickly—that he was not, as he usually was in these situations, relaxed and confident. He waited a few seconds, but she waited too, her gaze steady, slightly bemused.

"Actually, we arrived here four days ago," he said, "but I wondered then—when I first saw the poster—about what happened."

"My husband Alex died three weeks ago."

Saul blinked. "I'm sorry. I didn't mean to be so glib," he said.

"He died in Paris, which was his favorite city," Katherine said. "We'd been to the opera—*Manon*—and we were drinking champagne, a custom of ours after attending opera—and of a sudden, he sat up in bed, opened his mouth wide—an enormous oval, as if, I've thought since, he was in a chorus, singing 'Gloria'—said a very quiet 'Oh!' and then he was gone. It was his heart, of course—his first attack, and his last. The pain seemed minimal, though how is one to know."

She took out a cigarette, handed Saul a matchbook so he could light the cigarette for her. "We decided to go ahead with the tour, Eugene and I—Eugene is Alex's brother—and all things considered, this seemed best."

"All things considered?"

"All things considered."

"I see that I've been indiscreet," he said. "I should leave."

"Why?"

The crisp directness of her question set him at ease. "I'm Saul Davidoff," he said, and he reached across the table to shake her hand. "I'm a physician. My wife and I are here for a few months—on a kind of mini-sabbatical. I work with AIDS patients."

"You have a wife?"

"Why yes. I thought I mentioned her."

"But only four times."

She laughed, and when she did, Saul found himself laughing with her.

"You look younger when you laugh," Katherine said. "Do you laugh often?"

"Not in recent years."

"But don't you think we should laugh more?" she asked. "Before his death, Alex—my husband—had not laughed for eight months."

"You kept count?!"

"Of course not," she said. "My goodness, but you're literal. *Je rigolais avec toi.*"

"I don't understand."

"I was playing—making a joke with you," she said. "You speak French, don't you? I would have thought, watching you with the waiter, that you did."

"I did—I do," he said. "Look—can we start over again? Your husband died three weeks ago. What then? Did you return to the States?"

"I shipped Alex back—his body, that is—but kept his cello. It's a Goffriller, and quite valuable. It's probably worth more than the two of us—the *three* of us, for that matter—alive or dead. Shall I tell you about it?"

"Please."

He sat back and, while she talked, he watched her mouth. Her lips—thin, wide, sharply articulated and slightly bow-shaped—reminded him of Garbo's, and he made a mental note to tell her this later on. It was the supreme and ever-effective compliment—to compare a woman's features to that of a movie star, especially to one from a bygone era: Lombard, Lamarr, Oberon, Astor, Del Rio, Harlow, Shearer, Gardner, Hayworth, Brooks....

"It was made in Venice, in the early eighteenth century," she said. "The body, neck, ribs, and scroll, as with most violins, are of maple. The top is of spruce, however, and the end piece, tail piece, and pegs are of rosewood. In all, there are thirty-five separate pieces of wood joined by glue, and the glue, you see—hide-glue, from horses—is the crucial element: it must give way and break before the wood does. Am I boring you?"

"Not possible."

"The soul of the cello, however—" she said, without acknowledging his response "—the technical term is just that—*l'âme*—a slender piece of wood that determines tone and timbre, perhaps a quarter of an inch thick, and set into the body between the back and the belly just below the foot of the bridge, is of pine. Goffrillers are the most valuable of cellos, and with good reason. Their tone is impeccable, and capable of an enormous range of shadings—brilliant, dark, light, and also, when needed, powerful. Alex often said that a fine cello is like a good woman: warm and capricious. Nor does it like to be forced. The less power you apply, the more you get. The weight of the bow alone can create sound."

"I was remembering the photo on the poster—for your concert," he said. "It seems to have been taken some years ago, yet I was thinking of how much more attractive you are now."

"In my maturity, yes?" she said, then continued: "Goffriller himself—Matteo Goffriller—despite his unique gifts, was never admitted into the instrument makers guild. Alex believed that his particular Goffriller—he called it 'Tiger' because of the closely striped grain on the back—was alive: that it changed with the seasons, that it was somehow learning the music *for* him when he practiced. But let me ask you this: If I continue to describe the cello—to lavish praise upon it—can I count on you to do the same for me?"

"Surely you know—have been told—that you're an exceptionally beautiful woman."

"Surely you know that you are, as young people put it these days, coming on to me."

"No—just using my powers of clinical observation to accurately evaluate the presenting situation."

"You said that you work with AIDS patients," she said. "So tell me: do I, at the start of my career as widow, remind you of those women in previous generations, afflicted with tuberculosis—the Camilles of their time who, wan, flush-cheeked, and dying, represented an ideal of beauty? Will AIDS now do for us what TB used to do?"

"Hardly," he said. "AIDS ravages those it visits in godawful ways, though if you were in the early stages—it has a long incubation time, ten years on average—there would be no visible difference."

In his mind's eye, he was seeing Ethan Goldstein. Ethan's body was swollen, his skull shaved, his face—as if afflicted with a severe case of psoriasis—flaking, scaling, crusting. There was an intubation tube down his throat, an intravenous line in his left arm, an oxygen mask over mouth and nose. Ethan's family—mother, father, sister, two brothers—were in the room with him, but Dale, Ethan's long-time companion, for whom he sometimes asked when consciousness returned, was absent.

"Actually—" Saul said "—do you mind if I change the subject slightly?—I think you'll find this of interest—one of my more extraordinary patients was a musician—a young man who was a musical savant."

"*Was*? Then he's no longer with us—"

"He passed away several years ago. He was twenty-nine."

"His instrument?"

"Yours—the piano—which must be why he came to mind. Most musical savants are autistic, of course: we recognize them early on by the fact that they're unable to relate to other children in basic ways.

71

Their particular genius, though, is not for calendrical calculations, or for setting long bus or train schedules to heart, but for music."

"When we traveled by train or plane," Katherine said, "we'd purchase a seat for Alex's cello, and, on wide-body planes, for example—across oceans—it would sit between us."

"As if it were your child?" Saul asked.

"We had no children," she said. "But please—I interrupted you—tell me more about these musical geniuses."

"Though they can hardly speak, many of them, or sign their names in any but the crudest way, they can, after listening to a sonata a few times—Beethoven, Chopin, Mozart—reproduce it faithfully. And more than faithfully—not merely by rote, but with what seems genuine musical feeling. Most show this talent before the age of one, most are male, they are all visually impaired, and they *all* play piano."

"You've studied them obviously."

"I knew Ethan."

"Do you know all your patients in the way you knew him?"

"I hope so, though AIDS patients will often wander from clinic to clinic and doctor to doctor, with stops in between that further debilitate them. And there's also this, that doctors have favorites too. Ethan was a favorite."

"But—" Katherine hesitated "—if you'll permit me a somewhat cold calculus, isn't it true that, like Ethan, all the patients who come to you die?"

"Well, we *all* die—but I understand what you're getting at. Until recently most of my patients did die, and most of what I did was palliative. Antiretrovirals, however, have made an enormous difference. Ethan was one of the last patients I lost."

"How sad," she said, "yet how wonderful. To have known so many people in their time of dying."

"In a strange way, yes," Saul said. "I often miss the years when the epidemic was exploding— when there was a sense of camaraderie that was *exhilarating*, when we were discovering things nobody knew anything about, when we were desperate to save the world, terrible as it can be—"He stopped. "Forgive me, please. I seem to be going down a road that's much too dark for such a pretty day."

"Still, you've had your own family. A wife—"

"—and two children, both grown. Sam and Julia."

Saul thought of telling Katherine that Julia had been a gifted pianist—had given recitals when a child, had been offered scholarships to summer music camps. Before she completed her junior year of high school, however, she had stopped playing and had never, as far as he knew, touched a piano again.

"Perhaps, where Alex is now, he and the boy—this Ethan—have found one another," Katherine said, "and the boy has replaced me as Alex's accompanist."

"How long will you be staying in Grasse?"

"We don't stay here. We *play* here. We're staying a few miles away, in Tourettes-sur-Loup. Do you know it?"

"My favorite in the area, actually, whereas Grasse, which has its merits, is—"

"Is what?"

"Camus called it the capital of barbers' assistants," Saul said.

"We're here until Sunday. There's our concert tomorrow night, and on Sunday morning we leave for Genoa."

"And between now and tomorrow night—?" Saul waited, and when she did not answer his question, spoke again: "You must be practicing together more frequently now that you have a new repertoire."

"I should correct what I said before, about your young man being Alex's accompanist. In the beginning, you see—Mozart, Haydn, Corelli—it was the violin and cello that were considered to be accompanying the piano."

"Have you thought of going on tour as a soloist?"

"To be alone on a stage has always seemed to me a kind of death. At the same time, however, I dread the possibility that I may now be linked to Eugene forever, but without Alex between us."

"Eugene is difficult?"

"Eugene is in love with me."

"And—?"

"And I'm not in love with him, though on the day of Alex's death I was a bit out of my mind, so that when we were alone after the ambulance had taken Alex away, and Eugene comforted me—" She stopped. "But why am I telling you this? Can you tell me that, doctor? Why do I feel so free to mouth off this way?"

"Trust," Saul said. "Or an intimation of trust."

"I doubt it."

"You've clearly been through an ordeal, and—"

"Actually, Eugene and I have a practice scheduled for later today." She glanced at her watch. "We prefer early mornings or late afternoons. What I was wondering, therefore, is this. We can continue our conversation, or—if you have the time and interest—I could make you a cup of coffee. The apartment I'm staying in has a splendid view—and that way you would also get to see Alex's cello."

When he awoke, Katherine was sitting a few feet from the bed, reading, and he saw, with relief—the shutters were open—that it was still daylight. Katherine wore a thin, peach-colored robe,. The cello, resting upright in its stand, was beside her.

"I can't make a decision," he said, "as to which is more beautiful— you or the cello."

"Well, given its age, the cello certainly has shown itself to have greater staying power," she said. She put down her book, sat beside him on the bed. "But we need to do something for you before you return home. Stay here, please."

She came back a minute later carrying a basin and pitcher. She poured water into the basin, dipped a washcloth into the basin, squeezed out excess water and, starting with his toes, began washing him. The washcloth was warm, almost hot.

"There's nothing quite like it, is there, when it's good the first time," she said.

"Camus once said that—"

She stopped his mouth with the palm of her hand. "I hope you won't be offended, but at the moment I'm really not interested in what Monsieur Camus said. I've made coffee, however, and we have some time—I don't have to meet Eugene until five, and it's not yet three."

She dipped the cloth in the basin again, began washing his thighs and groin. Saul placed his hand between her legs. She lifted his hand, set it back on the bed.

"Your hands are strong," he said.

"We have Messrs. Czerny and Hanon to thank for that."

"What I was thinking, a moment ago—when I awoke—was of Meursault, in *The Stranger*, and of how, in prison, the days become both long *and* short for him, yet always the same day."

"This is your prison, then?"

"If you hadn't told me it was not yet five—"

"Not yet three," she said.

"Not yet three then. But if you hadn't told me, I wouldn't have known what day it was—whether I'd been sleeping for two minutes, or two hours, or had slept through the night."

She kissed him on the chest, then let herself lie there. "When I have this—you and me, in this way—I feel I can go on," she said.

"I don't understand."

She sat up abruptly, as if someone had struck her.

"Most of all, I took pleasure from our conversation," she said. "I've been thinking of your question, as to why it is we don't seem able, as a species, to think long-term, and I wish I could come up with answers. The question seems important to you."

"And I wish I could buy that estate for you—the one you were telling me about—the one where the woman presided over her salons. What was her name?"

"Viardot. Pauline Viardot. Pauline Viardot-Garcia."

"If you sold the cello, would that give you enough money to buy the property you need?"

She stood. "Let me get the coffee. You need to be alert on the drive home."

When she returned, he sat up. "The French are a very practical people, particularly when it comes to love, don't you think?" She handed him a cup, sat beside him. "'It's not the night of love that matters,' they say, 'but the cup of coffee in the morning.'"

"But it's not morning."

"You would notice that, wouldn't you," she said. "And think of divorce. In the States these days, five minutes after a married man or woman falls in love with someone else, or grows tired of his or her mate, they divorce, the family is destroyed, and the children, when there are children involved, affected for the rest of their lives. Here, though things are changing somewhat—Americanizing, if you will—a man can still have his *petite amie à coté*, a woman can have her liaisons—her *cinq à sept*—and families stay together. Much more practical—much more *sane*—don't you think?"

"I've been married to the same woman for nearly forty years."

"Which reminds me," Katherine said. "Tomorrow evening after the concert, please do not come backstage to congratulate me."

"Because—?"

"Because if you come backstage, your wife will know at once."

"And tomorrow, before the concert? I could—"

"I am occupied all day tomorrow."

"Then this afternoon was—?"

"Yes."

"Talk about short-term," he said.

"If my dream comes true—of having a salon like Viardot's—I promise to invite you. The salon was in her country home, near Baden-Baden. She built a small theater there which she called *le théatre de pomme de terre*. She and her children put on operas and operettas, some of which she wrote. Admission was one potato. If you'll remember to bring a potato—"

He set his cup down on the night table, pulled her down to him, his hand on the back of her neck.

"You have an admirable quotient of violence in you," she said a short while later. "I like that."

"I noticed."

"I've talked with Eugene about our recreating an evening like one at Viardot's salon. We might perform some of the duets she composed for piano and violin. Perhaps some songs her sister Maria performed. Her sister was a brilliant singer who died before she was thirty. It was her death, in fact, that gave birth to Viardot's debut, for when Maria died, Pauline, who was sixteen at the time, took her place."

"Camus called his twins—his children—'plague' and 'cholera,'" Saul said.

"Then he was not quite as sentimental as I thought," Katherine said. "But it's interesting you've chosen as hero a man who is a writer, and not a doctor. Why not someone like Schweitzer, or this man Paul Farmer, who works with AIDS patients in Haiti? Or even someone like Chekhov or Maugham, who were doctors *and* writers?"

"I don't know," Saul said.

"You must be an excellent doctor," Katherine said. "I can't recall the last time I met a man—especially one in your profession—who would say 'I don't know' with such ease. Speaking of writers, though, did I mention that Turgenev came to all of Viardot's salons? He was severely depressed, and Viardot would try to charm him out of his depression. Have you ever suffered from depression?"

"No."

"You're a lucky man then," she said. She paused, and when she spoke again, she did so as if reciting from memory. "Turgenev was madly in love with Viardot and followed her from Saint Petersburg to Baden-Baden, and then to Paris. He lived next door to her and her family, in fact—her husband and their children—until his death. Clara Schumann said that Viardot was the most brilliant woman she ever met. Before marrying Louis Viardot, who was twenty-one years her senior, and director of the *Théatre Italien*, and before retiring from the stage, she was herself much in demand as an opera singer. She had a three octave range. Like her father, she became a great teacher to other singers. She was also fluent in Spanish, French, German, Italian, English, and Russian, and if you don't stop me I will go on and on and on, *singing* her praises, so to speak, and—"

Saul kissed her, traced the contours of her face with his index finger.

"I know Paul Farmer, by the way," he said. "I don't know him well, but we've met. His wife and daughter live in Paris. Given his work, however, not just in Haiti but in the Soviet Union, he doesn't get to spend much time with them."

"I've known his type of man," Katherine said. "Admirable, to be sure, but we wouldn't want all our men—or all our doctors, for that matter—to be like him, would we."

Saul tried to draw Katherine down to the bed again, and when he did, she stood.

"I think we should leave things as they were," she said. "Actually, Eugene and I will be performing one of Viardot's favorites tomorrow night—Fauré's 'Berceuse-Romance.'"

She stepped away from the bed. "You should go now," she said. "The afternoon has been wonderful. You are a dear and fascinating man. I will think of you often."

"Do you say that to all the boys?" he asked.

"Don't be vulgar," she said. "Please. What we had *was* wonderful. Now it's over, and we must be practical. I will think of you often, and with great kindness."

Eight

When Saul arrived home, Tolle was in the garden, asleep, a book on her lap. He kissed her, softly, on the lips.

She opened her eyes. "My prince," she said.

"Your *Jewish* prince," he said. "And your Jewish doctor."

"Same thing," she said. "What time is it?"

"Just past four."

"My goodness. Did you—?"

"All put away. I was able to get fennel, and a most healthy looking *rouget*—it should be very sweet."

"And you had a good time?"

"*Tellement plaisant*," he said. "I shopped. I wandered. I had a lovely *prix fixe* meal. I read *Nice-Matin* and the *International Tribune*, I dozed in a café...."

"Just what the doctor ordered, yes?" she said. "Or the doctor's wife."

Tolle yawned, raised her arms, stretched and, her eyes closed, smiled. When she was coming out of sleep this way—drowsy, child-like—he felt especially affectionate towards her.

"Same thing?" he asked.

"Perhaps," she said. "But oh—we have news—and it didn't come to me in a dream. While you were gone we had two visitors."

"Tell me."

"Jerry Ravitch," she said. "He's still living in the same house, but he has a new and larger studio he's eager to have us see. It's on the road to Cabris. On one of the last good pieces of property available that he could afford. He wondered if we noticed that the village has more than tripled in size since we were last here, as has Cabris—Cabris even more than Spéracèdes. Mostly rich Germans buying villas."

"What other cheerful information did he bring?"

"That he heard we'd returned, which news thrilled him. The man does love you, Saul."

"Probably," Saul said, "although my impression was that he loved you a bit more than he did me."

"Oh?"

"Didn't I once catch him making a pass at you, in their kitchen?"

"Only once?"

"Yes—but I only *caught* him once."

"True," Tolle said. "Still, I invited him for dinner tomorrow night."

"But we were planning to go to the concert in Grasse tomorrow night. I bought tickets."

"Is that so important? It's just a concert, after all, and Jerry—"

"Okay, okay—how is the guy?" Saul asked.

"His usual antic self, though he *has* aged. He's eighty-five."

And the second visitor, Saul wondered: *Fiona?* And if she *had* come by, how would she have identified herself—a doctor? a colleague? one of his former residents? And what reason could she have given for being here?

"You don't believe I *intentionally* forgot about the concert, do you?" she said.

"No."

"I thought you'd want to see Jerry. You and he were quite close, after all. Michelle died—what was it, four years ago now?"—and we've been out of touch so much of the time, which is why—"

"Of course we'll see Jerry tomorrow night. And of course I'm delighted he came by. It's only that—"

"It's only that you wanted us to be alone, at least for a while longer. You wanted this to be *our* time—time away from everyone and everything."

"Yes."

"I sensed he was hurt that we'd returned and hadn't let him know we were here," Tolle said. "I started to tell him the story of why—your letter to the President, the shameful way the medical school reacted—but I thought *you* would want the pleasure of telling him what happened. It's the kind of thing—the letter—*he* might have done."

"Did he say as much—about not having heard from since we arrived?"

"No. But I *like* that."

"You like *what*—that he hadn't heard from us?"

"No. 'The Story of Why'—the words I used when I said, 'I started to tell him the story of why.'"

Saul thought of the smoothness of the cello to his touch, and of how surprisingly warm the wood had been. He thought of what Camus had written—or had Camus been quoting someone else: Flaubert? Stendahl?—about how unfortunate it was that extremely beautiful women always surprised us less the second time we were with them.

"You said we had another visitor," he said.

"Yes," she said. "A man who said he was a patient—perhaps a former patient. He's here on vacation—in Cannes—and learned that you were here also."

"Did he give his name?"

"Dale something—Peckrath, I think—in his early or mid-fifties, I'd guess. We talked for a while—he's a dancer—*was* a dancer—and he seemed to know that I'd taught ballet. He also made a point of telling me how wonderful you've been with friends of his—dancers—whose numbers, as we know, have been disastrously reduced by the AIDS epidemic."

"Yes," Saul said.

"Do you know him?"

"I know him."

"He said he'd stop by again in a day or two."

*

"Well, you both look truly magnificent," Jerry said. He stepped back, in the way he might have stepped away from a canvas were he painting their portraits. "I like you in silver hair, Tolle—distinguished, elegant, ethereal—and you, Saul! Tolle tells me you'll be sixty-eight in a few weeks but to these keen eyes you don't look a day over sixty-seven."

They were standing in the kitchen, Tolle preparing dinner, singeing peppers and turning them with wooden tongs while Saul opened a bottle of white wine.

"Only listen," Jerry went on. "Did you hear the one about the old man, weeping away on a park bench…?"

"No," Saul said. "I didn't hear the one about the old man weeping away on a park bench."

"Well," Jerry said, "his friend comes by and asks him what's wrong, and the old man tells him he's fallen in love. 'She's twenty-seven, and drop-dead gorgeous, and every morning before she leaves for work, she makes love to me. And at noon she comes home and she's kind to me again. And in the evening she makes dinner, and we watch TV, play a game or two of Canasta—she's not into Pinochle, but nobody's perfect—and before sleep she makes wild love to me, and…' And at this, the old man again burst into tears. 'So what's the problem?' his friend asks. 'It sounds like paradise. Why are you crying?'"

Jerry paused for effect, then continued. "'Why am I crying?'" the old man asked. 'Why am I *crying*? I'm crying *because I can't remember where I live!*'"

Saul raised his glass. "To old friends," he said.

"Speaking of old friends," Jerry said. "I have a proposal. I know you've been cooking up a sumptuous dinner in honor of our reunion, and I know we have lots to talk about—so much to say and not to say, right?—but this time you'll be here for a few months, so here's the deal. There's a concert I'd love to go to in Grasse tonight, and I thought maybe the three of us could go together."

"The Turetzky concert?" Tolle asked.

"How did you know?" Jerry asked.

"Because we were planning to go. When you came by yesterday, I was so happy to see you that I forgot to—"

"Hey—there's time for *everything*," Jerry said. "We're in the *midi*, after all, and if we can't be *dolce far niente* here, what's the point? And it's still early. So—*d'accord*? We'll drink, we'll eat, and then we'll go—?"

"Fine by me," Tolle said.

"Kate's an old and very dear friend," Jerry said.

"How dear?" Tolle asked.

"Ah," Jerry said, a finger to his lips. "You would ask that, wouldn't you?"

"Actually," Saul said, "we saw them in Brooklyn several years ago when they were a trio."

"There's that too," Jerry said. "I haven't seen Kate in five or six years, but her husband died recently—I read it in the *Tribune*—so when I saw they'd be playing here, she and her brother-in-law, I bought a ticket, only when I was here yesterday and you invited me for dinner, I forgot, and then—"

"We wondered why they were no longer a trio," Tolle said. "How sad for her."

"Not really," Jerry said. "Sad for *him*, certainly—but where he is now, he doesn't know that."

"Tolle's very concerned about you," Jerry said. He and Saul sat in the garden while they waited for Tolle to call them to dinner. "When I stopped by, and after the usual hello-how-are-you-it's-been-ages-and-oh-how-I-missed-you and the rest, what she talked about mostly was you."

"Should I be flattered?"

"Come on, come on," Jerry said. "Don't be hard-assed with me. She's worried you're heading for a major depression, and that you're—"

"—in denial," Saul said.

"Exactly. She mentioned a letter you wrote to the President."

"I told the President he was a murderer," Saul said.

"*No shit?*"

"No shit."

"That's *all?*" Jerry asked. "You wrote to the President and said, 'You're a murderer'?"

"Not quite," Saul said. "The letter had to do with cuts in funding for AIDS programs."

"Tolle said you've been doing important work—innovative stuff about using TB clinics to screen for AIDS, and that you've been going to South Africa several times a year. She's proud of you, buddy, and—better yet—she still loves you. Did you know that?"

"Yes."

"But it doesn't seem to make you happy."

"Should it?"

"In most cases, the love of a good woman is supposed to make a man happy."

"Then I suppose the news isn't *all* bad," Saul said

"Hey—lighten up," Jerry said. "Come on. I'm your old Brooklyn asshole buddy—talk to me. *Talk* to me! What ails you? Why so snappish?"

"I've been thinking of working in South Africa for longer periods of time," Saul said. "I can make a difference there."

"You make a difference *wherever* you are—but okay: South Africa. You've been there before. You like them. They like you. God knows, they *need* doctors like you. So what's the problem?"

Saul smiled. "I can't remember where I live," he said.

Nine

Tolle and Saul were in the garden, Tolle talking about how generous Katherine had been the night before. Katherine had had students like Julia before, she said—gifted young people who had not played piano for years—but if the early training was there, there would be embers she could fan into flames. And the fact that Julia had given up the piano completely was a good sign for it spoke to her passion *for* the piano.

After Genoa, Katherine and Eugene had concerts scheduled in Milan, Florence, Venice, Umbria, and Siena, and then—a return loop—in Menton, Monte Carlo, Avignon, Lyon, Nancy, and Paris. When she passed through the region again, she could meet with Julia if Julia were visiting. And if Julia did not visit, when Katherine returned to the States in early April, she could see her there.

"And perhaps," Saul said, "she talked of meeting Julia here so she would have a pretext for seeing Jerry again."

"She doesn't strike me as a woman who would need a pretext," Tolle said, and talked again about how much she had enjoyed the evening— after the concert the five of them had gone to a restaurant for a late dinner—and of how, when she and Katherine were alone, Katherine had told her that Eugene had been pressing his affections upon her.

"Ah—a levirate marriage in the offing," Saul said. "How wonderfully old-fashioned."

"She's known for years that Eugene cared for her," Tolle said, "and when she performs with him now, just the two of them, she does feel something akin to love for him, though this is probably due to the fact that to make music with another person, and to do so at what she called an *exalted* level—is the only thing that has ever given her true happiness."

"So much for her recently departed husband."

"Oh please," Tolle said. "We're not talking about a passionate liaison, after all. She and Eugene have known each other forever, they're our age—perhaps a few years younger—and—"

"More coffee?" Saul asked.

"What she said about music—and about passion—made sense to me," Tolle said.

"—and I think you and I both know what it means to have a passion in life," Saul said.

"And to lose it?"

Tolle picked up their cups, walked into the house, up a staircase, and into the kitchen. She set down the cups, began to make a new pot of coffee.

Do you remember, one morning, when we talked about places in Africa, Asia, or South America where we might some day wake up together? You told me about your village, about the time you taught in a school for young Jewish children, and about how much you'd loved New York City—how much you would love to show me around New York in the way I had shown you around Paris.

"Had I ever, in Brooklyn, been to Greenwood Cemetery?" you asked. And before I could decide whether or not to ask ask if your other American friend, Patricia Blake, had given you a tour there, you talked about walking along the Bowery, and of your delight in seeing elderly women still performing the old bump-and-grind, and—what touched me—your telling me that what you loved most of all was the enthusiasm of New Yorkers, after which, almost apologetically, you said there had, however, been one

quality that, to your surprise, you found lacking in Americans, especially in young Americans—present company excluded, of course, you said—and that was passion.

Were you being merely polite by not including me? I had some skills, a few talents—but neither as dancer, choreographer, or writer did I have exceptional talent—innate gifts that could compare with those of other women I knew. Even my sister Claire, about whom I rarely talked back then—even she, when still a child, showed more talent in one toe than I had in my whole body. But I hesitated to tell you these things, and to add that what I did have, and in abundance, that might make a difference if I lived long enough was passion. And I was not talking about the passion that came with making love, for wonderful as that was, I assumed that kind of passion was fairly common, and hardly exceptional. I wanted to talk about this with you, but...

"Hello again."

Tolle turned toward the door, and saw Dale standing on the other side of the glass doors, one of which he had opened.

"Oh—it's you," she said

"Yes, it's me," Dale laughed. "Who else could it be?"

"I meant it's you—the man who came by two days ago," Tolle said. "The dancer."

"Former dancer," Dale said.

"Same here," Tolle said.

Dale looked past Tolle. "*Bonjour, Monsieur le Docteur,*" he said.

"How long have you been here?" Saul asked.

Tolle turned toward Saul, whom she had not heard enter the kitchen. "This is the man I told you about who came by the other day," she said.

"You do remember me then," Dale said.

"Of course."

"I'm pleased."

"I asked you a question," Saul said.

"I've been here a few minutes—five perhaps," Dale said. "I saw you in the garden, but since you and your wife were engaged in what seemed a private conversation, I didn't want to interrupt."

"What can I do for you?"

"You might offer me a cup of coffee."

"Just tell me what I can do for you, Dale."

"I've made enough for three," Tolle said. "Please do join us."

"I make it a habit not to go where I am not welcome," Dale said. "That said, I will state the occasion for my visit, which is that I've been staying in Cannes and have been having some alarming symptoms."

"Yes—?" Saul said.

"I went to a hospital in Cannes last week—*Les Brouissailles*—do you know it?"

"No."

"I was more than a bit desperate, which is why I went, but after I put myself in their hands, I began to *truly* despair," Dale said. "I decided to return to the States, but before I purchased my plane ticket I took the precaution of telephoning so that I could set up appointments at the clinic—I had hopes you would see me—and it was fortunate I made the call because they informed me that you weren't there—that you were here."

"They gave you my address?"

"Of course not."

"But you turned your charm on somebody, and—"

"Must we go down such a road?" Dale asked. "I'm here, Doctor Davidoff, and I need your help."

"Talk to me then."

"Shall we adjourn to the garden?" Tolle asked, and even while she found herself irritated by Saul's response to Dale, she was aware that he was already being the good clinician he'd always been—that he was scanning Dale's face: hair, scalp, eyes, mouth, skin—and putting aside whatever feelings he had *about* Dale so that he could begin to search out signs and information that would enable him to be helpful.

While, for several minutes, Dale and Tolle talked about dance—they were seated in the garden—and about dancers they had known, or

JAY NEUGEBOREN

known of, who had succumbed to the AIDS virus—Saul remained silent. Then, standing, he put out his hands, palms up, and Dale let his hands rest on them.

Saul rolled the knuckles of each of Dale's fingers between his own thumb and forefinger, and he would, Tolle knew, from conversations through the years, and especially during the early years of the pandemic when she had sometimes visited him at the hospital (in exchange for his visits to her Stamford dance studio), that Saul would be checking for tell-tale rashes, for spots that would indicate the presence of a bloodstream infection, for nails that, ragged and/or dull, signified the presence of anemia.

"Does that hurt?" Saul asked.

"A bit. Yes."

"Tender when I do this?"

"Yes," Dale said, "but you haven't asked about my symptoms."

Saul turned Dale's hands over, then let go. "Why don't you sit," he said.

Dale sat while Saul palpated his neck, then felt along the back of Dale's head and along his forehead, cheeks, and jaw. Using a flashlight he had brought down from the kitchen, Saul looked in Dale's mouth, eyes, ears, nose, and throat, and while he examined Dale, he asked questions: How long had Dale been in Cannes? Had he been taking medications and if so what were they? Trouble swallowing or keeping food down? Any night sweats? Weight loss? Muscle soreness? Fever or fatigue? Gastrointestinal distress? Unusual problems urinating or moving his bowels? How about his sex life—active? quiescent? Had he been drinking heavily or doing drugs? When was his last check-up, and did he know his T-cell scores? Any other symptoms he thought Saul should know about?

Dale said he'd been having severe migraine-like headaches, with auras. His vision was often blurred, and he sometimes sweated through the night. He *had* lost weight, *had* been feverish, and for some time now had had a series of infections in his mouth.

"If memory serves, that would be oral candiasis, correct?" Dale asked.

89

Saul shrugged.

"Herpes zoster perhaps?"

"Perhaps," Saul said. "But there's little point in speculating. We won't know for sure without tests."

"I chose not to let them run any tests at *Les Brouissailles,* but as you've doubtless guessed, I *have* been involved with a man—it's why I came to France—though I add at once that we've both been monoga-mous—pathologically so—since we met."

"Glad to hear it."

Dale took a deep breath, spoke again: "In the interests of full dis-closure, I will admit to having had several lovers in the time between Ethan's death—three years and two months ago by exact count—and before, some fifteen months and three days ago, I met Gerhard. He's an Englishman, despite his name—his mother was German—and we've been at pains, quite literally, not to jeopardize his health. I'm on three major medications: two nucleosides and a protease inhibitor, and also—something I almost forgot: I have trouble walking sometimes—a peculiar kind of vertigo that comes over me when I least expect it." Dale exhaled. "So. What do you think, Doctor?"

"I think you're a sick man," Saul said. "But we knew that several years ago, when I was seeing both you and Ethan."

"And now?"

"Now? Now my best guess is that the virus has diversified—"

"—like my stock portfolio?"

"When the virus is homogeneous, as it usually is in the early stages, our immune systems can cope more readily," Saul said, "but when, as it replicates, it spins off new viruses, the immune system is over-whelmed—much slower at developing responses than the virus is at creating variations."

"Therefore—?" Dale asked.

"Without a new set of tests," Saul said, "we can't know *how* sick you are, and I wouldn't want to change the regimen you're on without knowing exactly what your T-cell count is, and where your CD4 and CD8 levels are. And I'd want to check for other things. Your lymph nodes are enlarged, and there's a swelling behind your left ear I'd want to look into."

"Me too. It's why I went to the hospital—what pushed me over *my* edge. And why I came to you."

"Have you made any arrangements to return to the States?"

"No. It's why I'm here. I was hoping you'd tell me what I should do next. Will you—*would* you?"

"My best suggestion is that you get on a plane and go home."

"But I can't."

"Gerhard?"

"If I leave him now, how will we know—either of us—if we'll ever see each other again?"

"Maybe he'll go with you."

"He can't."

"He can't—or he chooses not to?"

"Is there a difference?"

"I wish I could have better news," Saul said. "The best I can do is to urge you to get back to the States ASAP. I'd be happy to call ahead on your behalf."

"I did love Ethan, you know," Dale said. "I miss him terribly."

"I'm sure that's true."

"You don't believe me, do you? You think I took advantage of him—that I was the worldly, cynical older man exploiting the innocent child. You think I infected him and killed him."

"I think no such thing," Saul said. "I'm sure you loved Ethan in your way. I'm sure you miss him. Of course."

"*In my way?!*" Dale exclaimed. "Please don't condescend to me, Doctor Davidoff. How would *you* know what I felt for Ethan?"

"I was very fond of Ethan. In fact—" Saul was about to say that he'd been talking about Ethan recently with a friend. "I think of Ethan often," he said.

"Do you feel guilty about him—about his death?" Dale asked.

"Why should I feel guilty?"

"Because you killed him."

Saul rose from his chair. "I think our conversation is over," he said.

"You should know that I've made an official request, through my attorney, for Ethan's medical records," Dale said. "I'm also in possession of a copy of Ethan's last will and testament—one his family has refused to acknowledge—in which he named me, and not his parents, as executor. I know what you did, Doctor Davidoff, and I know why you did it."

"I asked you to leave."

"With pleasure."

"This is why you're here, isn't it?" Saul said. "There's no Gerhard. You never went to the hospital in Cannes."

"Wrong on both counts. Gerhard is waiting for me in the village. He accompanied me to the hospital. We've discussed Ethan's medical history in detail—in England, Gerhard was employed as a nurse—and he's well aware of the ways in which you turned Ethan's family against me, and of how and why you prescribed an overdose of opiates. You did overdose Ethan, didn't you, Doctor Davidoff? When you put him on the painkillers, you knew you were giving him more than enough to induce respiratory depression."

"Enough," Saul said. "You're deranged—"

"*I'm* deranged?" Dale laughed. "Am I the one who wrote to the President and called him a murderer?"

Saul took a step back. "How did you hear about that?"

"The *President* a murderer?" Dale said. "Please, Doctor Davidoff. Projection, yes? Projection at work, I would submit. And doubtless Ethan is not the only one you—"

"I want you out of here now," Saul said. "Do you hear me? *Now!*"

"*Calme-toi, mon vieux,*" Dale said. "We wouldn't want to have to take *you* to the emergency ward at *Les Brouisailles*, would we?"

Tolle put out her hand to Dale. "I hope you feel better," she said. "Please let us know if there's any way we can be of assistance."

Dale shook Tolle's hand, then drew her to him, embraced her, kissed her once on each cheek. "You've been most kind," he said, "and I'm certain we'll see one another again. As they say, Doctor Davidoff— my people will be in touch with your people."

*

"So," Tolle said, "the question's here again: what then is to be done?"

"Nothing," Saul said. "He's nuts—he was always nuts."

"Still, if he *is* the executor, and if he *has* hired a lawyer—"

"That's why God created malpractice insurance," Saul said.

"I think you should take his threats seriously."

"Maybe yes, maybe no," Saul said. "Or maybe we'll get lucky and he'll kick off before he goes to court."

"You'll only make yourself feel bad if you think that way," Tolle said. "You're too kind a man to wish even your worst enemy dead, especially when he's your patient."

"You'd be surprised," Saul said.

"That's true," Tolle said. "I would be."

"The bastard blindsided me," Saul said. "But *why*? Tell me *that*, please. Why did I forget what he was like with Ethan, and how he..."

"Hey!" Tolle said, and she put the back of her hand against his forehead, then took his left hand, at the wrist, and felt for his pulse. "I thought so. Your heart's racing, and to judge from the way you look, as if you're about to explode—your blood pressure must be way up."

"Big deal," Saul said, and he pulled his hand away. "I'm upset. Sure. Wouldn't you be?"

"Perhaps."

"Maybe he'll die before he gets back to Cannes," Saul said. "Maybe he'll come around a curve too fast, hit an oil slick, ram into a tree, smash through a guard rail, tumble down a *corniche*. There's a world of possibilities out there. It happened to Camus, to Jimmy Dean, to Princess Grace, to Princess Diana, to Isadora Duncan—and only a few miles away—right down there, in Nice, remember? But he *is* sick—*very*—and he did follow me here."

"Look," Tolle said. "I don't know much about this guy—"

"This creep."

"This creep," Tolle said. "Fine. And I assure you I will not let him

93

into the kitchen while I'm making dinner unless he's with Jerry *and* Gerhard—"

"Cut it out."

"But I have something else to tell you—something I should have told you yesterday, but I didn't want to spoil our reunion with Jerry, or our evening with Katherine and Eugene, and—"

"And—?"

"And the news is that someone *has* followed us here," Tolle said. "Correct that—that someone *is* following us here."

"Surprise me," Saul said.

"Julia."

"Julia."

"She's coming to the South of France and may, in fact, already be here."

"Which explains Katherine's seeming act of generosity last night," Saul said. "Nevertheless, this is terrific news—a family reunion. Is Sam planning to join us too?"

"Julia's pregnant."

"Then we'll soon be grandparents," Saul said. "Obviously, Julia's ready, and I think I can handle the responsibilities, especially if Julia doesn't have AIDS, but even if she does, I can get her and the child the best and most advanced experimental treatments available, so that—"

"*Stop it,*" Tolle said. "Just stop. And stop grinning at me that way—"

"What way is that?"

"The way you take pride in proving just how insufferable you can be when you set your mind to it."

"Still," Saul said, "it is a good idea—to stop it. You have my vote. I'd like to stop it. In fact, I'd like to stop *them*—all of them: Jerry, Dale, Gerhard, Katherine, Julia, the President..." He leaned toward Tolle, spoke in a whisper. "You wouldn't happen to have any cigarettes on you, would you?"

"If you're serious about cigarettes, I'll walk into town and get you some."

"I'm serious about everything," Saul said.

Tolle closed her eyes.

Nobody smokes anymore—that is, people still smoke, but not in public places, and I wonder sometimes, especially in winter, when I see them huddling outside bars and restaurants, if you would have seen these laws as ethically just—the good of the whole violating the freedoms of individuals, which includes—your area of expertise—the freedom to kill oneself. There are times—days, weeks, months—when I do get shut of imagining the car exploding against the tree, you rocketing out its rear window. When Saul was going on about Dale—fantasizing his death—and I used the word 'explode' to describe the way his anger was making his face red—I was there again, and being there this time did not make me unhappy. Or rather, I wasn't unhappy for you since it may have been a gift not to have known the moment of your death until it was there.

As for me, I want to know the day, hour, minute, and second of my departure in advance. So that I can choreograph it? Perhaps. Speaking of which, I'm considering telling Saul about my early years as a dancer—before I settled on classical ballet, and before I began designing ballets that I and others could perform. I never told you about those years, and not because I chose not to, but simply because we didn't have the time. But we do now. So perhaps instead of it always being, as you famously put it, too late—fortunately—it's also true that it's never too late. Un-fortunately.

Saul was breathing more easily. Tolle gave him what she hoped he'd find a reassuring smile, and when she did, Saul stood, walked to her, put his arms around her from behind, then let his hands slide into hers.

"You won't get away from me so easily," he said.

"Poor baby," Tolle said.

"Poor *serious* baby," he said. "But I have an idea. Perhaps what we should do, you and I, is to get away for a few months—to go some some place far away—some place where we were happy once upon a time, where nobody can find us, where nobody knows us except for a few select friends, and—"

"Julia may be here soon."

"Ah Julia," Saul said. "Our wonderful, peripatetic daughter about whom I have several questions: If she decides to give up the child—to un-grandparent us before our time—what will we do? What *can* we do? And—equally important—how will we feel?"

"I'll talk with Julia," Tolle said, "and perhaps she and I will go away for a while, just the two of us. Would you mind?"

"No."

You were so impressed with the fact that my mother had been a dancer with Le Ballet de L'Opéra de Paris that I didn't want to spoil things by telling you that after she left L'Opéra, and after a short stint with Merce Cunningham's troupe in Paris, she played in musical theatre all across the United States—pleasant if banal stuff—and that it was while I was on tour with her—for I danced and sang in these productions as did my sister Claire—that my sexual education began and flourished.

"At the end," Tolle asked, "*did* you prescribe opiates for Ethan?"

"Yes."

"If Dale went to court, would his case have any merit?"

"Yes."

Tolle was surprised that Saul answered without hesitating, and when he buried his face in her hair, she wondered if he would now begin to cry, and if so, would his tears be merely a self-serving mechanism whereby he allowed himself to believe that because he wept, he was a truly compassionate human being.

Camus, now sitting where Dale had sat, arched his eyebrows, the message clear: *Be kind*—or in the language of the beloved playing fields of their youth, both his and Saul's—*Play fair.*

My mother put me in ballet class before I was four years old, and Claire, who was three years younger than I, began a year earlier, when she was three. Claire was, as I mentioned, a wonder, and more than a wonder for, like some of the great dancers I had the good fortune to know—Allegra, of course, but also Fonteyn, Kirkland, Marakova, Ulanova—she had a fierce work ethic and loved nothing in life more than she loved to dance, and nothing more than dance except to be able to dance perfectly. Though no less passionate than I was, she was more disciplined and, as you and I agreed, there are no artists more disciplined than classical ballet dancers.

My father was doing quite well in those years—raising thoroughbreds that were competing at the best racetracks in America, primarily on the East Coast—Suffolk Downs, Belmont, Saratoga, Aqueduct, Pimlico— and, the highly profitable dividend from having them race at these tracks, being able to charge handsome stud fees when his horses serviced the mares of other horsemen. Also—crucial to keeping their marriage at least nominally intact—he did well enough to be able to hire help so that my mother was able to resume her career.

She feared, with reason, that she had lost the ability—technique, physical strength, stamina—to recover skills that had lain dormant and had also diminished because of age and two pregnancies. She knew it would be futile to attempt a comeback as a classical ballerina, or to stay on with Merce Cunningham, given the unique rigors of dancing in his company, for nobody, Balanchine included, was more demanding of his dancers than Cunningham. So she auditioned for parts in musicals and operettas. She had a good if not spectacular voice, its timbre sweet and distinctive, and excellent musical instincts.

She began by performing in the Tanglewood area of Massachusetts (we were living on the first of several horse farms in the western part of the state), and also in summer stock theatres that, in Western Massacusetts, southern Vermont, New Hampshire, and Maine, were in abundance in those years.

It was not long before she was playing principal roles—first in summer stock and regional theatres, and then in touring companies. When I was twelve years old, she received an offer to tour nationwide in Victor Herbert's Babes in Toyland. *The tour ran for two-and-a-half months— from early November to late January (*Babes *rivalled* A Christmas Carol *as traditional Christmas fare then), and ever the tough businesswoman (my father would brag to one and all that she was a far better and tougher businessman than he ever was—emphasis always on 'man'), she was able to negotiate an excellent contract, with Claire and I written in—we had both been doing ensemble work in plays such as* South Pacific, Oklahoma, *and* The King and I, *that called for child performers—and with the assurance, in addition to salaries for our participation, of comfortable living quarters for the three of us in each city we would visit.*

The tour began in Kansas City, Missouri. I was well developed for a girl of my age, and had already been fending off the advances of men in the companies, especially older men who would promise that the two of us could keep 'our little secret,' and who seemed to want little more, as several of them put it, than for me 'to lend them a hand.' My mother had always loved being the center of attention, had earned the right—by her beauty, talent, toughness, and wit—to be the center of attention. She flirted with everyone, nor did she discriminate in terms of age, gender, or sexual preference. She would be as likely to flirt with a custodian in a hotel or a cashier in a diner as with an actor or director, and I thought of what went on in front of my eyes, and Claire's, not as innocent, but as natural: it was simply the way she was—her smile flashing, her hands touching whomever she was talking to, her tongue flicking devilishly at the corners of her mouth. She was the star, and stars—male or female—were to be adored, flattered, admired, and entitled to what she referred to as any and all perks that came with the job. And those perks clearly included being affectionate in public (and in private, as I would learn) with whomever she chose. When I once plucked up my courage and asked if she thought our father would mind the way men kissed her both on stage and off, she laughed and told me that our father not only wouldn't mind but had encouraged her to be as friendly as possible with anyone who might prove useful to the furtherance of her career, and, thus, to the economic well-being of our family.

Most evenings after dinner, whether we were in performance or rehearsals, I would be charged with babysitting Claire—or rather, so Claire would not feel she was being treated as my 'baby sister,' our mother would tell us that we were mature enough young women to take care of one another, and that should we need her, we were to go to the concierge of the hotel (if there was one), or to its lobby (when a lobby existed), or simply knock on doors until we found a member of the troupe who would know where she was, and would alert her to our needs.

To be left on our own made us feel quite grown-up, of course, and exhausted as we generally were from the demands not only of the rehearsals and performances, but of the endless packing and unpacking as we moved from town to town, along with practicing on our own whenever we had time so that we could improve enough to eventually become stars like our mother—we usually fell asleep long before our mother returned.

One evening, however, I awoke and was about to go into the bathroom when I heard talking. I stopped, got on my knees, peered through the keyhole in the bedroom door—the kind that could be opened and closed with a skeleton key—and saw that my mother and two members of the company—a man and a woman—were on the couch and were naked. From the way they were giggling and hanging all over one another, and from the bottles on the coffee table, I assumed they were **very** drunk. I recognized the woman as being an older actress named Marjorie Nussdorf, who played the Queen of Hearts (our mother played Little Bo Peep), and the man one of the Toy Soldiers, a boy of sixteen or seventeen named Tim who hung out with a group of young men who preferred one another's company to the company of young women.

The next thing I knew, the three of them had fallen from the couch to the floor, my mother was on her hands and knees, Tim was climbing on my mother's back as if for a piggy-back ride, and Marjorie was bending over Tim, her mouth glued to his butt, where—was it possible?—she was licking him between his cheeks. They were mumbling things I could not make out, and suddenly Marjorie lunged forward and made Tim and my mother collapse onto the floor. The three of them rolled away from one another, and a few minutes later, after they had put their clothes back on, Tim left.

Then my mother and Marjorie clinked glasses, and drank, after which my mother declared that for her the greatest pleasure lay in the challenge— the challenge—of getting these beautiful and beautifully endowed young chorus boys to want to have sex with her more than they wanted to have it with one another. Yes, she loved being able to bed down her leading man in every play in which she appeared—this went without saying, and was, she thought, the obligation of any true professional—but it was being able to turn on these young men, and to give them an experience they would never forget—and forever desire to repeat—that gave her the greatest pleasure.

Marjorie and my mother clinked glasses again, drank, set their glasses down, embraced, and kissed for a long time, after which my mother remarked on the fact that as pleasurable as this was, such activities were *always immensely more pleasurable when they had as audience a young man like Tim.*

"Or your husband?" Marjorie asked, and my mother said that when the tour was over, perhaps Marjorie could visit in Massachusetts and the three of them could have a party of the kind she and Tom—that was my father's name—loved. She had often brought some of her women friends home with her so that, after dinner, and after the girls were asleep, she could, at home, have the kinds of pleasures she had when on the road.

Saul, who had nodded off for several minutes, woke and told Tolle to forget about the cigarettes, that what he needed was a nap, and that she could, if she wished, join him. He left, and Tolle smiled at Camus, who, to her delight, had lingered, and was standing by the mimosa tree. She closed her eyes, and touched herself with her fingers to see if, by telling him her *Babes in Toyland* story, she had been able to arouse herself. She had not. Perhaps, though, if she thought of the first time she had performed the lift-and-lick maneuver so dear to the hearts of male and female ballet dancers, she would succeed. Better yet, she thought, why not do what she had thought of during her first weeks with Saul and, once or twice, during their first time in Spéracèdes: teach him to do the maneuver with her. The problem she had foreseen whenever she'd had the urge to do so, was that she had feared that doing so might have led him to ask about other games she'd been playing before they met.

Although Saul had never seemed the jealous type—a refreshing quality in a man—she gathered from the little he did tell her that his sexual experience had been limited, and so she had decided not to risk revealing to him details of her experiences. But surely such considerations had by this time become irrelevant, and since Saul was still fit enough to lift her, and she weighed only a dozen or so pounds more than she had when in her prime, instead of seeing her lift-and-lick days as something that might trouble him, why not offer the maneuver as a gift—an experience that might, in addition to lifting her, do the same for his spirits.

It was doubtless Dale's visit that had reminded her of gay dancers she'd known—for she had known them, young and old, in the same ways her mother had, and had played 'front door-back door' with many of them. All the dancers had been having affairs with one another back then, and in all predictable variations and combinations. She assumed her mother knew what was going on, though she had pretended— or had chosen—not to know. Nor had her mother, despite—because of?—her own experiences ever seen a need or reason to question, counsel, or caution her.

Nor did her father. One afternoon when she was fifteen or sixteen, she recalled, he had found her in an empty horse stall doing it with two stable boys, the boys taking turns, and he had simply stood there, slapping a riding crop against his palm, though how long he had been there watching she did not know, and after the boys pulled up their pants and ran off, he had cautioned her about infection—the horses did crap there, after all, he said—and added that if she was going to do what she'd been doing she should, goddamnit, at least do it at night and in a clean place where people who happened to be passing by wouldn't trip over her.

He had probably been very drunk—he had always been able to consume enormous quantities of alcohol yet never *appear* drunk, though he would in mid-sentence sometimes, suddenly pass out and fall down. 'See?' her mother would say each time this happened—a tired joke even the first time she used it—'Your father always knows when to stop.'

But her father may not have even remembered the scene he had come upon that afternoon, or what he had said to her. By then, everything, with the exception, strangely enough, of working with injured horses, had come to bore him. The only times she ever saw him show interest, much less tenderness, in anything were when he tended to a horse afflicted with minor conditions such as Hunter's Bump. Hunter's Bump was a common ailment in horses that was brought on by taking off or landing wrong, thus causing a small protrusion on a horse's spine—a ligament tear—that would be irritated by a saddle and rider. Her father had loved to walk these horses, to talk with them, to tell

101

them everything would be all right, that they would soon be racing with the wind again. He would brush them down, feed them apples, sing to them, and nurse them back to health, after which he would turn them over to the grooms for rehabilitation, and when the rehabilitation went too slowly or failed—when the purse money and stud money ran dry—sell them off.

Tolle opened her eyes and saw that Camus was gone, and she wondered if he'd become bored with her. Though why wouldn't he, given that she'd become bored too—not with *telling* her stories, for it pleased her to be able to find words that could conjure up memories of actual events, and do so with seeming clarity—but with the reality of the experiences themselves, which had become, in all senses of the word, common.

Even before she met Saul, she'd become tired of the sexual games she'd been playing and, in the part of her she thought of as more French than American, had begun to long for that good cup of coffee in the morning that would accompany the kinds of conversations she'd had with Camus and would come to have, at least during their first year or so together, with Saul. She had, through most of that first year, been grateful for his love, and for the excitement of *being* in love. And later, when the feelings of love—infatuation?—had faded, Julia and Sam arrived, and to her surprise, she had been grateful for their existence—had found enormous fulfillment in raising the children, especially during their early years: nursing them, bathing them, holding them, putting them to sleep and, while they slept, staying in their rooms and, for hours sometimes, simply staring at them. She had not, as far as she could recall, ever resented the fact that their existence was the cause for her having to take yet another step away from a dance career already in partial eclipse. She had loved being a mother and, thanks to the income Saul earned as a physician, the luxury of being a *full-time* mother. When Julia had passed her third birthday and Sam was thirteen months old, however, she hired part-time help, and resumed her career: teaching dance several days a week, and occasionally participating in performances by modern dance companies in and around New York City.

But how long ago and faraway those years seemed! Also—not least of all—the children more or less successfully launched into the world, and her life with Saul having become defined by boredom and distance, and no matter who bore responsibility, and in what proportions, by the parallel lives they'd come to inhabit, she was once again grateful to Saul, this time for the pretext he gave her—the occasion—for doing what she'd been longing to do for years: to return to France so she could end her days in a place she loved. *L'appel du vide*—the call of the void, of non-existence—Camus had used the common French phrase to denote that sudden desire, more rational than impulsive, to veer off the highway, or jump off a cliff. Though in their absurdity, he said, such desires usually began in the heart long before the mind became aware of them.

How strange to still feel she was in love with a man she had known briefly nearly a half-century earlier, especially since she was—Camus had noted this on their first day together—such a rational, even *anti*-romantic woman, one at pains to deride in herself, or those she was close to, any least impulse toward sentimentality. Through the years, conjuring him up now and then—imagining his responses to her thoughts, feelings, and decisions—had provided her with what, for a while, her experience in therapy had provided: a safe place where every morsel of shame, embarrassment, rage, resentment, or vulnerability was permitted, and without being met with either advice or judgment.

It occurred to her, too, that she *did* still have feelings of affection, or perhaps love, for Saul, or believed she did, especially when, as had happened earlier in the day, she could watch him attend to a patient. This—his extraordinary qualities of observation and intelligence, his genius for diagnosis, his courage in working with AIDS patients—allowed her to admire him in the way she admired Camus for *his* gifts: his writing, his courage as a man who was engaged—*engagé*—in the political life of his times, his empathy for the dispossessed of the world, and—a quality he shared with Saul—his sense of how contingent and accidental everything in life was—and also the extraordinary (because an ordinary quality in *ex*traordinary men?) tenderness they were each capable of feeling for those individuals they knew and loved.

Saul loved his patients, she thought, the way Camus had loved his

103

friends. And Saul loved her, she mused, the way Camus had loved not only her, but *all* his women, even, as he had so endearingly put it, those he had loved simultaneously.

Simultaneously? How else translate *en même temps*, the phrase Janine Gallimard said Camus had used to describe romantic liaisons that had occurred *at the same time* though not at the same time *in the same bed.*

She smiled, and was aware that she was thinking fondly of Saul— of having a vague yearning for him. Given all that was going on, would he be relaxed enough to reciprocate? Perhaps she could talk with him about Claire and see if that might get him to talk about his brother Martin, and if talking about Martin might both distract him from his present worries, and enable him to open up about what, below the obvious—Julia's pregnancy, Dale's arrival—was troubling him. Martin had died at the same age Claire had died—twelve—though in an accident, not of an illness—and the commonality of their losses had seemed more magical than tragic when, their second or third night together, she and Saul had exchanged basic information about their families, including the effects on them of having become, before they were out of their teens, their parents' sole living children.

Yet neither of them, as far as she could recall, had ever talked about *missing* their siblings, or about love *for* their siblings. Saul seldom mentioned Martin, and though she had talked at length about Claire when in therapy, she had made a deliberate choice not to talk about Claire with Saul. How strange and, she now believed, how stupid. Because she had cut herself off from her parents did not mean she had had to cut herself off from her memories or feelings for Claire—feelings that, of course, had survived and intensified in the years following Claire's death. It was an omission—an absence—that, in the time that remained, she might try to correct.

She stood and was about to go back into the house, determined, with gentle probing, to get Saul to talk about Martin when, glancing back over her shoulder, she saw that Camus was now sitting in the chair Dale had sat in.

She sat across from him and decided it would be good to talk with him about Claire before she talked with Saul, so she could refresh her memories and, perhaps, stir up feelings attached to the memories—to feelings that lay hidden *within* the memories—and thereby, as wife and as friend, enable Saul to call up feelings she believed he had repressed for most of his life—feelings that were, she conjectured, the source of at least a portion of the hostility he had sometimes showed toward her, and toward the children.

Some of this was doubtless the ordinary 'survivor guilt' any brother, sister, mother, father, husband or wife might feel following the death of a close family member, and some of it—most of it?—was probably attached to feelings he'd had about having a wheelchair-bound father who—at least in the overt symbolic role the father represented—could have created in a young son unacknowledged feelings of impotence. Add to this the death of Saul's younger brother, and the displacement of feelings of helplessness that, as with the father, could have accompanied this loss, and one could infer some essential sources of Saul's choice of vocation: of a life spent rescuing and caring for the sick, the wounded, and the dying.

But why, now, such random ruminations? Why these glimmerings of feelings for and about Saul and *his* psychological patterns and history? And why this slender shift in *her* feelings, one that did not do away with her desire to take leave of the world, but which—simultaneously?—allowed her to take what pleasures she could before she left, and—more!—allowed her to be willing to be of use to others and, even, to *give* pleasure? Also: in what ways, if any, did the salient facts of Saul's childhood—the disabled father, the dead brother—that had entered into his choice of vocation also become the source of what in him remained: the often ingenious ways they'd come to detach themselves *from* one another, the quasi-adolescent romantic feelings he could still regularly express towards her.

She could not recall two consecutive days passing without his telling her he loved her, and this was, she told herself, no matter its shallowness, origins, or rationale—or his marital infidelities—no small thing for any man married as long as he'd been married to still feel for a wife. Nor was there any reason, she decided, other than her own habits of four decades, not to show her appreciation for his sustained expressions of love. Also—at least as important—a conversation with him about Martin (was he afraid, as with Martin, that anyone he loved—her!—might at any moment be taken from him?) might allow *her* to understand more fully the ways in which the loss of her sister had formed *her*. For, in her determination never to be owned by anyone, or by any feeling or, even, by any memory—and that included the memory of her time with Camus, which, by count, had amounted to a mere eighty-one hours— the importance of Claire in her life, and the loss of Claire *from* her life, had been something that was still a mix of feelings she was reluctant to explore or acknowledge.

Camus, she was pleased to notice, seemed in no hurry to leave.

My sister Claire died of cancer—bone cancer, which was, then as now, not an uncommon cancer in children—when she was twelve and I was fifteen. At the farewell service—she was cremated, her ashes strewn on a stream that ran through woods that bordered the western part of our property—my mother, holding me close to her while I sobbed away, was stoic. My father wept inconsolably, and all through that day and evening kept repeating that he would never forgive himself for not having spent more time with her.

During the last year of Claire's life, when she was not resting—the bottom half of her body, from the waist down, covered always with a blanket following the amputation of her left leg, so that I never saw what I both longed to see and was frightened of seeing—we spent most of our time together reminiscing about our years on the road, and talking about shows we'd been in—Babes in Toyland, The Mikado, and Showboat had been her favorites—and about performers we'd known.

One day she asked if I remembered the time she asked if I thought she was old enough—this happened the day before her eleventh birthday, and several months before we learned of her diagnosis—to let boys kiss her. Several of them had tried, and others, including one who claimed he had already kissed me, had asked if they could kiss her. She said she was inclined to let the boys who asked to kiss her do so, but she wanted to know—she was ever a direct and uncomplicated child—what the best ways of kissing were. Some of her friends had said that boys would try to put their tongues in her mouth, and she wondered, if this was so, if she should let them, and what doing so would feel like.

A year or so later, and two weeks before her death, when she was failing rapidly, she told me that she had let four boys kiss her, and had let one of them touch her breasts, though not on the inside of her leotard. She said that she had liked kissing, and she thanked me for whatever I'd said that had helped give her what she regarded as a precious gift.

She had been accepted into the New York City Ballet School, whose dancers were being trained to be in the Corps du Ballet for Balanchine's New York City Ballet Company, five months before her eleventh birthday, and if not quite the prodigy dancers such as Allegra and, later, Gelsey Kirkland, were, Claire was nevertheless a superior talent, and was being prepared for becoming a member of the Ballet Company, and eventually, or so our mother claimed Balanchine had told her, for principal roles.

By the time she became ill, I do not recall being jealous of her successes or her future prospects. In a strange way, I had become, or taught myself to become, grateful for my accident, and grateful to our father for having brought it about, since the impossibility of ever being as good as Claire having become a physical impossibility, I was relieved of any realistic hopes concerning a classical dance career.

The fact that Claire would leave the world before she had fulfilled any of the large expectations the world (or our parents) had for her probably removed any remaining element of jealousy or envy—jealousy of her achievements, and envy for who-she-was—and yet, simultaneously—ah that word, mon chèr Albert—gave me predictable feelings of schadenfreude: secret and wonderful frissons of happiness. At the same time, her illness and death, while making part of me rejoice—a part of me I despised because I rejoiced—also deprived me of whatever small measures of affection I had been receiving (or had ever hoped to receive) from my parents.

Claire was not only the center of their attentions, but her condition brought with it daily accusations of imagined acts of meanness I'd committed, and—as intelligent as my parents were, they were devoid of anything resembling psychological sophistication—they would ask, bluntly and repeatedly: 'Why are you still alive when Claire is dying?'

Only once did I have the courage to reply. My father had put Claire to sleep for an afternoon nap, and asked me why the hell a no-good little slut like me was still alive when Claire would soon be gone. I replied, with remarkable sangfroid, that there were several familiar sayings that might explain the situation: The first, of course, was the commonplace about only the good dying young, and the second was the equally common notion that people like me—and like him—were simply too mean to die.

He slapped me across the face, to which not unforeseen act I responded by simply standing there and telling him that no matter how many times he hit me, I was not going to die before Claire did, and that he could bet his last dollar on the fact that no matter how many times or how hard he hit me, I was not going to cry.

And I didn't.

Ten

Saul had been commenting on the fact that whenever he saw tears in Fiona's eyes, his stayed dry, and that when she saw tears in his eyes, hers stayed dry. They were sitting in a diner in Harlem on a snowy morning a few days before Christmas, and by way of response Fiona had pointed to the street sign outside the window—St. Nicholas Avenue—and remarked on its grim appropriateness to the day, given that the woman whose funeral they had just attended was a twenty-two-year-old mother of three whose children, ages five, four, and two, were also HIV-positive.

The woman lived in Brooklyn—on Myrtle Avenue, in the Bedford-Stuyvesant section—but her parents lived in Harlem. Thus the venue for the funeral and, despite the occasion, why the moment seemed to Saul, in memory, a mid-winter idyll: he and Fiona sitting across from each other, drinking strong coffee, eating heaping portions of eggs, sausage, grits, and home fries, talking about their patients, then laughing about how—*his* theory of the day—it was cholesterol that *strengthened* the arteries, holding them together and greasing them so as to enable blood to flow more smoothly.

They laughed again when he told her about Ishmael Martinez. Ishmael was a forty-six-year-old Puerto Rican man—a plumber, a father of four, grandfather to three, and a cocaine addict who had been clean for nearly a decade—a man with, Saul said, the sweetest disposition in the world, and a man, at the time, whose infection had just begun to enter his brain. The day before, after Saul had asked him how he was feeling, Ishmael had said to him, with a shy grin, "I was thinking that, since we know each other so long, Doctor Davidoff, you don't have to call me Mister Martinez any more. You can call me Ishmael."

Saul recalled Fiona's full-throated laugh—head thrown back, mouth wide open—and the way her mouth had opened wide again, in astonishment, several hours later when they made love. Making love with Fiona had always been most intense—deepest, wildest—after funerals. As relaxed as they were with each other at the hospital, without coyness or embarassment, and as easily as they could talk with each other wherever they were—at the clinic, on wards, in funeral homes, in restaurants, in bars or diners—when they made love, he recalled, they rarely said a word. That silence—that world without words—now seemed the most precious thing they shared.

Thinking of Fiona again—worrying about her—he had been unable to fall asleep, and so he had returned to the garden just as Tolle was coming up the stairs, saying that *she* was ready for a nap.

"But let's talk first," she said, and took his hand and walked with him back into the garden.

She had been thinking about her sister Claire, she said, and thinking about Claire had set her to wondering if, in recent years, he ever found himself thinking about Martin. He replied by saying that he often thought about Martin—that when he'd had a patient who was in his or her early teens, and was dying, he would sometimes imagine Martin's face superimposed on the patient's face. He said that after Martin died, his parents never, at least in his presence, mentioned Martin's name again. He said that for several months after Martin's death he had met regularly with Miss Cameron, a guidance counselor at school, that she had been helpful, and that he had made some choices during those months—good choices, as it turned out—that were choices he might not otherwise have made.

"Such as?" Tolle asked.

"Deciding definitively to become a doctor," Saul said. "And less important things that seemed pretty large at the time, such as leaving the football team so that I wouldn't risk serious injury. I was a pretty good ballplayer—was slated to be starting halfback my senior year on a good Erasmus team—but the possibility that I might be injured, and the pain this would cause my parents, made me decide to quit. Also, for the same reason—not to hurt my parents any more than they were already hurt—I stopped dating a non-Jewish girl they disapproved of."

"Did you miss Martin?"

"Oh sure," he said. "It was no fun to be left alone—to be the sole source of my parents' worries."

"And their joys?"

"Maybe."

"Same here," Tolle said. "After my sister died I did everything—well, almost everything—to be *a good girl* so that I wouldn't cause them any more pain than they'd already endured, and . . ."

"And—?"

". . . and what I think happened was that by never, or almost never, making waves or confonting them when they were nasty to me, I became more of a secret bad girl."

"You a bad girl? *Really?*" Saul said. "I'm shocked."

"You've benefited from that in some ways," she said. "Or at least you used to, but—I'm serious now, and please consider this a start on something resembling an apology—or rather, a start on having us talk about things we've almost never talked about. Now that we're here once again, however, far from home—"

"Talk is fine," Saul said. "But sometimes no talk is even better. You know the line—heard songs are sweet but those unheard—"

"—are sweeter," she said. "Could be. But I did have something I wanted to tell you about and show you—a gift I brought to France with me that, for a long time, I've been thinking of giving you."

"Show and tell—one of my favorite games," he said, and he stepped behind Tolle's chair, bent down and inhaled the pale lavender fragrance of her hair, yet did not find himself wondering about ways in which she'd been *bad* once upon a time. He had never cared much about what she, or other women had done with other men before they were with him. Although he and Tolle had each made a few vague allusions to their sexual histories—it seemed to him a conversation women expected at the start of an intimate relation in those days—he had cut her off after a short while by telling her that he thought it best to let the past remain the past. At the time, he recalled, she said she agreed with him in principle, but perhaps people *should* know these things so that they could more truly know one another, and, more important, so that they could avoid moments later on when having kept their previous lives hidden from one another might, in a crisis, lead to revelations that could stir up large feelings of jealousy and betrayal that would have the potential to sabotage relationships and marriages.

Things had been different with Fiona. She had come to his office one afternoon—this was before they became lovers—to talk about another resident, a friend of hers who was bent out of shape because, suspicious of her boyfriend, she had searched for and found a journal he kept, and had gone off the deep end when she read about various women he'd been sleeping with. This was, Fiona said, a reason the friend might have seemed uncharacteristically unfocused during the previous week or two, and after Saul had thanked her for letting him know so that he could, as the friend's supervisor, take this into account, he and Fiona found themselves talking about the insanity of jealousy, and about how ridiculous it was for men and women to go berserk because of relationships they'd had, or might have had, with others. It derived, he suggested, from what he thought of as "the illusion of possession."

"There's that—" Fiona agreed "—especially with guys who want to own you. I mean, there *are* betrayals that hurt and can set the jealousy genes in motion, sure, but what I've never been able to understand is how you can be jealous of someone's *past?*"

Thinking about Fiona, and then about Ethan—whom Fiona had known—he couldn't avoid thinking about Dale, and he found himself wondering why he'd been so passive with the guy, why he hadn't simply slugged him or, better yet, told him he thought it was a good idea to go to court—that a trial might be just the thing to bring the right kind of publicity to bear on incompetent doctors.

"I don't mean to cut off our conversation about Claire and Martin," Tolle was saying, "but I just remembered something else you should know—that Julia called to say she's made plans to stay in Saint Rémy, at the hospital, or whatever it is—a kind of nursing home or retreat run by nuns that Van Gogh stayed in during the last year of his life," Tolle said. "She'll work there in exchange for room and board."

"Will she visit us?"

"She expects us to visit her."

"And the abortion, if there's to be one?"

"She suggested what she considers an equitable division of labor: You handle the medical part, I do the counseling."

"Julia *can* be very practical at times," Saul said. "But—a reason I couldn't fall asleep before—I was thinking about our visitor—Dale— and that led to thoughts about Ethan, and that led to the realization that when Ethan died he was younger than either Julia or Sam are now. He was one of the last AIDS patients I had who did *not* die of natural causes."

What a strange phrase, he thought—*of natural causes*. What else do we die of? Viruses are natural. Bacteria are natural. Infections are a natural response to pathogens, cancers are natural products of cell division. War, disease, drought—hurricanes, earthquakes, plagues: these were nothing if not natural processes springing from forces that bore us no *personal* malice.

Maybe Julia had decided to stay at Van Gogh's hospital, or whatever it was, because she was terrified of something going wrong during an abortion, and fantasizing the worst—that she might not survive, and might, therefore, be living in the last year of *her* life, and wanted to be where Van Gogh had been at the end of *his* life. A strange but, for Julia, given her temperament, not a surprising choice.

He also wondered if Julia would expect her brother Sam to come to France and attend to her the way Van Gogh's brother Theo had attended to him. He missed Sam—loved his son for his refusal to follow one of the straight-and-narrow paths others his age were following, for his contrariness and spontaneity—qualities he often felt *he* lacked in large ways. And he missed Ethan, he realized, in the way he missed Martin. It was easy, of course, to miss Ethan, and to feel a love for him of the kind he had felt for Martin since, like Martin, Ethan was dead, so that his love for them could not be complicated by anything they did, or by his response to anything they did. In the same way that it was easy for him to love Martin and Ethan, so was it easy to love the others—the thousands of men, women, and children he had treated, all of whom were now dead. He wondered if, away from the daily round of work, and with obligation-free time stretching out before him, he would be capable of remembering all, or almost all, their names, and come up with a list, year-by-year, the way he'd often made year-by-year lists of women he'd known, and if he'd be able to match former patients to specific diseases—brain cancer, liver cancer, lung cancer, TB, pneumonia, heart disease—the way he sometimes matched, and ranked, women he'd known to the ways in which they had given him pleasure: orally, anally, intellectually, emotionally....

He thought about the prospect of Katherine returning in a month or two, and imagined the three of them—he, Katherine, and Tolle—in the garden, enjoying a candlelit dinner, finishing off a splendid bottle of Saint Émilion, after which Katherine and Tolle excused themselves and retired to the bedroom. When he saw himself entering the room a while later, Katherine and Tolle were in bed together, and they parted to make room for him in what would be, for that evening, the fulfillment of the most banal of male fantasies, yet one that for him—for the young, inexperienced man still very much alive *within* him—retained the power to arouse.

Camus, he recalled, had considered having an affair with Simone de Beauvoir, but decided against it not because of his friendship with Sartre—this was before their famous feud—but because he imagined that once he and de Beauvoir were in bed together, she would talk nonstop before making love, while they made love, and, especially, *after* they made love.

Saul heard a clanking noise, looked up, and saw Jerry standing on the terrace, a wooden broom handle in one hand, a pink ball in the other. Jerry tapped the broom handle against the iron railing.

"Anyone for stickball?" he asked.

"When I was twenty and Picasso was in his thirties," Jerry was saying, "I told myself that by the time I reached thirty, I'd be better than Picasso. When I was thirty, I said that when I reached forty, I'd be better—and more famous—than Picasso. And when I reached fifty, I said, 'There's still time—I'm doing remarkable stuff, that other guy is *kaput—finito!*'... but when I reached sixty, I said, 'Nah. You're a good painter, Jerry—you *shmear* well—but let's face it, you're never going to be better than Picasso.'"

Saul was in Jerry's new studio, which was about thirty feet wide and forty feet long, and had skylights and large windows that could, when shades were raised electronically, let in an abundance of the magnificent Mediterranean light Jerry loved—and while showing off his studio, and some of his recent paintings, Jerry talked about their dinner the night before, about how lovely Katherine had looked, and—to Saul's surprise—about the on-and-off affair Jerry had been having with her for more than thirty years.

Saul admired the studio and the paintings, said that the new paintings seemed less abstract than his work had been in earlier years, and that he could discern, in the lush textures—the very *speed* with which color had been applied—incipient shapes: men, women, children, buildings, cars, bridges, trains. He stood in front of one of the larger canvases, said that what fascinated him was that the painting clearly suggested a New York City skyline—a subway train on an elevated line—but that the colors were from the south of France: that the trains looked as if they were made from the kind of stones used in Spéracèdes and neighboring villages to build houses. He also liked the

115

reversals—the sky looking as if it were made of clay while the ground looked the way the sky could look after a mistral: crystal clear, almost translucent.

"And you're not laying on the paint quite as heavily as you used to," he said.

"I put away my palette knife," Jerry said, "along with other things. I don't have a computer. I don't have a cell phone. I don't have a regular telephone anymore—a landline—and I haven't renewed my passport."

"But what about your daughters and your grandkids—one of your daughters is in the States, isn't she?"

"Elise lives in San Francisco with her husband. Their children, Anou and Eric, both married, live nearby in Oakland. They try to visit me once a year, though they don't often succeed. Georgette lives near Toulouse with her new husband—her third—and her daughter Nicole lives in Marseille with a nice guy who drives trucks. They come by now and then when they remember where I live. In between we exchange letters."

"And in an emergency?"

"At eighty-five, what could constitute an emergency?"

"When we first met, I used to envy you, you know," Saul said. "I'd think—here's a guy who wakes up every morning and does what he loves."

"Romantic claptrap," Jerry said. "I *hate* painting. You think I'm having *fun* every day? Painting is painful, buddy. By the time I figured out what this was all about I was nearly seventy, and it's been a ball-buster ever since."

"Then why do it? Why do you *keep* doing it?"

"Why do I do it? Because I'm a neurotic Jew," Jerry said. "Because what else do I know how to do? What else *can* I do at my age—become an orthodontist? But let me ask you the same question, my friend. Why do *you* do it—why do you spend your life taking care of people who are going to suffer and die no matter what you do?"

"First of all," Saul said, "they don't all die anymore. Second of all, I can relieve their suffering and prolong their lives. Third of all, I can help them *in* their dying—can help them find meaning in the experience, and—"

"Spare me the violins, okay?" Jerry said, and then, like a traffic policeman, put his hand up. "Okay, okay. Despite the small barbs I enjoy throwing your way, I do admire what you do. But I also agree with Tolle about you being depressed, which is why I'm taking the opportunity to bust your balls. I mean, what greater pleasure in life than to kick a guy when he's down? I'm still very competitive, you know. You're not the only guy in this room who grew up in Brooklyn."

Jerry walked to the far side of his studio, took out a bottle of wine and two glasses from a cabinet. His movements were stiff and unsteady. Rheumatoid arthritis? Saul wondered. He pictured an MRI of Jerry's nervous system, the inflamed linings, the swollen joints. There were new medications and exercise regimens he could recommend, and, worst-case scenario—*best* case, given Jerry's flair for the dramatic?—he could recommend that Jerry strap wooden boards to his hands the way Renoir and Monet had.

Jerry poured wine, raised his glass. "To two old Brooklyn farts," he said.

"To two old Brooklyn farts," Saul said.

"I mean, you could have had an easier life—shilling for drug companies, being a plastic surgeon, face-lifting WASP women, bobbing Jewish noses—"

"Plastic surgeons work with kids born with birth defects, and with burn victims," Saul said. "They restore faces of men, women, and children who have none."

"Or you could become a *bon vivant* like me," Jerry said. "I'd wager you'd have a gift for it the way I do. We could stroll together along the Promenade des Anglais or the Croisette, picking up chicks. You could tell them what a famous artist I am, and I could tell them what a famous physician and letter writer you are."

"Tolle told you about the letter."

"She was proud of you for writing it, even though it's taken a toll,"

Jerry said. "Or rather—*her* opinion—it was because other things were taking a toll including—ha!—Toll-*e!*— that you wrote it."

"The letter was only a pretext," Saul said. "If I hadn't written the letter, I would have done something else to get us to come back here. It was time."

"Coming back, yes," Jerry said. "Thank you. So. Coming back to my suggestion about the ladies, and about the secret of my success *with* the ladies through the years, you're curious, right?"

"Of course. What's the secret of your success with the ladies?"

"Glad you asked," Jerry said. "What I would do a few minutes into a flirtation—and the great venues for flirtation have always been gallery openings for my paintings—was to say to a woman, 'Listen—I think you and I are probably going to to have an affair,' and I'd add a comment to make it seem I was *just* flirting—being playful because of the occasion—but it saved a lot of time for everybody, and the women, even when they protested, which happened rarely, were always flattered."

"Katherine then," Saul said. "You started with her this way?"

"With Katherine there was no need," Jerry said. "I cared for Katherine from the first moment I saw her. Katherine is the great love of my life. I would have left Michelle for her."

"Well, she's a free woman now—"

"—who had her eye on you last night."

"Come on," Saul said. "She's fresh from her husband's death, and then there's Eugene, and—"

"Cut the bullshit," Jerry said. "Knowing you, you probably banged her already. I saw the looks you gave her last night. More than that, though, did you see how she ate it up—having three of her lovers buzzing around her, all of us yearning to sup at her fountain of delights."

"The painters you used to compare yourself to—" Saul said "—Picasso, Cezanne, Matisse, Chagall, Modigliani—the ones who lived in this part of France—they're all dead, Jerry."

"But you're not," Jerry said. "Which is why—even though I'm pleased that you're still competitive with me, as your not-so-sly comparison makes obvious—I'm pissed at you for not playing stickball with me today. I would have whipped your ass." Jerry jabbed Saul in the stomach with the pointed end of a paintbrush. "Not bad, Saul—but a tad soft." He whacked his own stomach with the flat of his hand. "I still get up at six-thirty, still do fifty-five sit-ups twice a day, morning and evening."

"I'm glad to know you're doing well physically," Saul said. "Only I noticed that when you walk—"

"'Doing well physically'? Ha! What does that mean at my age?" Jerry asked. "I'm more like an old car. When it's gone two hundred thousand miles and you ask it how it feels, it coughs." He laughed. "So here's another one I was saving for you. I was walking along the Croisette a few days ago, and this old man stopped me. 'Listen,' he said, 'I've been meaning to ask—my memory's not what it used to be—but tell me: was it you or your brother who died last week?'"

After Jerry had opened a third bottle of wine, a treasured 1988 Chateauneuf-du-Pape, he said that one of the things he loved most about Katherine was the manner in which she dispensed her favors—generously and unapologetically, and with more discretion than deception.

"Speaking of deception," Saul said. "Do you really believe this Gerhard character is CIA?"

"You don't listen," Jerry said. "I didn't say he was CIA. I said he's MI6, but low level. He's been on the Riviera for years, peddling this and that. There's lots of these birds around. If they like the cut of your ass and you ply them with a few drinks, they'll confide—*shh!*—that they're agents, and make you swear to keep the information under your hat. It's the giveaway that they're worker ants—pissants all."

"But maybe this creep Dale's nonsense about suing me was a cock-amamie tale so he and Gerhard can inveigle their way into my life and send in a report declaring that I am not, in fact, going to off the President."

"What I liked about your letter," Jerry said, his head resting against Saul's shoulder, "is that you called that *yutz* in the White House a murderer—actually, you see, I was *for* going into Iraq in the beginning: we rid the world of a major piece of shit while showing the bastards in the Middle East that if they fuck with Israel, we'll bomb the crap out of them—but what I liked *most* about your letter is that it brought you here so we could hang out and get drunk together. It's been a sweet plus in my golden years—to have become a quiet, happy alcoholic."

"The way I look at it—" Saul said "—Tolle said this to me in a different context—is that noble as it is to save lives and help those less fortunate than ourselves, if we do *not* drink our wine today—this most excellent wine—poor and sick people in Africa and Asia will *not* suffer less."

"Sounds like Kant," Jerry said. "The moral imperative inverted."

"Pure *cant* if you ask me," Saul said, pronouncing the word 'cant' with a Brooklyn accent.

"Ah—my cue for one of the world's shortest jokes," Jerry said. He paused, and then: "You're still *very* pretentious, you know."

"*Moi?*" Saul exclaimed.

"You remembered!" Jerry said. "That pleases me—that when I'm gone, some of my bad jokes will live after me. And Tolle—oh my, my friend—except for the white hair—no, let's call it silver—she's as gorgeous and fetching a woman—as *desirable* a woman—as I've ever known. You're a lucky man."

"On some days," Saul said.

"Of course, of course," Jerry said. "You two were the envy of all eyes when you first arrived here. I didn't know a man who didn't want to be in your pants. And she was, at least when it came to the war in Vietnam, and to racism, as passionate a woman as I've ever known."

"Tolle was always a singularly intense woman," Saul said.

"When the country shut down in sixty-eight was when I most wished you were here. Can you believe it, Saul? *We had the whole fucking country shut down!*"

"You had the whole fucking country shut down," Saul said.

"Ah—but I told you the tale when you visited a year or two later—seventy? seventy-one?—when Tolle was pregnant with your daughter."

"Julia."

"I made my way up to Paris—nothing much was happening down here—and it was amazing—one of the most exciting moments in life for an old lefty like me," Jerry said. "Michelle was with me, and she was the one who first mentioned Tolle, how Tolle would have been in the front lines, digging up bricks and tossing the *pavés* at the *flics*, maybe even working with Cohn-Bendit—"

"Maybe sleeping with him," Saul said.

"Anything to help the revolution and increase morale," Jerry said. "As Katherine used to say about *her* liaisons: so little pain for me—so much pleasure for them."

Jerry talked about *les évenements de mai*—and about the time Daniel Cohn-Bendit, the leader of the student rebellion, announced that he would hold a press conference. He did this at a time when it appeared the coalition of students and workers might prevail, when de Gaulle and the government were in retreat—a time when it seemed that a revolution in the very way the nation was organized, where people at all levels of society would participate in the decisions that affected their lives, was about to take place, and when those, like Tolle, who were working in the civil rights and anti-war movements, were believing that what was happening in France could also happen in the States.

Exiled by the government, Cohn-Bendit had secretly made his way back to France, and when the media showed up in large numbers at his press conference, they were met by nine students, who declared, one after the other: '*We are Dany.*'

"'The great danger lies in a revolutionary moment which tends to become just another passing show for our consumer society,'" Saul said.

"Good memory, my friend," Jerry said.

"Tolle posted the words on our fridge," Saul said. "Despite her good taste and love for the finest things a doctor's wife's money could buy—despite how beautifully appointed with fine art and gorgeous furniture our home was, how fashionably she dressed, yet she loved to hold forth about the pernicious influence of *la societé de consommation.*" Saul said. "Which leads me to the great question of the evening: Shall we pee?"

Saul felt woozy and deliciously light-headed. Was it really more than thirty years since he and Jerry had hung out together this way? And how long since he'd seen Fiona? He tried to calculate, but the years sloshing around in his head, found he could not do so with certainty. He blinked, watched the horizon tilt slightly. He thought of how beautiful Tolle had been once upon a time—and still was, with or without fashionable *couture*—and he thought of the softness of Fiona's hair. Fiona may not have been as pretty as Tolle when it came to basic elements of physiognomy, but he had always thought her more *uniquely* beautiful, and recalled something Tolle herself had once said to him— read to him from a novel she was reading—that explained the difference: about how she had sometimes felt being born with near-perfect looks had been a curse—that beauty and being beautiful were not the same thing.

A beauty has no faults in her face, Tolle had said, but the face of a beautiful woman could have faults that served to deepen her charm. A remark, at the time—he had probably been telling her once again not only that he loved her but how much he still loved *looking* at her—had only deepened his love for her.

Saul unzipped his fly and thought of the way Fiona would, when riding him, lower her head and, one side to the other, sweep her hair back and forth across his face and chest. By now most of her hair was probably gone, and if, in addition to chemotherapy, and the debulking, she had had her ovaries removed, that would, years ahead of schedule, have brought on menopause. Would she be having hot flashes, and if her hair grew back in, would it be white—or silver— the way Tolle's was?

Saul heard Jerry unzip his fly, and then, with pleasure, he listened to the soft whistling sound they made by pissing together on the grass.

*

When Saul noticed that his toes were becoming numb—it was February, after all, and not May—he went inside, found a blanket, returned, and wrapped the blanket around Jerry.

"You're a truly kind man," Jerry said, "no matter what others may say about you."

"Shh," Saul said. "Jerry's sleeping."

Despite how much he'd had to drink, Saul felt remarkably clear-headed. To the north, where the Alps began to rise, the night sky was brilliant with stars. When he saw a dying star shoot across the heavens in a long, falling arc, he thought of Fiona and the moment he did, he noticed a wraith-like figure moving across the landscape, by a stand of trees at the near edge of Jerry's property. He pictured Fiona wasting away, wandering in darkness, searching for him. Because cancer cells multiplied faster than bodily tissues, they were especially vulnerable to radiation. But those bodily tissues that also divided rapidly—the lining of the digestive tract, the cells in hair roots and skin formation—were, not unlike cancer cells, were also highly vulnerable to radiation.

The figure in the garden, Saul now saw, was an old woman in a white dressing gown, what the French called a *robe de chambre,* and she had a dark kerchief tied around her head. Did the woman, like Fiona, wear the kerchief because she too was suffering the after-effects of radiation? He pictured Camus' body, littered with scars from years of pneumothorax injections, and then found himself imagining Fiona in a nondescript hotel room, trembling from chills and fever. When she opened her mouth, would he find lesions? Would her skin be covered with small bruises? And if he could conjure up all the side-effects she'd be subject to—the multitude of ways she was becoming increasingly frail and unattractive—would he desire her less?

"*Bonsoir, messieurs,*" the woman said.

Jerry opened his eyes—"*Bonsoir,* Madame Amione," he said. "*Ça va bien? Tu n'as pas des soucis, j'espère...*"

Madame Amione clutched her gown tightly to her body, explained

123

that she had received a telephone call for him, and that he was to give a message to a Monsieur Davidoff. Monsieur Davidoff's wife wanted him to know that they had an unexpected visitor—*quelqu'un imprévu*—and that he return home as soon as possible.

Jerry thanked Madame Amione, introduced her to Saul, told her that Saul had visited Spéracèdes many years before—several times—that he was a physician, and that the two of them were the best of friends—that they were like brothers.

Madame Amione apologized for having disturbed them, said good night, and left.

"Then you do have a phone, I see," Saul said.

"Phone *service*," Jerry said, and expained that Madame Amione was a widow who lived in the house next to his, and that he had given her phone number to Tolle in case she or Saul needed to reach him while they were in Spéracèdes. But he was glad she had stopped by because her visit reminded him that he'd intended to talk with Saul about her.

One afternoon about ten days before Saul's arrival, Jerry explained, Madame Amione had knocked on his door and announced that she had decided to give him the opportunity to buy her home. She would sell it to him under a French system called *viager* whereby Jerry would pay her a large sum now, plus a monthly stipend, after which, as *viagère*, she would be permitted to live in her house rent-free until she died. A widow, she had suffered a long list of illnesses, including, within the last year, some form of cancer—stomach, liver, lungs—he couldn't remember which. What he hoped to do was to borrow against *his* home and studio—both were fully paid off—in order to buy Madame Amione's home and in that way he would be able to leave each of his daughters a home of their own.

"So what I wanted to ask," Jerry said, "was if you'd be willing to go over Madame Amione's medical records, give her a brief physical exam, and give me your best estimate of how long she's likely to be around."

"When it comes to love and death, the French are a most practical people," Saul said.

"*Très pratique*," Jerry agreed. "So you'll do this little favor for me?"

"No."

Jerry sighed. "You're still such a moralist, Saul."

"This isn't about morals," Saul said.

"Then why not?" Jerry said. "The law's the law, and it's one where everyone's a winner. She gets a chunk of money, a lifetime annuity, and free housing—and I get a bargain, my daughters get an inheritance they don't have to fight over, and—"

"—and I have to go," Saul said. "We have a visitor."

"That guy Dale again?"

"I hope not."

"Who then?"

"It might be Julia," Saul said. "She's in France."

"Julia," Jerry said. "Tolle told me that she's had some troubles. Sorry." He put a hand on Saul's arm. "But hey—we've had a lot to drink. How are you going to drive home?"

"Carefully."

Leaning on Saul, Jerry stood, and embraced Saul.

"What I said to Madame Amione is true, you know," he said. "We are like brothers. I've always thought of us that way."

"Which brothers?" Saul asked. "Cain and Abel? David and Jonathan? Groucho and Zeppo?"

"Approximately," Jerry said.

"Approximately?"

"Madame Amione has a brother, you see—a true son of a bitch who might try to make trouble," Jerry said. "And there's a son too—a *papillon* of *papillons* who shows up whenever he needs a monetary transfusion. But I checked it all out with a lawyer, and the good news for us both—because I think she loves the idea of sticking it to them— is that she can do anything the fuck she wants with her house while she's alive."

Saul withdrew from Jerry's embrace, walked toward the house. He pictured Madame Amione lying wide awake on her back, wondering how soon it would all be over. He pictured Fiona, stumbling in the dark, falling down across a threshold that led to the bathroom. He imagined worms crawling through her arteries, plague rats feeding in her bowels.

"Think of it this way," Jerry said. "You wanted to be a man like Camus, right? I remember how you worshipped him. You wanted to be a man who, through all the vicissitudes of life—war, books, plays, tuberculosis, revolution, and the rest—never stopped loving and delighting in women."

"Approximately," Saul said.

"So cheer up, my brother, because the good news is that, in this most important category anyways, you've succeeded."

Eleven

Tolle had set the flowers Fiona brought, blue and yellow irises, in a vase, and then, while Fiona nibbled on some cheese and olives, and sipped tea—Fiona said she dared not attempt wine since the effect on her digestive system might be more spectacular than either of them would enjoy—Tolle had telephoned Jerry's neighbor, after which she had gone downstairs to the room that led into the garden, made up the bed, and put fresh towels in the bathroom.

Fiona's hair, tied in a blue paisley kerchief, Tolle saw, was dry and straw-like, wisps of ash-gray among shades of brown. Her eyes were bloodshot, the circles under them a dull shade of purple, and when Tolle said that Fiona must be tired from the journey—that she seemed fatigued—Fiona replied that she looked that way only because she *was* fatigued, and had asked if Saul had mentioned the possibility she might be visiting them, or the reason for a visit. Tolle said she remembered Fiona's name—recalled that Fiona had been one of Saul's residents at Kings County Hospital—but that he had not mentioned a possible visit.

"It figures," Fiona said, and explained that she had been diagnosed with and treated for ovarian cancer, and that Saul had probably seen no need to share the grim news until he knew, definitively, that she *would* be descending on him. She had arrived in France two days ago,

ostensibly to attend an international AIDS conference in Bordeaux—
she *had* stopped in Bordeaux to consult with a specialist her oncolo-
gist at Yale-New Haven Hospital had recommended—but had really
come because she knew Saul was in France. What had happened, she
explained, was that when she learned that because of a letter Saul had
written to the President, a copy of which he'd sent to several colleagues,
he'd been "granted" time-off from the hospital, she had decided to visit
him—the conference in Bordeaux was merely a ruse so she could take
time-off from *her* position at Yale-New Haven Hospital—since he'd
not only been her supervisor and mentor, but was a doctor whom she
could count on to be ruthlessly direct with her.

"I am in great need of ruthlessness," Fiona had said. "Not to mention sleep. Nothing more urgent, so when Saul returns, please do not
have him wake me. He and I can talk—confer—in the morning."

Tolle said that Saul was visiting with a friend, and suggested Fiona
wash up and make herself at home downstairs in what passed for their
guest room.

"Thanks," Fiona said. She started to stand but, obviously hesitant
to leave, sat again. "You were a dancer, weren't you," she said.

"I was a dancer," Tolle said.

"And you knew Albert Camus."

"I knew Albert Camus," Tolle said. "But how—?"

"Your husband talked about Camus a lot," Fiona said, "especially
to first year residents, when he would tell us about how *The Plague* had
inspired him to specialize in infectious disease, and how—he seemed
very proud of this—his wife had actually known Camus."

"He never told me he talked about me with his residents," Tolle said.

"He wouldn't," Fiona said. "You had to really push with your husband if you wanted to get him to talk about himself in any *personal*
way. But I pushed, of course—I've never been known for being shy—
and he told me that when you were a dancer you created a ballet *about*
Camus."

"That's true," Tolle said. "But that happened a *very* long time ago—"

"—and that before you had children," Fiona said. "Your

128

husband—Doctor Davidoff to us—was very proud of his children, and of you for the way you raised them—for giving up your career in order *to* raise them."

"That's not quite true," Tolle said. "I think Saul often idealizes things."

"You bet he does," Fiona said. "It's what makes him special to all of us—that he never stops admiring people who—like him, right?—hold up an ideal, and do what they do because they have a *passion* for their work and for justice the way Camus did, and—I guess—the way you did."

Tolle laughed. "A passion for a career as mother and wife?" she said. "Hardly. In fact, I would say that Saul was more devoted to our children than I was, except—perhaps—in the very beginning, when they were infants. I liked our children better before they could walk and talk."

"I don't believe you," Fiona said, "because I think you knew exactly what you were doing in giving up your career so your husband could advance *his* career—it's what most women of your generation did— and guess what?"

"What?"

"In your case, it turned out to be a pretty good deal," Fiona said. "Maybe not for you, or for your kids since he was away so much, but for his patients, his students, and—here's Fiona Casey's grand thought for the day—for the millions out there who had AIDS and who will have AIDS, now and forever."

"I admire the work my husband did," Tolle said, "but I don't agree with you that Saul has accomplished what he has because of sacrifices *I* made. I made my own choices quite freely, and did not, in fact, give up my career because of Saul, or because of his career."

"Glad to hear it," Fiona said. "And hope I didn't offend by using the word 'sacrifice.' In truth, you don't strike me as a woman who would have sacrificed her life or career for a guy, or even for her family, but how would I know?"

"Do you have children?"

"Negative," Fiona said. "Thus, q.e.d., I *wouldn't* know, would I. So what I should probably do is to head downstairs to dreamland instead of invading your privacy with my cavalier, facile, and ill-informed judgments." She stood, then sat again. "Only with—"

"—only with time running out, you figure what the hell, right?"

Fiona looked startled for a moment, and then burst into laughter.

"Exactly," she said. "You are *exactly* right!"

"We have a daughter, Julia, who's somewhat younger than you," Tolle said. "Julia is thirty-two years old, and she too is in France, and is, in fact, having her own difficulties, though not difficulties that can compare with yours."

"I'm forty-one, and I used to look lots younger than my age, but with all the crap they've been juicing me with, I look like shit, and don't tell me I don't. Your husband will probably be shocked to see me in this state, but hey—here I am."

Tolle wanted to reach out and touch Fiona, but despite Fiona's rather surprising—alarming, given its cause?—openness, she held back. She didn't want her words or gestures to be taken for anything resembling pity. Strong-willed and autonomous as Fiona seemed, she was clearly in need of a large dose of consolation or she would not, given her state of health, have made the long trip in order to meet with Saul. In the place of pity, consolation, or banal homilies, however, Tolle wondered what she could offer that might lift Fiona, if only fleetingly, from her doldrums—that might, perhaps, even *please* the young woman.

"You remind me of my daughter," Tolle said.

"How so?"

"You're brash and volatile," Tolle said. "You have a no-nonsense streak, both of you, that can land you in trouble, but that can also be your your saving grace."

"Saving grace," Fiona said. "I like that."

"I didn't mean to imply that—"

"Hey—you don't have to watch what you say with me," Fiona said. "We know the score. And so does your husband. Like I said before, maybe that's why he didn't tell you about the possibility of my showing up. I mean, why spread lousy news when there's so much of it out there already, especially given what *he's* been through with the idiots at the hospital freaking out because he did what every sane and honorable person should be doing. And you know what else?"

"What else?"

"I like talking with you," Fiona said.

"Same here," Tolle said. "That is, I like talking with you too."

"I mean, it's as if we've been given a special dispensation because of what's going on with me, and because we're here and not there, so that we're outside of time somehow and can be having a conversation we might never have had otherwise, and you know what else?"

"Tell me."

"I like talking with you because I sense that you get me—that you understand what I'm saying and why," Fiona said. "So here's something else I've been chewing on that I wanted to run by you that has to do with Camus, and it's something I'm not sure I should talk about with Saul. I wouldn't want to—I don't know what—to disillusion him or take away things that he believes in...and..."

Seeing Fiona struggle to find words, *and* to keep her eyes from closing, Tolle considered suggesting, again, that Fiona wash up and get some rest—that they continue their conversation in the morning—but she sensed that it was important to Fiona that she say what she had to say *before* Saul returned. Clearly, the young woman looked up to Saul—admired him in the unreserved way that Saul admired Camus.

"And what, Fiona?" Tolle asked. "Please. Try me, and then we can talk about whether or not you'd be disillusioning Saul."

"Of course I'll tell you or I wouldn't have brought up the subject," Fiona said. "It's pretty obvious stuff, something he might even agree with me about—who knows?—but what I've been wanting to tell him is that I think *The Stranger* and *The Fall* are much better novels than *The Plague.*"

"Me too," Tolle said.

"*Really?*" Fiona said. "You're not just saying that because—"

"Really," Tolle said. "I'm not just saying that because."

"Okay," Fiona said "Then I think I'd like to try a glass of wine and the consequences be damned. I mean, what the hell, and I'm feeling better, thank you very much, even though part of me is fast asleep. Can you tell?"

What was more accurate, Tolle told herself as she poured two glasses of wine, was that Fiona admired Saul not in the way he had admired Camus, but in the way *she* had. And just as, in the present moment, nothing could seem more ordinary and natural than to be sitting at a kitchen table with this young woman and talking *about* Camus, so nothing, at least in memory, could seem more ordinary and natural than to be once again seeing herself walking and talking with Camus in Paris. At the same time—but why?—she was also seeing herself as a child of five or six, in ballet class, practicing basic positions and movements—five positions for the feet, five positions for the arms, and then: *plié, relevé, sauté…*

Or was it Claire she was seeing?

Fiona was talking about why she believed *The Stranger* and *The Fall* were better novels than *The Plague*—less didactic, more mysterious— and Tolle recalled listening to Jerry make much the same argument late one night—this was during their second stay in Spéracèdes—holding forth about what Saul seemed to have missed: that although *The Plague* was set in Algeria during an epidemic taking place in the fifth decade of the twentieth century, it was not primarily about disease, but about the struggle against fascism.

Camus had begun writing the book in 1942, Jerry pointed out, a year after Germany had defeated and occupied France, and a year during which he was recuperating from a siege of tuberculosis and living by himself in Le Panelier, a hamlet outside the town of Chambon-sur-Lignon. Camus' wife Francine had returned to Algeria, so that Camus was that year living in the way the people of his novel lived: in a situation of enforced isolation, his life threatened by a plague-like disease.

Having Doctor Rieux ask the novel's key question—*How does one behave in a time of plague?*—was, Jerry explained, merely Camus' way of showing how people in France had behaved during World War Two when they were effectively quarantined from the outside world and were faced with the daily realities of oppression and mass murder. Just as the people of Oran had, in *The Plague*, to devise strategies to cope with a disease that was devastating their community, so the people of France had had to devise strategies to cope with an invading and omnipresent enemy. They had had to choose, in effect, whether or not to acquiesce to evil, or to risk their lives and endanger their families by joining the Resistance.

Tolle kept her eyes on Fiona, yet she hardly heard what Fiona was saying. Instead she was recalling that during the conversation about *The Plague* that evening, she had had the impulse to interrupt and say that although she and Camus had talked about many things during their three days together—three days during which they had spent a large percentage of their time in bed—she could not recall him ever talking about *The Plague*, its *meanings,* or about the meanings of *any* of his novels. At Saul's urging, however, she *had* talked about her ballet that night: about how she had met Camus in the Café de Flore, how she had told him about the unfinished ballet she was working on, how he had agreed to visit Nijinsky's tomb with her, and about how it was that what she termed this "brief encounter" had provided the impetus, and the missing piece—Camus himself—for what would become the heart of her ballet.

And when she and Jerry went out on his porch for a breath of fresh air later on, she had again felt a desire—a desire more mischievous than confessional—to *épater* Jerry with the story of her time in Paris with Camus.

"I wish I could have been with you and Camus in the cemetery that afternoon," Jerry had said. "and I wish even more that I could have seen the ballet he inspired—could have seen you take a curtain call…"

"It was wonderful," Tolle had said. "*Sublime*, really. And how *I* wish…how I wish that…"

"Ah, but if wishes were kisses," Jerry had said and, cutting her off and taking her in his arms, he had kissed her in a way that was more than friendly.

"Another time," she had said when they separated.

"*Donc,*" Jerry had said. "*À la prochaine* then…?"

"No," Tolle had said. "What I meant was that *that* was another time."

"Is it too late then—*fortunately?*" Jerry had asked, and she had been aware at once that his reference to the final line of *The Fall* was a line *he* would think she would fall for.

"It is, in fact, much too late—" Tolle had replied "—so get over yourself, buster."

She had left him on the balcony and gone back inside, and she could still recall his look of astonishment, especially at her calling him "buster," which, it occurred to her, was an appellation Fiona—or Julia—might have used with guys they'd wanted to get rid of.

She knew her reading of the novel was hardly original, Fiona was saying—that Saul probably knew pretty much everything she, or anyone else, would have to say about Camus.

"Probably," Tolle said. "And he knows what I think. We've talked about the novel often—about how the Occupation, the Resistance, and the role of the Vichy government gave rise to the novel's birth—so no reason *not* to talk about it with him."

"I figured—but thanks for letting me go on about it—for listening to me," Fiona said, after which her eyes closed, and her head bobbed twice before coming to rest on the table.

Dale did not credit the virus for his insanities, he said. Still, his threats about litigation and Ethan's death were, of course, sheer nonsense brought on by his state of desperation.

"And of denial," Gerhard said.

While Saul palpated the glands along Dale's neck and under his arms, Gerhard, a tall, thin, dimple-chinned man, stood by the door as if, Tolle thought, he were guarding it.

"Gerhard's right about that too," Dale said. "After we saw you last week, I persuaded myself that I probably had a bad case of flu, that this too would pass, *et cetera ad nauseum*—which turns out to be the key phrase, since I've been vomiting three or four times a day and can't seem to keep *any* food down."

"Which is why I urged him to see you again," Gerhard said.

Saul asked Dale to walk back and forth across the room, then to close his eyes and touch his right finger to his nose. Dale did as he was told—walked back and forth, then closed his eyes and tried twice to touch his nose, his finger jabbing the cheekbone below his right eye each time.

"I was never much of an athlete," Dale said. "Terrible eye-hand coordination."

"Magic Johnson contracted AIDS too," Saul said.

"But he's still alive."

"So are you," Saul said. "But look. As I said last time, the main thing is to get as accurate a diagnosis as we can so we can come up with a viable treatment plan. If you're set on not going back to the States, I can refer you to some people in Paris, or in Bordeaux. And there may be somebody in Nice."

"I keep remembering what Ethan was like at the end," Dale said.

"But you didn't visit him at the end," Saul said.

"Perhaps I did when you weren't there," Dale said.

"Or perhaps not," Saul said.

"And there's another thing," Dale said.

"Yes?"

"I'm scared."

"Of course," Saul said.

"But also—some good news—despite my condition and the many ways it has depleted me, I have not, as Gerhard can testify, lost my capacity for jealousy," Dale said. "Even when the angel of death is flirting with me outrageously, if I notice Gerhard merely glancing at another man, or—worse still—if I imagine him with other men after I'm gone—my jealous reaction seems able to make me completely forget my bodily ailments."

Saul went to the sink, washed his hands. "Is there anything else?" he asked.

Tolle was surprised by Saul's reaction—by his cold *lack* of reaction. Whenever she had seen Saul interact with patients in the past—and with family members, or other doctors—he had been warm, sympathetic, scrupulously polite. But the crispness of his responses to Dale—the harshness—suggested that he was himself more depresssed and, Dale's word, *depleted* than she'd realized. Or perhaps—*her* good news?—a side of his character she had seen rise to the surface now and again through the years, especially when dealing with their children— he did possess a fair amount of what Fiona said she had come to France in search of: ruthlessness.

"Not really," Dale said. "Just that, sad thought, I really would resent leaving this world, which does seem to suit me so well much of the time."

"I wish I could have better news for you," Saul said.

"Do you really?" Dale asked.

"Yes."

"Why should I believe you? You gave Ethan false hope, after all."

"I did no such thing," Saul said.

"Don't bother to defend yourself, Doctor Davidoff," Gerhard said. "When he gets like this, the best thing is to ignore him. He's really not himself these days."

"Then who is he—" Saul asked "—and what does he want?"

"The very questions I often ask," Gerhard said.

"And what do *you* want?" Saul asked. "What *intelligence*, let's call it, are you after?"

"I want Dale to live," Gerhard said.

"Then see that he gets back to the States," Saul said, "or to a good hospital here."

"I'm doing my best," Gerhard said, "but you happen to be the only doctor he trusts now. Given the scene he created here the other day, I will add that it is most generous of you to be willing to see him today. But surely, having examined him twice, you have at least a preliminary medical opinion—an impression."

"My best guess is that it's neurological," Saul said. "There's definitely an opportunistic infection at work—at least one—but until we run tests, we won't know if they're treatable or not."

"But it came on so *fast*," Dale said. "A few weeks ago, I was…"

Saul put his hand on top of Dale's, and Tolle watched how this literal laying-on-of hands made Saul relax—how it seemed to instantly moderate his hostility.

"…I was feeling just fine, Doctor Davidoff," Dale said. "I truly was, and I can't tell you how happy it felt simply to be *alive*, but now…"

"Look," Saul said. "The tempo—the rate of onset—doesn't tell us anything, really. The infection could be focal, or it could be generalized, but we won't know that until we get a diagnosis. Think of it this way—" he laughed "—maybe it's just TB."

"*Just* TB?" Dale exclaimed.

"I often tell patients when they present the way you do that we can always hope it's TB. Because sometimes, although we can't fully *cure* TB, we *can* send it on a long vacation. Or it might be toxoplasmosis. We can treat that. Or if it's a tumor, we might be able to stop its progression. But until we get a diagnosis—"

"Is the clinic open?" Fiona asked.

Although Saul seemed momentarily shocked by the arrival of a woman he didn't recognize, Tolle watched him regard Fiona with his usual kind, professional smile. Then, apparently remembering that Tolle had told him Fiona had arrived the night before, and realizing the woman *was* Fiona, he blinked—aghast at how terrible she looked—after which, recovering quickly, he offered Fiona a warm, collegial smile.

"Doctor Casey, I presume," he said, shaking Fiona's hand. "So, yes, the clinic is open this morning, and we appreciate your being able to join us here even though, as I've been informed, you're on holiday."

Fiona air-kissed Tolle twice, French-style, before turning to Saul.

"Pleased to be here, Doctor Davidoff," she said. "And I want you to know how much I appreciate the hospitality Mrs. Davidoff showed me yesterday evening when I arrived unannounced and in rather *mis*-shapen shape."

Saul introduced Fiona to Dale and Gerhard, explained that Dale had been one of his patients at Kings County Hospital, that he was HIV-positive, that his former partner, whom he believed she had known—Ethan Goldberg—had died of AIDS three years before, that Dale was on holiday in the south of France, had experienced some alarming symptoms, had learned that he too was on holiday, and was nearby, and had solicited his help.

"Fiona trained under me at Kings County Hospital," Saul said. "She's an AIDS doctor, director of outpatient AIDS programs at Yale-New Haven Hospital."

"Perhaps then, two heads being better than one, a second opinion would be helpful," Gerhard said. "I do not mean to impose, doctor, but if you could see your way to giving Dale a cursory exam, I'd be most grateful."

"Would you?" Dale asked.

Fiona looked at Saul. "Your patient, doctor," she said.

"He's my patient, yes," Saul said, "but take him...*please?*"

"Not funny," Dale said, and turned to Fiona. "But may I ask *you* a question first?"

"Shoot," Fiona said.

"Are you HIV-positive?" Dale asked.

"Negative," Fiona said. "Why would you think so?"

"I don't mean to offend, though it appears I often do," Dale said, "but you look like women I know who are HIV-positive. You seem, well, *depleted* is the word that comes to mind."

"I *feel* depleted," Fiona said, "but I know I *look* haggard, frail, and not-long-for-this world. So let's avoid diplomacy and euphemism, all right? What *I* have is ovarian cancer, and I've been through surgery, radiation, and chemo. Enough information?"

"Oh dear," Dale said. "If I had known, I certainly—"

"But now you do," Fiona said, "so what I want you to do is to be a good boy and to open your mouth without letting words emerge from it."

"My goodness," Dale said. "You've quite the bedside manner."

"To repeat—no words, please," Fiona said, and she began to put Dale through the same basic exam—mouth, nose, ears, eyes—Saul had put him through.

"Your impression?" she said to Saul when she was done.

"Your patient," Saul replied.

"All right then," Fiona said, and she spoke rapidly: "Given the ataxia I observed when you walked across the room, along with your evident lack of coordination, I'd say your condition is probably neurological, emphasis on 'probably,' and that what you need is a full work-up so we can discover the *kind* of infection that's chosen you, and get an accurate diagnosis. As Doctor Davidoff always taught, *everything* begins in diagnosis."

"And often ends there?" Dale asked.

Fiona sat, handed the flashlight she had been using to examine Dale to Saul, and opened her mouth wide.

"And now me, okay?" she said.

"Coffee first?" Tolle asked.

"Sure," Fiona said. "Strong and black, please."

"Did you sleep well?" Tolle asked.

"Not bad," she said. "But I *did* sleep, which is a major plus. It's wonderfully quiet here."

Saul sat next to Fiona, took her hands in his.

"I'm very glad to see you, you know," Saul said, "and I apologize for not alerting Tolle to the possibility that you might be arriving, but—"

"Shh," Fiona said, and she rested her cheek on the back of Saul's hands for a moment, then looked up at Dale and Gerhard.

"He is the kindest man in the world, did you know that?" she said.

"It's why I'm here," Dale said.

"Me too," Fiona said, and she smiled at Dale for the first time. "Then again, you have to remember that although, medically speaking, Doctor Davidoff and I are thought of as AIDS doctors, death is our true specialty."

*

"After I visit Julia, I'm thinking of going to Algeria," Saul said. "I want to visit Mondavi, and try to find the house he was born in. And Oran, of course. Tipassa also, where his friends erected a memorial to him. And—longer range—and for a longer stay, though not directly connected to Camus, I'd like to go to South Africa again."

"Are these announcements or invitations?" Tolle asked. She was sitting up in bed.

"Whichever you prefer," Saul said. "I'd love to have your company, but I suppose for an American these days—for an American *Jew*, even a half-Jew—North Africa would not be high on anyone's travel list."

"Oh come off it, Saul," Tolle said. "It's not that, and you know it."

"Then what is it?"

"It's that we've talked about making these trips each time we've come to France, or thought of coming to France, starting with the first night we met, so that makes it how many years?"

"You're upset with me," Saul said.

"I guess I am," Tolle said. "But I'm tired of hearing about an odyssey we seem destined never to take, and I'm wondering why in heaven's name you're bringing it up now when we have a very sick young woman sleeping two floors below, a very sick former patient of yours showing up whenever he feels like it, and a pregnant daughter who's not far away and who's facing a bunch of lousy choices—either to have a shotgun wedding to a guy who may not be the father of her child, to become a single mother, or to have an abortion."

"Points well taken," Saul said, and he sat on the bed, next to Tolle. "I *am* upset I guess—you're right—and covering it up with the old nonsense about following in the wake of Camus, which—I agree, you may be surprised to learn—I'm starting to realize may be an illusion, and may also—"

"*May* be an illusion?" Tolle said. "What else could it be but an illusion, and if—"

"Let me finish, please," Saul said. "Yes—it may be an illusion, but

140

it's an illusion that allows me to see us the way we were once upon a time—when we were young and in love, and when one of the things that made us feel the way we did—that made our connection so magical—so *beshert*, as the French like to say—was that we had him—Camus—in common, even though we'd come to our love for him in very different ways—and that we had each thought, independently of one another, of one day paying homage to him by visiting all the places he'd lived in, and perhaps, if we had the time, of re-reading books and essays he had written *in* the places where he'd written them, but now that…"

"Now that we're older and wiser—?"

"Exactly," Saul said. "Now that we're older and wiser, what I've decided to do instead—I made the decision when I was with Jerry the other night, and he voted for the idea—as I just told you—*if* you were listening—is to visit Julia, and then to *think* about going to North Africa."

"Did Jerry charge for the consultation?" Tolle asked.

"Hey—" Saul said "—why the sharp tongue?"

"Because," Tolle said.

"Because why?"

"Because I'm as upset as you are," Tolle said. "So fine—let's go visit Julia."

"I thought we might take Fiona with us," Saul said. "I talked with her before—before she went to sleep—"

"When you tucked her in?"

"*Jesus!*" Saul exclaimed. "What is with you this evening? Look—I know I've been a pain in the ass—a depressed dolt ever since I sent off that fucking letter—and before that too, but I'm *glad* I sent it because it brought us here, and, as I said before, it's given us a chance to *repair-the-marriage*, as they say these days—but then Julia comes along with her news, and Dale shows up, and now Fiona—"

"Tell me about Fiona," Tolle said. "You have a plan, I trust."

"The plan is to stop in Saint Rémy, perhaps have Fiona meet Julia if that seems wise—find out what the situation there is—and then get Fiona to Bordeaux and on a plane home."

"Maybe she and Dale can return to the States on the same plane."

"Stop it," Saul said.

"You're right," Tolle said. "I should stop it, and just tell you what I think, which is that it's probably best if you visit with Julia by yourself. It's always been easier for her to talk with you than with me—don't protest—and no matter what I say, Julia will be sure to use my presence to prove that I don't really care, that I'm just there to agree with whatever you say—or for you to agree with whatever *I* say—in order for us to present one of our vintage false-but-united fronts. And also, in case you think I didn't notice, and was not, as you suggested, listening to you—I *did* like your use of the term *beshert*."

"Are you sure about me visiting Julia without you?" Saul asked. "I really *would* like us to go to St. Rémy together."

"I'm sure," Tolle said.

"I may suggest that Dale see a man Fiona and I know at Yale—Friedland—who's the best when it comes to cases like his," Saul said. "If Dale should come by again while I'm gone, tell him to call me, or—a better idea—I'll leave the information about Friedland with you. Would you mind?"

"I don't mind anything," Tolle said.

"Not even me?"

Tolle smiled. "Don't push your luck, buster," she said.

What Tolle was thinking was that when she conjured up memories of their times together—in the café, in the cemetery, in her hotel room—though it seemed ordinary and natural, in memory, to be with Camus again, she sometimes, as now, had trouble recognizing or *seeing* the young woman at Camus' side, and this made her wonder if perhaps *she* was the real ghost. The *real* ghost? She liked the phrase, and what occurred to her was that she might write a story—a novella?—about that young woman, her meeting with Camus, and the invention of a ballet about him and Nijinsky. Here and there, someone might remember the ballet, but it hadn't been performed anywhere in decades, and the story she would write would not, as story, have that much in common with the ballet since it would be about Camus and the young woman more than about Camus and Nijinsky.

Fiona was clearly in love with Saul, and Saul was clearly fond of her—devoted *to* her—and it occurred to Tolle that if she was jealous, which she knew she was, though mildly so, she was jealous not of Fiona but of Fiona's ability to *feel* love for Saul. What she was also thinking was that for all of Saul's talk about colleagues who screwed their young nurses, residents, and interns—for all his talk of not shitting where you eat—maybe he had been no different from them, and had thoroughly enjoyed the aromas and tastes he found in the garden of young women that had blossomed anew at his hospital every year for the past three to four decades. What she was thinking was that maybe what Saul loved was simply declaiming *words* about shitting and eating—that he got off on using Brooklyn street-talk to put down a practice that he either envied profoundly, partook in with gusto, or took pride in rejecting sanctimoniously.

What she was thinking, too, was that in feeling irritable towards him maybe—*maybe*?!— she was covering up her envy for Fiona's ability to feel whatever she felt, and—more fundamentally—covering up her own sadness for the *loss* of the ability to feel anything like what Fiona might be feeling, whether for Saul or anyone else. Still, her concern for Julia and Fiona was real enough, since when it came to children, and she was aware that the night before she had thought of Fiona in the way she thought of her children, as she had long ago concluded, there was no safety—there was only love and worry.

She looked past Saul, hoping that perhaps Camus would appear, but realized that in this moment—Saul beside her, holding her hand and needing from her whatever it was she resisted giving to him— she didn't *want* to talk with Camus. When he'd shown up recently, he hadn't had much to say anyway, so to hell with him too…

"I spoke too quickly before," she said. "The truth is, I'm not sure about *not* going with you to visit Julia, though with Fiona in the car with us, I'd probably be less hostile towards you than I am this evening."

"Let's, as lawyers say, take it under advisement, all right?" Saul said. "And let's have a drink. We have a good bottle of Côtes du Rhone downstairs that I bought when I was in Grasse. We can celebrate the fact that in this house where, as Fiona noted, death is the specialty, you and I are still very much alive."

"Good idea," Tolle said. "And perhaps, if we don't drink *too* much—we'll need to maintain our balance—I can give you that gift I talked about yesterday."

Twelve

They came upon the village of Entrevaux from the east, the way he had first come upon it with Tolle nearly forty years before, and once again it took Saul's breath away. Hearing his rasped intake of air, Fiona put her hand on top of his, and he responded by pulling to the side of the road and turning off the engine.

"Are you all right?" Fiona asked.

Saul heard dull, irregular thumpings, then the faint sound of rushing water, and he wondered for an instant, if the sound was coming from within—if his blood pressure was shooting up as it had been doing occasionally in recent months. In a silence that seemed unearthly—he felt as if he and Fiona had been transported to a place covered with a large, transparent dome, one that let *in* light, but that kept *out* all sound—he realized, with relief, that the sound of rushing water actually *was* the sound of water: of the Var River, which, probably overflowing from spring rain and mountain runoff at this time of year, would be surging nearby.

The village of Entrevaux seemed, as ever, an apparition: from a cluster of perhaps a hundred closely-set stone-walled houses that seemed to grow from the ground itself, their red tile roofs bright in the late morning sun, a walled road zigzagged up the side of a pyramid-shaped mountain. Situated at the top, some fifteen hundred feet above sea level, was a medieval fortress from whose ramparts one had a three-hundred-sixty degree view of the surrounding countryside.

"I'm okay," Saul said. "I'm excited is all—it's just very exciting to be here again, and to be here with you."

They got out of the car and walked toward the part of town where he hoped to find the inn he and Tolle had once stayed in, and where, were it still there, they could have lunch. The village was preternaturally quiet, shutters on most homes closed while people were inside eating their midday meals and preparing for, or already taking, their *siestes*. The stores in villages like this, as in Spéracèdes, he explained to Fiona—butcher shops, bakeries, groceries, gift shops—closed down for two to three hours midday, and all afternoon on Wednesdays.

They found their way to the far side of the village, walked along a path that bordered the Var River, passed the drawbridge—down, as he remembered it had been the one time he had been here—that was connected to an abandoned fortress. Beside the drawbridge, a few feet from the river's bank, three small green-backed turtles sat on a single flat rock.

Under the bridge, where the river narrowed, the water, coursing downstream, foamed with increasing turbulence. He thought of boiling water, and reminded Fiona of a parable he had used when lecturing residents—did she remember him doing so?—about the fact that if you placed a frog in a pot of boiling water, it would jump out, but if you put it in a pot of cold water, lit a fire under the pot and let the water come to a boil slowly, the frog would stay where it was, and would die.

He had used this familiar fact to alert his students to the ways in which living creatures, human beings included, seemed to have been programmed by evolution to be able to respond to acute crises but not to chronic conditions, not to thinking and acting in terms of long-range effects and consequences. This short-sightedness was deadly when it came to medical care, he'd come to believe, where neither the government, medical groups, hospitals, insurance companies, nor his own hospital thought long-term, where the premium was always on efficiences dictated by profit margins and cost-effective ratios, and where, therefore, doctors were paid more for procedures—to shove things down people's mouths or up their assholes—than they were to do the essential: to take good histories so as to get to know their patients and to be able to put new and presenting symptoms in the context of a patient's story. But how get to truly *know* a patient when the system was geared, even for those who *had* health insurance, which most of his HIV-infected patients did not, so that the doctor a patient saw one time was rarely the doctor he or she saw the next time?

It was the same, Fiona said, at Yale-New Haven. And it was also the same, he'd come to think—did she agree?—with matters beyond health care: the belief that we were going to have a quick, neat, and complete victory in Iraq—to shock and awe the enemy into submission without having to think about or deal with the aftermath of our invasion; or the delusion that we could keep polluting and using up the planet's resources—water, air, oil, coal, minerals, wetlands, forests—without regard to consequences and future generations.

And so, he explained, when the Bush administration pushed for a delay in giving grants to the UN Global AIDS Fund—of an amount that was, as a percentage of Gross National Product, the lowest amount any developed nation was contributing—something in him had snapped and he had written and sent off his letter to the President. The only thing he had left out of the letter—a minor regret—was what he had thought would seem a self-serving appeal to self-interest: the deadly truth, given that viruses were now frequent flyers—passengers moving around the globe easily and with astonishing speed—that what happened in South Africa, South America, or the South Pacific, affected *us*. We were, none of us, islands entire unto ourselves, and we were, none of us, safe. Whatever spread across poor nations would eventually spread across wealthy nations. It behooved us then, even for *our* own well-being, to think of others, to think long-term, and to be generous. And he'd also wondered while writing the letter—a sign of his ragged state of mind that day, and the depth of his frustration and outrage—if we were somehow destined as a species never to think in our own long-term interests—if there were some underlying biological reason for our inability to respond to situations, conditions, and events implicated and predictive of situations that could do us in—if we possessed some kind of innate biological death wish that was leading, inevitably, to our self-destruction.

Saul watched the turtles slide from the rock and disappear, one following the other, into the river, and only when the third one was gone did he become aware that Fiona had, for some time, been leaning against him.

"It's too quiet," Fiona said. "I mean, does anyone live here anymore?"

"I think I heard a dog bark," Saul said.

"Did you?"

"I'd forgotten how dead these villages are—" Saul said "—very beautiful but very dead."

"So what I think, doctor, is that all this talk about death is finally getting me down," she said.

"*Finally?*" he said.

"And also that I am very, very tired."

Saul had forgotten, once you were in the interior of these villages, how little light came through. The houses were constructed with thick walls and few windows, he remembered Jerry explaining, especially *villages perchés*—villages like Cabris and Entrevaux—in order to keep out cold and wind in winter, and sun and heat in summer. In these villages, originally built on the sides of mountains and high above valleys to protect their communities against invasion, most of the windows to the outside had been added in the years after the villages had lost their military function.

They walked slowly, Fiona's arm in his, and came upon the inn he and Tolle had stayed in. Entrevaux had only three passageways that could legitimately be called streets, only one of which, the street on which the inn was situated, was wide enough for automobiles, and Saul left Fiona at the inn, saying he would bring the car around and return as quickly as he could.

He untied the kerchief from Fiona's head, threaded his fingers through the dry tangles.

"It's remarkably ugly, isn't it," Fiona said.

"Not to me," Saul said, and he kissed her.

Her lips were warm, and he probed her mouth as if, he found himself thinking, his tongue were an enormous cotton swab. He flinched at the thought, started to pull away, but Fiona held tightly to the back of his neck, after which she lay back down, let her hand rest lightly on his lap.

"Desire waning?" she asked.

He shrugged.

"Not to worry," she said. "As far as we know, ovarian cancer isn't a sexually transmitted disease."

"But everything's different."

"Because I'm dying?"

"Because I love you."

"I suppose, in your way, you do," Fiona said.

"In my *way*?" Saul said. "What's that supposed to mean?"

"I've been thinking about us a lot—" Fiona said "—about the near and far of it all—and what I've concluded is that I'm not sure I exist for you."

"Oh come on," Saul said. "You're incredibly dear to me, and if—"

Fiona stopped his mouth with the flat of her hand. "Just listen," she said. "I know you care for me, and when you tell me you love me, I believe you. Hey—why not? I'm very loveable. But what I think is that I don't exist for you in the same way Tolle doesn't exist for you. I think that we all—all your women—wind up as mere affects of *your* needs and desires."

"That's quite the indictment."

"Not at all," Fiona said. "You're a guy like other guys—and maybe if you didn't idealize us so much you'd desire us less. Who knows?"

"'Who knows' is right," Saul said.

"Look—I need to tell you these things," she said. "But first tell me about this plan you still have about going to Africa to visit places where

149

Camus was born and grew up. I remember you quoted something to me from him the first time we made love, so how could a girl ever forget, right?—something he said *about* love."

"It's inscribed on the memorial to him, in Tipassa," Saul said. "'Here I understand what they call glory: the right to love without limits.'"

Fiona covered her mouth to stifle a giggle. "He really wrote that, and you really think, in my delicate condition, let's call it—though not as delicate as your daughter's—that I'd go there just to look at a piece of stone with sentimental tripe like that on it? I mean, maybe it worked when I was completely gaga over you, but—"

Saul stood. "You're enjoying this too much," he said. "You like getting even, don't you?"

"Getting even?" Fiona said. "Getting even for what?"

"For what?" Saul said. "For not staying with you. For not leaving Tolle. For not encouraging you to have the child."

"*Our* child," Fiona corrected. "But good fucking god, Saul—that was centuries ago. I mean, can't you even permit me the consequences of *my* choices? Do you want to take credit for the infiltration of my ovaries too?"

"Probably," Saul said.

"Thank you," Fiona said. "But look—it would have been a mistake to have had the child. I believed it then and I believe it now. I mean, think about it for a minute: if we'd had the child, what would have been the *sequelae*? We would have screwed up your kids and family, complicated my life considerably, and fucked up both our careers at a time when people needed us."

"Points well taken," Saul said.

"If you'd divorced and we'd married, we would have wound up the same as most couples: frustrated, resentful, bored, and miserable. What's that other thing Camus said—about proofs of love—about there being no true love but only proofs of love?"

"That wasn't Camus," Saul said.

"Well, whoever it was, he must have been French," Fiona said.

"But really, Saul—how sustain anything like romance—like whatever we had when we had it—when we'd have had to be talking about custody schedules, or the rising tide of diapers and flatulence? And you can bet your sweet ass Tolle would have wreaked some delightful vengeance on us."

"She's not like that."

"Oh no?" Fiona said. "My money says she'd be more like that than either of us. And another thing you should know, while we're at it. I could have had children after you, but I chose not to. My decision, and a good thing given where I am now. In truth, I never met a guy, present company ex-cluded, I would have *wanted* to raise a kid with, and if I'd had one on my own, and departed on the schedule I'm on now, my family would have moved in and—as you may recall—my father's whereabouts and state of inebriation are two wonders of the modern world, my mother is useless, and my sisters are sad and ridiculous human beings with sad and ridiculous problems that will never be solved this side of the grave…"

Fiona's voice trailed off, her head fell back on the pillow. Saul felt Fiona's forehead, went to the sink, ran a cloth under cold water, returned to the bed and washed her face and neck. Fiona's eyes closed, opened, closed again. Saul had never met her father, but he had met Fiona's mother once, at a meeting Fiona had arranged in a cafeteria in Brooklyn, on Flatbush Avenue. Her mother was an heavy-set, overbearing Irish woman who, dressed in a hooded sweatshirt and baggy dungarees, looked more like a man than a woman, and who declared it a rotten shame that Fiona had become a doctor instead of settling down and raising a family the way Fiona's sisters had. And Fiona's sisters, each with three or four children, and each with husbands who drank heavily, beat them occasionally, and played around on them frequently, had agreed with their mother—had regarded Fiona as a stuck-up snob who thought she was better than everyone else. "Our family's just your typical Irish cocktail," he recalled Fiona saying: "one part violence, two parts lamentation, three parts guilt, and a large splash of venom."

Saul sat next to the bed, watched Fiona, and realized he was happy in the way he'd been when Julia and Sam were children and he'd watch them while they slept, and he also recalled things Fiona had told him when they were first coming to know each other: how, working her way through college and medical school, she had struggled to keep the demons of booze and promiscuity at bay, and of how, despite the nasty ways they treated her, she was constantly going on rescue missions to her mother and sisters for their crises.

So that who she was, it occurred to him, was exactly the kind of person Camus had in mind when he wrote about the right-to-love-without-limits. He wouldn't argue about Camus' words with Fiona—what point in upsetting her?—but why shouldn't he continue to believe what Camus believed: that in a world where cynics and self-styled 'realists' prevailed, all the more reason to hold on to notions others might find naïve, sentimental, or romantic.

As if on cue, Fiona opened her eyes. "Speaking of romance," she said, "I meant to add, and don't be offended—that I'm glad we haven't made love, and it's not because of the cancer or my lack of romantic feelings towards you, but because of Tolle."

"I figured," Saul said.

"Really?"

"Really."

"You chose well there, my friend, young as you were at the time," Fiona said. "You do have good taste in women."

"Present company *in*-cluded?"

"Oh yeah," Fiona said. "I mean, now that I know her, I wouldn't want to cheat on her."

"But you already did—*we* did."

"Hey—I was young and impetuous," Fiona said. "And you were irresistible. All the female residents were hot to trot with you, you know." She turned onto her side, facing him. "But tell me something else, doc, and don't be evasive. Who do you think will go first—me or Dale?"

Thirteen

The figures were heartening, Saul knew. During the Revolutionary War, forty-two percent of Americans injured in combat died of their wounds. During World War Two, thirty percent of those wounded died. During the Vietnam War and the Gulf War twenty-four percent of those injured died. And now, in the wars in Afghanistan and Iraq, despite enormous increases in the deadliness of the weapons being used, the figure had dropped to ten percent.

Several of Saul's former interns, residents, and post-doctorate fellows had been called to service in the war in Iraq, most of them assigned to FSTs (Forward Surgical Teams) and out of boredom, loneliness, fear—and friendship—they wrote to him. The efficiency of the technology, like the evolution in the care of the wounded, he learned, was astonishing. Each FST was able to set up a functioning hospital within less than an hour. The FSTs could deploy tents that, by being attached one to the other, would form nine-hundred-square-foot facilities and would each contain four ventilator-equipped beds and two operating tables. Supplies, stored in backpacks, contained sterile instruments, anesthesia equipment, medicines, drapes, gowns, catheters, and handheld units that enabled doctors to obtain hemograms and to measure electrolytes or blood gases from a single drop of blood.

Each FST also carried an ultrasound machine, an oxygen concentrator, portable monitors, transport ventilators, units of packed red cells, and stretchers.

The basic strategy was not for definitive repair but for damage control. Teams packed off liver injuries, stapled perforated bowels, washed out dirty wounds—whatever was necessary to stop bleeding and control contamination. Abdomens were left open, laparotomy pads left inside wounds, bowels left unanastomosed while patients were sedated and ventilated. Physicians tried to limit surgery to two hours or less before shipping soldiers off to one of two Combat Support Hospitals in Iraq, after which those requiring more care were sent to level IV hospitals in Kuwait, Spain, or Germany, and—when more than a month's worth of treatment was necessary—back home, usually to Walter Reed Hospital in Washington, D. C., or to Brooke Army Medical Center in San Antonio, Texas. The average time it took to get a soldier from the battlefield to the States was four days; during the Vietnam War the average had been forty-five days.

Charlie Teitlebaum, a forty-two-year-old surgeon born and raised in the same Brooklyn neighborhood in which Saul had grown up, had not been one of Saul's residents, but while doing his rotation in internal medicine at Kings County, he and Saul had become friendly. At the time, Charlie had been going through a difficult stretch—his wife, Doris, diagnosed with manic depression, had been in and out of mental hospitals frequently during her late teens and early twenties (Charlie only learned this *after* they were married), and, following their move to Brooklyn, had begun throwing tantrums during which she would physically attack him—screaming, punching, scratching, throwing things. (Three years after Charlie left Kings County for a position at Boston's Beth Israel Hospital, she had, on her thirtieth birthday, committed suicide by hanging herself in a barn that adjoined the bed-and-breakfast in Camden, Maine, where she and Charlie had spent their honeymoon.)

When, during rounds, Saul, noticing how uncharacteristically distracted Charlie seemed, had suggested Charlie come see him, and when Charlie came and Saul had asked the obvious question—*Is every-thing okay?*—Charlie had begun talking, and had kept talking for the next hour and a half. (The previous night, while, eyes closed, Charlie was practicing tying off ligatures in his wooden knot-box, Doris had plunged a potato peeler into his shoulder.) Saul met with Charlie daily for a while, sought him out when Charlie stopped coming to see him, and began bringing him home for dinner.

Saul had surprised himself with Charlie. Good Jewish boys from Brooklyn that they both were, the mere *idea* of taking the initiative in terminating a marriage was anathema. But Saul talked with Tolle about Charlie, then met with Doris and Doris' doctors, and concluded that Doris would, with the years, decompensate more frequently and more severely. And so Saul had questions for Charlie: If you stay with her, will you be able to finish medical school? Can you see yourself living with her for the rest of your life? And: If you think her life will continue to go down the tubes, why the duty—the *need*—to join in her descent?

Three months later, Charlie divorced Doris, and a year after that he remarried. His second wife, Eva, a pediatrician, was on the Beth Israel Medical School faculty, and by the time Charlie had completed a six-year residency in general surgery at Johns Hopkins in Baltimore, followed by a two-year fellowship in surgical oncology, they had had three children. By this time, too, Charlie owed the Army a dozen years of service.

In 1999 Charlie was assigned to Walter Reed, where he distinguished himself in general and oncological surgery. In October, 2001, less than a month after the attacks on the World Trade Center, Charlie was sent to Afghanistan with a medical team that accompanied the first troops landing there.

After a year-long tour in Afghanistan, he returned to Walter Reed, and three years later was deployed to Iraq. From Iraq, he wrote Saul every three to four weeks. His FST, within a four-month period of its arrival, he reported, traveled more than twelve hundred miles. Medical teams had been designed and trained for swift, mobile military operations, but the war in Iraq was proving to be slow-moving and protracted; blast injuries from suicide bombs and land mines increased, bringing about higher incidences of penetrating wounds, mangled extremities, and blindness. Charlie saw astonishing rates of pulmonary embolism and deep venous thrombosis, and, what alarmed him most, a near epidemic of multi-drug resistant *acinetobacter baumanii* infections.

On October 30, 2004, less than three weeks before Saul received Fiona's letter and sent off his letter to Bush, he received a letter from Charlie's wife Eva. Four days prior to Charlie's scheduled departure from Iraq, she wrote, while making his weekly telephone call home from outside his barracks, he had been hit during a rocket-propelled grenade attack. Despite the FST's best efforts, Saul told Fiona—repeating Eva's words—they were unable to revive him.

"So that means that later this year, Charlie and I can have a Kings County mini-reunion," Fiona said.

"Don't," Saul said.

"Why not?" She jabbed Saul in the side, and when he winced, she did it again. "Come on—why *not?*" She worked her fingers into his ribcage. "Ticklish?"

"No," he said. "Jewish."

They were traveling west on the autoroute and were, Saul estimated, about a half hour from Aix-en-Provence, where they planned to stop for lunch.

"So it wasn't only *my* letter that got you going—" Fiona said.

"I'd forgotten the effect the news about Charlie had on me."

"Which effect was—?"

"Anger. Rage. Outrage."

"No sadness? No tears?"

"Tears too. Sure. Mostly, though, it seemed senseless—without meaning."

"Charlie was just doing his job—being *responsible*—the way you taught us," Fiona said. "What do they call it in bioethics—fulfilling his *deontologic obligation*, right?—that if called upon to heal, you have to say yes because you may be the only one capable of performing that particular act of healing. Charlie was a good guy. He was smart, cute, and shy, I remember—like you."

"*Shy?*"

"Well, you did overcompensate prodigiously," she laughed. "You and Charlie—two Brooklyn *mensches*—and I'll bet where he is now he's changed and that, emulating his mentor, he no longer considers himself bound by marital vows."

"How can you be certain?"

"Because I know what men are like," she said, and she slipped her hand under Saul's shirt.

"Come on!" Saul said, pushing at her hand. "I'm driving and—"

"And what? You'll crash and kill us? Hey—that way Charlie and I will get to be together even sooner, or—hmm—maybe the three of us might…"

"A heavenly *ménage à trois?*"

"Sounds fine to me," Fiona said, and she rested her head against Saul's shoulder. "It's only my hands and feet that have been turning numb lately, not my brain." She put her hand on her stomach, winced. "Now that I'm here—now that I've seen Spéracèdes—I can see why you love it so, and when I was walking around town exchanging "*M'sieu-dames*' with everyone, I kept thinking about how they all know each other, and how their families have known each other for generations."

"They know each other, sure," Saul said. "And sometimes they hate each other too. Feuds go on for generations. Jerry can tell you stories that—"

"Those were the only times I was jealous," Fiona said. "Jealous and pissed off. When you talked about your times in Spéracèdes with Tolle, I'd find myself wishing I'd had what she had—not marriage, or the kids—but just some easy, free time together, where…"

Fiona stopped talking. "Ouch," she said.

"'Ouch' for jealousy?" Saul asked.

"No. Cramps."

"Bad?"

"Very."

Saul pointed to an overhead sign: *Aix-en-Provence 30 Km.*

"Not far now," he said.

Fiona extended her right arm, palm against the dashboard to brace herself.

"Hey—are you okay?" Saul asked.

"I am, but my stomach's not," Fiona said. "We'd better stop."

Saul slowed down, drove the car onto the highway's shoulder. Fiona got out, leaned on the front fender to keep from falling.

"I should have warned you earlier," she said, "but I thought it would pass."

Then she was vomiting profusely—stuff shooting out of her mouth and onto the road, some of it splashing onto her shoes. Saul put his arm around her, massaged the back of her neck.

"Oh shit," Fiona said, looking down. "And I mean it literally—that's shit I'm vomiting, Saul. Fuck! Fecal material. Smell it."

"Let's get you to a hospital."

Fiona held her stomach, let out a long, raspy breath, vomited again.

"Easy now," Saul said. "Easy. Deep breaths."

Fiona wiped her mouth with the back of her hand. "There's blockage—right, doc?" she said. "An intestinal obstruction would be *my* diagnosis. When the stuff wants to go down and out the back way but can't, it decides to reverse direction and go back up, right?"

"Let's get you to a hospital."

"Damn! I didn't want you to see me like this."

Saul took a bottle of water from the car, wet his handkerchief, started to clean Fiona's face. She snatched the handkerchief from him, wiped off her mouth and chin, blew her nose, then poured water onto her shoes, swiped at them.

Saul helped her back into the car, placed his hand on her abdomen, tapped on it—she didn't resist—and heard what he didn't want to hear: a sound like that coming from a hollow drum.

"Distended as hell," Fiona said. She sucked air, then sipped water. "Dehydration—another promising symptom. It's great to be a physician at a time like this, don't you think? Nice to really *know* something for a change—to be able to predict the future with a not unreasonable chance of being right."

Saul drove back onto the highway, pressed on the accelerator until the speedometer showed that the car was moving at a hundred-and-twenty kilometers an hour.

"Headaches lately too," Fiona said. "Thought I'd mention them. Listen to the patient and the patient will give you the diagnosis—isn't that what we were taught? Really *nasty* headaches the last few nights, and damn!—I'm messing up your plans, the time you intended to spend with your daughter."

"There's a hospital in Aix," Saul said. "We can stop there. In the meantime—"

"Forget Aix," Fiona said. "I was this way in the States, and with decent intervals between sieges. Well, it *passed*, right? So, based on *past* experience—hey, doc, I got off a good one, and isn't it remarkable how the presence of death can enhance one's potential for gallows humor—I should be okay for the next two to three hours. That means we can get to Saint Rémy, get me to a doctor there—"

"To a hospital."

"Okay. A hospital, but in Saint Rémy, please, because if I have to stay over in Aix, it'll screw up your reunion with Julia, and if it does, we have to think of the toll that will take on *me*."

She opened her window, let Saul's handkerchief fly away.

"Hey!" he said. "If a cop's out there—"

"Then we'll get an escort," she said. She touched his hand. "I'll be okay till Saint Rémy. I promise."

When Fiona woke, they were in Aix-en-Provence, driving along an avenue that bypassed the center of town. The avenue was lined on both sides with tall plane trees, their limbs, pruned back severely in early winter, looking, Saul thought, as if they had been amputated.

"Traffic willing," Saul said, "we'll be in Saint Rémy within an hour."

"Okay," Fiona said, "Only when we get there, I don't want some French jerk shooting me up with a lot of drugs, or shoving things up my butt. The French do that more than we do, I hear."

"The French like their suppositories."

"When they talk it's all going to sound like gibberish, so how will we know *what* they're doing. How will they know what's wrong?"

"I'll translate."

"Well, consider the good news: no conflict for us about hotel registration—no temptations there, no awkward explanations to Julia…"

Saul let his right hand rest on her stomach. "We're really doing okay?"

"*We?*" She put her hand on top of his. "I do like it when you use that word. But hey, you sweet man, don't be scared. *I'm* not. I'm in pain, for sure, but I'm not scared. Pain is okay—it means I'm still here. So why aren't I scared, you may ask?" She sighed. "Because I'm with the man I love. I mean, what some women won't do to get their guy."

When they arrived at their hotel—the Villa Glanum, named for a nearby Roman ruin and situated on a road that led to Saint Paul de Mausole—Saul brought his suitcase into the reception area, gave the man at the front desk his name, told him he had a reservation, that he was a physician, that he had a friend who was very ill, and that he had to get her to a local hospital as quickly as possible, after which he would return. The man replied that there was no hospital in Saint Rémy—that the nearest hospitals were in either Arles or Avignon, each of which was about a half hour away.

Saul recognized the name of one of the hospitals in Avignon— Hôpital Henri Duffaut—and asked the man to write down directions and also to telephone his daughter, Julia Davidoff, at Saint Paul de Mausole and to let her know that there was a medical emergency he had to attend to, and that he'd call as soon as he could.

A few kilometers outside of Avignon, near Chateaurenard, Fiona grabbed Saul's arm, pointed to the car door. Saul pulled to the side of the road and Fiona opened the door, bent over, vomited again.

"Less shit, more pain this time," she said when they were back on the road. "I'm puking air now. Good old dry heaves—I remember them well."

"What you said before put me in mind of something Camus once said—"

"Are you trying to distract me, doctor?"

"Of course," he said, and continued: "What Camus believed lay at the heart of so much that was wrong in the modern world—fascism, Nazism, totalitarianism—was what he called the cult of efficiency and abstraction."

"Well, when it comes to medical care, I'm in favor of efficiency."

"He believed we gave ourselves license to kill millions of people because we gave ourselves license to have certain thoughts," Saul continued. "He liked to tell the story of an apartment in Paris the Gestapo rented where, when a concierge was setting things in order, oblivious to a man and woman who were tied up and bleeding, and she was reproached by them, she responded by saying that she never paid attention to what her tenants did."

"Well, you sent your letter, and I sent mine," Fiona said.

"And Eva—Charlie's wife—sent hers," Saul said.

Saul followed directions, but when they arrived in the center of Avignon, at the fortress-like walls that contained the Palace of the Popes, traffic suddenly stopped moving.

"More blockage?" Fiona asked, and began to sing: "*Sur le pont d'Avignon. La la la la—la, la la la—la...*"

Saul glanced sideways, saw that, eyes closed, Fiona was biting down hard on her lower lip. As soon as they made their way to an intersection, he took a left turn and, remembering a time he'd been here with Tolle on one of their outings, he calculated that he could save time by back-tracking and taking side streets.

He drove south for several blocks, then west until he reached a street he thought would lead to the hospital. When, a few minutes later, he saw signs for the university, he felt a wave of relief: the hospital, he recalled, had adjoined the university. Following signs for the university, he drove along a narrow street until he saw the hospital on the left hand side—a large red brick building with green slate mansard roofing.

He pulled up in front—looked for signs directing them to the emergency ward, but found instead a large bronze plaque stating that the building, designated as a national monument, housed administrative offices for the University of Avignon.

"Shit!" he exclaimed.

"That's *my* word," Fiona said.

He rolled down his window, called to several young people, and asked where the hospital was. They told Saul that there was no hospital here, but that there was a hospital on Rue Raoul Fallereau—Hôpital Henri Duffaut—on the other side of the Palace of the Popes, by the Durance River.

"My problem, I decided—one of them, anyway," Fiona said, "is that I became attached to you at an early and vulnerable age."

Behind them, cars were honking. Saul pictured Charlie, in a makeshift phone booth, lifting a receiver, smiling in anticipation of talking with his wife and children, of telling them he'd be home in less than a week. Saul looked for a phone booth, saw one about twenty yards away, opened the car door. Had he brought a phone card with him?

He ran toward the booth, heard people shouting at him, then heard the staccato blasts of a whistle. Fiona was calling to him, pointing to a policeman on a motorbike signalling to Saul with a white-gloved hand to return to the car. The policeman, dark-skinned and unsmiling—Algerian? Moroccan?—ordered him to get back into the car and to leave at once.

Saul explained that he was an American physician, that he was looking for Hôpital Henri Duffaut, that the woman with him, also a physician, was ill and needed to be taken to a hospital immediately, that he'd been about to telephone for help. The policeman, his visor raised, leaned forward, stared at Fiona for a moment, nodded, took out his mobile phone, spoke into it and, after informing Saul that Hôpital Henri Duffaut had been relocated to another part of the city more than twenty years before, gestured to Saul to follow him.

"The thing with no name," Saul said.

"*What?*" Fiona asked. "What the hell are you talking about?"

"The thing with no name—it's what South Africans call AIDS."

Saul followed the policeman until, at the third intersection, they came to a wide cross street where two police cars were waiting, their flashers swirling. The policeman on the motorbike pointed to the cars and, as sirens began blasting on and off, he waved goodbye. Saul followed the police cars.

"I like listening to you speak French, by the way," Fiona said. "I meant to tell you that. Later—there will be a later, right?—will you talk to me in French? And I liked the policeman's gloves. For my first communion, I had a beautiful pair of white kidskin gloves my grandmother gave me. Did I tell you about her? She accepted me always—*liked* me—for who I was. If not for her…" Fiona doubled over, tried, without success, to keep from moaning. "God but it hurts, Saul. If this is what labor's like, I'm grateful I never…"

She coughed, shook her head back and forth almost violently, as if by doing so she could shake the pain from it.

"We're almost there," Saul said.

When they arrived at the hospital, its façade a flat surface of Mondrian-like squares in yellows, blues, and reds, and turned into the driveway that led to Emergency Services, two men in green hospital garb were waiting on a ramp, a gurney next to them.

"We haven't talked about it, but I've been thinking a lot about forgiveness recently, especially with regard to my parents," Fiona said. "People make such a big deal out of it—that it's the highest form of something or other. In the Zen stuff I do from time to time—between boyfriends—I try to go there: to realize that she's just being who she is the way I'm being who I am—to divest myself of all this ego crap, but…"

Saul heard an ugly gutteral sound rumble from her throat. "Sorry about that," she said. "But we should talk about forgiveness, you and me, okay? I forgave *you* a long time ago, by the way. Forgave my sisters too. But so far I can't find it in me to forgive my father *or* my mother. I mean, why should there be forgiveness for unforgivable acts? Why forgive people who willfully *hurt* other people?"

Saul turned off the ignition, went to Fiona's side of the car, where hospital aides were already helping her onto the gurney.

Fiona lay down, reached for Saul's hand. "That doesn't make me a bad girl, does it?" she asked.

Saul kissed her on the forehead, inhaled the foul residue of her vomiting.

"Come on—you can do better than that," she said.

Saul leaned down, kissed her on the mouth. Her lips were ice-cold. At the doors that led into the hospital a security guard stopped him. Saul took out his wallet, showed the guard a card that identified him as a medical doctor. He said it was essential that he be with Fiona so that he could provide information to the doctors about her condition.

A policeman was beside Saul, telling him that he would park Saul's car and bring the keys to the nurses' station in the emergency room. Saul entered the hospital, spotted the gurney at the far end of the corridor, saw that the staff was already checking Fiona's vital signs, moving her along. They disappeared behind swinging doors. Saul pushed through, watched two men lift Fiona and place her on an examining table. They began cutting away her clothes, listening to her chest, attaching wires. They moved quickly, efficiently.

A young man, a clipboard in hand—his ID tag identified him as Clément Hémon, M.D.—asked Saul if he could tell him what happened. Saul identified himself as a physician, and he began, quickly, to give the man Fiona's history, to tell him about the cramps, the headaches, the pain, the vomiting.

A woman in a white lab coat was probing Fiona's stomach, asking her questions, in English: Did this hurt? When had she last moved her bowels? How often had she been throwing up?

Doctor Hémon thanked Saul, conferred with the woman in the white lab coat. Saul went toward them but was held back by an aide who told him that Doctor Joussaume—the woman who was examining Fiona—would speak with him in a few minutes.

Doctor Joussaume took Fiona's hand in her own. "We're going to take you into surgery as soon as we can," she said. "We'll sedate you. Do you have any allergies? Do you know your blood type? We will test for it, of course, but if…"

Other personnel now entered the room, two of them transferring Fiona to a gurney again, rolling her away. Fiona waved to Saul. Saul started toward her, but was held back by another man.

"I'm Doctor Rosenthal," the man said, in English.

Saul spoke in French, as clearly and rapidly as he could, telling the doctor what he had told Doctor Hémon: that he was a physician, that Fiona had cancer of the ovaries—*cancer des ovaires:* the words were cognates—virtually identical, Saul explained—that she had exhausted all the usual lines of treatment—stages one, two, and three—that during their drive to Saint Rémy—they had begun in Spéracèdes, a village near Grasse—she had begun regurgitating fecal matter.

Fiona was a physician, he continued, and had been his student at Kings County Hospital. The two of them had been on their way to visit Saul's daughter Julia, who was working at Saint Paul de Mausole, in Saint Rémy. They had planned to stop in Aix for lunch....

Doctor Rosenthal made no attempt to interrupt Saul, and Saul wondered why he couldn't stop talking. And why was he imagining that the doctor was going to ask him if he would like to repair to a small *bistro* nearby so that they could have a drink and a cigarette together? What Saul wanted to know—a request, he said—what he had been trying to say—he *would* get to the point, he added apologetically—was that he would very much like to be there when they performed the surgery.

Then he was hearing Jerry's voice, after Saul had told him about Dale's second visit and the exam Fiona gave him, Jerry telling the story of a man who, upon waking one morning, tells his wife of twenty-five years that she's the most miserable, loathsome, ugly woman he's ever known. A few hours later, all contrition, the man calls home to apologize. Surprised to find his wife home in the middle of the day, he asks what she's doing there. "I'm in bed," she tells him. "What are you doing in bed?" he asks. "I'm getting a second opinion," she replies.

Doctor Rosenthal was saying that they had paged Doctor Coursaget —an excellent surgeon—and that Doctor Coursaget would arrive within a half hour. If Saul wished to attend the surgery, he would, of course, grant him this courtesy.

165

"The reason I wanted her to be treated at *this* hospital," Saul explained, "is because I remembered that you've done AIDS research here. That's why I recognized the name of the hospital, although I can't recall who the doctors were who did the research, or what the protocol was, I regret to say."

"Doctors Émile Anacréon and Nguyen duc Duy, most probably," Doctor Rosenthal said. "They have been at the—how do you say?—the forefronts of research on antiretrovirals and their interactions with methadone, since many of our AIDS people are also drug users."

Saul said that he too had done research and published papers on methadone treatment for people who were drug users and HIV-infected, and as he spoke—still unable to *stop* speaking—he realized that all the while Doctor Rosenthal was talking to him in English, he had been talking to the doctor in French.

The doctor shook Saul's hand. "Your friend is very sick," Doctor Rosenthal said, "but we will do our best for her."

It had been many years since Saul had been present for a major surgical procedure, and feeling like a small boy allowed into the world of grown-ups, he watched with fascination as Doctor Coursaget and his assistants opened Fiona's belly, found the dilated loops of bowel through which nothing—neither liquids nor the gaseous content of her intestine—was flowing, located the tumors blocking the intestines, and cut them away.

The music coming from the speakers was slow jazz, a woman—Sarah Vaughn? Dinah Washington?—singing a song he thought was called "Dreamy." Doctor Coursaget was humming to the tune, was now removing his gloves and his mask, was nodding to an assistant, asking the assistant to finish up.

The assistant gestured to a nurse, who pressed a button, the music changing to something louder, and with a more savage, driving beat—what Saul thought was called hard rock.

"We did the best we could," Doctor Coursaget said to Saul. "Your friend will need to stay in the hospital for four or five days, and I believe she will, for a while at least, benefit from some alleviation of pain. After that..."

166

The doctor shrugged, gestured with his hands, palms upturned, in a way that indicated there really was not much that he or anyone else could do for Fiona.

"It is often quite difficult to close up a woman after this particular surgery," he said. "So, as you can see, I have left the truly hard work to my younger colleague, Doctor Maubert, in whom I have great confidence. He will clean up her abdomen, of course, and inject warm saline solution into the cavity. We made a decision not to remove her uterus—a consideration of the extra time involved and possible post-operative complications. These would be negligible in most instances, but given your friend's condition, if we..."

Saul had stopped listening. He looked around: the operating suite was impeccably modern—as high-tech as any he had ever seen. He watched Doctor Maubert bend down over Fiona's stomach and imagined Charlie stitching up soldiers in a tent in Iraq, and he wondered: If he had known the day would end this way, would he have chosen to tell Fiona about Charlie?

Doctor Coursaget was telling Saul that he himself would be checking in on Fiona at least once every day. Saul moved away from the doctor, toward Fiona. He saw Doctor Maubert reach inside Fiona's belly, after which the room began to go dark, the floor to rise towards him.

"Come with me, please," Doctor Coursaget was saying, his hand gripping Saul's elbow.

Saul wanted to push the man away—*why are you so smug, you bastard?* he wanted to ask. *Why the fuck are you laughing?*—but all he could do was see, again, the pale, gloved hands vanishing inside Fiona's body, the dull gray-pink of her skin.

He sat on a bench, his head between his legs, and could not recall having walked from the operating room to the corridor in which he was now sitting. Doctor Coursaget sat beside him.

"It happens to all of us," Doctor Coursaget said, a hand on Saul's shoulder. "There is no need to be embarrassed."

Saul sat up, drank from a glass of water Doctor Coursaget offered.

"She's okay then?"

"We did the best we could," Doctor Coursaget said again. "She will be in the recovery room for a while, and you can visit with her there. We sedated her quite heavily, however, so I do not expect that she will wake for several hours."

A few minutes later, the doctor stood, shook Saul's hand, and left, and as Saul walked toward the exit—he would retrieve the car keys, then go to the parking lot and get Fiona's suitcase—he realized that not only had no one asked for payment, or for either of them to fill out forms, but that no one had even asked that he or Fiona show proof of insurance.

Without meaning. He had chosen not to elaborate on those words when Fiona had asked about his reaction to Charlie's death. *Without meaning.* If Julia decided not to have the child, perhaps she and Fiona could share a room while they recovered from their surgeries. Perhaps the hospital would give them a two-for-one deal. When he spoke with Tolle, he could ask her to drive down to Jerry's house and ask Jerry how Madame Amione was doing, for if she too were in need of a surgical procedure...

Saul retrieved the car keys, walked outside and, momentarily blinded by the bright winter sun, felt as if he had walked directly into a wall of pure white light. He felt dizzy, held onto a railing. He needed food and water, he knew. But he also needed to telephone Julia and Tolle, to go back into the hospital and check on Fiona, to inquire about payment and insurance. Would Dale and Gerhard have stopped by during the day? If Dale had his lab tests done at Hôpital Henri Duffaut, Saul would be able to evaluate the results immediately. *Without meaning.* Camus had been right, although given her condition there would be no reason to say so to Fiona. But, as Camus had often maintained—what, in Saul's opinion, lay at the heart of his philosophy of the absurd—seemed true: in a world where one could no longer believe either in God or in reason, it *was* often difficult to know how to behave—to know what to do.

Fourteen

"Being on Van Gogh's turf has obviously inspired you," Fiona said to Julia.

"The sunflowers were my father's idea," Julia said.

Fiona handed the flowers back to Julia. "I feel better—groggy as hell, but better," she said. "Would you mind asking one of the nurses for a vase?"

Julia took the flowers, left the room. From under the sheets, tubes ran to plastic pouches, and a drip—glucose? morphine?—ran from Fiona's left wrist to a bag of clear liquid that hung from an IV pole.

"She's lovely, Saul—and it's apparent how much she adores you," Fiona said. "But then, who wouldn't?" She took his hand. "You were wonderful yesterday."

"Just doing my job," Saul said. "You're the one who's wonderful."

"This is the first time I've met one of your children, so I can see why you always…" She wiped at her eyes with the back of her wrist. "Forgive me—I'm sorry for losing it this way, but since I woke from surgery, I've been *highly* emotional…"

"Unlike the way you usually are, right?"

"What I thought about first thing when I woke, was that it *was* a good idea to visit you," Fiona said. "If I'd been by myself, I'd probably be dead by now."

"Not true."

"Take some credit. I mean, think of it this way—you've probably added *months* to my life." She laughed. "It would be sheer hell to have my family around now, my mother clucking over what a shame it was that I was going to die without having given her grandchildren, or my sisters…"

"Shh," Saul said. "Don't."

Julia returned, set the vase of sunflowers on a window sill. "When you're discharged, would you like to visit Saint Paul de Mausole?" she asked. "I could show you Van Gogh's room, though it's not clear that the room they say was his was actually his. But from the window you can see what he saw when he painted. It's still pretty much the same: a wheat field, a stone wall enclosure, cypress trees, hills."

"I'd love to," Fiona said.

"While he was there he tried to kill himself by drinking lamp oil and sucking the paint out of tubes," Julia said.

"Do you like the taste of paint?" Fiona asked

"Haven't tried it yet."

"I'm a lawyer, by the way," Julia said.

"I'm sorry—" Fiona said "—not that you're a lawyer, but that I'm a bit out of it. Your father told me you were a lawyer, that you went to Columbia Law School, that you clerked for a judge in D.C., that you were slated to become a partner in one of those old New York white shoe law firms, but why are you here—?"

"I took an extended leave of absence."

"Hey—so did I—and so did your father!" Fiona said. "See? I *knew* we had lots in common. What we don't have in common, though, me and your father, is that I've never been known for being diplomatic. So I was wondering why you came *here*. Why Saint Rémy?"

"I'm here because I'm pregnant," Julia said. "And because I read Van Gogh's letters—the ones he wrote to his brother. I'm here because he spent the last year of his life in Saint Paul when it was a lunatic asylum, which it still is, except for the part that's a museum, though they call it a sanitarium now. I'm here because he wrote that Saint Paul was the most peaceful place he'd ever been in, and when I read his letters, I knew this was the place to come to while I decided whether or not to have the child."

"And have you decided?" Fiona asked.

"The book was a birthday present from an old boyfriend who was an artist."

"Always a good idea to take away something tangible from each failed relationship—" Fiona said "—a habit I tried, though with mixed results, to make into ongoing policy."

"Reading the letters also pushed me into talking with *my* brother— Sam—and he encouraged me to come here," Julia said. "We talked about Van Gogh, and his time at Saint Paul, and about the wonder of it: how somebody who was so totally crazy could also be so phenomenally productive."

"But Jules—" Saul began "—his painting gave his life *meaning*. Lots of people who go through difficult times, and who—"

Julia's eyes grew large. "Did you *hear* that? Did you hear what he called me?"

"He called you Jules," Fiona said.

"I've been trying my whole life to get him to stop!" Julia said. "I mean, why can't he call me what I want to be called?"

"Sorry," Saul said.

"But why can't he *stop*?" Julia asked. "And why—"

"He can't because he can't," Fiona said. "But he has to stop now because I'm very tired, and I need to sleep. Before you leave, though, tell me: have you made a decision—will you have the child?"

"Van Gogh painted more than a hundred-and-fifty paintings at Saint Paul in less than a year," Julia said. "He made *hundreds* of drawings too, and this was while he was hallucinating, on isolation, locked into water tubs—and what astonished me was how *clearly* he could write even while he was so screwed up. Therefore, being considerably screwed up myself, I thought that if I could drink in some of the same stuff he did—the colors, the light, the hills, the walls—*not* the paint— that maybe things would clear up and slow down, so that—this is

171

my long way of answering your question—I could figure out what I wanted to do."

"Sounds like a plan, but I *am* tired, and…"

"We'll go—sorry, sorry—but I can't slow down, can you tell?" Julia asked. "I can't slow down. Sometimes I get started and I can't slow down, like now, whether it's talking, or shopping, or calling people—I do that a lot: I go to my address book some days and just start with the letter 'A' and call up everyone I know, everyone I've ever known, and—"

"Do you tell them all that you're pregnant?" Fiona asked.

"God no," Julia said, and laughed. "I may be crazy, but I'm not *stupid*."

"You never were," Saul said.

"I never was which?" Julia asked.

"Both."

"He always says the right thing," Julia said. "Have you noticed?"

"And most of the time he *does* the right thing," Fiona said. "Still the good Jewish boy. But didn't you also choose to come here because your parents were nearby?"

"Yes."

"When I was in your situation, I kept wishing I had parents I could go to."

"Did you have the child?"

"No."

"Are you sorry?"

"No."

Saul put his arm around Julia's shoulder and, to his surprise, felt her lean into him.

Julia moved to the bed, kissed Fiona on the cheek. "We'll come back later, okay?"

"Okay—that would be good."

"And guess what?" Julia said. "I feel better too."

"Well, enjoy the feeling while you can," Fiona said. "In the meantime, pray for my bowels. As soon as they cooperate, I'm out of here."

Julia pointed to the large parking lot that took up most of the town's center, and told Saul that several mornings a week, the lot, along with many of the side streets that radiated from it, was transformed into a market.

"I could be happy living here," she said.

"Who wouldn't?" Saul said.

"It's a real *village*, with the kind daily life you and Mom said you had in Spéracèdes—a place where you can shop every day for the things you need for that day, and where you know the shopkeepers, where their children are friends with your children, where—"

"You don't have any children."

"It has all the perks of a larger city too," Julia continued. "Museums, music festivals, art galleries. Lots of writers and artists live here, and it's not far from major cities, and from the sea, and—"

"But it has no hospital."

"That's why God created Avignon," Julia said.

Saul smiled. "You're in a good mood, aren't you?"

They were at a café, an electric brazier beside their table giving off enough heat to enable them to sit outside.

"What could be bad?" Julia said. "I've just made an amazing new friend, I'm far from my law office, my phone, and my computer, and I'm in a beautiful village in the south of France where—lucky me—I'm having a fashionable late-afternoon drink with my father."

"And you're pregnant."

"Oh *that!*" Julia said, and waved the subject away.

"You didn't answer my question."

"You didn't *ask* a question."

Saul leaned across the table. "Julia," he said.

"*Dad,*" she said, leaning toward him in the way he was leaning toward her.

"Look. We've *got* to talk about what you're going to do. I have no intention of telling you *what* to do, of course, but—"

"You know what?" Julia said. "How about, instead of you telling me 'the choices are mine but you just want to make sure I understand

173

the consequences and the et-ceteras,' you just tell me what you think. How about—even better—you tell me *what to do*! It would be a relief, believe me, to have somebody just take over."

"I need more data," Saul said. "What week are you in? Have you had an ultrasound yet? Do you love the guy? Does he know?"

"Last question first. He doesn't know *and* I don't love him. I surely had the *hots* for him, but I thought about it and concluded that if I never saw him again, it wouldn't be too soon. I don't *miss* him. He's much more neurotic than I am—and profoundly irresponsible. He'd make a *lousy* father—the kind of guy who'd say, 'You deserve to have your career, dear, so I'll stay home and play Mister Mom'—and I'd arrive home to find him zoned out in front of the TV—yes, he's a pothead too—the house a wreck, the baby ass-deep in poop and puke, and—"

"Do you want the child?"

"Maybe."

"Not good enough," Saul said.

Julia looked away. She lifted her glass of wine, then set it back on the table. "I probably shouldn't be having any alcohol," she said. "Why didn't you stop me?"

"You're a big girl," Saul said. "And one drink won't cause birth defects. All things in moderation."

"Including moderation, right?" Julia sighed, put up a hand to indicate that she didn't want Saul to say anything. "I know you mean well and yes, I did come here because I wanted to be near you and Mom, and I'm sorry if I'm being difficult about this."

"You're angry."

"Maybe." She smiled. "I mean, who *isn't*? It's what makes the world go round, as far as I can tell. But look, can I ask you a question, and if I do, will you tell me the truth?"

"Try me."

"You and Fiona were lovers, weren't you?"

"Sounds more like a statement than a question."

"Here's another: is she really going to die?"

"Yes. She's really going to die. We *all* die—no exceptions, it seems —but the odds are good she'll die a lot sooner than you or I will."

"How long does she have?"

"Three months," Saul said. "Four maybe—six, tops."

"I like the way she talks to you. Mom talked to you that way sometimes, but in your daughter's opinion, not often enough, so maybe *that's* why I'm angry. Why couldn't you have fought and divorced the way the parents of all my friends did?"

"Did you feel left out?"

"Alienated and deprived," she said. "Mom sent me a copy of the letter you sent to President Bush, by the way. She's very proud of what you did."

"It's just a letter," Saul said. "I didn't *do* anything."

"But sending a letter like that is out of keeping for the father I know—it's you being a little bit outrageous. It's you *not* doing the right thing, *not* saying the right thing and—" Julia stopped, waved her hand in front of his eyes. "Dad? *Dad?!* Are you *listening* to me?"

"Of course. You like it when I don't do the right thing or don't say the right thing."

"No." Julia shook her head. "No. You can parrot my words back well enough, but you're staring at that woman over there. It's rude."

Saul *had* noticed a woman sitting a few tables away: a dark-haired woman, her short hair parted to one side—in her mid-forties, he guessed—who was drinking coffee and reading a newspaper.

"I thought she might be someone I knew," Saul said. "She looked familiar."

"They *all* look familiar."

"Sorry."

"I hate it when men do that," Julia said, and, nearly knocking over her glass of wine, leaned forward and slammed her fist on the table. "I absolutely hate it when they pretend to be listening while ogling another woman, and when a guy does it to me what I want to do is to pull an ice pick out of my handbag and jab it in one of his eyes. If we could do that to every man who thinks he has the right to stare at us that way, and if—"

"Stop it, Julia. People are staring at *you*."

Julia sat back. "Okay," she said. "I'm done for now. But I meant what I said before—I wish you'd be that way more often—that you'd be more like that guy who wrote to the President—like the guy who made up those crazy fairy tales for me before I went to sleep that I could tell to my friends and..."

Saul saw her eyes well with tears, and while he was aware again of how much she resembled her mother physically, he was even more aware of how much—in the guileless way she talked, in her energy— she reminded him of Fiona.

"The Princess and the Pea Shooter?"

"That was a good one," Julia said. "Whenever a guy got fresh with her, she loaded up and shot him in the eye and—hey, maybe that's why I've always wanted to—"

"Any morning sickness?"

"No."

"Been to a doctor?"

"Sure."

"Okay," Saul said. "What I think is that you should have the child."

Julia grinned. "Thank God," she said. "I was hoping you'd say that. So okay: here or there?"

"There."

"Do I tell the father?"

"Not necessarily. If he finds out he has a son or daughter, there could be legal complications. We need to know more first—to inform ourselves."

"What if I don't do what you say—what if I *don't* have the child?"

"Then you don't."

"Was the child Fiona alluded to—the one she didn't have—yours?"

"Yes."

Julia took a deep breath, nodded.

"Thank you, Dad."

"For what?"

"You *are* a good man, you know. Mom always said so, even when

176

she was pissed at you. Maybe not the best Dad in the world to *us*—you were away so damned much, and playing around, and—"

"Now wait a minute," Saul said.

"Oh Dad, it doesn't matter. I think it may have mattered to Mom at the beginning—she never said anything to me, but..." Julia stopped. "When I think about marriage—about finding a guy I'd want to have children with, and when I think about my age—past thirty—*wow!*—I mean, the idea of making love to one man and one man only for the next twenty or thirty years seems ridiculous. I don't get how people do it."

"Maybe they don't."

"But then there's all the secrecy, and lying, and sneaking around, and hurt feelings. It all seems so stupid."

"What's the alternative?"

Julia shrugged. "Living in France?"

Saul laughed, and he thought about Tolle, and imagined her laughing with him. He glanced toward the woman he had glanced at before, thought of the gift Tolle had given him before they had gone to sleep the night before, and of how, afterwards, they had been laughing so hard they had been unable, for a while, to resume making love.

"I've been angry with you—sure—but not for that," Julia said. "For that—and this may sound crazy, but meeting Fiona confirms it—I'm actually happy for you. I mean, it surprises *me* that I feel this way. But we both know how Mom can be Miss Siberia, everything locked up inside her until *boom!*—and you *did* work so damned hard all those years, going out to save lives every day, and when—"

"*Save* lives?" Saul said. "Not at all. Mostly they died. For every life I saved—prolonged, at best—at least a hundred died. Look. In just the short while we've been sitting here and talking, *thousands* of children have died of AIDS. More than eight thousand people *a day* are dying of AIDS—"

"I don't need to hear this now, okay?" Julia said. "Because I want to talk about *us* and about *me*, not about people I don't know and will never see. Because what I was starting to say before was that you being such a good man made it hard on *us*. Harder on Sam than on me. He's really intimidated by you, in case you haven't noticed. Given who you are—how can he *ever* live up to you?"

"He doesn't have to. He just has to be Sam."

"*No!*" Julia slammed her hand on the table again. "You don't get it, Dad. You just don't get it, do you? You're so fucking righteous and *correct. That's* the big problem. I mean, are you *ever* wrong? Have you ever done *anything* wrong?"

"Evidently—to judge by your anger—I've done lots wrong."

Julia leaned back and smiled broadly. "But not lately," she said. "So let's have another drink, you and me."

At the hotel, Saul had tried several times, without success, to reach Tolle. Maybe she was in the shower, or had gone for a walk and left her cell phone at home. Maybe she was writing and had turned off her phone in order not to be interrupted. Or maybe—more probable—she was having dinner with Jerry.

But it didn't matter. He was happy sitting at the café where he and Julia had had their drink. To his invitation to have dinner together, she had pleaded fatigue, and so, by himself, he had enjoyed a splendid, leisurely dinner—*paté de campagne, blanquette de veau,* a salad, wine—a dinner made more splendid, he thought, *because* it was leisurely, and because it gave him time to think about his visit with Julia, and about the gift he had received the night before from Tolle. The restaurant, about half full (the woman who had been sitting nearby was gone), was exceptionally quiet. He and Tolle had often remarked on the fact that the general noise level in French restaurants was considerably lower than that in American restaurants. Why, they'd wondered, did Americans—young people especially—seem always to be *shouting* at each other? And they had noted that in France couples often sat side by side instead of across from each other. He also recalled Jerry commenting on the fact that the French brought their dogs to restaurants but left their children at home—one of many examples that showed why the French, unlike Americans, rarely looked back on their childhoods with affection. The French neither worshipped nor idealized childhood—what children looked forward to in France was escaping *from* childhood.

Saul could see himself arguing with Jerry about this—if it were so, why did French youth style themselves after American youth—but to what end? What Saul preferred to do was what he was doing now: to be alone, and to be thinking of his visit with Julia. For just as knowing she would die in a few months seemed to have given Fiona license to be more blunt than usual, so being pregnant—and being set adrift from familiar moorings—seemed to have allowed Julia to say things to him—to criticize him and to praise him in ways she would never have done in New York.

To reconcile one's vices and virtues, Saul recalled Camus saying, was the very definition of knowing how to live, and remembering this, it pleased Saul to think that it wasn't so much that it was possible for Julia to *say* these things that was heartening, but that she felt free to *think* them. Saul ordered a favorite dessert—a *tarte tatin,* caramelized apple pie served upside down—and coffee, and recalled how almost childlike Tolle had been the evening before, when, so as to not chance waking Fiona, she had taken him by the hand and led him out of their bedroom and down into the garden in order to present him with his gift. They brought the bottle of Côte du Rhone with them, along with a single wine glass. It was an unseasonably warm moonless night— there were no street lights on the road, and all lights in their house were out—so that nobody would see her present him with a gift she hoped would please him, she said, and one that would, she allowed, also provide a measure of pleasure for her.

She asked him to strip down to his underpants, then took off all her own clothing except for her undergarments—panties and bra— and explained that she would now show him a *pas de deux* that had been a favorite of young ballet dancers. She believed he was strong and stable enough, and that she was still light and fit enough for them to succeed. In order to perform this particular variation of a *pas de deux,* she would show him, first, how to do a classical lift so as help her to rise onto his shoulders, or above his shoulders. There was nothing to worry about, she said, since the ground was soft, there was no ceiling to be wary of, and also because being able to achieve this particular *pas de deux*, as with any *pas de deux*, was more a question of physics—of leverage and angles—than of muscle.

There were, she explained, two basic lifts—an arabesque lift and a shoulder lift—and his responsibilities would be the same for both: he was to place his right hand on her waist, above her hip, but not on her stomach—slightly below her ribcage—and, when she went into a classic arabesque position, her right leg firmly planted and on toe, her left leg extended straight back and parallel to the ground, he was to place his left hand under her thigh and be prepared to lift—in the way, for example, a waiter would lift a tray of dishes, but to be sure not to grab with his fingers. He was to bend his knees slightly in a *plié*, and when he lifted he was to do so in a single motion and extend his arms straight up and parallel to one another. She would ease the lift by rising on her own—jumping lightly—and once she was airborne, so to speak, he was to slide his right leg a bit to the right and plant it as solidly as he could. In the air, while ascending, she would decide whether to sit on his shoulder—a simple act, really, like sitting on a chair—or to continue upwards towards heaven.

She had had him practice lifting her—an inch or two off the ground, then several inches, then a foot or so—and after they shared a second glass of wine, she told him that the time had come. On the count of three—"*Alors—l'heure est venue!*" she said—he bent his legs slightly, lifted, and she rose above him almost weightlessly. He was amazed to find her floating beautifully above him… an instant later, however, he felt his left arm start to give, felt the two of them totter, felt her begin to descend, one hand gripping his left shoulder while she turned her body so that she was facing him instead of away from him, and while her legs were still spread wide in an arabesque, her sex—but when had she removed her panties?—was suddenly close to his mouth.

"*Taste me!*" she said. "Please taste me, Saul. Taste me *now*."

He had tasted her for, at most, a half-second, after which his right hand slipped, she pushed off, and they tumbled to the ground.

"Are you all right?" he asked.

"Never better," she replied, and had asked him why he had stopped doing what she had told him to do, so he had rolled on top of her, and with his tongue had luxuriated in her strong, pungent juices, after which he had mounted her, poured wine into her open mouth, told her how much he appreciated her gift—'the *lift-and-lick pas de deux*' was its official name, she informed him—and assuring her he was determined not to lose his balance this time, he had pulled her to her feet so they could make a second attempt. They stood, they drank, and when he put one hand on her waist, and his left hand under her thigh, she had giggled, stumbled, and sat down on the ground.

"Are you *serious* about wanting to try again?" she asked.

Sitting next to her on the ground, he said that he was game if she was, and she said she was very game—possibly very *gamey* too, though that was for him to know—and then had begun babbling about not believing that they had actually, if only for a millisecond, done what they'd done, and at their ages, and when he mounted her and tried to penetrate her, she was giggling and laughing so hard that he lost heart and dismounted. They had lain side by side for a while, holding hands and looking up at a sky now star-streaked, and had complimented one another on their ability to have performed a maneuver she had not performed for eons, and he had never performed, and one at which dancers a generation or two younger could not always succeed because they laughed too much, or were too drunk, or because they couldn't stop giving directions—'*Higher! Lower! Closer! Not **too** close!*' —so that they would usually revert, Tolle said, to more traditional modes of pleasure.

They heard a siren—police? fire? ambulance?—and Tolle wondered aloud if, for what they had just done, the authorities were coming after them. The sirens stopped, then started again.

"We should probably go in," Tolle said.

"But not yet," he said, and he rested a hand on her right leg. "Do you miss those years?"

"Which years?"

"The years when you were a dancer."

"No," she said.

"Not at all?"

"Not at all."

He stroked her leg gently. "I forgot about your accident," he said. "Sorry."

"Why sorry?" she said. "If I'd continued in ballet I would have been, at best, a good but ordinary dancer, never a principal," she said. "Instead, I was able to choreograph and produce an original ballet, to meet Camus, and to teach several generations of girls and young women, along with a fair number of professionals, and thereby enable them to become more accomplished dancers."

"Gifts," he said. "You were always a gift giver."

"Curious," she said. "Because, as you've often remarked, there's nobody more self-interested than I am, nobody more..."

"More what?"

"Selfish."

"Ah—but 'self-interest' and 'selfish' are not the same thing," he said. "Your parents may have accused you of being selfish, especially after your sister became ill, but—"

"We've been over that, so let's not spoil *our* moment," she said. "Also, there's something else I've been thinking about."

"There's something else you've been thinking about," he said.

"If not for the accident and for the loss that came with it, which, I admit, seemed enormous at the time," she said, "I would not have met you, and fallen in love with you, and married you. You and I would not have brought Julia and Sam into the world, and I would not be here with you now—happy, and sweaty, and a little bit drunk," she said. "And do you know what else?"

"What else?"

"I don't believe that even Balanchine, were he our age, or *any* age, would have dared to attempt what we've just attempted."

"We were awesome," he said.

"We *are* awesome," she said. "And do you know why?"

"Because you're an excellent teacher?"

"Perhaps," she said. "But also because you're an exceptional student, especially considering your very late start at this new career. And do you know what else?"

"Tell me."

"We were awesome because you never protested," she said. "You believed."

"A good boy does what he's told," he said.

"Please do not reduce your heroism to a truism," she said. "It does an injustice to my brave and courageous husband—"

"True," he said.

"—and I won't allow it," she said. "At rehearsals, according to Allegra, Balanchine used to say to his ballerinas, and with his thick, sexy Russian accent, '*Vat are you saving it for?*' And in my opinion, what we did this evening—"

"—would have made made him applaud your teaching skills, and—"

"—your willingness to go all-out—along with your hitherto dazzling, hidden potential, which was enhanced by what Balanchine demanded of his dancers, as all good ballet teachers do: *obedience*—obedience to the formal details of classic techniques and routines."

"I take direction well," Saul said.

"Though not always, thank the lord," Tolle laughed. She propped herself up on an elbow, looked down at him. "You didn't protest because—my opinion—you were *open*, Saul. Because you let me care for you and show my love for you the way *I* wanted to love you and not the way *you* wanted to be loved—and do not interrupt, please, because I also want to say that I'm proud of you, and grateful to you, for the admirable courage you've shown in accepting your gift, and also for something else I've been intending to say—for having gone and *written* your letter to the President, since if not for that letter, we wouldn't be here, and—how best to put it?—we would never have exchanged our gifts, and also…"

Her voice trailed off.

"Also—?"

"You make me happy, and I admit to being somewhat surprised that you do."

"I make you happy."

"And I'm also surprised that I'm able, with you, to *be* happy."

"That's good," he said. "Very good."

"Would you pour me another glass of wine, please?"

He poured wine, they drank, and he held the bottle upside down to show her that it was empty.

"I am feeling pleasantly drunk, and quite young," she said. "No. Correct that. What's so great about being young, after all? Would either of us like to be Julia or Fiona's age again? Or Sam's? So, let me take it from the top: I am feeling pleasantly drunk, and quite—a better word—youth-*ful*."

"And the moral," he said, "is that it *is* better to give—to be *able* to give—than to receive. Is that what you're trying to tell me?"

"Oh shut up and kiss me," she said then, and they kissed, and she pulled him onto her, and while they made love, she told him several times—words he had not heard for years—that she loved him.

When he woke from a sweet post-coital nap, Tolle's head on his shoulder—she was snoring lightly—and realized they had fallen asleep together in their garden, he found himself remembering being in a quite different enclosed area in South Africa. There to consult with AIDS workers in Cape Town, he had gone on several walks to villages and encampments that could be reached neither by cars or motorbikes. Hiking to these places with health care workers—carrying backpacks that contained antiretrovirals, and umbrellas to shield themselves from the sun—he had been happy, and had felt something he would have hesitated to ever state aloud to anyone but that he told himself he could now tell Tolle: simply—as he occasionally felt at the hospital when pressures eased—that he was doing what he had been put on earth to do.

What he could not make sense of at the time—and when he again pictured himself walking across a valley lush with tropical greenery to a Zulu compound near a river that eventually would flow into Table Bay—was how such a phenomenally beautiful landscape could be home to such a phenomenally deadly disease. In memory, the South

African hills that rose up at a distance from the valley were not unlike the hills that rose up around Spéracèdes—the Southern Maritime Alps that, further inland, would become the Northern Maritime Alps and, eventually, the Swiss Alps—and even as, in his mind's eye the night before, and again now, sitting at the café, the South African landscape became more and more beautiful, what he found himself imagining was that the people who inhabited this landscape, and were afflicted with the HIV, were not merely suffering and dying, but were, one at a time, rotting.

He saw himself in a compound where, through a translator, he was explaining to health care workers and villagers how to take antiretrovirals, how many to take each day, and when to take them. Then he was being shown, with pride, a stone-fenced cattle crawl in which there was one cow and a scattering of chickens.

And when he recalled the manner in which the people there had expressed gratitude to him—one hand holding onto the wrist of the hand that, palm upturned, received medications from his hand—he imagined strands of hair falling from their skulls and drifting into the air, skin falling away from their bones in patches, teeth dropping from their mouths and landing one at a time, in soundless puffs of dust, on the dirt of the cattle crawl.

Fifteen

The best time to plant a tree is twenty years ago. The second best time is now...

The words of the African proverb kept repeating themselves in Tolle's head. When Saul had returned from South Africa two years before, those words—in addition to toy animals and a colorful necklace made from empty soda cans—were his gift to her, and it was only now, after *her* gift-giving the evening before, that she began to sense what the words meant to Saul, and why he had given them to her.

The best time to plant a tree is twenty years ago. The second best time is now...

How truly dear of him, she thought, and how closed off and distant I've been from him—and from myself—not to have received them more openly. But why these feelings *now*?

"Saul?"

"Hey—good morning," he said. "I tried to reach you after my visit with Julia so I could share the good news—that she's decided to have the baby—but by the time I got back to the hotel last night—I treated myself to a dinner in town where I kept thinking about *our* lovely time, and wishing you were with me—it was late, and—"

"Julia called," Tolle said. "She gave me the news, which I agree is wonderful, and we had a good heart-to-heart for which, it seems, I have you to thank—and I also heard about Fiona, so no need to repeat that grisly tale, but there are *so* many things I want to say to you, Saul, and—"

"—and I *miss* you," Saul said. "I miss you, and I keep thinking about us, and—"

"I miss you too," Tolle said. "Of course. But I'm going to forgo the pleasure of elaborating because something has happened here in the village, and it's important that you return as soon as possible."

"Of course," he said. "But I promised Julia I'd visit with her again—she wants me to to see where she's living, and to show me around—and I want to go back to the hospital to visit Fiona, and—"

"Have you seen the news, on television—or read the morning paper?"

"I just woke up," Saul said. "Tell me—"

Tolle spoke quickly: "The village doctor's wife and eight-month-old daughter were murdered yesterday, allegedly by the *femme de ménage* who cleans house for them. The *femme de ménage* is from Algeria, and according to this morning's newspaper, she is supposed to have bludgeoned Madame Bertrand and the daughter to death, after which she wrapped them in bed linens, poured oil on the linens, and set them on fire."

"*Jesus!*"

"Allah, I'm afraid, would be more like it."

"Look. If *we* start thinking that way—"

"Forgive, please," Tolle said. "I'm upset—a bit disoriented, in truth. I walked into the village this morning to get a newspaper, and there were slogans spray-painted on the walls in the center of town saying 'Allah is Great,' and 'Death to the Jews,' along with a swastika, and—"

"Where did you stay last night?"

"Here," she said. "Jerry was with me—we had dinner together, and he insisted on staying. But I'm scared, Saul. The police are everywhere—in town and on all the roads in and out of town—and TV crews have begun to arrive too, and rumor has it that Le Pen himself is coming to Spéracèdes, doubtless to tell his followers the usual France-for-the-French garbage, and how all of France's problems are caused by dark-skinned immigrants and—"

"—and by Jews. When in doubt, blame the Jews," Saul said. "When you're in love, as the saying goes, the whole world is Jewish, so I suppose since the whole world is *not* Jewish…"

"You sound like Jerry when you talk this way," Tolle said, "and I wish you'd stop."

"Sorry. But—"

"I'm scared, Saul—*very* scared, and I want you here," she said. "When I was in the village this morning, none of the North Africans were to be seen—the women weren't washing clothes or shopping, and the men who work on the roads and do the gardening were nowhere in sight either. It was eerie—small groups of women huddled together, and not just the old women who are usually there, and they were all whispering to one another. I've never felt more like an outsider."

Saul said he would make quick visits to Julia and Fiona, and then head for Spéracèdes. Tolle told him that according to the paper—and from what Jerry saw on television—there had been reprisals up and down the coast, from Menton to Marseilles, bands of vigilantes going into North African neighborhoods and smashing windows, burning homes and cars, looting stores. The doctor and his wife—Doctor Bertrand, not the Doctor Bertrand who was here during their first stay in Spéracèdes, but that doctor's *son*—had a second child, it seemed—a four-year-old son who had been in a *maternelle*—nursery school—when the murders took place. The funeral, Jerry had informed her, was scheduled to take place in Spéracèdes tomorrow.

When Jerry gave her the news about the decision to have the funeral as quickly as possible—a political decision, he noted, and not a decision based on an affinity for Jewish traditions—and about the doctor's surviving child, and added that, for such eventualities, as he frequently maintained, it was always good for parents to keep a spare, she had screamed at him that he was as sick as the people posting their

188

hate signs, that his habit of making jokes out of everything disgusted her and had always disgusted her, and that she never wanted to see him again. Jerry had left, saying he would close up his house and studio, and that she should be careful, and trust no one. He *knew* the French, and they were, none of them, to be trusted—not villagers, not the government, not the Army, not the North Africans, and not the police, who were, he reminded her, not local to Spéracèdes or the *midi*, but part of the national defense forces.

She did not tell Saul about how she had lost it with Jerry, and what he had said to make her lose it. And she did not tell him that when she had been in the the village square, which, at seven A.M. was already crowded with villagers, police, journalists, and television crews, she had overheard two elderly women talking about having been near the doctor's house soon after the event, about the odor the burning bodies had given off, and, to their surprise, about how incredibly sweet it had been.

Waiting for the funeral cortege, they stood in front of their house, on the road that led from the church to the cemetery. Two helicopters hovered in the sky, the whirring of their blades a muted rumble that sounded, Saul said, not unlike sounds he might hear were he listening with a stethoscope to a patient's innards. Tolle held tightly to his hand, and thought of how, only two nights before, they had been below, in the garden, Fiona asleep nearby in the room next to the garden. Had it been Fiona's presence—her *brave* presence given the gravity of her illness—that had made a difference, and had made Tolle feel suddenly loving and compassionate towards Saul? Loving *because* compassion-ate—because she had been able to put aside her own needs, desires, and moods and thus begin to understand, but in a new way, what *his* life had been like all through the years of their marriage?

Perhaps. And perhaps Julia's condition, despite what Tolle knew to be her ingeniously clever defenses, had also been a contributor to the easing of something inside her, to the sense of possible renewal—of understanding why, in her life, and in the words that continued to drone on in her head, it seemed a good time to plant a tree.

189

Behind metal barricades, crowds three and four deep lined both sides of the road, and policemen, in pairs and on horseback, were stationed along the route. Church bells had been ringing steadily. The sky was dark, without sun or the imminence of sun. The air was cold, near freezing—the radio had predicted thunderstorms—and on the terraces that rose toward Cabris, the undersides of leaves on olive trees appeared in the light breeze to have been brushed with silver.

At four separate police checkpoints, Saul told her when he arrived home the evening before, he had been asked to get out of his car, had his passport and driver's license taken, had his car and body searched, and had been questioned rigorously: What was his purpose in being in France? Why had he rented a house in Spéracèdes, and how long had he been there, and how long did he intend to stay there? Was he acquainted with the woman who was being charged with the murders, or with other Algerians who lived or worked in the village? Did any of them do housekeeping or gardening for him? Was he allied with *Médecins Sans Frontières* or Amnesty International…?

The police returned his license and passport at each checkpoint, and so Saul had concluded that his letter to Bush had *not* led to his having been placed on any governmental watchlists. Proof, he said, using the same words he said he'd used with Julia, that it was *just* a letter—an innocuous one—and not an act. Tolle had been massaging the back of his neck—they were in bed—and she had responded by saying that, with all due respect, she begged to disagree.

He had fallen asleep before she did, and while he slept, she had become slowly but acutely aware of the fact that the act that had given them so much pleasure the night before was, in the work that had been his for more than three decades, also the cause of death, and of enormous suffering. She had wondered if this—an awareness she had not experienced since the early months and years of the AIDA epidemic, of how deeply involved he had been in a life informed hourly by the deaths of individuals he treated and knew—was also responsible somehow for what seemed a slight shift in her feelings.

It was a shift that, while they waited to see coffins pass by that would contain bodies of people neither of them knew, began to seem more than slight. She was aware, too, that even as she waited for the coffins, and for friends and family of the deceased to appear, she was resenting the fact that what was happening—with Fiona, with Julia, and, especially, with her and Saul—was being displaced by events external to them.

Jerry pointed across the road, to the four-story-high Hotel Soleillade—a hotel that, despite being on an unpaved road, was the tallest building in the village other than the church—where police sharpshooters, in flack jackets, were positioned on the hotel's roof and in some of its upper story windows. "When I was in Paris, and this was a long, long time ago," he said, "I remember looking out my window—I had a second floor apartment on the Boulevard Raspail—and seeing a funeral come by—and a large black hearse, and mourners in top hats, and a brass band playing Beethoven's Fifth Symphony."

The bells had stopped ringing, and police on motorcycles now cruised by slowly, along with journalists, photographers, and television crews. They were followed by four policemen on horseback, then by a phalanx of several dozen police marching in lock-step. Behind them came two teams of horses, one following the other, each team pulling a coffin—a large coffin first, a smaller one behind it—each coffin covered with a garland of braided red and white flowers.

"The French are really good at this," Jerry whispered. "They're terrible at many things, but when it comes to ceremony, they're absolutely terrific."

Tolle ignored him. To have sent him away when he arrived earlier in the day, she had reasoned, would have meant telling Saul about the stupid jokes Jerry had made, and about her tantrum, and might thereby, if Saul sided with her, which she knew he would, have compromised a friendship important to him. Saul put his arm around her shoulder, pulled her close, and this simple gesture brought tears to her eyes, and she told herself not to ask why. She heard Julia's voice again—"I know it sounds crazy, Mom," Julia had said when she called the day before, "and I know with all that's happening, hormones and stuff, that I'm not my usual self, but I think—and I'm not talking about sex—how can I, given my situation and hers?—but I think I'm falling in love with Fiona"—and she recalled her own response, saying that she had *already* fallen in love with Fiona—how not fall in love with a woman so brave, attractive, funny, and especially—despite all, and despite the irony of the phrase—full-of-life?

Tolle shivered, and Saul pulled her closer, but she was shivering now not because of the funeral cortege, or the cold air, or because she was imagining Fiona's sad situation, but because, thinking of lying on the grass with Saul two nights before, she had a sudden flash of memory—a recollection of the moment, after her fall, that her father, beside her on the ground, and then above her, had begun kissing her and trying to open her mouth with his tongue.

Do we ever get over these things? she wondered. Despite all her years on the couch, all the memories and feelings she had dredged up, talked about, *re*-experienced—many of which she had not even known she *had* until they surfaced—why did such brief moments still possess the power to make her doubt who she was, and why she felt, thought, and acted the way she did? And why had Saul, through all the vicissitudes of his career, and of their life together—why had he rarely slackened in his expressions of love and affection for her? Why had he never lost his boyish, optimistic ways of engaging in, and being *engagé* with, the world?

These were not, she concluded, unattractive qualities in a man with whom she seemed destined—a thought she had not entertained for a very long time—to grow old together. Then too, it occurred to her, and she smiled inwardly at the thought, Camus, Saul's long-time rival for her affections, would be in his nineties by now, a chain smoker afflicted with tuberculosis whose chances of still being around, even had he survived the car crash, would be slim indeed.

Behind the lines of police, at a distance of some fifteen to twenty yards, a crowd of mourners now appeared. The man in the center of the front line, a tri-colored sash across his chest, was, she assumed, Doctor Bertrand. Hatless, and wearing a gray three-piece suit—Tolle gauged him to be in his mid-to-late-forties—the doctor was strikingly handsome in the manner of an Italian movie star, with wavy, greying hair, deep set eyes, and a square chin. His arms were linked with the arms of two elderly women, one to each side of him, and the elderly woman to his right had her arm linked in the arm of a much older woman who walked with difficulty, dragging her left leg slightly. Doctor Bertrand stared straight ahead, and from the proud way he carried himself, he might, she thought, have been a hero returning to his hometown in order to witness a statue being unveiled in his honor.

A young boy, in suit and tie identical to Doctor Bertrand's, walked several feet to the doctor's left, hand in hand with a middle-aged woman. A priest in a long black robe walked to Doctor Bertrand's right, and in the line of people immediately behind Doctor Bertrand walked four other priests, along with three women in brown-and-white habits, this group followed by a group of two to three dozen others, the women in dresses and topcoats, the men in suits, some of the women pushing baby carriages. Despite the chill in the air, Tolle noticed, none of the men wore coats.

Jerry said something about how, at French funerals, the mistresses of dead men often walked arm-in-arm with the widows.

"Summer afternoon," Tolle heard herself say, perhaps as a way responding to the irritating irrelevance of Jerry's observation with a remark that would seem equally irrelevant.

"*Summer?*" Saul said.

"Summer afternoon," Tolle repeated. "I was just remembering that Henry James thought those were the two most beautiful words in the English language."

Dale and Gerhard, on the far side of the crowd, waved to them—gestured to indicate that they'd meet them down by the main road. The speaker, on a platform in front of the village's school, was talking about the National Front's *mission civilatrice*—its civilizing mission—and about how the two great dangers facing France were unemployment and immigration. Three million unemployed Frenchmen, he declared, were three million immigrants too many! What had happened in

Spéracèdes would soon be happening not only in Paris, Marseilles, or Lyon, but in every village where good and honest Frenchmen and Frenchwomen lived. North Africans and others from that continent were draining France of its resources, causing crime and death, undermining the integrity of French national identity.

The French nation grieved with Doctor Bertrand and his family, he declared. In such a dark time, however, there *was* hope and there *was* light, for the National Front had solutions to France's problems: repatriate these immigrants, restrict their access to French citizenship, create and deploy a special National Guard to prevent civic unrest and subversion....

Camus, Tolle thought, would not have been surprised by such a speech, or by the enthusiasm of the crowd. While France was, in the early years of the war, occupied by Germany and was shipping its Jews to the concentration camps, Camus had been teaching Jewish children in a school in Oran, and had taken pride in doing so. After the war, he had often spoken of Algerians—a remark Saul loved to quote—as being "the Jews of France."

She saw that some of the people cheering most enthusiastically were villagers with whom she exchanged friendly greetings when she walked to and from town. The speaker—not Le Pen, who had sent his regrets—was listing items on the National Front's agenda: reintroducing the death penalty, criminalizing abortion, blocking France from further integration with Europe, encouraging French women—their patriotic duty—to have more children. Saul touched her arm, pointed to one of the placards: *Pour le SIDA—SIDAtoriums.*

"Does that mean what I think it does?" he asked Jerry.

"Sure does—according to these birds, people with AIDS are to be placed in special camps," Jerry said, and added: "Even if they're Jews."

"I'm afraid irony won't sell well today," Tolle said. "We should leave. I'm feeling distinctly uncomfortable—sick to my stomach actually."

Many of the founders of the National Front had been members of the Nazi Waffen-SS and of terrorist OAS Algerian settlers organizations, Jerry said, and did Tolle and Saul know that Le Pen had called the gas chambers "a minor footnote" in the history of World War Two? Tolle looked at other slogans on other placards: *La France et les Français D'Abord... La France pour les Français de Souche... Non à l'Islamisation...*

A speaker was recounting the story of Joan of Arc, the National Front's patron saint, who had martyred herself to prevent British domination of France. He spoke of the ways ethnic minorities would soon dominate French life, and of how all those who championed them— the Left, the Socialists, the Communists, the trade unionists—intellectuals, feminists, homosexuals—were contributing to the degeneration of the nation.

"Are you coming?" Tolle asked.

"No," Saul said.

"I'll meet you back at the house then. I'll ask Dale and Gerhard to join us," Tolle said. "It's not safe for them to be here."

Monsieur and Madame Antonetta, who owned one of two *épiceries* in the village, approached. "I am very happy to see you here today," Monsieur Antonetta said.

Tolle had seen Monsieur and Madame Antonetta walking with the crowd of mourners, and she asked if Madame Bertrand and her daughter were relatives. Monsieur Antonetta said that yes, Madame Bertrand was—*had been*, he corrected himself—his niece.

Tolle and Saul offered their sympathies, and Monsieur Antonetta thanked them, and said that the reason he was happy that Saul and his wife were here was because they could now see for themselves the problem that the good people of Spéracèdes, like good people everywhere, were facing in France.

"Intolerance," Saul said. "Yes. It's despicable."

"*Intolerance?*" Monsieur Antonetta asked. "How intolerance? What we have in common with you Americans—our great and unfortunate bond—is the knowledge of what happens to a society when it refuses to take strong measures to save itself."

"Uh-oh," Jerry said.

"I don't understand," Saul said.

195

"Tolle's right," Jerry said, a hand on Saul's arm. "Time to head for the exits."

Saul pushed Jerry's hand away. "Tell me about what we have in common," he said to Monsieur Antonetta. "Please."

"I speak, of course, of your Negroes," Monsieur Antonetta said. "You set them free within your borders more than a century ago, yet you are still paying the price. They rape your wives and daughters, they steal your cars, they destroy your cities—"

"Excuse me," Tolle said, and to Saul: "Please come."

"I want to hear more," Saul said to Monsieur Antonetta, "because it seems to me that you and I have *nothing* in common. I would, in fact, be ashamed to have *anything* in common with you."

"Are you then—how do you say it in your country—" Monsieur Antonetta asked "—a lover of niggers?"

In his left hand, Saul held one of the flyers that the National Front had been distributing, and, with a backhanded swing, he lashed out at Monsieur Antonetta, but Monsieur Antonetta, a stout man who stood at perhaps five-foot-four, jerked his head back with surprising quickness so that the paper fluttered past his nose.

"You are not French, sir," Monsieur Antonetta stated calmly. "If you were, you would understand what we live with here. I admire you greatly, you know—you Americans. In Indochina first, and now in Iraq, you have been the defenders of the West—of Christian civilization—whereas our leaders..."

"I am, for your information, a Jew," Saul said. "And so is my wife..."

Monsieur Antonetta made a slight percussive sound—*Pouf!*—across his lips, as if to say: Well then—that explains everything, of course, doesn't it?

"Don't say another word," Jerry said.

Tolle looked toward the speaker's platform, where a man was now holding forth about the necessity of repealing anti-racist legislation—the so-called *liberticides*—about giving the police more power, about ridding the nation of the scum that was fouling its waters, about the sacredness of the nuclear family....

196

"Shame!" Tolle shouted. "Shame…! *Tu as honte…tu as honte!*"

Saul gripped her arm. "This time I'm not staying on the sidewalk while I watch you walk out onto the avenue," he said, and he stepped in front of Tolle, and began shouting.

"*Shame!*" he cried. "*Shame…! Shame…! Shame on you! Shame on all of you! Tu as honte…! Tu as honte…! Vous avez, tout le monde, honte…! Shame…! Shame…! Shame…!*"

A squat, heavy-set man pushed Tolle aside while another man wrenched Saul's arms behind him. Policemen quickly surrounded Saul, pushed him forward. Tolle tried to get to him, but a policeman grabbed her by both arms, from behind, told her to be careful and not to move. A tall man, in jacket and tie, and with a trim, white goatee, stood in Saul's path. Someone yanked Saul's head back by the hair and when he did, the man with the goatee, grinning broadly, and cursing in French about Saul's mother *and* wife, drew back his fist and smashed it into Saul's face. Tolle struggled to free herself from the policeman, and looked around for Jerry. Were Dale and Gerhard nearby?

Tolle watched the two policemen who, one to each side of Saul, had been escorting Saul from the crowd, suddenly push him to the ground and step aside. Curled into a fetal position—Saul was lying, she realized, on one of the village's *boule* courts—she watched people scream at him, pound on him, kick at him. Police returned—a group of five this time—and pressed the crowd back, then shoved and carried him toward a waiting police van. Tolle tore at the hands of the policeman who held her—scratched him with her nails, kicked backwards at his shins—and when the policeman loosened his grip, she broke loose and ran after Saul, but stopped when she saw him, about to enter the van, turn and, his face covered with blood, wave to her. Although they had attended many civil rights and anti-war demonstrations together in the sixties and seventies, this was the first time either of them had ever been attacked *physically.* She returned his wave, sensing—*knowing*—the pride he was already taking in the fact that he had acted so as to cause the police to take *him* away this time.

In addition to a broken nose—Gerhard kept reminding Saul to

keep the ice-pack pressed to it—one of Saul's eyes was closed most of the way, and when he coughed or laughed, Tolle watched him wince as the pain from what Saul and Gerhard agreed was probably at least one broken rib—shot through the his body. Despite the lidocaine, Gerhard warned, the procedure—putting a dozen or so stitches into Saul's upper lip—would still sting.

While Gerhard worked on Saul, Tolle listened to Gerhard and Jerry exchange views about the state of the world: about corporate greed and short-sighted policies that were bringing about the dying of the planet; about Muslim fundamentalists who raised their children to kill other people's children; about global warming and the coming inundation of cities and continents; about ongoing epidemics of AIDS, TB, malaria, and dysentery that would kill millions....

If the bastards who organized today's demonstration ever took over, Dale declared, they'd make the Holocaust seem like a holiday. Osama bin Laden, Le Pen, Bush and his crowd—Muslim fundamentalists and Christian loonies—they were all mirrors of one another, he said: ideological idiots with the wherewithal to destroy those who didn't submit to them.

Gerhard sighed, said that Dale was talking his usual doomsday rubbish. What was happening had little to do with ideology. We *always* live in interesting times, Gerhard said, the difference now being the *wherewithal* people had with which to visit their meanness, stupidity, and incompetence on others. Although Fanon had been correct too, he added: when people were so poor and miserable that they were beyond life and death, why should the lives of others be worth anything to them? Led by malevolent imbeciles, nurtured by religious idiocies, and well-armed, the wretched of the earth would, while bringing about their own self-destruction, destroy everyone else with them.

"Can we count on that?" Jerry asked.

"Alas, no," Gerhard said. He stepped back, admired his work. "There!" he said to Saul. "In a few years you'll be as good as new."

Tolle poured wine for herself, then kissed Saul on his swollen, newly stitched lip. "My hero," she whispered.

"Speaking of holocausts," Jerry said, "did you hear about what happened when Abe and Becky went to Auschwitz to celebrate their fiftieth wedding anniversary?"

"I'll return in four or five days to remove the stitches," Gerhard said to Tolle. "Unless you prefer to do the honors."

"So Abe and Becky are on a Hadassah tour—Vienna, Prague, Budapest, Cracow—" Jerry said "—and by the time they get to their hotel, they're having this spectacular knockdown drag-out fight, but then there's a banging on the door, and people are shouting—'The busses are here! The busses are leaving for Auschwitz!' So cut, and it's six hours later, and Abe and Becky come back to their hotel room. They sit in silence for a while, until Abe says he's sorry for what he said about her and about their marriage—that seeing what they've just seen puts things in perspective. Will she forgive him? 'Oh I forgive you,' Becky says, wagging a finger at him, 'but I want you to know that you *ruined* Auschwitz for me!'"

Saul started to laugh, stopped abruptly, closed his eyes.

"No more jokes," Tolle said. "And yes, I'll take the stitches out."

"The lips heal quickly—lots of blood in them," Gerhard said. "But you had best check out the eye with an ophthalmologist. Sometimes as the swelling goes down, the retina can begin to tear away."

Dale reached into a canvas bag from which Gerhard had been taking first-aid supplies, and withdrew a syringe.

"Put it away," Gerhard said.

"Guess what's in here," Dale said to Saul. "Can you?"

"HIV-infected blood," Saul said.

"Correct," Dale said, and he moved toward Saul, syringe in hand, as if he were going to stab him. "And guess what you get for giving a correct answer?"

Gerhard seized Dale's hand, bent his thumb backwards.

"Take it *easy*," Dale said. "All I wanted to do was to needle him a bit."

"And *inject* some humor into our situation?" Jerry asked.

"Spare us," Tolle said. "Please."

"Well, our good doctor is the only one *you* seem to be able to keep in stitches," Dale said.

"Very good, but—" Jerry said.

"And you should know that I was ready for them if they molested us," Dale said. "I would have stabbed them *all*."

"—but a question," Jerry continued. "Is the stuff in there *real*?"

"Oh yes," Gerhard said. "It can get quite—how do you say it?— *hairy* for us sometimes, especially late at night. There are hooligans who cruise around in gangs and delight in gay-bashing, so just as women carry pepper spray, we carry this."

Dale put the syringe back in the canvas bag, took out a small CD player and headphones, and sat on the floor, by the staircase. "What I do at times like this is to listen to the music Ethan loved—" Dale said "—Schubert, Mozart, Prokofiev, Satie—oh how he loved Satie!— Shostakovich and Scriabin too—and whenever I do, what I think, sadly, is that the music Ethan played will live on after him, but the knowledge that was in his fingers is gone forever."

"Speaking of music," Jerry said, "I forgot to mention that I had a message from Katherine saying that she and Eugene will be returning soon. And her good news—that she's in negotiations to buy a large farmhouse nearby, on the Siagne." He put a hand on Saul's shoulder. "Shall I let her know of your troubles?"

"No thanks," Saul said.

Jerry said he was relieved that the police released Saul so quickly. There were no law enforcement personnel in Western Europe nastier than the French. Still, he worried that if Le Pen's people learned that Saul was living in Spéracèdes, they might go after him. The best thing, therefore, might be for Saul and Tolle to move, at least temporarily, to another village or to a hotel.

"Maybe," Saul said. "But first I have to go to Avignon and Saint Rémy—to see Fiona and Julia."

"*We* have to go," Tolle corrected.

"Of course," Dale said, "for how can Doctor Davidoff drive safely with one eye, especially on *French* roads with *French* drivers?"

"In the kingdom of the blind…" Jerry began.

"*Tais-toi!*" Tolle commanded, and she sat beside Saul, offered him wine from her glass. He drank, said he was sorry to have caused her so much trouble. She put an arm around him, told him she was *almost* as proud of him for what he had done on this day as she was for what he had done two days—two nights—before.

"I *am* eager to see Julia," Saul said. "And Fiona."

"Me too," Tolle said, and she thought of the South African saying, and of the new life growing inside Julia, and then of what Saul had explained to her: that most South African women who were infected with the HIV had only one lover. Most South African women were monogamous, he had explained, but their men worked in industries where their labor was needed—sugar, gold, diamonds—and so the combination of migrant labor and an industrial society had proven to be the deadliest of marriages. As men moved around the country and returned home periodically, they carried with them the infections they acquired, which infections they passed on to their wives, who passed the infections on to their children.

Sixteen

Saul walked to the window, opened the shutters, saw that it was dark outside, sometime between midnight and dawn, he estimated, given the sparse scattering of lights in the valley. There was a glass of water and a small container of pills on the nightstand, with a note from Gerhard telling him to take two pills every four hours and not to forget to see an ophthalmologist.

His head throbbed, and when he tried to take a deep breath, pain zigzagged along his ribcage. Slowly, one step at a time, he made his way down to the kitchen, and to the room below the kitchen, where he found Tolle, asleep. She turned over, spread her arms.

"Come to me," she said. "Please."

"In a minute," he said, and went into the bathroom, urinated—no pain there, at least—then returned, and lay down.

"You fell into a deep sleep, and I didn't want to chance rolling over onto you after *I* fell asleep, so I came down here," she said. She reached under his shirt, rubbed his chest gently. "To repeat: I was very proud of what you did. It was a very *stupid* thing to do, but at least somebody stood up to those bastards."

"What time is it?" he asked.

"Shh—let me worry about things, all right?" Tolle said.

"Fine," he said.

"I called Julia while you were sleeping, and I told her what happened," Tolle said. "She told me she visited Fiona, who is doing quite well apparently."

"I may sneeze," Saul said.

He inhaled rapidly several times—shallow breaths—but could not stave off the sneeze, and when he sneezed pain roared through him.

"Gerhard advised getting a chest X-ray," Tolle said.

"Why?" Saul said. "Whatever they find, the treatment—*no* treatment really—will be the same."

Tolle said that Gerhard had said the same thing—that there was not much one could do for cracked ribs—but that it was a good idea to confirm what they assumed. He had left bandages and tape, and had told Tolle to wrap Saul in the bandages so as to at least blunt *some* of the pain. He had recommended warm compresses for the eye, and said that Saul should keep the eye covered with a patch—a makeshift one he'd taped there—to keep foreign objects from irritating it. The pills he left were Tramadol, which he preferred to Percocets, though he warned that they could prove addictive.

"Here," Tolle said, and she patted her shoulder. "Rest your head here."

Saul rested his head on her shoulder, let his good eye close, let his mind wander. He saw cypresses, their deep, swirling greens, and recalled Julia telling him that Van Gogh had described them as being like Egyptian obelisks.

"I *do* love you," Tolle said.

His right hand resting on Tolle's bare stomach, Saul lay on his left side, which, though tender, seemed to have no broken or cracked ribs. He recalled Camus saying that to truly love someone was to accept growing old with that person, but noting that he, for one, was incapable of that kind of love.

He smiled. He slept. He woke. He slept again.

He listened to the sound of Tolle's breathing, to the strong, slow beats of her heart, and took pleasure in the warmth of her body, the softness of her skin.

"I remember one patient," he said when Tolle's eyes opened. "He was reduced to a skeleton of himself in his last days, with growths on his skull and in his mouth. He had been a distinguished mathematician at C.C.N.Y., his lover had abandoned him, and his family had disowned him, and he had taken last rites. When I sat with him at night, just the two of us, he kept repeating—as if to comfort *me*—that everything was going to be all right, that he was reconciled to his fate, that my being there made him feel loved and forgiven."

"Because you gave him hope?"

"Perhaps," Saul said. "In those days, though, I was essentially a therapeutic nihilist. I *had* to be. Because nothing worked, and they all died, and they died miserably—not just patients, but doctors and nurses I worked with, men and women I admired and loved—and do you know what was hardest of all?"

"Tell me."

"Their gratitude."

"I can understand that," Tolle said. "You sat with them in their last hours, you held their hands, you visited them in their homes, and you endured their rage—you used to tell me how angry some of them were."

"Wouldn't you be?"

"Shh," Tolle said. "Don't upset yourself."

"I love you too, you know," Saul said. "And it was very good—even exciting, actually—to hear you use those three words again."

"Yes," Tolle said. "Although I often didn't *like* you, I always *loved* you. And I never loved you unconditionally since it's my belief, as you know, that the only unconditional love is the love that exists between mother and child, and—don't protest—can *sometimes* exist between father and child. And you might also be interested in knowing—now that I'm feeling free to talk with you this way, and not, I hasten to add, because you're wounded—that there were a fair number of times I thought of leaving you. But I always loved you."

"Remarkable," he said.

They made love after breakfast—more exactly, given how restricted his movements were, Tolle made love to him, and he had found the experience—of being made love to while helpless—exciting. He had insisted on driving to Saint Rémy by himself. Lots of one-eyed men did well in the world, he argued, and it was important, given his conversation with Julia two days before, that he have time alone with her before the three of them got together. The same, he said, was true for visiting with Fiona.

Tolle taped his ribs before he left, but by the time he was twenty-five kilometers from Aix-en-Provence, the desire to scratch himself had become uncontrollable and, at a rest stop, he took off his shirt, unwound the bandages, and scratched away. His right eye was still closed most of the way, and he was seeing occasional flashes of light at its edges, like pale bursts of summer heat lightning. His nose remained swollen, his jaw sore, his lip tender, his body bruised here and there, yet he found himself relishing the discomfort, for it was the constancy of the pain, like the extraordinary fatigue he had known during the early years of the AIDS pandemic, that was making him feel more alive than he had in a long time.

When he arrived at Saint Paul de Mausole and identified himself to the woman at the front desk as Julia's father, the woman told him that Julia had departed that morning but had left a letter for him.

He drove to the Villa Glanum, where he'd made a reservation the night before, and went to his room. He unpacked his suitcase, took two pills, removed his eye patch, wet a washcloth with warm water, and lay down on the bed, the washcloth across his eyes.

When he woke, the room was dark and he could not remember, at first, where he was. He reached to the side to turn on a lamp, found none, reached further and nearly fell from the bed. He repositioned himself and lay without moving until the pain subsided. The flashing lights, at the edges of his right eye—tiny jagged darts of white—were arriving with what seemed increasing frequency. He wiped his face with the washcloth and, noticing that his shirt was nearly drenched, realized that he had been perspiring heavily. He sat up, set both feet on the floor, let himself become accustomed to the dark. He felt dizzy, nauseated, disoriented. He walked to the door, turned on the overhead light, opened the shutters. Bright light poured in. He checked his watch, saw that he had slept for nearly three hours.

The major news, Tolle said when he telephoned a few minutes later, was that a woman who was apparently Doctor Bertrand's mistress—she had mingled with the family and other mourners at the funeral, and had been residing at the Hotel Soleillade—had been seen, early mornings, walking arm in arm with the doctor. And the Algerian woman, through a lawyer, was maintaining that she had not been in the doctor's home on the morning his wife and child were murdered, that it had been her day off, and that the police had coerced her into making false statements.

Tolle was eager to hear about the drive, and about how he was feeling, but she was running late, she said, and had promised to meet Jerry, who had telephoned a half-hour before with more news of what he had named 'L'Affaire Bertrand.' They were going to drive down to Cannes, have drinks with Gerhard and Dale at the Hotel Carlton, and indulge in what she supposed would be, no matter the horrific events that were its excuse, little more than vulgar gossip. As Saul well knew, she hated people who loved this kind of gossip, but given recent events, and with Saul gone, she welcomed any pretext to get out of the house, and away from Spéracèdes.

He said he might return sooner than expected—he would explain later—but he hung up without telling her that Julia was no longer at Saint Paul de Mausole.

He picked up Julia's letter from the bed—he had fallen asleep on it—and he went to a small *secrétaire* near the window, opened the envelope, withdrew the letter, unfolded and flattened it. The pages were damp and, along the right edge, stuck together. The letter was written on Saint Paul de Mausole stationery, a drawing of the cloister at the top of each page.

Dear Dad:

I've decided to have the child, and to have it by myself—without, that is, calling on you or Mom or anyone else to be with me and do things parents—or spouses—usually do.

But not to worry: I still have grade-A health insurance from my firm, and when it comes to medical care, they do, as you know, order these things better in France.

But to the what, the why, and the how. I need—crave—some time alone—to sort things out, to come to terms with matters I've been—not running away from exactly, but not fully facing up to. I trust you'll respect my decision. But you should know that I appreciate your concern and that—

Whoa! Cancel that language. I appreciate your love, Dad. I know you are, as we say these days, there-for-me—always have been, always will be, even when (as I couldn't resist pointing out when we were together) you were not there bodily.

I'm glad we had our time together, glad I made the decision to come to France, and glad to hear—this news via Mom, with whom I talked this morning—that you two are communicating. Communicating?! Lord, how I hate that kind of language—makes me feel my teeth are scraping against a chalkboard—but I want to get this letter written so I can be out of here before you arrive.

Mom knows of my decision, and she didn't try to talk me out of it. It does occur to me that perhaps I'm giving you my news in writing because I'm afraid that if we talked I might go soft. Whether you're aware of it or not, you do have the power to intimidate.

My hormones are a bit out of whack these days—first trimester was a piece of cake mostly, but for the last week or two the baby has been causing alternating waves of bliss and blues—intense alertness and an equally intense desire for sleep.

I'm rambling. Had I more time, as the saying goes, I would have written a shorter letter.

A thought: although our being together was crucial to my decision—your nonjudgmental acceptance went a long way toward my nonjudgmental acceptance of myself—I'm clear-minded about the fact that this is first and last about the child. The way I see it is that I've been given a real chance, and ready or not—prepared or not—*chance has decided to favor the child. I'm not into the lofty* 'experience of motherhood' *some of my friends seem to aspire to. I'm into bringing a life into the world, and nurturing that life as best I can.*

Mom told me about what happened at the demonstration, and I checked the newspapers, and there you were, identified as 'unidentified American tourist'—and let me tell you: this 'unidentified American tourist' won my *heart! I wish I'd been there, and I hope you press charges (the local rag said two men were taken into custody for assault), and that in the future you'll figure a way to do what you do less self-destructively. That you* still *believe in things is amazing given all you've been through, and that you* act *on your beliefs is inspiring.*

I'll keep in touch because I know that afterwards I'll want your approval and (even) your praise. Mom is, and always has been, no secret, a mystery to me, as she hinted in a remarkably frank conversation we had, she often is to herself! But for now, I've decided to make Fiona my designated go-between/messenger. It's a true miracle how close she and I have become in so short a time. No surprise, perhaps, given the situations we're each living in, though mine is not, of course, grave in the way hers is.

As we know, she may not be here when the child arrives, but by then perhaps I'll be ready to settle down, you'll be healed, and Mom's evolution to a warmer, gentler, more approachable Mom will have evolved.

*'Settled-down-somewhere-*in-France' *is what I should have written. That's another (interim) decision. I like being in a place where nobody knows me, and where* privacy *is valued and respected. My French is competent and getting better, and trying to phrase my thoughts in another language also seems to have the effect of clarifying them for* me, *making them into objects that haven't come from me.*

Also, fyi: I intend to make inquiries concerning employment on this side of the Atlantic: EU, NATO (why not infilitrate from within?), American law firms and corporations with offices in France. Like you and Mom, I'm nothing if not resourceful, and when I set my mind on something…

Also: when there are two of us, I'll have less liberty to indulge my desire to save others the way I did, if briefly, at Saint Paul de Mausole. This need to rescue others—Mom excepted?—does seem to run deep in our family, but—whoa again!—I just looked at the time and see that I need to pack, pick up my rental car, and blow this joint. But be assured that once the baby's here, I intend to shed this willed isolation. Did you know, by the way, that Van Gogh's brother Theo died only six months after Van Gogh did? And he was the "normal" one: a wife, a child, a home, a career, the ability to care for his own family as well as for Van Gogh. Van Gogh's last letter to him, where he credits Theo with being part of the creation of his work, was written four days before he killed himself.

Before the baby comes I intend to make a pilgrimage to Auvers-sur-Oise, where the brothers are buried next to one another. Which reminds me to tell you that I've been in touch with my brother. Also that I hope you'll take a suggestion from your daughter and read Van Gogh's letters some time. Here, to tempt, a sample:

'For cooping up all these lunatics in this old cloister becomes, I think, a dangerous thing, in which you risk losing the little good sense that you may still have kept. Not that I am set on this or that by preference. I am used to the life here, but one must not forget to make a little trial of the opposite'.

Both Fiona and Mom mentioned the possibility of your chucking the Kings County job and going to South Africa to continue your good work there.

I applaud.

You will, I expect, be seeing Fiona soon. Drink from her strength, Dad. And from her love.

And give her mine.

Je t'embrasse très très fort.

Julia
(aka Jules)

Saul turned off the main road at Chateaurenard, drove through the town, found smaller country roads. At an auberge on a narrow two-lane road, he stopped for a late lunch. Before visiting Fiona, he hoped to visit the cemetery where Vincent and Theo were buried, but when he inquired as to where it was located, the *propriétaire* informed him that Auvers-sur-Oise was nowhere near the auberge, but, as best she could recall, northwest of Paris.

After lunch, Saul took a short walk, perhaps a quarter-mile, to a small cemetery he had noticed on his way in to the auberge. There were fresh flowers on several graves and, as in Spéracèdes, silver- and gold-framed photographs of some of the deceased attached to gravestones. At the far end of the cemetery, an elderly woman, on her knees, was pulling weeds.

He imagined strolling through the cemetery with Julia—or Tolle—and musing on stories of people buried here: on what the pre-ponderance of certain family names, along with the years of birth and death, suggested. He found himself wishing he could do with both of them what he had rarely done: tell them about his mother, father, and brother, about his grandparents and aunts and uncles, and about what things had been like for him when he was a boy growing up in Brooklyn.

For better *and* worse, the major part of his parents' social life had centered around family. His mother was the third child of seven, his father the seventh child of eight, all their brothers and sisters had had children, and they all, with one exception—his father's eldest brother, who had migrated to the Bronx and was never talked about—they all lived within walking distance. Most weekends and holidays were spent with family. He had had several dozen first cousins whom he saw regularly at these get-togethers, but had, with the years, lost touch with almost all of them. And Martin was gone too, and he could not remember that he—or his parents—had ever again, after the unveiling of the stone above Martin's grave on the first anniversary of his death, visited the cemetery where he was buried.

Saul's father had died before he and Tolle met, and his mother had died when Julia and Sam were five and three—Tolle's parents died at about that time too, though she had not seen either of them for more than a decade before their passing, and did not go to their funerals—so that Sam and Julia had lived most of their lives without grandparents and also, given that neither he nor Tolle had living siblings, without aunts, uncles, or first cousins. How sad for them, he thought, and he wondered if Julia's desire to be alone, and to live in a place where nobody knew her, was somehow connected to the absence in her life of extended family.

When childhood memories arrived, as they were doing now, he thought mostly of friends, not family—of guys he'd grown up playing ball with—and he thought of them with warmth and affection. He had been happy when he was playing ball. He had been happy when he was hanging out with teammates after a game. He had been happy when he was travelling with them to and from games on buses, or in cars, or by subway. Like Camus, Saul often thought that the essentials of his moral code—his sense of fair play, his reverence for loyalty, his work ethic, his drive to succeed and to win—had been formed in the streets, and on the playing fields of his childhood.

The elderly lady who had been tending to a gravesite was now pushing a small wheelbarrow his way, the wheelbarrow overflowing with sticks, branches, weeds. Saul asked if she needed help, and when he did, the woman recoiled physically. She was toothless, he saw, and as she hurried past him she shook her head angrily and muttered something unintelligible to him in what sounded like the *patois* elderly villagers in Spéracèdes used. He nodded and—but only in his mind— tipped an imaginary hat to her.

In the restroom of the auberge, he washed his hands and face and, lifting the eye patch, examined his eye in the mirror above the sink. The eye was still swollen and bloodshot, rimmed in intriguing shades of purple, red, green, and blue.

According to the *propriétaire*, Saul was about forty minutes from Avignon, and he could get there by taking several small roads, connecting with D15, which ran along the Rhone, and following D15 north.

A bouquet of white and purple tulips he had bought to give to Fiona lay on the seat beside him, next to Julia's letter. He remembered peeling apart the stuck pages of the letter so as not to tear them, and when he did, he remembered the description, in medical school, that a doctor lecturing on ophthalmology had made of a detached retina: that fluid passing through a retinal tear could lift the retina from the back of the eye in the way wallpaper could peel from a wall.

When a patient presented with symptoms of an increase either in the number of floaters, or of a seeming veil or curtain moving across their field of vision—*or of flashing lights*—it was imperative that the patient be seen by an ophthalmologist immediately. Once the retina began to peel away from the back of the eye, the peeling could accelerate with astonishing swiftness, and best results were obtained if the detachment were repaired before the macula—the central region of the retina responsible for fine and detailed vision—detached. If not promptly treated, retinal detachment could result in permanent vision loss.

The problem, he recalled, was not that they couldn't repair the retinal detachments and tears. That part was fairly routine: the surgeon would suck the fluid out from behind the retina, push it flat against the back of the eye with gas, then tack it down—cauterize it—and, if necessary, stabilize the retina with silicone stripping around the eye. But if the macula peeled away, it could cause irreversible damage to the eye's photo-receptors. He remembered the analogy the doctor had used: if you dug up a piece of sod from a lawn and left it exposed for a day or two, or even a few hours on a hot day, after which you tamped it back down, it usually stopped growing. So it was with a retinal detachment not attended to in a timely fashion.

If he went to the emergency room before he saw Fiona, he knew, he might be whisked directly into surgery and not get to see her. Therefore, he decided, he would visit Fiona first, then telephone Tolle, after which he could walk down to the emergency ward and have someone examine his eye.

He was feeling dizzy again, and knew he should not have had wine with lunch, but he was determined to press on. He felt his good eye close briefly several times, and to keep himself awake—alert—he began thinking of famous one-eyed people, starting with those who wore patches. There were Moshe Dayan and Sammy Davis, Jr., of course—and he remembered that Peter Falk, Rex Harrison, and Edgar Degas had been blind, or nearly blind, in one eye. The jockey who rode Seabiscuit to the Triple Crown had been one-eyed, as was the sports commentator Dick Vitale.

He realized that he was making lists the way he did when he could *not* sleep (of women he'd known, of line-ups of teams he'd been on, and line-ups of teams he'd cheered for like the Brooklyn Dodgers and New York Knicks), but making them of one-eyed men. He heard a car horn blare several times, saw that he was veering off the road and heading straight for a stone wall. He braked hard, stopped the car. He blinked, took short, quick breaths, and when the pain in his chest and side receded—and after he looked ahead and was relieved to see that the road was *not* lined by plane trees—he started the car again, and concentrated on staying awake and keeping his good eye open. He recalled that a man named Post—*Wiley* Post—the first man to fly a plane around the world by himself, was one-eyed, and that there'd been a quarterback for a Rose Bowl team who had been one-eyed, and an old-time one-eyed boxing champion, Harry Grebs, and a one-eyed Philadelphia Eagles quarterback named Tommy Thompson, and....

All he wanted to do was to rip off the bandage that covered his eye, but when he lifted his hand to do so, he realized there was tape across his wrist, and that a tube, rising from his wrist, was attached to an IV pole.

"Well, in my opinion, you'd look much more dashing with a *black* eye patch," Fiona said.

"You're dressed in street clothes," Saul said.

"I've been discharged, and I'm going home," Fiona said. "All is well."

"For the time being," Saul said.

"For the time being," Fiona agreed.

She rose from her chair, pointed to a vase of tulips on the window sill, told him the flowers were a gift, her room to his. He asked how long he had been in surgery.

"About an hour," Fiona said. "I talked with the surgeon, a bright young Lebanese man—his English was excellent, and with the loveliest liquid French accent—and he thought it best if you stayed over until tomorrow. Sometimes they do the surgery as outpatient, but given the severity of the detachment, along with your general physical state and your age…"

"My *age?*" Saul protested. "He didn't really mention my age, did he?"

Fiona smiled. "Given your general physical state—you do look like damaged goods, sad to say—*and* your age—he wanted you to stay overnight."

"But *you've* been discharged?"

"We've reversed roles, at least for the moment. Good news, don't you think?"

"You're too cheerful," he said.

"And he asked if I knew when you'd last had a stress test."

"Because—?"

"Because when they did a routine EKG, they found some problems—abnormalities on the ST segment, and some pathologic Q waves, which he thought indicated you may already have *had* a heart attack."

"Shit."

"He advised an angiogram, and stenting the arteries if they find significant blockages, which he feels fairly certain they will."

Saul wiggled his wrist, pointed to the IV line. "Sedation, right?"

"Right."

"And you—you're *really* feeling better?"

"Much."

"But look—I have a room in Saint Rémy, and it's paid for," Saul said. "You could stay there until I get out, and then…"

"I'll check into a hotel in Avignon—that way I can be here tomorrow when Tolle arrives, and when—"

"Tolle knows?"

"You telephoned her before surgery, or don't you remember?"

214

"I'm groggy as hell—*dans le cirage*, as the French say. And *very* disoriented." Saul shook his head from side to side. "The drugs were great, though."

"Remember the time you and I got high at the AIDS conference in Stockholm, in that marvelous room at the Hotel Diplomat, and we were looking out the window when an armada of hot air balloons came sailing through the sky and—" Fiona stopped abruptly "—and I'm also staying because I want to meet your son Sam, who'll be here tomorrow. Julia telephoned him and filled him in on what's been happening. He's bringing a friend he wants you to meet—her name's Felicia. They're flying into Nice Airport, where Tolle will pick them up, and they hope to be here by midday."

"A family reunion," Saul said. He closed his eyes, recalled the elderly woman cursing him in the cemetery, and of the thoughts he'd been having about family—or, more exactly, about the *absence* of family. "Maybe that's the *real* reason I wrote the letter to Bush—so I could wind up in a hospital in France that would give my wife and children a reason to convene—what do they call it these days?—a *destination* reunion." He closed his good eye, touched the bandage. "What was the doc's prognosis?"

"Fifty-fifty you'll retain some vision, mostly peripheral, but that's a conservative estimate in order not to raise false expectations," Fiona said. "You might do better. The macula was totally detached, and you had three major tears, so there'll probably be extensive scarring."

"And tell me about Julia. She's feeling all right?"

"Julia's fine—rather full of herself, in fact, and very full of the life she's bringing into the world," Fiona said. "When a woman's pregnant, the eyes look inwards, or so I've heard. I spoke with her after the surgery and assured her you weren't in any immediate danger."

"But she's gone, yes?"

"Yes," Fiona said. "We talked a lot about her decision, and about you and Tolle too—about your marriage, about how both you and her mother had talked with her about trying to *repair* the marriage—"

"Before or after we repair the body?"

215

"She's a wonderful young woman, Saul," Fiona said, "and I think she's made a good decision, though she and I agreed we should think of it as a *reversible* decision. And I'm not talking about *having* the baby, but about *where* to have it. You can be very proud of her."

"I am."

"And you're going to be a grandfather," Fiona said. "Are you prepared?"

"Probably."

"Julia said—" Fiona stopped, moved away from Saul's bed "—Julia said that if I'm still here when the baby comes, she'd like me to be the child's godmother."

"If you're still here—? Julia actually *said* that? I don't believe it."

"You're right," Fiona said. "*She* didn't say that. *I* said that."

"You also—I think I'm just now hearing what you said before—" Saul gestured to the IV, as if to explain his mental lapses "—but I think I heard you say you're going home."

"Yes," Fiona said. "I'm going home. I've had a lot of time to mull things over these past few days. I'll stay in town long enough to say goodbye to Tolle, to meet Sam and Felicia, and then it's back across the waters."

"No South Africa then?"

"No South Africa."

"Anything I can do to make you change your mind?"

"Probably not. Some dreams really *don't* come true," she said. "And do yourself a favor and look in a mirror, Saul. You're a total mess."

"Enough then, I suppose. You mulled, and you decided that the possibility of time together for us is *kaput*," Saul said. "So be it."

"But *no* protest?" Fiona said. "You didn't *want* to spend at least a *few* torrid weeks below the equator with me so that…"

She stopped, swallowed hard, waved a hand at him to indicate that although she couldn't say anything else, she didn't want *him* to say anything. She moved to the window, looked out for a while, then came back and sat on a chair next to his bed. Her eyes, to his surprise, were clear and dry.

"There's a certain freedom in all this," she said. "I can still dissemble—still say things to others I know aren't true. I haven't lost that skill. But I can't lie to myself anymore."

"Do they know?" he asked. "Your family, I mean."

"I told Megan—she's my oldest sister, the one who comes closest to being sane."

"And—forgive—but you talked about an angiogram—did the doctor schedule it yet?"

"Didn't ask, don't know." She shrugged. "But the way I see things is that even if we could go to South Africa together—or, failing that, to Bimini or Tuscany, which, given the shape we're *both* in, seems unlikely—having met Tolle and Julia, I couldn't do it. Was I tempted? You bet. It's why I came here, after all..."

"It's why you came here," Saul said.

"The way I see it, though, it's as if I've been living out the adult version of one of those Make-a-Wish things where kids about to die get to play basketball or be in a rock band with one of their heroes. But the thing of it is, not only couldn't I tolerate the possibility that what I did would hurt *them*, though I suspect Tolle's beyond hurt and Julia's beyond cynicism, but I couldn't take the chance of hurting *you*."

Fiona stood, put up a hand to indicate that she wasn't finished saying what she had to say, and when she spoke again it was clear to Saul that she had been preparing her words carefully.

"We'd have our idyll, I suppose, say all kinds of wonderful, foolish things to one another—feel profound, sublime feelings about the meaning-of-it-all—love, of course, and all flesh being grass, and intimations of mortality and immortality—but then what? I'd be wandering up there in the happy hunting grounds, and you'd be back at square one, and with your lone marital bridge burned. So that with me gone—and your heart broken forever, yes?—who'd be left to love you and take care of you? Who would *you* be able to love?"

"You. Julia. Sam. Tolle."

"Because another conclusion I came to," Fiona continued, "is that what's really hard is not when nobody loves you but when you have

217

nobody *to* love. With all their faults—my mother and sisters—I love them still. And there's Julia too now, and this way I wind up having that, you see—loving Julia, loving you, others—and it makes a lot of things that were never okay, okay."

"Like—?"

"Because there's this too," Fiona said. "That you and Tolle have stuck it out so long it would be stupid for you two not to ride off into the sunset together. You've too much sheer history together, and soon you'll have a grandchild, and then maybe more. And Tolle has not only been writing up a storm, but she's been sketching out new ballets, so it wouldn't be a good time to add unnecessary conflicts to *her* life."

"New *ballets?*" Saul said. "That's news that hasn't reached me yet."

"What I also decided," Fiona said, "is that I don't want to die in a strange land. As my Aunt Rose, who didn't get to America until she was in her forties, used to say—and she lived north of Boston in a gorgeous part of New England—'The hills are very beautiful, but they're not mine.'"

"Sounds like Spéracèdes," Saul said.

"This way I'll be back in my own room where my mother, who's exceptionally skilled at gloom, doom, and guilt, will get some welcome absolution for all the real and imaginary wrongs she's inflicted on me," Fiona said. "I mean, look at it this way—*her* way: if she hadn't been a terrible mother, would my life have turned out as badly as it has?"

Saul started to speak, but Fiona put up a hand.

"I'm almost done," she said. "Truth be told, it'll be a treat to let her do for me now what she didn't do then. Retribution? Vengeance? Some *schadenfreude* at work? Maybe. Do I have other options? Could be. It's not a bad deal, really—familiar setting, my sisters cooing, chirping, and weeping around me while working their butts off to cheer me up. Lots of nieces and nephews telling me about their lives, the girls confiding secrets to their dying aunt…"

Saul waited, and when it was clear Fiona had finished saying what she'd wanted to say, he spoke.

"So you've worked it all out," he said. "It *is* the best of all possible worlds, and your going home to die is—forgive the word—the *living* proof, right?"

"I think your envy's beginning to show," Fiona said. "But the other thing—what I wanted to tell you most of all is that I couldn't have known this—couldn't have known *what-to-do*—unless I'd written the letter to you. First I had to write the letter, and then I had to come here."

She leaned over, kissed him on the mouth, quickly.

"Mister Split-Lip—that's what I'll call you from now on," she said. "Mister Split-Lip. So hey—thanks for being here when I needed you."

She stood, turned, walked to the door, and left.

Saul drifted in and out of sleep, but when he opened his good eye again the men were still there, staring down at him. Doctor Chehade, who, he recalled, had performed the eye surgery, reached under the sheet and took Saul's hand in his own.

"It was as I thought," he said, speaking in English. "Your left anterior descending artery was seventy percent occluded, and both the left coronary artery and the circumflex artery were approximately sixty percent occluded. There is also evidence of a prior myocardial infarction—a *silent* heart attack, I believe you call these events—involving the inferior and inferolateral walls. Am I correct, Doctor Guérard?"

A lime-green surgical mask dangling around his neck, Doctor Guérard nodded, then spoke in French. Struggling to comprehend what they were saying, Saul asked the doctor to speak in English.

"Ah yes, well when I saw what was occurring—occurring with the occlusions, yes?—I went ahead and did the angioplastys. Three. *Coated* angioplasty—stents, you call them, I think—so there should be minimal fibrosis—scar tissue from the inflammatory, yes?—and for the rest, I am not worried."

"Why should you be," Saul said. "It's not *your* heart."

"*Je ne comprends pas*," Doctor Guérard turned to Doctor Chehade. "Did I use the wrong language?"

Doctor Chehade explained that Saul had been making a joke.

"*Ah—tu rigole avec moi!*" Doctor Guérard exclaimed. He beamed with pleasure, put his hand over his heart. "That pleases me—it shows that your spirit is remaining vital and that you will make the recovery well. It is always a good warning when the patient is to joke with the doctor. *Donc.* It was my correct decision not to do the *pontages*—the grafts—with your chest opened up. Yes."

"Where am I?" Saul asked.

Doctor Chehade said that Saul was lying on a gurney in a hallway because the bed in a new room they had assigned him to was broken. As soon as it was fixed, he would be moved there.

"When can I get out of here?" Saul asked, and when he did—the residue of a dream?—he saw tribesmen on horseback, hypodermic syringes, like knives, clenched between their teeth. "Out there—*dehors, la-bas—*"he said "—people are dying—"

"In here too," Doctor Chehade said, and turned to Doctor Guérard, who said that he wanted Saul to remain in the hospital for at least one more night to allow time for the anesthesia to wear off.

"*Then* I can go?"

"Of course. But you will need someone to fetch you," Doctor Chehade said. "Also, given the surgery to the thoracic region, along with your rib fractures, we strongly suggest you wait at least two weeks before you drive an automobile."

"Three full weeks would be preferred," Doctor Guérard said, and added that he would visit with Saul later in the day—that he wanted to talk with him about a cardiac rehabilitation program. He had already arranged for a hospital nutritionist to talk with Saul about losing weight and maintaining a healthy diet. In addition, he would confer with Saul about "*le stress*"—about his work schedule when he returned to the United States, about his high blood pressure, his sexual activity, his smoking.

Saul pictured victorious horsemen riding toward the horizon and leaving behind them, on what had been lush, green playing fields, the mutilated, dismembered bodies of pregnant women. He told the doctors that his wife and son would be coming to visit soon and that they could take him home.

Saul cranked a lever so that he was in a sitting position on the gurney, and he became aware, for the first time, of a weight on his leg. He lifted the sheet, saw that a sandbag—to prevent bleeding—had been placed over his thigh where Doctor Guérard had inserted a catheter into the femoral artery. There was no light coming from the window at the hallway's end.

He looked over his shoulder, towards where he assumed a nurse's station would be, but saw only a long, dimly lit corridor, the pale glow of what he assumed were television sets coming from rooms on both sides of the hallway, but without sound. Was everybody asleep? Had they forgotten he was there? Had he died and been transported to some medical purgatory where he would spend eternity waiting in a silent corridor—a world without words—for a bed?

He thought of climbing down from the gurney in order to find a nurse, but if he pushed the sandbag aside in order to stand up, he was afraid he might bleed onto the marble floor, or become dizzy and pass out. *A world without words* wasn't that what Fiona had named the hours they had spent together *away* from hospital, clinic, AIDS patients, and funerals? Perhaps if he had to stay in or near Hôpital Henri Duffaut for a while, he could be of assistance—take histories, review medications, share research and program strategies, or, better yet, help with grant proposals. If he was going to stay in South Africa for any substantial period of time and be useful there—a vague notion that seemed to have quickly become an imperative—he had best begin thinking about money: about how and where he could raise funds for projects he wanted to initiate.

If Tolle came with him instead of Fiona, perhaps she could help with schedules and paperwork and still have ample time to work at her writing. Or was she really intent on creating and producing new ballets? For a brief moment, he found himself wondering if Fiona had been hoping to fake him out, and that when he arrived in Cape Town she would be waiting for him at the airport. Perhaps she'd find a shaman, a witch doctor, or a *sangoma*—a traditional healer who could bring about a miraculous, extended period of remission…

A handsome man, dressed in a suit and tie that reminded Saul of the suit and tie Doctor Bertrand had worn on the day of his wife's funeral, was smiling down at him. Saul was not aware of when the man had arrived or of how long he had been standing there. All Saul wanted to do was to sleep: to sleep more, to sleep again, to sleep deeply and to dream the kinds of dreams he had dreamt all through his medical school years—dreams where he'd receive secret information concerning a cabal going to destroy the world—dreams where he'd inform others that if they followed him, they could escape and be saved. They'd move down staircases (orange and black corrugated steel, like those of his Brooklyn elementary school), run across meadows, slash their way through forests, find out caves, underground chambers, and subway tunnels that lay below vast deserts where they could remain undetected until he'd marshalled the weaponry—bazookas, machine guns, long bows, tanks, submarines, and hypodermic syringes filled with deadly chemicals—with which to defeat the forces of evil that were bearing down upon them.

"Sleep is of utmost importance at a time like this," the man standing beside his gurney was saying, "and so I am grateful that you have slept so well. We French, you see, still believe in the *cure de sommeil,* which I understand finds little favor in your country even though it has proven quite helpful in specific situations, and has been particularly effective for women."

The man then explained that this induced narcosis usually lasted from ten days to two weeks, and that though the person slept, on average, twenty hours a day, he or she did not do so in darkness or in total silence. In previous generations they had used barbiturates to bring about sleep, but now they used combinations of anti-anxiety and anti-depressant medications, along with *hypnotiques*. What was essential to the cure was that patients be removed from the ordinary anxieties that pressed upon them, that they be put into prolonged states of calm in which they would be cognizant not only of the protection and safety the doctor was providing, but also of the real world that could be perceived, at a distance, through the veil of sleep and dreams.

"Who are you and why are you telling me this?" Saul asked.

"I am Doctor Chehade," the man said. "I was waiting for you to awaken in order that you and I might have a conversation before I leave. Also, I would like to take a look at your eye again."

"I didn't recognize you without your uniform," Saul said.

Doctor Chehade laughed. "I agree with Doctor Guérard —the fact that your sense of humor has not departed is an excellent indicator of regeneration."

"Why am I still here?"

"We did not want to disturb you while you slept. But come—I will take you to your room."

Doctor Chehade, whose voice, in English, was quietly reassuring— he could hear Fiona saying it had a seductive, liquid quality—reached below the gurney, unlocked the brake and, holding the IV pole with one hand, began pushing Saul along the corridor.

"I was able to obtain a private room for you, which is one reason for the delay," he said. "But I also wanted to talk with you of something existent on a more personal note."

In the hospital room, Doctor Chehade offered Saul his hand, and when Saul stood up in the space between bed and gurney, he felt his knees begin to give way.

"I'm weak," he said. "The journey from the gurney, right?"

"You have not eaten for many hours," Doctor Chehade said. "But I have ordered a special dinner for you. I think you will be pleased."

"Thanks." Saul sat on the bed. "You've been very kind, Doctor Chehade—very considerate."

"It has been my pleasure, for a man of your eminence." Doctor Chehade smiled. "I took the liberty of searching for you on the Internet, you see, and I state now that it is an honor for me to serve you. The work you accomplished several years ago in South Africa is especially noteworthy for it serves as a reminder to me to consider seriously the filing of an application with *Médecins Sans Frontières*, an organization that at this time benefits only from my modest financial support. And you are also a man of Jewish descent, am I correct?"

"Yes. But why—?"

"My parents were friendly with a Jewish man—Austrian, not Israeli—when I was a young boy in Beirut. He was a merchant involved in silk and linens, and we ate in his home upon occasion. I am Christian—not Muslim, or Druse—and thus did not have restrictions against eating pork, and neither did this man and his family. His name was Emanuel Mandelbaum, and he was a most gentle man, yet quite modern. He loved electrical appliances and had acquired many, especially for his kitchen—vegetable choppers, small ovens, *grillades*, egg boilers. In his basement, he repaired appliances for friends and neighbors. I recall bringing him a toaster that had ceased working—it was of the kind with flaps on each side that opened outwards—and staying with him while he repaired it. He was a fastidious man, and, remembering the deftness of his fingers again—they were quite small and what I think you call 'stubbed'—it occurs to me now that he would have made an excellent surgeon."

"Was he a survivor?"

"A survivor?"

"Of the camps."

"Of course."

Doctor Chehade reached into an inside jacket pocket and, like a magician, so deft were his moves, he withdrew a piece of equipment which he quickly attached to his forehead. It was a head lamp, Saul saw, and it gave off a long rod-like beam of pure white light. Doctor Chehade directed the beam of light onto the palm of his left hand so that he could adjust its intensity. Then he came nearer to Saul and removed the bandage from Saul's damaged eye, after which, very gently, he probed the area surrounding the eye with his fingers.

"Very good," he said. "Excellent."

He turned out the room's overhead light, closed the door. In his left hand he held a small piece of glass, which he moved back and forth in the space between Saul's eye and the light that came from the head lamp.

"No more split-lens ophthalmoscopes?" Saul asked.

"We have not used those for many years," Doctor Chehade replied. "This is a convex lens, you see, and creates a *virtual* image, but an image that is indefinitely more accurate."

"You mean infinitely—*infinitely* more accurate."

"You are correct."

The lens, which Doctor Chehade rotated between thumb and forefinger, looked to Saul like a large cat's eye. Saul closed his good eye, and when he did, saw nothing but grey, as if a sheet of slate had been slipped into a slot behind his retina in the way a photographer slipped a photographic plate into a camera. The slate put him in mind of city sidewalks made of squares of what were called *blue* slate, and this evoked memories of playing a game called Chinese handball, where, in an alleyway, you slapped a ball, on one bounce, against a wall so that it landed in square sidewalk boxes, to left and right, that other players guarded. There were rarely slate sidewalks in alleyways, but in front of several buildings on his block where he and his friends played boxball, hit-the-penny, and a baseball game where you tossed the ball low, with spin, across three boxes....

When Doctor Chehade had finished examining Saul's eye, he replaced the bandage with a new bandage, after which he washed his hands.

"Yes," he said.

"Yes?"

"It is as I thought—the healing has already begun, but we will not know for some time yet how much regeneration we have. You may dispense with the bandage tomorrow, nor will you require an eye patch afterwards. I have ordered eye drops—antibiotics, to prevent infection and inflammation—and I am confident that you will regain, at the least, some portion of your peripheral vision."

"And after that—?"

Doctor Chehade shrugged. "Who knows? Time, Doctor Davidoff. Time must become our friend. In four to six weeks, we will perhaps know more. But I would look forward, frankly, to a healing period of at least several months."

"Great," Saul said. "And I had a heart attack too, correct?"

"A minor infarction which is, as we say truly, of little or no consequence. Doctor Guérard estimates that it occurred some time within the past twelve months. Perhaps you recall some unusual indigestion, or some fleeting pain you attributed to exercise, or—"

"S.B.D.," Saul said.

"S.B.D.?"

"Silent But Deadly—what we called silent flatulence when I was a boy."

"That is very good—I will remember it," Doctor Chehade said. "S.B.D.. But Doctor Guérard is not concerned about your heart, for it is a kind of miracle—what we call the wisdom of the body, yes?—how one can function and live on with only minor portions of the heart muscle remaining alive. Doctor Guérard will urge you to change your habits, but if you do or if you do not, we expect you will reach a ripe maturity. Were there a danger more imminent, he would not release you back to the world."

"Great news," Saul said, and saw that in his dream people he'd been trying to save had been wearing grey T-shirts with pink lettering—*HIV POSITIVE*—that men and women wore during protest marches he had witnessed in Cape Town. Chanting and singing, arm in arm, the marchers had proclaimed their medical status proudly. He also recalled being invited to a dinner by one of the doctors at the hospital, being seated next to a man named Joseph bin Laden—this was *after* 9/11—and wondering if this charming, cultivated man, who was one of Osama bin Laden's brothers, and who had created the bin Laden Institute for the Study of Islam, knew that Saul was a Jew. Then he was seeing a banner—*IMAGINE IF HITLER HAD WON*—that conjured up a phantom Nazi triumph, remembered being a bystander at another march in Cape Town, this one organized to recruit volunteers to the Taliban....

"Often the fibrosis of the retina can cause a tension—a *tractional* detachment—that may cause the retina to detach again, sometimes repeatedly," Doctor Chehade said. "Still, I am optimistic."

"Why?"

"*Why?*" Doctor Chehade laughed. "Because I am an excellent surgeon and an optimistic human being—that is why!" he declared. "And because I like you. But let me ask you something else—my true reason for remaining until you regained more completely your consciousness. The question I have been preparing to offer to you is this: What are your allegiances to the State of Israel?"

"Excuse me?" Saul said. "What does the State of Israel have to do with my surgery?"

"I feel a responsibility, as a man of Middle Eastern origin—a man from a civilized Arab nation—to talk to my Jewish friends about this when occasion presents itself. I talk with you as I have often talked with colleagues in the hospital who are of Jewish extraction. I trust you will believe that I am not singling you out."

"I'm an American," Saul said.

"Of course you are."

"And a Jew. Yes, I'm a Jew."

"Well, I knew that, but I am glad you have decided to clarify your status. Honesty is a requirement of any true friendship."

"What I meant to say is that I'm a Jew, but not an observant or practicing Jew," Saul said, and immediately wondered why he was offering this information. "Being Jewish does not inform my ordinary, waking life in any particular way," he went on. "I don't go to synagogue or observe the holidays—not even those most Jews observe—what we call the High Holy Days, the New Year and Yom Kippur, our Day of Atonement."

"I understand," Doctor Chehade said. "Of course. You need say little more. I have met Jewish people such as yourself—Americans as well as French and English—and their habits of living conform to your description. You should be assured that I remain a great admirer of your people. Sometimes I think that I admire you more than many Jewish people themselves do—those who, *malheureusement*, seem to have forgotten who they are, and where they come from, and why they are here."

227

Doctor Chehade steepled his hands below his lips. "You are, you see, a people who believe in One God, who is, of course, the God of all creation. You are a people with great respect for learning, and with traditions of charity, justice, and hospitality very much like those of my own people. You have stayed together—a true community, with common bonds, beliefs, and rituals—despite oppression and plagues, and without, until this past century, a land of your own. The most excellent doctors I have known, both here and in my own homeland, have been Jewish. I am proud to call myself your friend and that you have chosen to listen to me, yet at the same time I recognize that you have become fatigued from your ordeals and also, perhaps, confused as to the direction of my discourse. Therefore, I will arrive swiftly at my conclusion."

Doctor Chehade stepped back and when he spoke, his voice became stronger, as if he were speaking not only to Saul but to other men, perhaps nine or ten of whom had entered the room and were gathered around Saul's bed.

"I feel it incumbent upon me, when I am with Jewish friends—and I want you to listen very, *very* carefully to what I say now—to inform you that although the State of Israel will, in the future as in the past, win many battles, it will not win the war. It cannot."

Doctor Chehade took Saul's free hand in both his own.

"I see that you are eager to fall asleep again," he said, "and I trust it is not because I am boring you. *Par conséquent,* let me end our dialogue by asserting that I understand that this has been a difficult time for you, and in such a time I do not intend to add to your burdens. Still, while you must understand that *I* certainly am not against you or your people, you must also understand that history is."

Seventeen

As soon as Tolle started pushing the wheelchair down the ramp and into the hospital parking lot, Saul tried to stand, but as he did, he tripped on one of the chair's foot-rests and when Jerry grabbed his arm, Saul slapped at Jerry's hand, lost his balance, and would have slammed face first into the parking lot's asphalt had not Felicia grabbed him around the waist.

"Whoa, big daddy!" she said. "Easy does it now."

To keep the wheelchair from hitting Saul or Felicia, Tolle pushed it sideways, and it now rolled downhill while she stood, immobile, with the others—Saul, Jerry, Sam, Felicia—and watched it accelerate, then crash into the side of a parked car.

"Wow!" Sam said.

"Shit," Saul said.

"Is it *your* car?" Jerry asked.

"No," Saul said.

"Then why be upset?" Jerry said.

Felicia put an arm around Saul's shoulder. "Are you all right, Doctor Davidoff? It's always humiliating, don't you think, even when you *know* it's not your fault, to fall down in front of others."

"Call me Saul," Saul said. "Please."

"And how are the ribs today, Saul?" Felicia asked.

"Ribs, heart, eye, nose, lip—who knows?" Saul said. He reached into his mouth, grasped one of his top two front teeth and wiggled it. "And I think one of my teeth is loose too."

"It must be time for that game of stickball," Jerry said. "More of a level playing field now—so how about my extra twenty-five years versus your newly acquired wounds—reasonable *handicaps*, wouldn't you agree?"

"Not funny," Tolle said.

"Maybe we can fold the wheelchair up and take it with us," Jerry said. "That way, you could roll around in it when we play—like, what do they call it when the gimps and cripples have their games—?"

"Special Olympics," Felicia said. "And you shouldn't talk that way about disabled people. You hurt them *and* you demean yourself."

"Just a joke," Jerry said. "As you can see, some of my best friends are disabled."

"Grow up," Felicia said.

Felicia had shoulder-length raven-black hair, broad Slavic cheekbones, full, sensuous lips, and was nearly as tall and broadly built as Sam, who was six-foot-four and had been a standout football player in high school and at Columbia.

Tolle was not surprised to see that Camus had joined them and was gazing admiringly at Felicia.

But did you notice that when she smiled at Jerry, there was malice in the smile? You have, of course, known your share of beautiful women, several of them American, though your wife, if I recall correctly, was descended from Berber and Turkish Jews, and was—something you took pride in— more truly Algerian than you were. What I'm wondering about, however, is whether Felicia considers her remarkable out-sized beauty a gift, or, as my own looks have been for me at times, a torment: a life of forever being stared at—or, more often, leered at; forever being coveted for what-you- look-like and not for-who-you-are; yet never wanting not to look as good as you can in order to excite admiration in others...

So you're here again with that half-smiling, knowing look I loved, and the question it never occurred to me to ask about you when we were together is also here, but about Saul: Is he, too, going to leave me, and at a moment when my own prospects seem suddenly bright?

And if not, am I fated to care for him in his dying in the way he's cared for others—to care for him—Julia might delight in this irony—as practice for caring for her child? And if I choose not to care for him, but to leave him, which thought has been hovering at the edge of consciousness since the day of the funeral, what then?

Hard to separate what's actually happening from what's happening in my imagination. In the hospital this morning—before I saw Saul, when I had little idea of just how old and wasted he'd look—I had this glimmer of—a notion **for**—*a possible story—about a couple who, in order to renew an empty marriage, agree to separate for a year, and never afterwards reveal to each other, or to anyone else, what they did during this year.*

Felicia strode ahead and examined the car's door, where the wheelchair had hit. "Several dings, but no major dents," she said. "I'll leave a note on the windshield with my cell phone number."

Tolle took Saul's arm, guided him down the ramp, cautioned him to take baby steps.

"Isn't she terrific, Dad?" Sam said. "She's really a take-charge kind of woman like Mom, and I figure that makes me the luckiest guy in the world."

"Glad to hear it," Saul said.

"And there's something else," Sam said. "Now that Felicia and I are together, I've discovered I'm actually *happy* to be with my family again. Though I regret the occasion, of course—your troubles—I'm certainly glad for the pretext. I wanted you to meet Felicia before this, but she put the brakes on—said we shouldn't present ourselves to you until we were clear about the nature of our commitment, and now that we are… well, we're *here!*"

"Thank you," Saul said.

"And our major good news is that we've set a date," Sam said.

"A date?" Saul asked.

"For the wedding."

"For the wedding," Saul said.

Felicia tapped lightly on the side of Saul's head. "*Hello?*" she said. "Anyone home?"

"Sorry," Saul said. "I'm in a bit of a fog. But yes—congratulations must be in order. So congratulations. I'm very happy for you both." He turned to Tolle. "Are you happy too?"

"I think it's wonderful," Tolle said as she helped Saul back into the wheelchair. "She loves our son and he loves her. What could be bad?"

"What could be bad," Saul said.

"Felicia's smart, she's beautiful, and—what she doesn't mind people knowing because she's a wonderfully *transparent* woman—" Sam began.

"*Transparent?*" Felicia said. "At *my* height and with *my* bone structure?"

"—and she has a winning sense of humor too, as you can tell," Sam said. "And also—what I *started* to say—she's smart, she's beautiful, and—what she's not in the least embarrassed about—she's rich."

"And *spoiled*—don't forget spoiled," Felicia said. "I'm used to getting my way. My sense of entitlement, which comes from being rich, attractive, and having doting parents, throbs in me like an overactive thyroid. But it's true too that I *adore* your son, and I knew right away—on our first date—that I wanted him to be mine. He's the kindest man I've ever known."

"Didn't someone else just say that?" Saul asked.

"Fiona," Tolle said. "It's the way she described you to Dale and Gerhard."

"Is Fiona gone?" Saul asked.

"Fiona's gone," Tolle said.

"I guess you can tell how happy—how *lucky* we are to have found each other and, more important, to have *recognized* our good fortune," Sam said, "and what we've decided is that a big June wedding would be too conventional—we want something more intimate and private— and it would also be too soon since you're not planning to be stateside for a while."

"Can Fiona come?" Saul asked. "Will she still be here?"

"Fiona's going home," Tolle said.

"Felicia's parents were scheduled to go on a cruise to the Far East in June, and though they offered to cancel, we saw no reason to have them do that," Sam said. "Her parents have been great about *everything*, by the way—told us not to worry ourselves over details."

"Like money," Felicia said.

"Have they met Fiona—" Saul asked "—or Julia?"

"We're not to worry about money so that we're free to think about our *happiness* is the way they put it," Sam said. "And the answer to your question is that they haven't met Julia *or* Fiona—or you and Mom, for that matter—but we're hoping that you and Mom—and Julia too, of course—will participate in our wedding in a significant way. We want you to be *players*, Dad."

"Although I'm not sure I understand this strange language you speak," Jerry said, "it all seems quite wonderful. But I have a question for you, Sam: do you know what young women in New York City do to get rid of cockroaches?"

"I give up," Sam said. "What *do* young women in New York City do to get rid of cockroaches?"

"They ask them for a commitment," Jerry said.

"Your compulsion to make jokes out of everything is quite irritating," Felicia said.

"She's incredibly blunt sometimes," Sam explained.

"Blunt and *offensive*," Felicia said.

"And that can be quite irritating too," Jerry said.

"You're right," Felicia said. "But I can get away with it because I'm an attractive young woman. The world cuts attractive young women lots of slack."

Tolle gestured to Jerry to open the car door.

What I was hoping, when Saul and I were in Spéracèdes again, was to tell him I'd been thinking somewhat obsessively about the South African proverb he gave me on his return from Cape Town. And I was also looking forward to talking with him about how surprised and pleased I was that making love could still give me so much pleasure, and asking him if he agreed, contrary to popular mythology, that sex—making love—became better with age.

But now, *Albert?*

Now that he's in the sorry state he's in—now that everything that's happening seems more and more absurd—not absurd in the sense you used the word—perhaps a better word would be bizarre *in the French sense of that word—but if he remains the same, or—more likely—continues to deteriorate, what point?*

"You *will* participate, though, won't you, Dad?" Sam asked. "I know you and I haven't been close in recent years, but Felicia and I would welcome your participation."

"*Par-ti-ci-pa-ti-on,*" Jerry said, pronouncing the word in French. "That was what the students wanted most of all when they tried to bring down the government. *La Participation.*"

Jerry started to talk to Felicia about *les évenements de mai,* and how the students and workers had come close to bringing down de Gaulle and the entire French government, but Felicia ignored him, spoke directly to Saul.

"We met your friend Fiona this morning," Felicia said, "and she told us that she expects to be seeing Julia very soon, perhaps later today, depending on how far she can get before she becomes tired."

"And after we spend some quality time with you," Sam said, "Felicia and I intend to stay with Julia for a while."

"Then Fiona's *gone*—?" Saul said.

Saul jiggled keys in the air, clicked a button several times until, at the far end of the parking lot, a car's taillights blinked several times. Jerry tried to get Felicia's attention—took her by the arm, and started to explain *why* what had happened in France in 1968 was so import-ant, and why—*his* theory—the revolution it promised had not come to pass, but Felicia told him to give it a rest, turned away from him, and walked toward the car with Sam, an arm around his shoulder while she whispered words in his ear that made him laugh.

I'm delighted you've returned, and at least as delighted—and *amazed—by Felicia, and by the fact that she loves my son and plans to marry him, though it's difficult for me to believe it's so. Although I've never been a great mother—in truth, I couldn't wait for the children to grow up and leave home—Sam always fascinated me. Was he really **my** child? Did I actually give birth to him? There were long stretches of time when I did truly adore him, almost as if he'd been given to me as a gift, but on loan. He was so extraordinarily open and credulous—had a childlike naïveté, a quality of—there's no other word for it—**innocence**—a boyishness that persisted well past his college years, and was, given my innate cynicism, a quality I was in awe of. Although he towered over everyone, he never, except when playing football, was anything but kind.*

Despite your belief in the absurd as being at the heart of the way things are in the world—in us—and although you were committed to linking private beliefs to public action, yet I remember you saying that in the end all truly important questions came down to individual acts of human kindness. Which leads me to believe you would have adored Sam too.

'There's not a mean bone in his body,' Saul used to say about him, and it's true. Despite his prodigious strength—and because of it, his gentle nature—his friends called him Sam the Lamb. But Sam married? And married to this stunning, intelligent, strong-willed woman?

Talk about absurd!

And yet… Did you hear the words Felicia just whispered in his ear, and how lovingly she did so? 'Oh you dear, dear man—do you know how much I love you?' And how happy Sam was to hear these words? And also, did you notice how easily Felicia brushed away Jerry's attentions? In this she reminds me of the ways I used to dispatch men who hit on me. But I can't help wondering about the obvious—were I or Felicia less attractive—less strikingly attractive—would Jerry or any man-on-the-prowl ever give us the time of day—ever pretend to be interested in us for anything other than our physical attributes?

Nothing new here, of course, and I fear—what I did not fear when I was with you—that my giving voice to these familiar thoughts will bore you. Though by your gesture, thank you, you seem to be urging me to return to what I was talking about a few minutes ago—to the story I was beginning to conjure up about a couple, and what I conceive of as their 'year between,' which year is, it occurs to me—do we detect a theme?—a ghost year.

They had reached the car, and Tolle took Saul's hand, helped him out of the wheelchair.

"Julia left after we had breakfast together this morning," Sam said. "She looks great, by the way—never better! Pregnancy clearly becomes her."

"Fiona never said goodbye to me," Saul said.

"Actually, she did," Tolle said. "She said goodbye to you yesterday at the hospital."

"Oh," Saul said. "I'm sorry. I was zonked out on the meds, I suppose, though I must say I enjoyed the way they made me feel."

Despite everything that's been happening—despite Sam and Felicia's presence, despite Jerry's nonsense, despite Saul's sad state, despite the weird chattering going on around me, along with the usual dark thoughts that were with me before that, the good news—the heartening news!—is that ideas and notions for stories, and for stories that might become ballets (in the ballet about the couple trying to save their marriage, for example, I see them going their separate ways at the end of Act One, and for Act Two, simply having a note in the program that says 'One Year Later')—and these ideas, and fragments of ideas, have begun crowding into rooms of my mind that have been empty far too long—rushing in and jostling one another for attention like lines in a Bach fugue, each new idea calling out: Look at me! Look at me! Look at me!

*   **Look** *at me?*

Correction then. **Listen** *to me. But 'look at me' seems apposite too, and I see by your smile that you're anticipating my next (and obvious) question. Would you—or Saul—have ever given me a second look if I'd been a homely young woman? And if either of you had not...*

And then I'm recalling what my mother would say to me when I was a child: that beauty is rare, and that those who possess it should never be indifferent to it.

"Then I won't ever see Fiona again, will I," Saul said.

Tolle told Saul to step up into the passenger seat, left leg first, and to hunch over in order not to scrape his head on the car door.

"It's better this way, right?" Saul said. "Tell me it's better this way."

"It's better this way," Tolle said.

"We met online," Felicia said.

Saul was sitting up in bed, Felicia and Sam close to the bed, Jerry in a chair he had turned around so he could straddle it and rest his hands on the chair's back. Tolle stood next to a window that looked out toward the Glanum ruins—ruins of a fortified Roman town that had been buried for centuries.

"On *line?* You met in a *factory?*" Jerry asked.

Sam laughed. "Not *on* a line," he said. "On*line*—on an Internet dating service—on Jdate."

"*J*date?" Jerry asked.

"'J' for Jewish," Felicia said.

"You're *Jewish?*" Jerry said to Felicia. "Funny, you don't look Jewish."

"But she does," Tolle said. "More than I ever did, certainly."

"In my opinion, Felicia possesses a unique and exotic Semitic beauty… and it drove me wild when we met," Sam said. "On our first date I couldn't stop staring at her."

"Nor did he try," Felicia said, "and I must admit that I didn't try to make him stop. Instead, I told him I was Israeli in order to see, given the reputation Israeli women have for being aggressive, how he'd react, and he responded with the happiest smile, and asked me what I'd done during my two years of military service—had I been a fighter pilot, a tank commander, or—?"

"The *real* reason we hit it off so quickly—" Sam said "—why our initial connection was so strong other, no secret, than our being tremendously drawn to one another sexually—was because of *you,* Dad. Because of AIDS."

Tolle touched Saul's mouth with her fingertips. "We should

237

probably unthread you some time today," she said. "What do you think, Felicia?"

Felicia examined Saul's lip. "I agree—the stitches can come out any time now," she said.

"Felicia's a doctor," Sam said. "But I told you that in the hospital, right? A *medical* doctor, although she doesn't practice medicine. She does research on HIV—on virus killers."

"Microbicides," Felicia said. "I work with David Ho—at the Diamond Foundation in New York. Do you know him?"

"I know David," Saul said. "He helped open things in China for better communication between our countries on AIDS. If I remember correctly, he went there with President Clinton."

"They've started some interesting research in China, especially with thermo-reversible gels," Felicia said. "The problem, however, as you well know, is that people can become so infatuated with the vaccines and microbicides, or so confident in the efficacy of antiretrovirals, that they forget their basics—condoms—which are the only tried-and-true way to prevent HIV. That's why the danger I foresee is paradoxical: that the availability of microbicides—whether as gels, creams, or suppositories—could result in a net *increase* in HIV infection rates."

"I agree," Saul said.

"Given that women now account for the majority of people living with HIV," Felicia said, "and that in most situations a woman's greatest risk comes from her husband or regular sexual partner—and that she has little power to insist on condoms—microbicides, which can be used *without* the cooperation or awareness of one's sexual partner, could prove a potent ally."

"See how brilliant she is, Dad," Sam said, "and how I can admire things in her that I've always admired in you? She's on the cutting edge of important discoveries and, more important, she does what you taught us *we* should do in life—*to make a contribution*—and so she just goes into the lab every day and does the work—no matter what—and she does it without ever despairing and without ever giving up hope."

"Speak for yourself," Felicia said. "I give up hope a hundred times a day. Don't you, Saul?"

"Sure," Saul said. "Especially when I'm sitting here doing nothing. But when I'm feeling better I hope to go to South Africa, where I can at least *try* to make a difference."

"And what I believe is *truly* incredible about our story," Sam said, "is that in most cases AIDS leads to suffering and death—but in our case it led to love."

Felicia rolled her eyes. "He's much smarter than he looks... or sounds," she said. "But to fill you in, Saul: where my own research focus is two-fold: first, determining the effect of microbicides on mucosal tissue; and second, and perhaps *more* daunting, coping with the sheer number of female volunteers we need to test each new product. Since a two-agent microbicide with seventy-percent efficacy potential needs four times the number of female volunteers single-component products do, the logistics of drug trials are becoming prohibitive. For one of my most promising candidates, for example—a product that, applied as a liquid becomes a gel once *inside* the body—about twenty million new infections might occur during the time it would take us to enroll the necessary twenty-thousand volunteers..."

Julia's gone. Fiona's gone. Madame Bertrand and her daughter are gone. Ethan's gone. Claire's gone. Martin's gone. My parents are gone. Saul's parents are gone. Thousands of Saul's patients are gone. And you're gone. And do you know what else? I wish all the people prattling away in this room were gone too.

I remember how you used to hate listening to your wife—Francine, right?—playing piano and practicing Bach, and Bach again and again, hour after hour, and how you'd take long walks in order to get away, walks during which you'd carry on some of your liaisons.

But what difference if they stay or leave, babble on, or go silent? And what difference—here, or in Spéracèdes, or in South Africa, or in New York—and with or without Sam and Felicia and Julia and Jerry—if Saul **never** *vacates this dopey state he's in?*

And how survive if I have to become his nursemaid, though I suppose

239

*I could hire someone to care for the basics, but if I did, he'd protest for sure, and I'd have to spend time training her, and there'd still be everything else—doctors, prescriptions, middle-of-the-night emergencies, hospitalizations, blood tests, X-rays—when my mind's on fire with ideas for new work. And—an obvious question—am I having this incipient burst of creativity—and yes to the question I see in your eyes about the **prospect** of liberation—because Saul is debilitated and disabled, and I'm suddenly sensing what it* might *be like to be on my own, and not to have to deal with him, not to have to always be planning my life while also taking **his** life into account...?*

Do you recall how, after we visited Nijinsky's grave, we talked about what it was like when ideas for new work came blazing through our minds, and how the only time we could extinguish those fires—let them fade to embers for a while—was to make love?

"Felicia's begun going around the country and giving lectures about AIDS," Sam said. "She lets people know how urgent the situation is in the way you did in your letter to President Bush. Are they aware, for example, that in the United States one person contracts AIDS every minute, and that worldwide, eight thousand people die of AIDS every day—more than five each minute, and—"

"Down, boy," Felicia said. "Go easy. Your father knows the data, and he needs to rest now."

"But I *like* hearing numbers," Saul said. "They comfort me."

"Well, *more than two million children* worldwide are infected with HIV," Sam said, "and half of them won't live past their second birthday. In South Africa alone, *more than five million people* are infected with HIV, and only one percent of those infected are receiving antiretroviral treatment."

"I'm sad because Fiona can't come with me to South Africa the way she hoped to," Saul said, "but perhaps Tolle will."

"No thanks," Tolle said.

"Or maybe you and Felicia can come with me, or go without me if I continue to have these stupid medical problems," Saul said. "You're my *kadishil*, after all."

"What's a *kadish'l*?" Sam asked.

"It's Yiddish for a son who says *kaddish* for his father after his father dies," Jerry said.

Saul reached inside his mouth, pulled out his loose tooth.

"*Look!*" he said.

"Open," Tolle said. She looked into Saul's mouth. "Does it hurt?"

"No."

"Could be the painkillers you're on," she said. "But give me the tooth and I'll put it under your pillow later."

Felicia brought Saul a washcloth filled with ice chips. "Suck on this," she said.

Tolle almost laughed out loud at Felicia's words, for they brought to mind a morning when she woke Saul up by going down on him— 'The Breakfast of Champions,' she'd said, alluding to advertisements that featured famous athletes praising a breakfast cereal—and swallowing his semen.

"Actually," Sam said, "I wouldn't at all mind going to South Africa with Felicia—to accompany her there while she does her work on AIDS. Isn't it wonderful, when you stop and think about it, how I've reversed the roles you and Mom had? Instead of becoming a doctor's *wife*—I'm going to be a doctor's *husband*!"

"Did you mind?" Felicia said.

"Mind what?" Tolle said.

"Mind being a doctor's wife—giving up your autonomy, along with possible careers in order that Saul could have the career he had?"

"I never gave up my autonomy because of Saul," Tolle said.

"That's true," Saul said. "Nobody has ever been able to tell Tolle what to do, or what not to do."

"Perhaps," Felicia said, and to Tolle: "But what did you tell *yourself* to do?"

"I was a dancer," Tolle said, "but then, because my body was compromised by an accident, I had to give up that ambition, and I became a teacher of dance."

"And you were a wife and a mother," Sam said. "At breakfast this morning, Julia and I were talking about what a terrific mother you were, and how you sacrificed your ambitions so that Julia and I, and Dad too, could fulfill ours."

Tolle stood. "I think I'll take a walk, and visit the ruins," she said. "They're still being excavated, and I hear they're quite fascinating."

Felicia put a hand on Tolle's shoulder. "The options women like me have now—and men like Sam too—simply weren't there when you were our age."

"I never forced you to do anything," Saul said. "You told me you *wanted* a conventional life—that you *wanted* to get married and have lots of children. I remember! It's what you *said!*"

Saul tried to get out of the bed, but a leg caught in the sheets and blankets, and he tumbled from the bed onto the floor.

Sam knelt at his father's side. "Are you all right, Dad?" he asked. He picked his father up, helped him back onto the bed. "Anything hurt?"

"Everything hurts," Saul said.

"From what I've learned from Sam, and from what I sense from our getting to know one another," Felicia said, "it's clear that you've always been wonderfully independent, and have always had your own mind about everything, but…"

"But what?" Tolle asked.

"But dependency is still dependency even if it's freely chosen," Felicia said

Eighteen

"What I heard," Katherine was saying, "was that there's speculation the doctor, whom I take it had been having an affair with a woman from Juan-les-Pins, may have paid the housekeeper to do away with his wife."

"Ridiculous," Jerry said. "The idea that having a mistress would constitute a motive for murder would be laughed out of court over here. What self-respecting Frenchman or Frenchwoman *doesn't* have somebody *à coté?* The rumor *I* heard is that it was some of Le Pen's people who paid the housekeeper, or her husband, to do the deed so that they could rile people up about the dangers of immigrants."

Katherine turned to Saul. "But other than those already dead, you seem to have suffered the most dire consequences of the event."

"You do look like shit, Saul," Jerry said.

"Hey—go easy on my old man," Sam said. "Somebody has to stand up to those bastards, and I'm proud my Dad was the guy."

"Thanks for the vote of confidence, son," Saul said. "And certainly I have to acknowledge that my act had a more immediate effect than, say, a letter might have had."

Tolle ruffled Saul's hair. "When his morbid humor surfaces, I know he's feeling better," she said.

Saul was still taking painkillers several times a day, and combined with the wine and the cool mountain air, they seemed to be conspiring to make him alert, and happy, in a way he hadn't been for the previous two weeks. Could it be, Tolle wondered, that the cause of his happiness—what was accelerating his recovery—was the knowledge that she would soon be leaving for the States, and—a happy by-product of her decision—would be seeing Julia and Fiona, and reporting back to him about them.

She was standing at the western edge of a veranda of what would soon be Katherine's new home. About a hundred yards below, the *Canal de la Siagne,* a canal that, for most of its length, Katherine had informed them, adjoined a walkable footpath, carried its water down to the coast—to Cannes—while the Siagne itself, twenty or so yards below the canal, flowed all the way to the Mediterranean. Tolle looked across a deep forested gorge to where, on a narrow road cut diagonally into the rocky hillside, a grey pick-up truck—the sole visible sign of life—was moving slowly downhill. How peaceful, and how beautiful, she thought, and then—how not?—she was hearing words Saul had recited to her several nights before when, after dinner, they stood on their balcony looking out across the valley toward the hills above Cannes—'The hills are very beautiful but they're not mine,' he'd said—a saying that, given the conversation they'd had at dinner, and the agreement they'd arrived at, she saw as his way of commenting on the fact that they would each be leaving Spéracèdes and *its* hills before long, and going their separate ways.

"True enough," Tolle had said, "but which hills are mine?"

"Good question," Saul had replied.

Alex's cello, a bright red ribbon tied under its tuning pegs, stood in the place of honor at the head of a picnic table, for it was because of an agreement to sell the cello that Katherine had received the money necessary to make an initial payment on the property and, the payment made and preliminary papers signed, had received permission from the property's owners to entertain friends here.

Saul was explaining to Felicia that he had first come to France because of Camus—because of *The Plague*—and because of the role it had played in his life, especially early on when, along with memories

244

of his father's polio-induced disability, it had inspired him to specialize in infectious diseases.

"Look, Saul," Felicia said. "I don't mean to rain on your parade, but as I told you before, I disagree with you about *The Plague*. In my opinion, it's much too self-servingly noble in its sentiments, and far too expository in its narrative. But the main reason—"

"But it's a great *story*—" Saul said "—an allegory, if you will, about—"

"Let me finish," Felicia said. "I couldn't buy it because it's about *one* outbreak of plague in *one* city, and about a doctor who's far too self-effacing and heroic to be credible."

"But what Camus believed," Saul said, "was that a plague could come to *represent* all the evils of the world and, thus, be like the world itself. For me, that's where his fiction, philosophy, and politics converge, because if people turn away from a plague—from evil—and are too cowardly to do something about it, then the only resort left—thus, paradoxically, Camus' *optimism*—an *absurd* optimism, certainly—is to rebel."

"I agree with Felicia," Jerry said. "And so did Jimmy."

"Jimmy?" Saul said.

"Jimmy Baldwin," Jerry said. "Jimmy thought Camus' novel was far too heavy—too simple-minded and didactic. We were having drinks in Cannes one day—he was living in Saint Paul-de-Vence then, and he'd come loping into the bistro with his little green Harvard book bag over his shoulder. He'd order Scotch and then more Scotch until he couldn't hold a glass in his hand. He'd get nasty with me sometimes too, as if, once he was smashed, he'd suddenly realize I was a white man. If white people got organized and were willing to make sacrifices—*material* sacrifices—then maybe the flaming sword that had been set down between the races—just *maybe* it could be extinguished and we could learn to live together."

"I'm confused," Sam said. "Are you suggesting that James Baldwin thought *The Plague* was about *racism*—about where responsibility for the *plague* of racism most truly lies?"

"Shh," Felicia said, and she put a blanket around Sam's shoulders.

"They're talking about dreams—about your father's dreams, and about James Baldwin's dreams."

"Speaking of dreams," Katherine said, "I've located a piano—a marvelous pre-war Bechstein that should arrive fairly soon, perhaps within the month. When Eugene returns to the States next week—to interview for positions at several universities—he'll take the cello with him and deliver it to the dealer in New York City who arranged for its sale. More important, however, is that Eugene's plan to return to New York reminds me to ask how things are going with Julia and Fiona. Jerry told me that Julia has returned to the States, and that she and Fiona are living together."

"I think it's great that Julia made the decision to go back to the States," Sam said, "and to be with Fiona until the baby comes, or at least until…"

Saul looked at Tolle, his expression telling her he was wondering why she had been so quiet most of the afternoon. "I'll be there soon too," Tolle said. "Julia and I are in touch nearly every day, and so far neither she nor Fiona have reported any new medical problems. They seem happy together, for which I'm grateful."

"What they need is luck," Sam said. "Felicia has taught me never to underestimate the role luck plays in life—like how *we* met. The way I look at it, meeting online is *truly* romantic, you see, because with thousands of options—all the possible people you can write to or get messages from, and all the computer-generated guides that tell you who you will and won't be attracted to—to actually *meet* one person in that proverbial haystack with whom—"

"As in 'a good roll in—?'" Jerry asked.

"—with whom you fall madly in love, and marry—" Sam said "—I think it goes against all odds and is therefore *incredibly* romantic!"

"Ah, my very own Sam the Lamb," Felicia said, and she roughed Sam's hair. "Speaking of luck, though, consider this: women are four times more likely to become infected with HIV during intercourse with an infected man than men are, so thank whatever gods are out there that it takes *multiple* sexual encounters for the virus to take hold most of the time. If not, the global pandemic would long ago have reached proportions beyond our imagining."

"I've often been consoled by the same thought," Saul said. "But what's come to interest me more than the mechanisms of HIV—how best to interrupt its life cycle, for example—are public health measures. Medications, vaccines, and microbicides will continue to improve, but what are we to do about the *behavioral* element—about the dreadful cultural, political, and social systems that are the more significant obstacles to prevention, care, and treatment?"

Tolle turned to Eugene. "Then you won't be continuing as a duo, I take it," she said.

"That's correct," Eugene said. "We may choose to perform together from time to time, here or in the States, but for a while we'll go our separate ways."

"Because—?" Tolle asked.

"Because we want to," Katherine said.

"Precisely," Eugene said. "We'll honor some of our contractual obligations on the continent, but even as we speak, lawyers are preparing what I suppose one would call our divorce papers. We were together, the three of us, for twenty-two years. Still, I expect the settlement to be amicable. We're getting what each of us wants: I'll have a steady job, without so much travel—"

"—and with access to an endless supply of gifted young female students," Katherine said.

"—and Katherine will have what she's always wanted—" Eugene said "—life in a remote, picturesque, and desolate part of the world and, best of all, a life free of the Turetzky brothers."

"How sad," Sam said. "I mean, after all your years together, and fresh from the death of a brother—and a husband—it's hard to even *begin* to understand what it must feel like to experience such loss."

"Not really," Eugene said, and he filled his wine glass and drank, after which he closed his eyes.

Katherine set out food—*tête de fromage, cornichons*, cheese, olives, bread—then asked Felicia to tell her about the wedding.

"I thought you'd never ask," Felicia said, and repeated what Tolle had heard before: that the wedding would take place in the oldest synagogue in the United States—the Touro synagogue in Newport, Rhode Island. There would be two rabbis officiating, and Felicia would go to *mikvah*—the ritual bath of purification—before the wedding. Sam had agreed to do the same, as her father had done before *his* marriage. And by then—the wedding was scheduled for the last day of October—'*Erev* Halloween,' Felicia joked—so that Julia, who would be maid of honor, would have given birth to her child. There were rabbinic rulings that forbade an unwed mother from standing under the bridal canopy, but if the rabbis refused to let Julia stand up for her, she would tell them to take a hike and would find other rabbis.

Both she and Sam would fast on the day of the wedding, and Felicia's brother, Raphael, would be Sam's best man. He too would attend the ritual bath, along with several of Felicia's uncles and male cousins. Under the wedding canopy, the rabbis would examine the wedding rings to make certain of their purity, and would *pretend* to examine the wedding contract. And what Felicia looked forward to most, she said, was walking around Sam seven times, once for each of the seven wedding blessings.

"She's always been able to walk circles around me," Sam said.

"Instead of gifts, we're asking our guests to contribute to one of several charities," Felicia said, "including *Médecins Sans Frontières* and my research center. And I'm trying to find some *private* research companies that are doing valuable work."

"Good luck," Saul said.

"Are you aware that only one percent of research money for HIV is going for microbicides?" Felicia asked. "And this is so, as you know, because pharmaceutical companies see no viable commercial markets for them in the *developed* world, and because they know that if they do come up with effective microbicides, they'll be pressured to distribute them cheaply in *third* world countries."

"It's been the same story with TB for more than fifty years," Saul said. "Because TB has largely been eradicated in the developed world, there are no financial incentives for drug companies to develop *new* TB drugs, so we wind up without new medications to treat the drug-resistant strains that keep emerging."

"I guess all you can do in the end is what you know how to do," Jerry said. "Take me, for instance. I know the world out there is corrupt and miserable, but the only thing I know how to do is paint. So I paint."

"I believe it's time for our toast," Katherine said, and she raised her wine glass. "To my dear friend Jerry Ravitch, who has had the wisdom to agree to allow me to be his benefactress—"

"—and muse," Jerry said.

"His benefactress and muse, then," Katherine said, "for he has consented to take up residence here, where I'll be transforming an old *cabanon* into the studio of his dreams."

"Jerry's going to *live* with you?" Saul said.

"Why the surprise?" Katherine said. "Jerry is one of the great undiscovered treasures of the art world, and also the oldest and dearest of friends."

"Emphasis on oldest," Jerry said. "But I'm stronger than ever." He glanced down, at his lap. "Now I can bend it."

"Katherine has often had a penchant for older men," Eugene said. "She seems to be have bought into the notion—greatly exaggerated, in my opinion—that wisdom comes with age."

"And speaking of older men—" Felicia said "—in his retirement, Mister Clinton, who's about your age, Saul, seems to have discovered AIDS religion." She blew air across her lips. "But he did dick when it counted. The man was a total disaster."

"I couldn't agree more," Eugene said. "He's probably the most charming disaster in American history."

"And that great environmentalist buddy of his, Gore, was no better—" Felicia said "—shilling all over Africa for drug companies the way he did."

"What bothers me," Saul said, "is that people like Gore and Clinton are often moved by suffering, yet they're moved by evil much less often, and evil's all around us."

Tolle was tired, and she was restless. Against expectations, Saul

249

had recovered sooner than she'd thought he would, and enough for her to have felt free to talk with him about going their separate ways for a while, which conversation she had begun by informing him she had made a decision to return to the States—to check in on Julia, of course, and Fiona—and also to talk with people in the world of dance, and enlist their support for a new dance company she intended to create: a repertory company that would encourage original works that combined the best of classsical ballet and modern dance. She had already been in touch with people she knew from her early years as a dancer, and also with several dancers with whom she had worked as teacher, some of whom—Kevin McKenzie, Suzanne Farrell, Gelsey Kirland, Mark Morris, along with her old friend Allegra Kent—were enthusiastic about her plans, and had promised to help.

Saul had not only assented to the idea of them heading off in different directions—she to the States, and he to South Africa—but, to help bring her company into being, had said she should feel free to draw upon their savings and investments. His reaction, however, had done little to quench the craving that was with her constantly of late—to have time for herself *now*: to be able to do her work on her own schedule, without interruption, obligations, or distractions, and to be away from everyone, and, above all, away from having to listen to people *talking*—to be away from so much sheer *noise*.

"But what about your new studio in Spéracèdes?" Saul asked. "You've been dreaming about it—planning it—forever. I can't imagine you abandoning it."

"Abandon it?" Jerry said, and he put an arm around Katherine. "Never! Although we've been inspired by our inspiring young couple, Katherine and I have decided not to marry, and have also decided—and please don't try to talk us out of it—not to have children."

"What a shame," Felicia said.

"We'll do our own variation of the Sartre-de Beauvoir *shtick*, but without benefit of marriage," Jerry said. "We'll be a loving couple, devoted to one another till death do us part, but we'll spend a good portion of our days, and some nights too, in our separate residences."

250

"The notion that Sartre and de Beauvoir had some kind of ideal marriage—that they made their marriage work by their famous *arrangement*—is nonsense," Tolle said. "The reason they lived apart was because they couldn't stand one another, and also because living together all the time would have compromised their ability to carry on their multiple affairs."

"Ah," Jerry said. "But the fact that the arrangement allowed them to *stay* married on a long-term basis is proof that it was, if not an ideal marriage, clearly an ideal *form* of marriage."

"The only *proofs* Camus believed in, he often said, were those he could touch," Saul said.

"Speaking of touch," Sam said, and he bent down, lifted Saul from his chair, gave him a bear hug, and kissed him on the mouth. "I love you, Dad, and sometimes I forget to show you how much I do."

"His *ribs*, Sam!" Felicia said. "Be careful—"

"What I was going to say," Saul said, "was that what Camus believed, paradoxically, was that plague also had its merits and advantages—that it could open people's eyes, make evil palpable, and draw on the best or worst in us."

"You agree with that?" Felicia said. "After all *you've* seen, especially since you were there at the beginning when nobody knew what the hell was happening—you still believe in sentimental drivel like that?"

"I do love you, Dad—" Sam said, and he kissed Saul on the mouth again, then helped ease him back into his chair "—even if you were never at home during those years for me and Julia—because what Felicia has made me understand is that you *couldn't* be at home."

"Shall we go inside?" Katherine said. "It's becoming cold—that happens here as soon as the sun goes down—and I need to bring in the cello. I can take it outdoors now and then, as on this splendid afternoon, but otherwise it will continue to reside mostly in the bathroom where it can breathe in the moist air necessary to its preservation."

Katherine walked toward the house arm in arm with Jerry, Jerry saying he would light a fire inside so they could continue to eat, drink, and solve more of the world's pressing problems. Tolle helped Saul up from his chair and, his hand in hers, walked with him toward the house. Felicia lifted the cello from its stand and carried it into the house while Sam went to Eugene, woke him up and, an arm around his shoulder, helped him walk across the veranda as if, Tolle thought, he were helping a wounded comrade from a battlefield.

Inside, Tolle sat at the foot of a handsome French country table, its dark, planked surface gleaming in the dim light. She found the darkness comforting, and found herself wishing for nothing other than sleep, silence, and solitude. Were Camus to join her, she told herself to remember to thank him for having given her the information about Sartre and de Beauvoir, although it was hardly news now the way it had been once upon a time.

Camus would have loved Katherine's new home, she thought, in the way he had loved the house in Lourmarin—for its rustic beauty, its openness, its simple combinations of wood and stone. Originally a farmhouse like Camus' home, Katherine's house had been built in the early eighteenth century, she had explained. Overhead, there were magnificent beams of chestnut *and* oak and, between the dining room and master bedroom, a closet that, to everyone's surprise when Katherine opened it, contained a small waterfall. Katherine said that a stream, diverted into the house and through this closet had, with its soft, constant rushing sound, been the telling detail in her decision to purchase, along with the fact that the house was already, as they could see, quite handsomely furnished. The owners, who lived in Paris most of the year, had been renting it out during the summer, mostly to Germans, and had themselves only lived in it during the colder winter months.

Tolle joined Katherine and Felicia in the kitchen where, on a large island, Katherine was setting out utensils, platters, bowls, plates, and food. Katherine had already prepared the basics for a traditional Provençale meal, she said: hard-boiled eggs, fish (boiled cod, baby octopus, crab, and shrimp), and vegetables (boiled potatoes, carrots, onions, fennel, beans). She asked Felicia to make the *aioli*—to break up two heads of garlic, to chop up the garlic cloves, add eggs to make a paste, and then to slowly add olive oil until the texture was that of a thick mayonnaise. She asked Tolle to arrange the fish and vegetables on separate platters, and she would set the table, put out the bread and wine, and see that the men did not feel neglected.

"On another day you might want to walk some of the nearby trails with me. They're like drovers' roads in rural England that, as here, were once used to transport livestock." Katherine laughed. "I sometimes think part of the reason I love walking the trails is so that I can, as I just did, *say* the word 'droveway...'"

"This is a dream come true for you, isn't it," Felicia said.

"And quite a *strange* dream at that," Katherine said, "since I've never been one to dream about the future, and certainly not about *my* future, and also because it's come true at a moment in my life, and at an age when, even *were* one a dreamer, possibilities for significant change would seem to have narrowed appreciably."

"I'm like you," Felicia said. "I never had dreams the way other girls did—to marry this guy, or live in this place or that place, and have two-point-three children."

"But what of your work?" Katherine said. "You seem a most knowledgeable and dedicated physician, and in a medical specialty hardly known for its happy endings."

"It's just work," Felicia said. "Good work for sure, but it's just what I do every day. I never *dreamt* of becoming a doctor. I decided to become a doctor because I thought it would be *useful* work—because, like Sam, I was raised to believe that whatever I did in the world nine-to-five Monday-to-Friday should be something that *made-a-difference.*"

"And it seems you have," Katherine said.

Felicia shrugged. "I *liked* science, and was good at it," she said, "so I guess just slid into being a doctor the way you slide into a comfortable old sweater."

"*Comfortable*?" Katherine said. "Surely working with people who, for the most part, suffer and die in godawful ways is the *least* comfortable of professions—"

"Unlike Saul, I don't work with them, or hold their hands in their dying," Felicia said. "I work in a lab, though I don't work there *because* I don't want to work with patients. It just happened that I found research more interesting and challenging—less boring—than seeing patients one after the other all day, and dealing with hospital bureaucracies. And I was good at it—better than I would probably be at what Sam's father has spent his life doing."

"And Sam?" Katherine said. "Surely, given the obvious—your exceptional beauty and other attributes—you've had many suitors to choose from, so that I'm curious—in what way did Sam, in the old-fashioned sense of things, win your heart?"

"Sam's a hoot!" Felicia said. "No offense, Tolle, I *adore* your son, but as I said, I didn't grow up dreaming about falling in love with Prince Charming, or what kind of honeymoon we'd have, and the rest of the *Modern Bride* nonsense. Perhaps it was because I was always so much *bigger* than everyone else, including most guys, who were usually into anorexic models like Veruschka and Twiggy, and maybe it was because—my parents' wherewithal being the key player here—I never wanted for anything. Whatever I wanted, I could have—the best schools, the best tutors, the best clothes, the best vacations—so that there was no hunger-in-the-belly the way there is for guys like Saul and Jerry, and probably—I'm guessing—there was for you and Tolle when you were young women."

Katherine dipped a finger into the *aioli*, licked her finger. "More oil, I think, and some salt and pepper."

Felicia turned to Tolle. "Did *you* have dreams when you were young—before you met Saul?" she asked. "I know you were a dancer. Sam told me that if not for a horseback-riding accident, you probably would have been a great ballerina."

"I had dreams, yes," Tolle said. "Not when I was *very* young—not, that is, when I was still living at home..."

"Because—?"

"Because I sensed that any dream I did have, and let my parents know about, would have been taken away: aggrandized, sabotaged, destroyed."

Tolle waited for either Katherine or Felicia to respond, but when, after a few seconds, neither of them spoke, and in order to put *them* at ease, she spoke again: "I've never talked much with Sam or Julia about my parents—their grandparents—because they were gone by the time Sam and Julia came into the world."

"How sad for them—" Felicia said "—and for you."

"Not really, but I suppose you had to know them to understand why I say that," Tolle said. "The short of a long story is that once I left home, I never had much to do with them, and by the time Sam and Julia came along—actually by the time I met Saul—my parents and I had stopped speaking with one another. It was a loss—of course—but in many ways, no loss at all."

"Do you think, now that Julia's going to have a child, and Sam and I, *after* we're married, will be having children too—at least we hope to— that you'll want to talk about this part of your life with us?" Felicia asked.

"Perhaps," Tolle said.

"*Perhaps*?" Felicia said.

"If it's important to you, of course we'll talk," Tolle said.

"We know how difficult—and whacky—all seemingly happy families are—how *alike*, right?" Felicia said. "And I'm not looking for a stroll down Nostalgia Lane where you remember all these warm, cute, cozy times together, and where—"

"My own belief is that nostalgia is often a veil for rage—" Katherine said "—a way people have of repressing the anger and frustration they felt when they were young and replacing their *angst* and confusion with scenes in which all the blood and gore, so to speak—all the nastiness— have been excised out."

"Still," Felicia said, "Sam and I think family is terribly important—"

"Emphasis on 'terribly'?" Katherine asked.

"Sam and I think it's imperative, especially for young couples like us, to understand where we've come from—" Felicia said "—to know something of our particular family history and how *who-we-are* has something to do with who our parents were and where *they* came from. Far too many of our friends seem to believe that the world—history itself—began a decade or so ago."

"Wise words," Katherine said. "But I'm not surprised to hear them coming from you, given how mature you are for a woman of your age.

You put me in mind of women in novels by Evelyn Waugh—do you know his work?—by your assurance, your manners, your indifference to the opinions of others, and by—how best to put it?—"

"—by my wealth?" Felicia said.

"Yes," Katherine said. "And here you underline my point for me— by your seeming lack of embarrassment about *all* matters, whether material or immaterial. But I *am* quite curious about what we were talking about a minute or two ago. Weren't you ever bothered that you *didn't* have dreams or at least daydreams, about boys, or about having young men show an interest in you?"

"Not really," Felicia said. "At least not as far as *I* know, although things did change after college when med students and doctors of *both* sexes showed interest, and that was okay too. I had a few relationships, and I enjoyed them more or less, depending on the usual variables, but I don't remember ever hoping a relationship would blossom into something else, and I don't recall being bothered by the *absence* of such a feeling. But then..."

"But then?" Katherine said.

"But then I met Sam," Felicia said, and she dipped a finger in the *aioli*. "Mmm—yum. I think it's ready, nice and sharp."

"*Aioli* is best when it's so sharp and hot it makes you sweat," Katherine said.

"Are we ready then?" Tolle asked, and she gestured to the platter of vegetables she had been arranging.

"Handsomely done," Katherine said. "I'll go in and finish setting the table, and see if our men are still awake." Katherine put two small bowls on the island. "But here, Felicia—divide the *aioli* into two bowls, would you, please?—one for each end of the table."

Katherine left, and Felicia began spooning the *aioli* from the large bowl in which she had been preparing it into the bowls Katherine had set on the island.

"This has been a real blast, hanging out with you and Katherine," Felicia said.

"For me too," Tolle said.

"But what I'm hoping," Felicia said, "and I trust you won't think me being invasive or disrespectful, but what I found most intriguing was what you said about your childhood, and how you had to hide yourself and go underground with your feelings—your dreams—in order to protect them. Truly, I can't imagine what that would be like, though I guess I can sense elements of it from having had a childhood that was opposite to yours in many ways."

"You were a lucky girl," Tolle said.

"Oh yes," Felicia said. "But as Sam likes to point out, the main thing about luck is to recognize it when it comes your way, and to be able to make a home for it."

"I agree with Katherine—" Tolle said "—that you're remarkably mature for your age—correct that: for *any* age."

"Let's not go *there* again, okay?" Felicia said. "Let's just say I showed great discernment in my choice of parents, but more important—more *intriguing*—is what *you* hinted at, and perhaps some day you'll be willing to talk with me about it—about why you felt that anything you valued could be taken away from you."

"Has Sam told you—this was long before he and Julia were born, and also before I met Saul—but did he tell you that I was sent away for a while when I was a young woman?"

"No."

"Of course not," Tolle said, "because—unless Saul told him—he wouldn't know, would he. But at the age of nineteen, I had what was then termed 'a nervous breakdown'—this was after the horseback-riding accident, and after another signal experience I won't rehearse now—a period when I was dangerously self-destructive. My parents put me in a private mental hospital, though they had all kinds of euphemisms for such places at the time, places where, in addition to sending those of us in need of psychiatric care, wealthy parents also sent daughters who were pregnant." Tolle laughed. "But what a combination! A garden of mad and pregnant young women walking across beautifully landscaped lawns, their aides and nurses trailing behind them…"

Katherine came back into the kitchen. "The men are awake and

257

eager for our company," she said. "If you bring in the *aioli*, Felicia, and you carry in the fish and seafood, Tolle, I'll bring in the rest. Jerry has lit the fire, and is attending to the wine."

"To be continued?" Felicia said to Tolle.

"Perhaps," Tolle said.

Without looking at either Tolle or Felicia, Katherine turned and left.

"Katherine could tell that we…" Tolle broke off. "Her manners are impeccable."

"*Impeccable*," Felicia said, pronouncing the word in French, "though I sense she can be quite ornery when she chooses."

"How lucky for Jerry, yes?" Tolle said.

"Yes indeed," Felicia said.

"'I was *not*, by the way, pregnant' is what I was about to say, although…" Tolle said.

"Although—?"

"My saying 'perhaps' is just a reflex that has to do with—well, with what I was alluding to before—with an old instinct, still here apparently, to hide whatever's precious to me."

"Although *what*?" Felicia said.

"Since Katherine will reappear at any moment," Tolle said, "for now let me answer by showing you the one place on my body where I agreed to reconstructive surgery."

Tolle held out her left arm, laid two fingers on a spot about five inches above her wrist.

"You cut yourself," Felicia said.

"But not *on* the wrists, which might have resulted in a successful attempt," Tolle said.

"Good surgeon," Felicia said. "Unless you pointed it out—and even when you do—I'm not sure I *see* anything."

"The surgeon did excellent work," Tolle said. "Neither of my children have ever noticed anything, nor have I ever asked them to look at what I'm showing you."

"I had friends who cut themselves," Felicia said. "This was in

258

boarding school—at Rosemary Hall—and though successful at calling attention to themselves, like you, they were unsuccessful at what they may have *thought* was their true intention."

"Saul knows, of course," Tolle said. "But neither Julia nor Sam do."

"They know what?" Felicia asked.

"Thank you," Tolle said. "And the answer is yes, that of course we'll continue our conversation."

"*Good!*" Felicia said. "And we'll have lots of time—lots of occasions, lots of years . . ."

"I know the last thing you expect or want from *me* is gratitude," Tolle said. "Nevertheless, I thank *you* because I see that I'm surprised, and surprisingly happy, to hear myself talking about something I haven't thought much about for years."

"Everything Sam has said about you, and more, is true, you know," Felicia said, and she gave Tolle's shoulder a firm squeeze, then picked up the bowls of *aioli* from the island. "You're a truly amazing woman and—the good news from my point of view—not at all an *uncomplicated* woman, and that's another reason I'm glad we're going to be family to one another."

Nineteen

When Saul awoke shortly after eight, opened the shutters, and walked out onto the balcony, Tolle was already in the garden, and she was talking with Dale. Dale, his arm in a sling, waved to Saul with his free hand.

"I come bearing news," Dale said.

Saul took the stairs down to the kitchen one step at a time since, his ribs still sore, any sudden movement could bring on spasms. Although the swelling around his eye had gone down, the promised peripheral vision was, thus far, proving non-existent and, his lips dry, he was afraid that if he opened his mouth too wide, the split, from which Felicia had removed stitches when they were in Saint Rémy, might tear open again.

He ran his tongue through the open space between his front teeth, and when he did, found himself recalling a retainer a dentist had made for Sam to preserve the space between two front teeth when Sam, three or four years old at the time, had fallen against the screen of a television set and knocked out one of his baby teeth. Given that his own teeth were not about to close in on one another quite yet, despite the receding gums that came with age, Saul figured he could forego a retainer. Tolle had suggested that, when he returned to New York after his trip to South Africa, he make an appointment with their dentist and arrange for an implant.

Saul preferred a bridge, he'd said, because he didn't want anyone drilling into his gums and bone. No matter what assurances dentists gave, he believed the possibility of infection—from the drill, the screw, bacteria, and the false tooth—was surely higher than they would publicly acknowledge.

In the kitchen, he took an empty mug from the drain rack and slowly, one hand against the wall, he descended the stairs. In the bathroom, he relieved himself, took several painkillers from the medicine chest, along with other pills—an ACE inhibitor and a beta-blocker that Doctor Chehade had prescribed to lower blood pressure to prevent arrhythmias, and guard against another heart attack.

An implant would also, given the number of visits required and the time needed for healing, take too long, and he had work to do. The prospect—the hope?—that he *would* find work to do, and lots of it, in South Africa—was what buoyed him and kept him going. He washed his hands and face, looked in the mirror above the sink, and imagined Fiona there, standing behind him. *Oh yes, my friend, we have work to do*, he could hear her saying, not when they had to put their clothes back on and return to the hospital, but when they would arrive in her apartment and would begin removing one another's clothes. *Oh yes—we have work to do, good work, life-affirming work....*

By this time, he knew, Fiona would be having more nausea, more bowel obstructions, more vomiting, more chills, more fevers, more mouth sores, and would be bleeding and bruising with increasing frequency. He looked in the mirror again, and cringed at the face he saw looking back at him: a one-eyed old man with a missing tooth, a scarred lip, a swollen eye. What woman would ever again be pleased to have him initiate a conversation? Mister Split-Lip indeed, he thought, and when he did, Fiona reappeared behind him, cocked her head to the side, and raised her eyebrows to show him she knew exactly what he was thinking.

HIV, like many men I've known, Fiona liked to say, was an especially *narcissistic* virus—in love with itself and with the image of itself it presented to the world, and also, allied characteristics from which

261

it derived its power, arrogant and predatory. Like all viruses, HIV was essentially a parasite; when it entered a body, it attached to CD4 lymphocytes—the white cells (and antibodies) that normally attacked and destroyed organisms they sensed as foreign. HIV never perceived *itself* as alien or unnatural, however, and once inside the lymphocytes, it would insert its own genetic material, after which it utilized the host cells to make copies of itself. This accomplished, it would break out of the host cells, enter the bloodstream, and set out on a search-and-destroy mission, invading other cells and creating billions of copies of itself, thereby inducing severe immune deficiency while simultaneously sapping the body's ability to stave off disease-causing pathogens.

For ovarian cancer, alas, nothing came close to being an equivalent of antiretroviral medications, so that the cells that were colonizing Fiona simply multiplied and took over, dividing, conquering, and spreading in a kind of biological *lebensraum*. And the treatments employed in futile attempts to do *them* in—surgery, chemo, radiation—were often as cruel as the disease itself.

Until now, he had been an excellent physician. Was it possible he also had the potential to become an exemplary patient? Were Fiona still in France, he might discuss this possibility with her. Or with Felicia. But Felicia too had returned to the States, and was spending weekends in Boston, with Julia and Fiona, and was also, Monday to Friday, back at work in her laboratory in New York, testing products, arranging for protocols, writing reports, creating initiatives.

And Sam? Sam was tagging along with Felicia, spelling her and Julia on weekends, staying in Boston all week long so that Julia could have some time off from caring for Fiona. Although he believed it went against nature to be envious of one's children—and thought of Felicia as one of his children—he knew he was envious of Sam for being able to spend his days with Fiona and Felicia, and of Felicia who, fortunate physician, dealt on a daily basis with what *might* work, and with what *might* make a difference. Her eye was on the test tube and the computer screen, and not on pustules, abscesses, and vaginal bleeding—not on dead mothers or dying children. Like other physicians and research scientists, Felicia lived in what he'd always thought of as a *cleaner* world, and one where there was a genuine possibility that chance occurrences—randomness, serendipity—could prove salutary. In her world there was always the possibility of the improbable breakthrough, which, when it arrived, could make exhaustion and tedium vanish.

In the early years of the AIDS epidemic, the good news for clinicians had often been that they had bad news, because bad news inspired their thirst for work, their dedication to their patients, their devotion to one another. Then too, bad news had been good news because, like HIV, it permeated *all* of life, and the only response, therefore—the only way to keep despair at bay—was to draw on one's rage, and to use the rage as fuel.

He dried his face on a towel, entered the garden. Were those buds he saw on the mimosa? Had Dale arrived to announce the coming of spring? Before Tolle could ask if he'd taken his medications, he opened his fist and showed her the pills, and when he did, he realized—this while she gave him a perfunctory good-morning kiss, asked if he'd slept well, if she could butter bread for him, and would he like it with jam—that it was proving a not unpleasant experience to have her be solicitous of his well-being, and the leisure in which to contemplate many things—his trip to South Africa, his son's wedding, his future grandchildren—and, not least of all, the infirmities of his body. He smiled inwardly, recalled lecturing residents about the alleged wisdom-of-the-body—the natural inclination and power of homeostasis, of the ways the body adapts to new situations and conditions in order to restore equilibrium.

Close to Dale, Saul saw what he had not seen from the balcony—that within the sling Dale's cast enclosed not only his arm, but his wrist and palm, and that two fingers were in surgical splints—and also that his face was badly bruised: deep purple periorbital hematomas around his left eye, a swollen nose, fresh bruises and cuts on his forehead and neck.

"You should see the other guy," Dale said.

"Why?"

"Because the other guy, as I've informed Tolle, is Gerhard."

Saul turned to Tolle. "Coffee ready?" he asked.

"Are you surprised?" Dale asked.

"Not really," Saul said.

"No?" Dale laughed. "Well, as with Ethan, when you gave *him* false assurances, I believe you're dissembling."

"Believe what you will," Saul said.

"It's all right to be *wrong* sometimes, Doctor Davidoff," Dale said. "Why must you doctors think you have to be *right* all the time?"

Why don't you just shut your ass and give your mouth a chance, Saul wanted to say.

"Why don't you tell me why you're here," he said instead. He gestured to Dale's arm. "Clearly you've already seen a doctor, so I doubt you've come in search of medical advice this time."

"You're right about that, because what I'm here for this time is for... for..."

"... is for friendship," Tolle said. She poured coffee into Saul's mug. "Dale is here because he's in need of our friendship."

"You were out earlier than usual this morning," Saul said to Tolle.

"Yes. I enjoy going into the village by myself in the mornings—" Tolle said, speaking in French "—when the shopkeepers are setting out their wares, the women gossiping, the children heading for school— when it seems, despite all, that the world *is* beginning again. The bread and croissants were still warm—I ate half a baguette on the way home."

Saul sat down across from Dale.

"I've been a good boy while you were gone," Dale said, "and I'm pleased to inform you that my T-cell count has been rising steadily. Gerhard, however, is quite ill. Appearances to the contrary notwithstanding, it's Gerhard who's been most in need of treatment."

"And what do you expect of me?" Saul asked.

"I *expect* nothing," Dale said. "So if I'm intruding—you've certainly had your share of troubles recently—I'll be on my way."

"On your way where?" Saul asked.

"Be kind," Tolle said, then turned to Dale. "With all that's been happening, Saul has not quite been himself of late."

"Then who have I been?" Saul asked.

"Gerhard has become dangerously violent," Tolle said, and she began going back and forth, mid-sentence, from English to French, French to English, and Saul sighed inwardly. Was he in for another siege of *her* mood-swings, where she went from elation to depression and back again, often without any seeming transition and, worse still, often without any awareness she was doing so. "He has apparently been going on some kind of wild spree, and—"

"'Wild' is putting it mildly," Dale said. "Gerhard has been getting into nasty brawls, tomcatting around, fucking anything that moves, frankly, and—"

"If I remember correctly, Gerhard has AIDS." Saul said.

"In full bloom," Dale said. "His T-cell count is below one hundred, and continues to descend more swiftly than the proverbial fall of a sparrow."

"And since he is, according to what you've told me, doubtless infecting others—"

"—even as we speak," Dale said.

"—perhaps we can see that he's arrested for attempted murder," Saul said. "Or stopped in some other way."

"What would you suggest?"

"I wouldn't," Saul said, "and I wouldn't because my dealings with the French police do not inspire trust, because he is not my patient, and because of the obvious—that his behavior is reprehensible, and nothing outrages me more—pisses me off—than people who *willfully* spread disease."

"My, my, but we're quite edgy today—moralistic too," Dale said. "Given what you've seen, I can certainly understand where you're coming from. Still—"

"I don't need your understanding," Saul said. "What I need is for you to leave. When you showed up here unannounced, I made a suggestion that led you to avail yourself of appropriate medical treatment. My wife has spoken of your need for friendship—but please explain why I would ever want to be friends with a man who has already, as with Ethan, knowingly exploited others, and who, in a less grave moment, has threatened my life."

"*Soit gentil,*" Tolle said, and she stroked Saul's arm. "Please, Saul. *Soit sage.* You upset me terribly when you become *faché* like this, *quand tu deviens totalement fou—*"

"I *was* a bit mad, I admit, and I've apologized for my behavior," Dale said. "And I was mad not just at you, but mad as in *deranged,* which, regrettably, happens now and again. I *am* trying to learn to control myself. In fact, at Tolle's suggestion, I've entered into psychotherapy with a charming woman I met at the English Library in Nice, and we're working, with mixed success, to get me to learn to curb some of my more antic impulses."

"Dale has been telling me about Gerhard," Tolle said. "About what he was like when they first met. I was astonished."

"As I was," Dale said. "I met him at one of the baths in Cap d'Antibes, and we adjourned to a bar, where we talked for hours—about Scott's *Raj* novels, about Klimt and Schiele, Bach and Mahler, Louise Bourgeois, and E. M. Forster—his favorite author, by the way, and this before any of us knew about *Maurice.* Still in mourning for Ethan, how could I *not* have wanted to be charmed—to be released from my grief? But then…"

"Then he saw the way Gerhard was living," Tolle said.

Saul looked at Tolle and found himself wanting to ask her if it were really true that they had fallen in love with one another once upon a time—that they had married, and had brought children into the world—and in order to calm himself, he did what he'd often done: he conjured up images of what Tolle had looked like on the afternoon they met. But now, it seemed, she planned to renew the life she'd had *before* they'd met—to create a dance company again, and it occurred to him that the dance company would be populated by beautiful young dancers, and that he would surely get to meet some of them. He doubted that any of them would be as beautiful as Tolle had been, or that any of them could make him feel what he had felt once upon a time. Still…

"Though he did not invite me to his home at first," Dale was saying. "It took several weeks, and many drinks, along with additional

266

transformative supplements, before I saw where he lived. When I did—when he let me visit him in his decidedly *un*-natural habitat for the first time—I thought I'd stumbled into the worst slum in Calcutta."

"Have you been to Calcutta?" Saul asked.

"No. But—"

"Calme-toi, mon mari," Tolle said. "Please."

Son mari? How interesting, Saul thought. Was it true that he was her husband, and that they were together today but that while everyone else in their intimate circle of friends seemed to be pairing off—Jerry and Katherine, Sam and Felicia, Fiona and Julia—they would soon be going their separate ways? He imagined telling Jerry the news. 'Yes,' he would say, 'my wife left me today. Or perhaps it was yesterday. I can't be sure…'

"This happened *after* he declared his love for me," Dale was saying. "I knew he hadn't been in love with anyone for some time—he claimed that after the one true love of his life died of AIDS, the only relationships he was interested in were of the sybaritic variety, and that if I had similar priorities, we could proceed. Things changed, of course, and I won't bore you with the how, why, and where, but once he confessed that he loved me, he disappeared. I sought him out, and discovered that he lived in what was little more than a mud hut disguised as a one-room apartment. How he managed to arrive at the hospital looking the way he did—handsome, clean, sparkling—is one of the great mysteries of life. He had surrounded himself with walls of canned food, mostly fish, that were stacked ceiling-high—tuna, herring, sardines, beans—alongside sprawls of books, dirty clothing, magazines, newspapers, neo-antique trash. The aroma was formidable. When I lay down beside him my first time there, he was mortified … and seriously enraged. Why hadn't I let him alone? he pleaded—along with other protestations. He was seriously ill—his T-cell count was approximately what it is now—and I … well … "

"You rescued him," Saul suggested.

"I'm not sure that's the word I would employ," Dale said. "But he did come around gradually, and with my encouragement he went on a regimen that enabled him to become the man *you* met. But now he's back to where he was, *status quo ante*, and—"

"—and even your love isn't enough to save him this time."

"That's my fear," Dale said.

"Well, life's rough," Saul said. "Even the chorus girls are kicking."

"*Stop it!*" Tolle said. "Just stop it with the ridiculous old Brooklyn nonsense you and Jerry wallow in. Enough, Saul. Enough."

"*Genug?*" Saul said, and he imagined Jerry, on the balcony above them, applauding.

"Doctor Davidoff *is* correct in that self-pity will get us nowhere," Dale said. "Gerhard *liked* chorus girls, actually—loved to go to the music hall when he was in London. His mother and father were old troupers, you see, and it surprised me, given how cruel they were to him when he was a boy, that he retained affection for a world that had been the stage for their cruelty."

My ass bleeds for you, Saul thought of saying, but saw that Tolle was glaring at him—daring him to come up with another of his Brooklyn schoolyard sayings.

"The facts are rather pedestrian," Dale said. "The father drank and beat him—beat the mother too, along with Gerhard's two younger siblings—and doubtless did other things I won't bring up this morning, though it appears I just did, didn't I?—and as you well know, if we've been abused when young, we often take pleasure in abusing others when we grow up, which induces yet more guilt and more pain and, of course—the ultimate aphrodisiac—more desire to do harm to others, especially those close to us."

"Once more then," Saul said. "I'm asking that you leave, and that you not visit me again. Try another physician—try the police, try the CIA, try the American consulate—but do not visit me here. This is my home, not my office, and in this home my wife and I are enjoying a much needed vacation."

"Needed and *earned*," Dale said, and rose from his chair.

Tolle put a hand on Dale's good arm. "Please stay," she said.

Saul started to stand, but the quickness of the movement produced a jolt of pain across his ribcage, and he sat back down.

268

"I asked him to leave," he said.

"Well I asked him to stay."

"Your wife lives here too, it seems," Dale said, and when he did, Saul felt rage—pure bile—rise inside him, and with it a wave of nausea. He closed his eyes and pictured Fiona again. They were nearing Aix-en-Provence, and he had stopped the car, and she was bent over, leaning against the car's front fender, and vomiting. He wished he could tell Fiona not that everything would be all right—she would call him a fool if he did that—but that he was ready to grant her wish to be with her to the end—that they could spend their time reminiscing about all they'd done together, and go on to tell each other things they had never told each other—tales from childhood, pleasant and unpleasant, along with things that, perhaps, and for good reason, she would not, where she was now, want Julia to know…

"I consider Dale a friend," Tolle said.

Saul recalled watching Doctor Coursaget's gloved hand reach into Fiona's belly, and pictured the doctor coming away with a coil of snake-like intestine that he tossed aside, after which Saul imagined a venomous snake-like coil unfurling inside him. Tolle was repeating what she had said about considering Dale a friend, and she was smiling in a way that made Saul think, once again, of how ridiculous it was that a woman her age could still be so strikingly beautiful and desirable. *Had she no shame?* He had a desire to return her smile with his own gap-tooth grin, after which he saw himself picking up a hammer and smashing her smile with it—shattering her perfectly aligned teeth—and were Dale to protest and cry out in horror, to begin hammering at *his* teeth. And wasn't loneliness, he recalled Camus writing, like a hammer blow that could shatter glass yet harden steel…?

He gave Dale his best professional smile. "But today's your lucky day because I'm off duty," he said.

"I don't understand," Dale said. "What does duty have to do with anything? You're *off* duty? But when and where were you *on* duty? And if you *were* on duty, what difference would it make?"

Tolle had an arm around Dale's shoulder, and was whispering

to him in French. Saul had always, from their first time in France, been proud to listen to Tolle speak in French—her French, and her Parisian French accent, were virtually perfect, and she would often, by the French, be taken for one of their own, which was a rare event for any foreigner, but especially so for an American. He sipped the last of his coffee, and thought of the first time he and Tolle had made love in France—in the hotel room above Le Petit Prince—and of how exciting it had been to listen to her purr to him in French, to say how remarkable it was that they were finally where they had hoped to be, and only a mile or so from the house where Camus, while recovering from a siege of tuberculosis, had lived for a year.

In his mind he gestured to Fiona in a way that let her know he was not going to blow his cool, and that she shouldn't worry about him. He would be going to South Africa soon, where he would be able to continue the kind of good work they'd done. And where she was going—and he was not wishing her an early departure, not unless the pain became exquisitely unbearable—he hoped she would remember to give his warm regards to Charlie Teitlebaum, whose swift, unforeseen end she might, with justice, be envying these days. He wondered how Charlie's widow and children were doing, and what the tally of dead in Iraq, soldiers as well as civilians, was of late. One benefit of being ill—of being out-of-it—and he assumed it was the same for Fiona, was to have stopped following the news on a regular basis unless, in Fiona's case, Julia, Felicia, and Sam had been keeping the television or radio on while Fiona, on increasing doses of drugs, moved in and out of consciousness.

"Farewell," he said to Dale, but without moving to shake the man's hand.

Bracing himself against the arms of his chair, he stood, and kissed Tolle once on each cheek. "*À très bientôt, ma reine—*" he said "*—à toute à l'heure, j'espère.*"

Then, as if fit enough to run a marathon or play a game of full-court basketball, he walked toward the house.

The doors to the balcony were open, and Saul could see past the iron railing to the valley, the hills, the coast, and the sea, but not to the garden below. Behind him, he heard Tolle enter the bedroom. He breathed in, not deeply enough to bring on spasms, but sufficient, he hoped, to help him calm down so that he would not show Tolle just how enraged he was, for if he did she would use that against him as she often had, and would make their argument turn not to the issues between them, but to whether he was or was not angry, and to where, in him, the anger—the repressed demons of his childhood, she was sure to say—came from.

"Whatever in the world possessed you to treat him like that?" Tolle said. "Talk about reprehensible! I am *furious* with you, Saul. Absolutely livid."

"Whatever possessed *you*?" Saul replied, "I asked him to leave, and you—"

"I *what*—?" Tolle asked. "I *disagreed* with you? Perhaps you didn't hear what Dale said, which is that this is *my* home too."

"Actually, it's not your home or my home," Saul said. "It's a vacation rental."

"Snide. When you're attacked, you become snide. A weak defense."

"Just trying to keep things clear. Wishes to the contrary notwithstanding, as your friend might put it, our *home* is in New York, not Spéracèdes."

"Look," she said, and she was speaking only in English now, and he was not sure what to make of that. Did it mean she would revert to her intense, super-rational self, or would the presence of her super-rational self itself be a sign that her incipient madness—always there, just below the surface—was ready to show itself forth and pour its wrath down upon him. "Are you going to stand there and stare out into the great void, or are you going to face me so we can talk about this like adults?"

"Blow it out your ass," Saul heard himself say.

"Brooklyn rises," Tolle said. "When in doubt—when in trouble —retreat to your old Brooklyn crap. Thank you but no thank you. I have been here before, and do you know what?"

"I'm sure you're about to tell me."

"Damned right."

"Damned *fucking* right is what you wanted to say."

"I have been here before and I think the kindest thing I can say is that you bore me," Tolle said. "We had a man visit us because he's going through hell and counted on some kindness—on some ordinary human kindness. The man he loves is about to die—"

"—while himself spreading disease and death."

"—the man he loves is about to die, has been putting himself in harm's way, betraying Dale with others perhaps—"

"*Perhaps?*"

"I would think a clinician as experienced as you might allow for hyperbole in a moment like this, for Dale is obviously feeling something else—something you just might recognize from your own life: *helplessness*—helpless to help someone he loves, helpless to help someone he wants to save. A modicum of empathy would be welcome. But empathy, alas, is clearly not your strong suit of late."

"Do you really believe he might have been exaggerating?" Saul asked.

"Weren't you the one who told me that his ability to distinguish lies from truth—illusion from reality—was unreliable?"

"'Fucked-up' would be the proper clinical term, I think. 'Pathological liar' would work too, though I must say that Dale was always incredibly convincing, even had me fooled for a long time. That's why, with his story about Gerhard, who knows how much was cock-and-bull, and how much real." Saul turned away from the balcony railing and, on instinct—a game-winning move, he told himself—he put his hands on Tolle's shoulders, kissed her forehead. "In any event, I *am* sorry," he said.

Tolle pushed him away. "You've become a smug son of a bitch too," she said. "In addition to which—worst of all—something I did not, in truth, expect because it goes against everything about you I've respected and admired—you've become *mean*."

"*Mean?*" Saul said. "I beg to differ, but I know you when you get this way, and I won't defend myself against inane accusations. More to the point, however, what did you *expect* when you turned against me—when I asked him to leave and you sided with him?"

"What are we—the Stalinists of American Marriage? You make a home in my pocket and I'll nest in yours?"

"It's just that I was under the illusion that husbands and wives are encouraged not to air their soiled laundry in front of others," Saul said. "Isn't that what they teach in Family Therapy 101—that couples should work out their differences privately? What was I supposed to do—fight with you in front of him?"

"Hmm—there *are* always choices, aren't there," Tolle said. "But let me ask *you* a question: Just what kind of banal united-front-couples-craziness do you think I subscribe to? And here's another one: Do you actually believe you know me? We've been married—what is it now, thirty-nine years?—and have raised two children together, and what I'm wondering about is if you actually believe that's given you the right to say you *know* me—to possess the *ability* to know me? Presumptuous, wouldn't you say?"

"Talk about snide," Saul said, then raised both hands in a gesture of surrender. "But I give, okay? You're much too word-clever for me, and the stuff about Gerhard spreading AIDS—combined with Dale's typical snotty tone—plus memories of Ethan, and of Fiona's swift decline—it all just got to me."

"You *embarrassed* me, Saul. He was our guest—*my* guest—and Gerhard had beaten him savagely, and he was hurting, and all you could do was…" Tolle stopped, waved a hand at him. "I need a cigarette," she said. "How's that? For the first time in centuries, I need a cigarette. Do you have one to spare?"

"I don't smoke."

"Bullshit."

"What do you mean—'bullshit?'"

"Oh come on, Saul—we're too old for this nonsense—things you do that you think I don't know about, things *I* do that I tell myself you don't care about."

"Like what?"

"Just forget it, all right? It's not what this is about. We're talking about *Dale*—about the way you treated him."

"What about how he treated me—a man who happens to be your husband, remember? What about the way he treated Ethan? What about all the other Dales out there—rich, privileged smart-asses who should know better but are—"

"Irresponsible?"

"That's one good word for it."

"Well, their behavior does keep you in business," Tolle said.

"Do you think I *want* people to get sick?" Saul said. "Do you think I wished the fucking AIDS epidemic into existence?"

"Of course not," Tolle said. "So don't bust a gut quite yet, all right? Especially in your fragile condition."

"*Fragile?*" Saul said. "Is that what this is about—that—"

"My goodness—have I pierced the man's vanity?" Tolle said. "You *are* fragile, Saul, but do you know what the good news is?"

"What?"

"*I'm* not."

True enough, he thought. Nor were the other women in his life of late—Katherine, Fiona, Julia, Felicia. They may have been old, ill, pregnant, or love-sick, but they were none of them fragile, and he found it reassuring—a gift—that, starting with Tolle, he had been surrounded during his recovery from his physical woes by beautiful, strong, and strong-willed women.

"That's good news, of course," he said, "though it does sound to me as if you're beginning to slip into one of those famous mood swings where you go up and down like a yo-yo—wild sex one day, lock-up the next—and where I'm supposed to be patient and make believe it's perfectly normal for you to talk about the wild adventures you and I are going on, or those you're going on by yourself—or about leaving you alone in your cave of gloom because if I don't you don't know *what* you'll do to yourself. And then..."

"And then what?"

"Forget it," Saul said. "I'm upset—Dale's visit stirred up a bunch of stuff—about him, Ethan, Fiona, and about Kings County and whether or not I'll be going back, or if they're going to find ways to jettison me definitively—and also, forgive my vanity, about my physical state and how it feels to be *me* now, and about how long it's going to take to be back where I want to be, or if I'm *ever* going back to where I can be useful to others again."

"Well I'm upset too," Tolle said, "and—perhaps, perhaps—just a tad out of line. It happens sometimes. But you *do* drive me crazy, Saul. You are a good and admirable person, I suppose—"

"You *suppose?*"

"—but also unbearably irritating. Remember when Fiona said you were the kindest person she's ever known?" Tolle said. "I agree, but what I've never been able to figure out is how somebody as kind—and smart—as you can be, can also be so incredibly stupid and insensitive at the same time."

"Thanks."

"But in these matters—a saving grace—you're also predictable," Tolle said. "For despite what a good, admirable, and kind man you've been—as doctor, father, and friend—you've also been predictable and boring."

"Aren't they the same thing?" Saul asked, but he felt himself wince, and not from his cracked ribs or swollen eye or split lip. He thought of replying, though not to her, that some of what she said had merit. He had done what had been expected of him, after all: he had become a doctor; he had married; he had brought children into the world and raised them. If not the most faithful of husbands—and he noted the omission of 'husband' in Tolle's list of what what made him good, admirable, and kind—he had fulfilled the primary responsibilities of a husband as he had of a father: to provide, and to protect. And when called upon to do for others—to be a physician in a time of plague—he had never abandoned or betrayed his responsibilities to patients and colleagues. Perhaps his problem—and Tolle's—was that he *had* taken the predictable road in life. Perhaps 'all the difference' in their life together did not come from the road *not* taken, but—and

275

here he thought of Camus, in the car with his editor and his editor's family—from the road taken.

In the context of their present conversation, however, he decided that an ironic way of putting things would be less than helpful. So he remained silent, and hoped she would not interpret his silence, as she often did when in the grip of her labile moods, as hostility.

"Let me put it another way," Tolle said. "Does a person have to be dying for you to be able to activate your sympathetic and empathic neurons? Do you have to be armed with a stethoscope in order to be human? How could you have *been* that way with him? I thought you guys from Brooklyn believed in fair play—in never kicking a guy when he's down?"

"Embarrassed *you*?" Saul said "How would you like it if you'd asked somebody who'd insulted you to leave our house, and I said—'Hey— don't listen to her. She's just my wife. I mean, we're legally married, and she was a good fuck once upon a time, but...'"

Saul watched Tolle study him, and when she tapped an index finger against her lower lip and, briefly, licked the finger, he suddenly found himself wanting to put an end to their argument by making love to her—slowly at first, but with increasing abandon: wildly, savagely, extravagantly—bringing her off again and again in the rolling orgasms she loved, and of choking her at the moment of orgasm to increase her pleasure, and even, afterwards, apologizing to her for the fantasies he'd had of doing violence to her. He imagined her resting her head against his chest, telling him how much she really *did* love him and, despite all the years together, his age, and his recently acquired infirmities, what a wonderful lover he still was—how strong, tender, and—as with his apology and the fantasies that had been their cause, how *un*-predictable....

"And do you know what else, as long as we're being so frank and open with each other?" she said.

"Tell me."

"You can go fuck yourself, because what I've decided is that you're never going to fuck me again."

276

"Hey—!" he said, and reached toward her. "Stop. Please stop it before—"

"Don't touch me. Don't ever touch me again," she said. "Because this is as good a time as any. Because—to repeat—what I've decided is that you're never going to fuck me again. Because why? Because I'm leaving you."

"What are you talking about?" Saul said. "Hey look. We're both upset—maybe it's the strain from all that's been going on—not just what happened to me, but with Julia, Fiona, Sam, Felicia, the murders, Dale and Gerhard..."

"You're forgetting our dear friends Katherine and Jerry and *their* new lives, which, you may recall, was a direct result of the death of Katherine's husband."

"Look," Saul said. "You've been great about taking care of me through all this, and I *am* sorry for what I said before."

"Don't be. It was refreshing to have you be real for a change."

"I know I can be a horse's ass sometimes," Saul said, "but it's been a blow—a series of blows—watching Fiona deteriorate, then being attacked, having to undergo surgery—"

"Surgeries. Plural, dear. Strive for accuracy."

"—being put on the disabled list, so to speak. Being compromised."

"*You've* been compromised?" Tolle laughed. "Of course. Now why didn't *I* think of that? Doctor Saul Davidoff has been compromised and will be on the disabled list for several weeks although he's expected to rejoin the team in time for the playoffs, and—"

"Stop it," Saul said. "*Please?* Let's calm down so we won't say anything else we'll regret. Let's have a drink—I know it's early—but let's have a drink. Or take a walk." Saul envisioned Katherine opening the closet that lay between the dining room and the master bedroom, saw words rushing from him, tumbling down the waterfall. "Remember the walks we used to take up to Cabris, or down to Peymeinade, or over to Saint Cézaire, or exploring the Roman ruins along the Siagne—picking wild asparagus and wild strawberries, collecting thyme and bay leaves, pulling rosemary branches from people's hedges? Remember

277

how we'd sniff one another's fingers afterwards—and the time we did it in the woods, in the hunter's preserve outside Cabris? Or perhaps we could go on an outing to some village we've never seen, rent a room in a hotel the way we used to and become lost in ways we loved to become lost—to become bathed in sweat and smells, or maybe it would be better to just go our separate ways, if that seems best to you—I do want to please you, to do what's best for us both—but perhaps a cooling off period of an an hour or two, or longer if you prefer, or..."

Saul stopped, wondered if the meds—the painkillers in particular—were the cause of his talking jag, and if, more important, what he said was *pleasing* Tolle. But if he were trying to please her, he wondered, why was he also so angry with her?

"You really don't get it, do you?" Tolle said. "Did you hear *anything* I said? And do spare us the stroll down memory lane. If you *truly* knew me, you'd know how little credence I put in nostalgia, which, as our friend Katherine so succinctly put it the other day is invariably a veil for rage. I recall an analyst I knew commenting on how bewildering it was to listen to people who had come to him because they were deeply troubled yet would spend endless, very costly minutes reminiscing about the alleged golden moments of their childhoods—whether their memories centered around your precious Brooklyn Dodgers, or grandma's chicken gumbo, or wonderful conflict-free family reunions, or..."

"I'm pouring my heart out, trying to get us back on track," Saul said, "and you're quoting second-hand wisdom dispensed by some second-rate shrink—not even your own guy who, to judge from the results, left some major work unfinished, and—"

Tolle laughed. "Well, that might well be true," she said, "and were he still with us, I might work with him on what you've just said, and what I felt *about* what you said, but do you know what?"

"Tell me."

"Whether he were or were not still alive, I would still be leaving you," Tolle said. "I've thought about it for years, of course, if on an irregular basis. Even before I married you, I thought about it, so how's *that* for intimations of late middle age recollected in early childhood?

But it's time. There's never a *good* time, after all. It's what he once said to me when, before *your* time, Saul, but in the period after I'd had my ballet performed in New York, I was involved for several months with a younger man. People often came to my therapist worried about the *right* way to break up with somebody. Was it all right to do it by phone? By letter? Did they owe it to the other person to do it face-to-face—to explain *why* they were doing it? And what my therapist said was that it didn't matter. All that mattered was to do it—to just *do* it—and that when you did, to try to be sure the break was clean and unambiguous, and that you didn't leave the door open even a crack. So I suppose—"

"Just do it," Saul said. "So it seems we were participating in what one might call *Nike*-inspired psychotherapy back then. How wonderfully *American*."

"—and I suppose what I'm doing this time is taking my own advice, so that *this* morning will serve as well as any other time or place. What was that saying you brought back from South Africa you loved so much, about planting a tree—?"

"That the best time to plant a tree was twenty years ago, but the second best time is now."

"I'll take second best then," Tolle said. "I'll stay here for a few more days to arrange what has to be arranged—to figure out how you can get around until you can drive again, make sure you have all your meds, get you a cell phone of your own. I'll talk with Jerry and he can probably provide services for most things a good wife would provide. In fact—and no offense to Katherine—I think you and Jerry would make a quite handsome couple."

"Now look here, Tolle—"

"Look *where*?" she said. "Look at you? Look at us? Look at Sam and Julia? Look at Fiona perhaps?"

"What does Fiona have to do with this?"

"Everything—" Tolle said "—and nothing."

"You're becoming too cryptic for me," Saul said.

"Oh Saul—come on, come on. I mean, how stupid do you think I am? How *blind*?"

"You have two eyes to my one—a distinct advantage. Two very pretty green eyes, in fact—green touched with hazel today. It must be the light, because…"

"For god's sake—do you think I care if you think my eyes are pretty? You *are* a ridiculous man, you know."

"A ridiculous man who still loves you," Saul said, "and who recently heard you say that you love him too."

"I do love you, Saul. I just don't want to *live* with you any more."

"But isn't that why we came back to Spéracèdes? I mean, sure—I know we've grown distant through the years, but—"

"Distant? Did you say distant?"

"—but I thought the reason we came back was so that, away from the usual pressures, in a place where we were once happy, we could become close again—we could *repair* things or, even better, *renew* things."

"We came back because *you* wanted to come back," Tolle said. "We came back because you wrote a letter. We came back because you leapt at the chance to get some time off, and you know what? You deserved it. You *earned* it. You were burnt out, Saul. How not? You'd been going nonstop, a hundred-plus hours a week, for years."

"But *you* thought it was a good idea to come back."

"Not really."

"*No?*"

"No."

"You did it because of me?"

"I did it *for* you."

"Because you loved me, right?"

"Because I loved you," Tolle said. "And because I thought it was worth a try."

"So let's try then."

"We already have, and—I don't mean to be unkind—but it's been *very* trying, and the truth is I'm getting out before I become as burnt-out as you."

Saul sat on the bed. "I don't know what to say," he said.

280

"Then don't say anything." Tolle walked past him, to the staircase. "Would you like more coffee?"

"Just like that? You tell me you're leaving me, but would I like more coffee?"

"What surprises me, really, is how quickly I got used to it," Tolle said.

"Used to what?"

"To you—to the way we lived our parallel lives—to your philandering, to your not being there, to your—well, to your not *being*."

"I'm sorry."

"For what?"

"I don't know."

"Thanks." Tolle said. "That was a good answer. 'I don't know.' More doctors should say that. More *men* should say it. And I guess I'm tired too, though not as tired as I may appear. But do you know what? I'm not disillusioned, or excessively cynical, and that's a surprise. Rather the opposite—especially when I'm writing, or thinking about writing, and even more these past few weeks when I've been thinking about stories I can turn into dance, and about a dance company that would perform the stories and give them life. It's been amazing, actually—please don't interrupt to tell me how happy you are for me, and how *supportive*—god, but I hate that word—but I *have* been happy to be back in Spéracèdes again, though the sad realization—what has spawned a few of the not-so-happy moods you've noticed—is that I'd have been just as happy—*more* happy, in truth—if I'd come here by myself."

"Because you found work you love?"

Tolle shrugged. "I suppose so. Yes. But…"

"It's like coming home, isn't it, when you find something you love—something you can't *not* do."

"But it wasn't the other women, I was going to say—not Fiona, or Katherine, or that young English thing who used to write your grant proposals, or—"

"Enough, okay? I get the point."

"Despite my alleged smarts, my list is doubtless incomplete, which is just as well. Because it wasn't the other women, you see—this may seem too fine a point—but more your need to have a secret life that, in the end, wasn't very secret. I think I could have accepted your being away from home so often, your being a workaholic, your not talking with me. Work—burying oneself in one's work—seems to be a mistress of choice for many men, yet—"

"Not talking with you? But I *always* talked with you—"

"Don't defend yourself. You *reported* to me, yes, but we stopped talking *with* each other—'communicating' is the operative term these days—a long time ago."

"Perhaps," Saul said. "I was tired. I was tired all the time. We always talked about the children, though, didn't we?"

Tolle did not reply.

"I *was* obsessed—I admit it—but that seemed a good thing," Saul said. "Still does—the way you're obsessed about your work now, the inspiration to return to the world of dance—and with the work set before *me*, obsession was a help—a compulsion too—and if I didn't do the work—"

"—somebody else would have done it, though not nearly as well as you did."

"Then *why*—?"

"Let me finish," Tolle said. "I loved you enough to endure all of that—and if it's any consolation—if knowing what I'm about to tell you might relieve some of your guilt, you should know that from the beginning—less than a year into our marriage, in fact, I wasn't idle either."

"Idle?"

"I began being with other men, including some of our friends and your colleagues, all of whom will remain nameless."

"You're kidding," Saul said. "Tell me you're kidding. You're making this up. I mean, you've become a fiction writer—a dreamer—and this is your way of getting a rise out of me—of getting even."

"That's guy-talk, Saul," Tolle said. "Why would I kid about a thing like this? I concluded long ago that you and I are probably not that different in these matters, though we're probably different in that I never loved anyone else—never needed the illusion that I *might* love someone else. Or perhaps my career in ballet companies along with my time in Paris made me more French about these things, made me think, as many French women do, that to make love with a man after dinner is simply like having a dessert that you could take or leave, depending often on the man's preference. So little pain for us—so much pleasure for them. Or—I don't recall the exact phrasing—but that love was like wine, and that the only way to appreciate a truly fine wine was to drink ordinary wines—wines that were *buvable*—on a regular basis. That way, when the exceptional wine came along, your palate, so to speak, would know the difference."

"The French have always—Jerry's famous dictum—been great at profound banalities."

"And banal profundities," Tolle said. "And there was always a connection between us—a physical connection certainly—call it chemistry, call it neurosis, call it whatever you choose. Who cares? It was your need to have secrets, though—to *sneak*—even with something as trivial as cigarettes—that wore me down and, frankly, pissed me off."

"But what about Camus?"

"Excuse me?"

"What about your affair with Albert Camus?"

Tolle sat down in the easy chair by the window. "Oh my," she said.

"You think I didn't know you had an affair with him, and how important it was to you. I wasn't a blind man back then, and. . . ."

"Oh my," Tolle said, softly. "Oh my."

"Oh my?"

"Of course you knew, and of course I knew you knew," Tolle said. "But that you can't, after all these years, let it lie—leave it *unsaid*..."

"But—"

Tolle put a finger to her lips. "Shh," she said. "Try to be quiet—to button that bruised lip of yours—try not to talk, all right? I'd be *very* grateful."

"I'm not your mother or father, you know," Saul said. "I haven't tried to take away anything and everything precious to you the way you used to tell me *they* would, and..."

"Please, Saul," she said. "I'm feeling much too sad for words right now, whether yours or mine. Can we please just sit here for a while, without talking, and without thinking—can we just *be* for a few minutes?"

"But—"

Tolle put a finger against her lips again. "Shh," she said, and closed her eyes. "Please. You've been a good and honorable man, but please, please be a good boy now and do what I ask without questioning it. Shh…"

There was a loud banging on the door below.

"But the way we've been talking now—letting it all hang out as the kids say these days, isn't *that* something?" Saul asked. "I mean, with all that's going on—my injuries, the ongoing AIDS pandemic, Fiona's death warrant, the war in Iraq plus the other wars, especially in Africa, that rarely make our headlines—not to mention the ongoing, deadly racism ever-present back home—with all that's going on, doesn't it make our troubles seem like an ordinary domestic squabble most couples who've been married as long as we have might have? Doesn't it put our problems in perspective? I mean, think of it, Tolle: how many couples can talk the way we're talking now? And what about our *history?* How can you just toss it all out the window? How can you act as if—"

The banging came again.

"I asked you for some quiet time," Tolle said, and then, again: "Oh my…"

"You're too cool for me," Saul said. "Too clear, too smooth, too clinical, and what I'm wondering is if, in that secret vault of yours you call a heart, there's *anything* about us you haven't already come to a conclusion about. Talk about distant."

Tolle stood. "You may be onto something," she said. "For longer than I was aware, I probably have been saving—husbanding?—a large portion of my passion—my feelings, my dreams—for my work, although I didn't always know I was doing so, or what that work might be. But the writing I've done so far, meager and flawed as it is, and now my plans for a dance company—the fancies about what I *might*, with some luck, create—when I think about such things, it's the only time—and here's an interesting notion—that I'm not in control. When my characters—my dancers—take off on their adventures and their flights, I'm lost." She went to the balcony, looked out across the valley, then turned back. "But I'm happy too. And what I think I'm happy about is that when I'm imagining others—and what *they* might be doing and imagining—I'm not being me."

Saul stood, then grabbed at his ribs, "Fuck!" he exclaimed. "I for-got—I got up too quickly."

He sat, pressed his eyes closed against the pain.

"Why don't *I* see who's at the door," Tolle said.

Saul looked up, expecting Tolle to reach down, to touch him, but she walked past him, to the door.

"But if you knew all these years," Saul said, "why didn't you say anything?"

"That's very funny," Tolle said. "'Why didn't I say anything.' Of course. You *are* funny sometimes, did you know that? Not in the way Jerry is, with his repertoire of set pieces, but funny nonetheless."

The banging came again, along with a man's voice. "*M'sieu-dame...? Allô...! Bonjour...! Monsieur Davidoff...? Madame...?*"

Tolle left. Saul stayed where he was, on the bed, motionless.

"It's the police—two young policemen," Tolle said when she returned. "They want to know if you've had any threats recently, and if you intend to press charges. They'd like to talk with you if you're available. They're very polite and proper—quite solicitous. What shall I tell them?"

Twenty

"How's Gerhard doing?"

"Better," Saul said. "His T-cell count's way up, as are his spirits. Dale's been extraordinary with him—patient, loving, and unbelievably kind. It's remarkable to see it when it happens."

"That love can be a force for good in the world?"

"Something like that," Saul said. "But who would have thought just a few years ago that people could be halfway through death's door and could be called back—rescued!—by these incredible pharamaceutical cocktails."

Jerry raised his glass of wine. "*Shehechayanu*—" he said "—that we've lived to see such a happy day."

Saul and Jerry sat side by side at an outdoor restaurant in Grasse—Les Arcades, in the Place Aux Aires—eating a late lunch. Earlier in the day—it was the second week of April—Saul had visited Dale and Gerhard in Cannes, after which he'd seen an opthalmologist in Grasse who had confirmed the diagnosis he expected: that he would never again have vision in his right eye.

"In South Africa," Saul said, "if we can get just one or two people in a village to take the antiretrovirals and stick with them, then when others see what's happening—their effectiveness—they'll begin to believe *they* can recover too."

286

"More easily than from a broken heart?"

"For sure."

"Speaking of which," Jerry said, "I meant to ask—have you been missing Tolle much?"

"No."

"Surprised?"

"Yes." Saul lifted an olive from his plate, popped it into his mouth. "It's amazing after so many years—the feeling of liberation—and not just because of the possibility of being with other women without all the old lies and guilt. Though actually, *that* need—for women, or more exactly, for the conquest *of* women—seems to have faded for the moment."

"For the moment?"

"Tolle and I are actually *communicating*—a buzzword she hates—talking about possible projects for me in Cape Town, about her ballet company, about wedding arrangements for Sam and Felicia, about Julia and the baby—"

"All well there?"

"Just fine," Saul said, and he looked toward the table where he had first seen Katherine. "But the same question back to you. Do you miss Katherine?"

"Terribly."

"Talk to me," Saul said.

"At first, I was enormously relieved," Jerry said. "Katherine can be *very* demanding, especially for an old geezer like me, but the last ten days or so I've been brooding, which goes against my religion, and I realized that during the few weeks we were together, I was a happy man. When I emerged from my studio, I'd find her playing the piano, and I'd plop down on the couch and lie there listening, and *doing nothing*—no small achievement for a Jewish Calvinist like me—and then, as if it were the most natural thing in the world, she'd come over to me, lean down, kiss me sweetly on the mouth, and…"

Saul saw the tears in Jerry's eyes. "Hey—no need," Saul said. "I was just curious."

"But it *is* curious—*vraiment curieux*—that I truly believed the two of us were going to ride off into the sunset together, especially since I'd never, through all the years of our on-again-off-again affair, cultivated long-term fantasies about us."

"*Never?*"

"Well hardly ever," Jerry said. "But to my surprise—more than I ever did with Michelle—I discovered that I loved our domestic life *à deux*—I loved knowing she'd be there when I was done painting, I loved going into the village together to do our *commissions*, I loved talking about what we were going to have for dinner, or about which trail to take on our afternoon walk. I'd even agreed to renew my passport. We were planning for a goddamned future, Saul—a *future!*—and ..." Jerry wiped at his eyes with the back of his hand. "But I'll be okay in a few years."

"I used to think that the loveliest thing about being in love," Saul said, "was that when you were in love you believed there *would* be a future."

"Ah, my dear and sentimental friend," Jerry said.

"That's me," Saul said, and—a way of reciprocating for Jerry's openness?—he thought of telling him about the conversation he'd had with Tolle at the airport in Nice, after Tolle's plane had begun boarding. Saul had wished her a safe journey, told her to give his love to everyone—Julia, Fiona, Felicia, Sam—and said he would keep her posted, would let her know how long he might be staying in South Africa, and when he planned to return to New York. Or perhaps, depending on how Julia and Fiona were doing, he might return to Spéracèdes briefly on his way to New York.

And surely, he'd added when Tolle did not respond, he would be back home in time for the birth of Julia's child—of their grandchild—and when he said this she had hugged him and kissed him on the mouth with great tenderness.

"I do still love you, you know," he'd said.

She had stepped back, shaken her head slightly from side to side, as if to say: *You don't understand anything that's been happening, do you?*

He considered objecting—saying to her unspoken words that he knew full well what was happening—but before he could find words, she spoke.

"The problem—" she said "—and I've been thinking about this for some time, and should probably have addressed it long before this, but better late than never, yes?"

"Sure," he'd said, and he was still, he recalled, holding her hand in his when he did.

"The problem," she said, "is that you've never had your heart broken."

He had thought she was kidding—that what she said was her playful way of telling him that their being apart for a while was, of course, merely temporary.

"And by abandoning me here in France," he said, "you're helping me solve my problem—is that what you're trying to say?"

"I'm not *trying* to say anything," she had said. Then she kissed him again, on the mouth—fast and hard—picked up her carry-on bag, turned, and walked toward the jetway that led to her plane.

"I can tell from your many questions about the future of *my* illusion," Jerry said, "that you're dying to hear chapter and verse as to how it all unraveled."

"Sorry," Saul said. "I was distracted. What you said about the future—about you and Katherine—put me in mind of something Tolle said."

"How not?" Jerry said. "I want to hear *everything*, Saul. But first, an abridged version of *my* fateful day. So. When we woke up together, I started in with my joke-of-the-day—this one about a retired couple, Abe and Becky, who go to a drug store in Florida where Abe asks the manager if the store carries certain items: bedpans, hearing aids, reading glasses, blood pressure monitors, diapers, Metamucil, Viagra, Gerotol—and when the manager says he carries all of them, Abe says, 'Good, because Becky and I are getting married, and we want to use your store for our wedding registry.'"

"Funny," Saul said.

"'*Not* funny,' is what Katherine said, and that I'd told her the same joke twice before, and that I was—get this—like fruit that's been lying around too long. Like my jokes, she said, I was probably too *mature* for her—a remark *she* found funny. Then she got out of bed. And what did I do to retaliate, an *alte kocker* like me?" Jerry laughed. "*I fell asleep*! And when I came into the dining room later on, she said she would be having lunch with a friend in Juan-les-Pins, and that when she returned she expected me to be gone. She handed me a folder in which I would find an accounting of items we'd purchased together, along with a check she trusted would be adequate reimbursement for my contributions to the household. 'Ah,' I said, 'so these must be my walking papers, yes?' to which she responded by—what else?—*walking*! I haven't seen her since."

"Her loss," Saul said, and he pictured Tolle disappearing in the jetway without turning back to wave goodby. He closed his eyes, caught the scent of garlic and butter, and found himself recalling a night, during their first week in Spéracèdes, when with Jerry, Michelle, and their two daughters, he and Tolle, sacks in hand, had hunted snails by flashlight. The snails were *huge*, some of them four to six inches long, and they were everywhere, crawling across roads and gardens, up and down terraces. And he remembered Tolle remarking on how agile Jerry was—how, even though he was old enough to be Saul's father, he looked and moved as if he were only a year or two older. When they were done hunting, they deposited their haul in a large wooden barrel, along with cornmeal and spices, and left the snails there for three days, after which, in Jerry and Michelle's kitchen, they had boiled the snails, blanched them with cold water, removed them from their shells, cut off the black pieces at the ends of their tails, sautéed them in garlic and butter, and, wine and talk flowing freely, had feasted on plate after plate of nothing but snails.

"To tell the truth, in the moment itself I was pleased to find I *could* walk away—without having to use a cane or a walker," Jerry said. "I came here—to Paris, not the *midi*—on a fashion shoot when I was twenty-five years old, you know. Imagine! Twenty-five years old, and in

Paris, with *shekels* tumbling out of my pockets, and women falling all over me, and the next thing you know it's sixty years later."

"But you look great…!" Saul began. "I mean, look at the shape *I'm* in, with…"

"You don't have to humor me, sonny boy," Jerry said. "I know the score, and the way I look at it, I've got maybe five percent of my life left—tops!—but you at a mere sixty-something, why you're still a spring chicken, and there's something else—another uplifting story I wanted to share. Beginnings and endings yes? Because the first time Katherine and I met, she was sitting at a table right over there, under the plane trees, where you were staring with your good eye only a few minutes ago. At the time, I was married to Michelle, and Katherine was married to Alex, and I sat down at her table, told her I recognized her—that Michelle and I had been to her concert in Cannes the night before, and what I found an incredibly refreshing aphrodisiac was how she would, to a complete stranger—*moi!*—say the most extraordinary things, and yet in the off-hand way she said them, she might have been talking about where she'd parked her car. And—what I've been getting to, and then we have to talk business, you and me—she asked if I agreed with her that the wonderful thing about making love as one aged—as with making music—was that depth of feeling gradually replaced virtuosity."

"Let's hope," Saul said, and he took out a pack of cigarettes, offered one to Jerry.

"Ah," Jerry said, taking a cigarette, letting Saul light it for him. "As the French like to say, 'A world without vice is like a woman without legs.'" He inhaled, blew a perfect smoke ring toward the sky. "And another wonderful thing about aging is that you don't have to worry about the future, since there's so little of it ahead."

An elderly woman—limping, hunch-backed—placed a card on their table that stated she was deaf, then began making signs with her fingers that Saul assumed were intended to represent letters of the alphabet.

"Get lost, you two-bit faker," Jerry said.

Saul reached for his wallet and when the woman came closer, Jerry suddenly clapped his hands—a loud *crack*!—next to the woman's right ear. Startled, the woman jerked her head back.

"See?" Jerry said, and he brushed the woman's card from the table.

"Hey—!" Saul said. "She's just earning a living the best way she knows how—"

The woman pursed her lips as if she were going to spit at Jerry, but before she could, Saul pressed two euro notes into her palm. Briefly, while Jerry glared at him, the woman fixed her eyes on Saul, not on the money, then limped off toward the next table.

Saul tapped on his wallet. "And for you," he said, "I'll trade your saying about a-woman-without-legs for a Jewish saying that was one of my father's favorites: 'Be kind, for everyone you meet is fighting a great battle.'"

"You're a disgrace to our tribe," Jerry said. "A guy who grew up where you did and is such an easy mark."

"Not really," Saul said. "I just…"

"Save it," Jerry said. "You *are* a good soul, Saul—Tolle often talked about that—how you could be dull as toast as a husband, but that you were a truly good man—*kind* was the word she often used to describe you—and that in her experience, that was a rare thing. Rare too, in my experience, is a wife, and I'm talking long-term, who not only cares about her husband but cares *for* him, which brings me to something else I wanted to share with you."

What Saul wanted was for Jerry to shut up. When Jerry got this way—angry, bitter, facetious, condescending and, worst of all, mean, as he'd been with the gypsy woman—Saul tried to resist the impulse to respond in kind, tried to come up with something that would get Jerry to stop, but without letting Jerry know he had unnerved him.

"So what I was thinking before," Saul said, "is that being here with you this afternoon—it's like we're two guys hanging out in a pizza joint or luncheonette in Brooklyn, shooting the shit about the usual—sports and girls—except that we happen to be in the south of France. Lucky us, wouldn't you say?"

"Lucky us," Jerry said. "But you can't fool this old fool by appealing to the illusory happiness of his youth. You're upset about stuff, Saul, as well you should be given all that's been happening, and what I was about to tell you is that a few days after Tolle lowered the boom on you, she stopped by my studio to talk—to commiserate with me about Katherine having lowered the boom on *me*, but also, and I wasn't surprised, to ask me to keep an eye on you. She's still very worried about you." Jerry paused, leaned back. "We were close, you know, me and Tolle. I valued her friendship greatly."

"Are we still set for tomorrow?" Saul asked, and he noticed as he tapped ash from his cigarette into the ashtray, that his hand trembled slightly. "We're playing for the stickball championship of the *midi*, correct?"

"Correct," Jerry said.

"Well, I intend to whip your ass," Saul said, "though it occurs to me that we don't *have to* play before I take off tomorrow. I may be back in a month or two—I'm not sure of my schedule yet—but if I am, we could play then. What's the rush?"

"The rush is I'm eighty-five years old and I want to play while I still have an edge—before your ribs are healed, or they fit you with some kind of bionic eye," Jerry said. "So here's the plan: I'll pick you up at noon. That way we can have our game, I can get you to the airport in plenty of time, and still be back in time to sign the papers for the deal on Madame Amione's property. That came through, by the way—did I tell you?"

"No."

"And a good thing it did, given my expulsion from Katherine's garden," Jerry said. "I know you raised those ethical eyebrows of yours about the *viager* stuff, but as we know, when it comes to that most important of life's trinities—love, death, and money—the French are the most practical people in the world, and unless Madame Amione has some secret way of cheating the angel of death, it's a good deal all around."

"And your daughters—are you still planning to give each of them one of the houses?"

"As soon as I can. Which will depend, of course, as much on Madame Amione's health, or lack of same, as on my decisions."

"But if they come to live here, where will *you* go—or will you live with one of them?" Saul asked. "What if...?"

"What if, what if," Jerry said. "As we used to say—if my aunt had balls we would have called her my uncle. But let me assure you, I do not intend to be a burden to my children, so I've worked something out—I've got plans, *mon vieux*—I've got plans out the wazoo. And also—" he tapped on the side of his head with an index finger "—what I just remembered is that I've picked out a painting for you as a farewell gift. Framed it too. I'll bring it with me when I pick you up tomorrow."

"But how will I carry it onto the plane?"

"It's small, will fit in your luggage, and is wrapped in protective bubble wrap. You're not the only experienced professional sitting at this table, you know."

"And what will I do with it once I'm there?" Saul asked. "I don't mean to sound ungrateful, but I'm renting an apartment in Cape Town from a medical student—he'll stay with his girlfriend—and he says it's quite small."

"What will you *do* with it?" Jerry smiled. "Why, you'll *worry* about what to do with it—you'll get, perhaps, more than slightly irritated with me, and so—the good news—you'll *think* of me, and you'll remember how, despite the ever-present competitive edge that lurks below the surface of our friendship, you'll remember how happy the two of us were while we were sitting here together on this delightful early spring afternoon."

Along with the painting he had promised him (gift-wrapped), and a broom handle (one end taped), a pink Spaldeen (a "hi-bouncer"), and chalk (for outlining bases), Jerry had also brought Saul three newspapers to take with him on the plane: *Nice-Matin, Le Monde,* and *The International Herald Tribune.*

"You'll be pleased to see—though 'pleased' is surely not the right word—*proud* perhaps?— that your fears about the war in Iraq seem to be coming true," Jerry said. "The so-called insurgency is making gains, there's still no legitimate or illegitimate government running the country, and our boys are dying on a regular basis, though in nothing near the numbers in which civilians are dying. According to *Le Monde*, more than twenty-five thousand killed in the first two years, and nearly fifty thousand wounded."

"Thanks for the good news," Saul said.

"Tens of thousands of demonstrators loyal to some Shiite *chasid* have marched through Baghdad to denounce our nation's occupation of *their* nation," Jerry said, "and on a note you can relate to personally, hospitals have become a favorite target of suicide bombers. Somewhere near a hundred-and-fifty Iraqis, including women and children, were killed by a suicide car bomb at a medical center in what they say is the single deadliest blast in Iraq's history. In addition to which—"

"Enough, okay?" Saul said.

"Well, given your optical impairment, and the difficulties you might have reading the small newspaper print—the *Tribune*'s coverage is disgracefully thin—I thought, as a man who rightly protested this insane war, and who, both as an emissary of our nation to the world, and as a citizen who will be returning to the States before long—I thought you'd want to be reasonably well informed."

"Go fuck yourself," Saul said, and then—to cover up the fact that Jerry had, once again, gotten to him: "You're just trying to distract me from our game—from an event that's *truly* newsworthy."

"Got me there," Jerry said, and he walked away and began chalking in their playing field by drawing a small, lopsided pentagon to serve as home plate, then chalking in a foot-and-a-half wide narrow rectangle for a pitcher's mound, and outlining twelve-inch squares for first, second, and third base.

In Grasse the previous afternoon, Jerry had suggested they play their game on the unpaved road in front of Saul's house, no matter—or, more to the point, *because of*—the attention their contest might attract. That way, he hoped, their game might become legend in the way a Black Mass Brendan Behan had once performed in the village square—Jerry had attended—had become legend. And he had announced the ground rules: any ball that went past the pitcher on the ground would be a single; a ball hit past the pitcher on a fly would be a double; a ball hit past the infield on a fly would be a triple; and a ball hit into the cemetery would be an automatic home run. Although they would be playing on Saul's home turf, in deference to his age, Jerry would pitch first and would, therefore, have last licks.

There would be no warm-ups, Jerry reminded him, and because there was no catcher, no overhead fast pitching. They would toss the ball in easily, on one bounce, and they would get three swings for each at-bat—a foul on the third swing would count as a strike—and if they chose not to swing, they would be responsible for catching the ball and returning it to the pitcher so that they wouldn't have to spend time chasing after balls that passed them by.

Jerry set a small portable tape player at the side of the road, and when he was done chalking in the bases and going over the ground rules—a crowd of boys and girls, along with a few old men, had gathered on both sides of the road—he turned on the tape player, which blasted out a static-laden brass band version of "The Star-Spangled Banner," after which Jerry cried out "Play Ball!" turned off the tape player, walked into the middle of the road—"Batter Up!" he called—and, taking his place on the pitcher's mound, tucked the ball under his armpit, spit on his hands, wiped his hands on his trousers, bent over, squinted toward home plate as if looking for a catcher's sign, and then, with a smooth underhand flip, tossed the ball toward Saul.

Saul was right-handed, so that when he stood sideways and to the left of home plate, facing Jerry and watching him toss the ball, he was looking at him with his good eye. The ball landed about fifteen feet away, rose in a high arc, then began its descent. The doctor in Grasse had been correct, Saul realized, for even though, with only one eye he had no true depth perception, he was able to gauge distance—to follow the ball's trajectory as if he were seeing it in three dimensions. The ball grew larger as it came toward him, and when it was several feet away, letter-high, Saul shifted his weight to his left foot, whipped the broomstick around, snapping his wrists quickly—this was where power was generated—and to his delight, heard a lovely, deep sound as wood connected with rubber and sent the ball soaring into the sky like a small pink rocket—rising and rising while all heads, including Jerry's, turned and followed its flight until it had passed well beyond the cemetery's stone wall.

For a moment everything was still, and then the children were running and screaming down the road toward the cemetery. Saul blinked, dropped the broomstick and, elated, trotted toward first base. When he had rounded all three bases and was heading toward home plate, he saw that Jerry was walking slowly to the side of the road.

Jerry bent down, turned on the tape player again, and this time a brass band poured out a lusty version of "La Marseillaise," which was followed immediately by "The Internationale."

"I was once a man of the left myself," Jerry said.

On the way to the airport, Jerry had said there was no rush since their game had been cut short by Saul's rude decision to show off, and also because he'd received a call the previous evening from his lawyer informing him that Madame Amione had had a last-minute change of heart, and had decided *not* to enter into an agreement with him about her home and property. When they arrived at the airport, however, Jerry had slapped a hand against his forehead—"*Schmuck!*" he exclaimed—and said that he trusted Saul would forgive him, but that he had to turn around and head for home for he suddenly remembered he'd forgotten to turn out the lights in his house.

"I need to turn out the lights," he had said, and added: "It's time." He reminded Saul of what he'd told him before—that he had a life-long obsession about making sure lights were turned out because all through his childhood, if he, or his father, or his older brother Stanley (long since gone, of pancreatic cancer), or his younger sister Norma (also gone, from breast cancer) left a light on, their mother would have one of her famed "conniption fits," screaming at them that she wasn't toiling away day-after-day and working her fingers to the bone in order to support Con Edison....

It was only when the pilot announced that they had just passed over the Mediterranean and would soon reach their cruising altitude of thirty-seven thousand feet, that Saul heard Jerry's voice again—'*I need to turn out the lights. It's time*'—and understood which lights Jerry had been referring to.

Thanks to Tolle, Saul now had a cell phone, but who could he call, and to what end? In the quintessential existential situation in which Jerry was now living—alone, his ties to others thinned to the point of non-existence; his relationship with Katherine having failed; his work having become, since his split with Katherine, tedious *and* frustrating; what audience he'd had for his work dead, dying, and disappearing; his body betraying and mocking him more and more each day; his deal with Madame Amione having fallen through and, thus, his attempt to do well by his children and grandchildren and to bring them close to him also failing; and now Saul abandoning him too—in this situation, no matter what anyone said *to* him or did *for* him, Jerry would still, Saul assumed, deflect all attempts at intervention, while acts of kindness in all likelihood would serve only to strengthen his desperate resolve, and result in his remaining steadfast in the belief that he was free to answer Camus' basic question whenever, wherever, and in whatever way he chose.

A flight attendant asked Saul if he would like a drink before dinner was served—red wine? white wine? champagne?—and he said he would appreciate a glass of red wine. The woman seated next to Saul said that she would have the same.

"You're an American physician, aren't you," the woman said.

"Yes," Saul said, and he extended his hand. "Saul Davidoff. But how—?"

"I recognized you from your newspaper photo," the woman said. "I hope you don't mind my mentioning it, but you *are* the man who was attacked during the demonstration in Spéracèdes, aren't you?"

"That's me," Saul said.

"I'm Isabelle Roussel, and I'm with the World Health Organization," the woman said. "There are some two dozen of us on the plane. We'll lay over in Cape Town for several days—meetings, and a visit to

298

Robben Island, to see where Mandela was imprisoned—on our way to a conference in Durban. Is that your destination?"

"No," Saul said. "I'll be staying in Cape Town for a while."

"Yet you're an American physician—"

"So—?"

"My research requires that I be in South Africa for meetings and a conference related to my work, but—I'm curious, and trust you will forgive my directness—why would an *American* doctor choose to go to South Africa at a time like this?"

"Sutton's Law," Saul said.

"Sutton's Law?"

"Willie Sutton was a famous American bank robber," Saul explained. "He was exceptionally clever, but occasionally he slipped and was caught, and when they asked him why he continued to rob banks, his answer was simple: 'Because that's where the money is.'"

"I see," Isabelle said. "And South Africa, of course, is where AIDS is."

Saul nodded. "Are *you* a physician?" he asked.

"I'm a statistician—an economist actually—what's called an econometrician these days. Given the work I've focused on, more of a *bio*-metrician than anything else. I have an appointment at the University of Montpelier but thanks to a grant I've taken a year's leave in order to work with the W.H.O. on a study having to do with what I expect you know something about: transmission patterns of HIV in migrant workers."

"Grim work," Saul said.

"But dull," Isabelle said, smiling.

Sitting in a window seat on the left side of the plane, Saul had to turn his head a full ninety degrees in order to see the woman, whom he judged to be in her early to mid-fifties. White-haired and slightly overweight, with strong, plain features, and wearing thick rimless glasses, she was neither attractive nor unattractive. She might have been, he found himself thinking, exactly what she was: an intelligent middle-aged professor.

"But how did you know I work with AIDS?" he asked.

"The newspaper noted that you were a physician, and here you are heading for South Africa. Why else would you be going there, unless it was for safari?" She gestured toward his left hand—to his wedding band. "Since you are a married man, if you were going on safari—on vacation—you would doubtless be doing so with your wife. Unless..."

"My wife is in the States, where our daughter is expecting her first child," Saul said. "And yes—I'm an AIDS doctor. In the States, I work at Kings County Hospital and Medical School, in Brooklyn."

Isabelle said she had visited New York ten months before for an international conference on malaria—her fourth time in New York, in fact—and had loved it as she always did. Not the most beautiful city in the world, she said—no Paris, Rome, or Prague—but a very *exciting* city. Her English was impeccable, and when Saul complimented her, she explained that she had been an *au pair* in New York City for eleven months when she was a young woman, and that English was the common language in her field of expertise and so she had been using it every day for many years. Their drinks arrived, and they continued to talk—about New York City, about their work, about past and future projects, and about people they knew in common, including, it turned out, several doctors Saul considered good friends: Peter Piot, director of the United Nations program on HIV/AIDS, and Gerald Friedland, director of AIDS treatment and research programs at Yale University.

When, to her question as to how long he would be in South Africa, he said was unsure—it depended on what projects he became involved in or could generate—and when she asked if his wife would be joining him in Cape Town, he replied that their timetable was contingent on the course of their daughter's pregnancy. Isabelle wore no wedding ring—no rings at all—and Saul did not ask if she were married or widowed, or if she had children or grandchildren.

When dinner arrived, Isabelle said that perhaps they could talk again after they had eaten, and she took out a copy of *Le Nouvel Observateur*, wished him a *bon appétit*, and proceeded to eat her dinner as if she were dining alone in a restaurant.

Saul picked at his food—he was not hungry, and he wondered if this was because of what he suspected, and feared, Jerry might do...or had already done. Other than that he was 'dull-as-toast,' and 'a good man'—whatever *that* meant—he also wondered what else Tolle had told Jerry about him, or if, it occurred to him, Tolle had even *said* these things to Jerry. Jerry had always been something of a bullshit artist, and he may have been inventing stuff so as to gain the upper hand—to intimidate Saul by making him jealous or, at the least, uneasy. It also occurred to him that Jerry might have wanted to make him *think* he was contemplating doing himself in order to make Saul, trapped in a plane high above the earth, feel some of what he was in fact now feeling: helpless and guilty.

But why was he worrying things so much? If Tolle had not been so absolute about their separation, and had not during their trans-Atlantic telephone conversations, persisted in her determination *not* to respond to his overtures about their working together at a reconciliation, would he have been *less* vulnerable to Jerry's digs, *less* worried about what Jerry might do?

And again, as he'd been doing since Tolle had flown off, he wondered if there were any truth to what she'd said about him not knowing her—not *truly* knowing her. But even if there were some truth to it, what was that nonsense about him never having experienced a broken heart? Didn't she remember the long talks they'd had about about the deaths of their siblings, Martin and Claire, and how he had told her in detail, especially during their first few weeks together, that he had been so saddened by Martin's death—so despairing—that he'd thought of following Martin into the next world? And too, all through his childhood and adolescence, what was he to do with his sadness given that his parents didn't allow Martin's name ever to be mentioned? And what could he do with the perpetual frustration he felt—and was encouraged by his mother to do so—that he had to be the perfect "good boy" in all things—household chores, school, appearance, manners—so as to accomplish the impossible: to make up for his father's polio-induced debilities, and for Martin's absence.

If he hadn't closed a door on that period of his childhood and locked away most of the feelings it generated, he recalled saying to Tolle—and saying what he did partly in the hopes of gaining the approval, sympathy, and love Tolle did actually come to bestow on him—how would he have ever gotten *anything* done, or achieved anything *of* his own and *on* his own in this life?

And hadn't Tolle told him—he could see her face again, full of what he took to be compassion and tenderness for what he'd been through—that what had been true for him had, in *her* family, been equally true for her?

Looking out the window and seeing nothing but soft fluffy gray-white clouds, he took comfort from the realization that he was far from people and places he knew—suspended between what-was and what-was-to-be—and was able to relax and let his mind drift freely more than he'd been able to in a long, long time.

He recalled how exciting it had been, their first evening together in the Chinese restaurant, to find not only that Tolle was pleased that he'd tracked her down at the police station—that a woman like Tolle might actually *like* him—but that they had a wealth of things in common, not least among them their shared passion—a mutual, magnificent obsession, they'd happily agreed—for Camus. And as adolescent and unreal as he'd come to believe her ongoing love for Camus was, he felt pleased to be able to acknowledge that what had frequently saddened *and* angered him was something he *had* been able to refrain from mentioning to her: his having lived for more than forty years with the knowledge, not that she'd had an affair with Camus, but that no matter what he did—or *who-he-was*—he would never be able to replace Camus in her heart.

But—he almost laughed out loud at the irony of the parallel—if he could acknowledge that Tolle would never replace Fiona in *his* heart—that he had enough room there for both of them because, sentimental fool that he was, he believed—like Camus?—that the more one loved the more one was capable *of* loving—then he decided he could live quite contentedly with what also seemed to be true: that even if she didn't know it, Tolle probably had enough room in her heart for both him *and* Camus.

Too bad, though, he thought, that he'd been unable to keep what he'd said to her to himself. Too bad, for sure. But perhaps, since he'd already forgiven himself for mentioning what he'd always known about her and Camus, eventually she would find a way to forgive him too.

He finished his glass of wine, asked for another and, glancing sideways, saw that Isabelle was reading an article about the tsunami in South Asia. He stared at the photos—homeless children, devastated villages, dead bodies—and considered tapping her on the shoulder in order to tell her what he was thinking; that, in the wake of the tsunami, which had occurred less than two months after he'd sent off his letter to President Bush, the offers of aid seemed to him to have constituted a kind of global pissing contest in which the United States and other nations, along with movie stars, rock stars, and assorted celebrities vied with one another to see who could raise and send the most money, the most workers, the most assistance.

He was, of course, for doing everything possible to help those left behind by the tsunami, but he also found himself thinking about what one would find if one went back to visit these people in a year, or in two, or in five: Where would the help be then for the reconstruction of lives and psyches? Who would be producing concerts and telethons, sending food, money, medicine, doctors, nurses, engineers…

The flight attendant brought him another glass of wine, and took away his dinner tray. He reached under his seat, took out the newspapers Jerry had given him, skimmed a front-page article in *Le Monde* about the war in Iraq, and realized that when Jerry had talked about Katherine (whom he had, on their ride to the airport, kept referring to as "The Widow Turetzky")—of how they'd met, and how things had ended—he could have told Jerry about how he and Tolle had met, and about how their years together had been book-ended by two ill-conceived and failed American wars: that they'd met at a protest against the war in Vietnam, and were parting, four decades later, because of the *sequelae* of a letter he'd written protesting the war in Iraq.

Beginnings and endings, did the man say?

When, a while later, a flight attendant took away their wine glasses, Isabelle turned to him and asked if it were true, from what he knew of South Africa, that men there believed they could be protected from HIV by having sex with a virgin, and that there was, *par conséquent*, a brisk business in securing and selling young women for this purpose.

Saul said that it was true.

Isabelle took out a sleep mask, said that she appreciated his frankness, and added that she appreciated even more what he had done during the demonstration in Spéracèdes—that it was an act of great bravery.

"Or stupidity," Saul said.

"That too," she said, smiling, "but—and this in no way takes away from what you did and, in fact, to my mind, makes it *more* admirable—I'm reminded that Aristotle considered bravery to be the mean between cowardice and foolhardiness."

"Ah, the famous golden mean," Saul said. "All things in moderation, including moderation—is that what you believe?"

"Well, for your sake—for *both* our sakes—I hope not," Isabelle said, "for if we did *all* things in moderation, what pleasure in life?"

She pushed her seat back, adjusted a pillow under her head, unfolded a blanket across her lap.

"But it *is* a rare to meet a man these days, whether French or American, who is truly *engagé*," she said, "and I will reiterate what I said before—that I admire what you did in Spéracèdes, as well as your going to South Africa to do your part to help contain the AIDS pandemic."

'What else can I do?' Saul thought of saying. 'I'm a doctor.'

He said nothing, however. Her insistence on repeating herself, he realized, along with her incessant showing-off, her name-dropping, her curious dragging in of Aristotle, and what he took to be an invitation he had no least desire to accept, was irritating him. Still, closing his eyes—the sleep mask over her eyes, Isabelle had turned away from him—he had every expectation that he would soon be asleep, and that he would—a happy thought—sleep more soundly than she would.

For although he was, after all, a sixty-eight-year-old man with cracked ribs, a broken nose, a split lip, a missing front tooth, and a heart condition—a man whose wife had left him, whose dearest friend in the world was dying of ovarian cancer, whose aging expatriate friend might in that very moment be performing the most absurd and definitive of acts—still, he was certain that he himself had many years of good work left in him, years in which he would comfort himself with the thought that although HIV and AIDS would be with us for the rest of human history, he would not.

Twenty-One

Because her visit with Julia had gone exceptionally well—Julia had been warm, talkative, ebullient, and affectionate—Tolle was dreading her visit with Fiona more than she had earlier in the day. For a while she had thought Julia might dread *any* mention of Fiona, yet when, halfway through their lunch Tolle said in passing that she would be visiting Fiona later in the afternoon, Julia had begun talking about Fiona—about her love *for* Fiona—in an effusive and passionate way she could not recall Julia ever talking about anyone or anything.

The time they had spent together, Julia said, was precious beyond understanding—ineffable, sublime, magical—and therefore could not be measured in weeks, days, hours, *or* words. Nor would she try to explain to Tolle or anyone else just how they could be measured, and she had quoted Fiona saying something about the nature of the ineffable being that it could *not* be expressed in words. What she *would* tell Tolle about, however, was the belief she and Fiona shared in the *sacredness of privacy*—Fiona's phrase—and in its relation to depth of feeling and, thus, to the possibility of true intimacy. Some of what they believed, and experienced, was in the letters they'd been exchanging since Fiona had been moved to a hospice, and perhaps one day she might share those letters with others. But for now...

While Julia continued to talk about Fiona—their letters, their last visit together eight days before—Tolle found herself thinking of what Camus had written to her in the last letter she'd received from him: about how it was only our will that kept us attached to others and, in a passage she'd long ago set to heart, about how contingent and accidental everything in what we called love or friendship was, for without love or friendship the world went back to darkness, and returned us to that great cold from which human tenderness had for a moment rescued us.

Hearing Camus' words again, she found herself wondering what Julia knew, or suspected, about her relationship to Camus other than that he had been the basis for a character named 'Camus' in a ballet she had produced a dozen years before Julia was born. And she wondered, too, as before, if Julia knew, or suspected, that Saul had been anything other than Fiona's mentor.

Julia was talking about how wonderful Felicia and Sam had been, how even though she felt just fine, and could easily get along without them—she had been sleeping well, had no nausea, had not gained too much weight, was swimming almost every day, and had been working regularly for a law firm on a *per diem* basis—she was pleased to have their company, and thrilled by their devotion to her. She absolutely *adored* Felicia, and was more than pleased to find that she and Sam were becoming closer than they'd ever been. And also, so it would not go unsaid, and she assumed Tolle felt the same, she rejoiced in the fact that Sam and Saul had, during the time in France, and since then, through e-mails and phone calls, begun to bury some old hatchets and were becoming close with one another. And these, she had emphasized, were only *some* of the most obvious things—the *large* things—that were making her appreciate the importance of family in her life, something she had, she confessed, never put much of a priority on.

Central to this, of course—her inspiration—was Fiona's example, for despite the fact that Fiona had, for years, been describing herself as a DCLC—a Devout Certified Lapsed Catholic—she had already had last rites performed, would allow a priest to give her the sacrament of extreme unction, and had agreed to be buried in the Catholic cemetery in Somerville where members of her family, on her mother's side, were buried.

"What cost to me?" Fiona had said, and it was the unadorned way she'd said it—no matter the complexities and ambivalences that might lie below her decision—that had initially caused Julia to reflect on her own relationship to her family. And these reflections had been profoundly influenced by Felicia and Sam, who, like Fiona, felt strongly about a life in which, for major life-events—birth, coming-of-age, marriage, and death—as well as for the daily, weekly, monthly, and seasonal rounds of ordinary life—there were rituals and traditions that tied us not only to one another, but to our past—to the people, history, and traditions that were ours by virtue of the families and communities into which we had been born.

When Tolle started to express regrets about not having provided anything resembling what religions and family—extended family especially—usually provided, Julia had stopped walking, and cut Tolle off by pressing two fingers against Tolle's mouth to silence her, after which she had given her a huge hug—they had had lunch at an outdoor café near Harvard Square, and were walking along Concord Avenue towards Julia's apartment—kissed her on both cheeks, grabbed Tolle by both ears, and pulled Tolle towards her so that their noses were almost touching.

"*I love you!*" she said then. "Do you *know* that? Have I remembered to tell you how *much* I love you?"

"I love you too," Tolle said, and added, "Of course..." and when she did, Julia had laughed, said she was aware she was making Tolle uncomfortable and, as they started walking again, had taken her mother's arm and had talked about how difficult she knew she'd been at times—her rebellious teenage years, of course, but even more the last dozen years or so, and that no matter what she'd done, especially with all those *guys* she'd had parading through her life one after the other, she had never felt abandoned—or judged—by Tolle *or* by Saul, and that was an incredible gift for which she would be forever grateful.

She and Fiona had had long talks about this since, never having had unconditional love from either of *her* parents. Fiona could understand, by its absence, just what it meant *to be* loved unconditionally.

Julia talked about having met Fiona's mother and four sisters, and said they were as described: her mother a vain, dull-witted, morbidly obese nervous wreck, and her sisters—except possibly for Megan—all nut-jobs, each one nuttier than the next. Fiona's father was long gone and, like Tolle's father—a grandfather Julia had never met—had been an abusive Irish drunkard without discernible redeeming qualities. By and by she would tell Tolle more about them, and perhaps Tolle could talk with her about *her* grandparents, and about the aunt—Claire—she'd never known, but that right now what she needed was to get home and take a nap.

But speaking of fathers, Julia said, reminded her that she'd had a conversation with *her* father—Saul—who had asked her to check in regularly on Tolle since he was worried about her being by herself in New York.

"Why would Saul worry about me being alone *now*?" Tolle said. "I've been alone many times when he was away at some medical convention, or at—"

"He worries about your *moods*, Mom," Julia said. "He worries about you becoming depressed. He worries about you hurting yourself. Not because he's in South Africa, or because of the troubles you two have been having, but because you've been depressed on and off your whole life, and that sometimes your depression—especially when you think you're *not* depressed—can rise up and do you in."

"I'm surprised," Tolle said.

"That he talked to me about your troubles?"

"No," Tolle replied. "I'm surprised about what he told you about how depression works in someone like me—that he noticed."

"And—?"

"And I've decided to hang around for a while so I can see what it's like to be a grandmother."

"And also to see if you can get a dance company started again, correct?"

"That too," Tolle said.

They were still several blocks from Fiona's apartment, and Julia stopped again, asked Tolle to give Fiona a hug and kiss for her and, depending on how conscious Fiona was, to explain again what she trusted Fiona had been told by one of Fiona's sisters, or by one of the nuns at the hospice: that Julia's doctor had strongly advised against her visiting Fiona for the usual reasons doctors didn't like pregnant women going into hospitals, nursing homes, or hospices.

She and Fiona, star-crossed lovers that they were, she said, would continue to keep romance alive by exchanging old-fashioned hand-written love letters the way other lovers did who were kept apart by the cruel jokes the gods delighted in playing on brilliant, beautiful, loving, and lovable young women.

"And we're all of the above, right?" Julia said, smiling.

"Indeed," Tolle said, at which point Julia said she had loved their time together but, assuring Tolle that she would be fine—that although she missed Fiona fiercely, she *enjoyed* being by herself these days, which was something new for her—she preferred to walk home the rest of the way by herself.

"I love you, Mom, but oh—I almost forgot to tell you—" she said, patting her stomach "—it's going to be a girl!"

"Oh my…" Tolle said.

"And I'm going to name her Fiona," Julia said, after which she gave Tolle a quick kiss, turned, and walked away.

Tolle found herself on Quincy Street, in front of the Harvard Faculty Club. She entered the Club, and an elderly, dark-haired woman welcomed her, asked if she had come for tea, which they would soon be serving in the library or, if she cared for something stronger, would she prefer to be seated in the conservatory.

"Actually," Tolle said, "I just wanted to *look* inside for a moment—I wasn't intending to enter. I seem to have lost my bearings a bit… but here I am, I suppose."

"Well, you are, aren't you, dear," the woman said.

"I used to come here a long time ago," Tolle explained. "When I was a little girl, I often came here with my father."

"Well, how lucky for you—and for us—that you found us again," the woman said. "But please do come in and rest for a while. And do at least take a glance at the conservatory, which was surely not here when either of us were girls. It's only been open for a few years, and we believe it's a marvelous addition, one in which we take pride."

Tolle let the woman lead her through the lobby, which looked familiar—lots of dark wood paneling and plush armchairs—into a sun-filled room where a glass cupola let in bright mid-afternoon light and illuminated a large moss-colored chandelier. Straw baskets and plant holders housing bamboo and ferns, white-arched trellises covered with fig vines, orchids on glass tables, an oriental rug in soft shades of salmon and teal at the room's center, striped pink-and-white fluffed pillows on wicker furniture, a massive bouquet of exotic flowers on a handsome buffet table, and the room barren of people...it took Tolle's breath away. Such an oasis of peace and quiet—of beauty—in a place that held some of the only pleasant memories she had of her father.

"It's lovely," Tolle said.

"Yes," the woman said. "It is quite something, we think. Others often have the reaction you're having, and that makes us believe our troubles were worth the effort. May I seat you at a table, or would you prefer to sit at the bar?"

"The bar, I think," Tolle said, and then: "I'm feeling a bit emotional, as you've clearly sensed. I just left my daughter Julia, you see—she's pregnant and lives nearby—I live in New York City—and only a few minutes ago she informed me that my grandchild is going to be a girl, and that..." Tolle stopped, set two fingers against her mouth "... and that her name is going to be Fiona."

"What a perfectly lovely name," the woman said. "My name is June. I'm the director of the Faculty Club, and I'm a grandmother many times over, so please allow me to offer you a congratulatory drink on this special day."

311

June seated Tolle at the bar, put down a place setting—napkin, silverware, plate, water glass—and informed Tolle that they would be serving complimentary appetizers in a short while.

"You've been very kind," Tolle said. "I'm a bit surprised at how nervous I am—how *affected*—a kind of delayed reaction to the good news, I suppose, although…"

Tolle looked past June, toward the entrance to the conservatory, and realized she was expecting—hoping—to see Camus enter.

"I'll leave you to your thoughts," June said. "If you need anything, now or later on, please do feel free to call upon me. Frank Corby, our barman, will be with you presently."

When the room was about half full—mostly middle-aged and elderly women, along with several men in business suits, but no students or young people—a man sat down next to Tolle at the bar, put out his hand, introduced himself as Mark Reilly, and began to make small talk. He wore a blue blazer and Harvard tie and, pointing to her empty wine glass, offered her a drink. Tolle thanked him and said that yes, she would appreciate another glass of wine.

The man continued to talk and when the wine came and he asked Tolle about herself, and what brought her to the Harvard Club, she told him what she had told June—that she was visiting from New York, that her daughter was living in Cambridge temporarily, and was pregnant, and that she had come here with her father—to the Club, not the conservatory—when she was a girl.

Her father had raised horses, Tolle said—thoroughbreds—and often, when one of his horses was running at Suffolk Downs, and especially—this was her recall of childhood days, and might not be fully accurate—when he'd had a winner they would come here to celebrate. Her father had loved holding forth about his horses, and also—what in her memory made those days so wonderful—had loved bragging about her to the other men.

Tolle said that on those days she had sometimes worn her favorite childhood outfit—a frilly white lace top, a pleated black satin skirt, and gold-tipped ballet slippers. To the man's questions—and his compliment: that she *looked* like a woman who had been a ballet dancer once upon a time—she said that yes, she had, as a child, and well into her adolescent years, been a dancer, and that her father had shown her off occasionally by having her do a few basic turns for the men.

She laughed, and said there was something else she was remembering that could, these many years later, be revealed: that although her father wore a Harvard tie, he had not gone to Harvard—had not even finished high school, in fact—and that he also owned ties that represented several of the other Ivy league schools—Yale, Princeton, Dartmouth, Columbia—and that before they left for Suffolk Downs—their horse farm was in the western part of Massachusetts—he would ask her to help him choose the tie-of-th- day. "'Would you fancy me a graduate of Harvard again,' he would say to me, 'or shall I be a Yalie this time?' and he would always add—the line I waited for—and with a wink, that his only true *ties* to Harvard and the other Ivy schools were, in fact... *ties!*"

"And I'll wager you another drink, and dinner too if, as I'm hoping, you're available, that he was an Irishman like me," Mark said.

"Oh he was Irish all right," Tolle said. "Thomas Callaghan Riordan of the County Cork Riordans."

"My family knew some Riordans," Mark said "and they were a rambunctious crew, even when they were *not* on the sauce!"

"Truth be told, with or without drink, my father was a cruel and nasty man most of the time," Tolle said. "And yet—I wonder why—those days with him, here and at the track, remain precious to me."

"I understand—oh I do," Mark said and, as if to emphasize how sympathetic he was, he let his hand rest on Tolle's lap.

Tolle stared at his hand.

"And I've won the bet, haven't I," Mark said. "So that you *are* available for dinner, I take it."

"No," Tolle said.

Mark unfolded his napkin, leaned toward her and, as he did, he dropped the napkin so that it lay above his hand.

"Ah but you're lovely, Miss Riordan," he said. "You must have been a great beauty in your time, as you remain, for you still have what it takes to set a man's blood to singing."

"Please remove your hand," Tolle said.

"And I have to say, if you'll allow me," Mark whispered, "that though I've met many a lovely lady in these environs, you've got that distinctive Irish charm that stirs both my heart *and* my loins."

Mark moved his hand along the inside of her thigh.

Tolle set down her wine glass, turned away from him, lifted a fork from the counter.

"Please remove your hand," she said again.

"And how I do love a lass who still has some fire left in her!" Mark said. "I had a feeling, when I saw you here by yourself, that—"

Tolle recalled a scene from a foreign movie—French? Spanish?— where a young girl, taunted at mealtime by another girl in an orphanage, stabs the other girl in the back of her hand, thereby nailing the girl's hand to their communal dining table. Deciding that using the fork would be too banal and melodramatic a gesture—that something more *personal* was required—Tolle set the fork down.

Touching the man's ear with an index finger, she gestured to him to come closer so that she could tell him something, and when he came closer, she blew into his ear lightly, then bit down on it until she tasted blood, after which she took the napkin he had placed on her lap, placed it in his hand, and had him press the napkin against his ear.

She stood, sipped the last of her wine—*pour refraicher la bouche un peu*, she thought—and walked toward the entrance where June, holding a silver tray of appetizers, was waiting.

"Thank you, dear," June said, in the same gracious manner she had used to welcome her to the Club. "You run along now, and enjoy the rest of your afternoon. We'll take care of this, and, I must add, we'll do so with great satisfaction."

Outside, to her surprise, she found that she was neither trembling nor breathing hard. She walked for several minutes until, at the intersection of Waterhouse Street and Massachusetts Avenue, she came to Cambridge Common. She sat and, happily, found herself part of a seemingly picture-perfect scene—mothers and nannies with small children, students playing frisbee, elderly couples strolling arm in arm, young lovers fondling one another—and she wondered how it could be that while they were doing what they were doing, and while she was taking pleasure in watching them, halfway around the globe young Americans of eighteen, nineteen, and twenty were dying even as, in concert with others, they were bringing about the deaths of untold numbers of other young men, along with thousands of men, women, and children who were not soldiers. And in South Africa, where Saul was now, hundreds if not thousands of people afflicted with AIDS and/or tuberculosis were suffering, and were dying excruciating, painful deaths, and elsewhere…

Once, when she and Saul were having after-dinner drinks in a favorite New York City French restaurant—a bistro on Broadway at 105th Street—Saul had done the arithmetic: if three-and-a-half-million people died of AIDS in a year, and you divided that by three-hundred-and-sixty-five, that meant that about nine-thousand people died of AIDS each day, and if you divided that by twenty-four, then you saw that about four-hundred people died of AIDS each hour, and if you multiplied that by the time they had been having dinner—two hours—you realized that approximately eight-hundred human beings had died during the time they had been eating…and that such figures did not take into account the untold grief and misery these deaths brought to all those who knew, loved, and were dependent upon these people.

Camus, she thought, would have responded to Saul's mathematical sermon more positively than she had—she never underestimated the planet's ongoing tragedies, she'd said, but please: does my *not* enjoying a glass of wine make life better for some poor person on the other side of the world?—and she looked around, and wondered if Camus might happen by and sit beside her so she could share her thoughts with him, and—what she longed to do—tell him about what she'd done to the man at the Harvard Faculty Club… or had Camus been there watching? And would he recall, on their last morning together—at a time in her life when she was still bold, brash, and wickedly self-confident—her warning him that although she would do all she could to make the two of them supremely happy, and happily productive, she could also be persistently ruthless?

Or had she said that she could be ruthlessly persistent? No matter, she thought. What *did* matter was that what she'd said to him about being ruthless had freed her to talk with him about a time she had decided to end her life, and of how reading his essays—not, curiously enough, his novels or stories, which she had told him she *preferred* to his essays—had enabled her to put away her vain desire to leave this world, a desire that had persisted intermittently throughout her life, and in its most recent incarnation, upon her arrival in Spéracèdes with Saul, had returned.

This time, however—she trusted Camus would not feel slighted—her desire to leave the world had departed not by reading his prose, but by watching Saul being attacked at the rally that followed the burial of Doctor Bertrand's wife and son. She thought of what awaited her on her return to New York—the appointments with the bank and realtors to finalize her taking a lease on a space for her dance company; her meetings with several people she hoped to persuade to be on her board, especially Carolyn Brown, who had been Merce Cunningham's principal dancer and was an old friend of Tolle's mother; and interviews and auditions scheduled for several young dancers and choreographers. On Friday evening she and Katherine would be having dinner—Eugene, with whom Katherine was staying while in New York for several performances they had scheduled, would not join them—and she and Katherine would be able to talk about Jerry and his sudden passing, news of which, but without details, Katherine had given her the previous week.

The more she thought about her return to New York, the more she became aware that no matter how long she sat in this lovely park on this enchanting spring day, Camus was not going to make an appearance. He had, clearly, made a decision not to visit with her today, but not *ever* to visit with her again—not *ever* to be there for her to talk with him—not even in his silent, ghostly guise…?

For the moment, she comforted herself with the thought that she could always reread his books and journals—and there were, still, unpublished journals that would eventually appear in print—and she could, as ever, conjure up memories of him and of their brief time together. The one that now came to mind—no surprise—was of the two of them at Nijinsky's tomb, her watching him caress Petrushka's stone cheek with the back of his hand. Without closing her eyes, she could hear his voice again, telling her that he had been drawn to Nijinsky's madness because it made him aware of his own desire, not to *be* mad, but to be able to leave reason behind and, thus, not to be in bondage to its dictates.

And she could, with pleasure, see his face again, so boyishly attentive, while she told him the story that had inspired her ballet, and of the time—after having lived as a recluse and madman for three decades, and in a time when he was not institutionalized, and in a moment when people were celebrating the end of the war—Nijinsky had gone out into the world once more, had come to life, and had danced again.

Tolle left the park, and began to find her way to Concord Avenue again—Fiona was living at Sancta Maria Nursing Facility, a hospice run by the Daughters of Mary of the Immaculate Conception—and what occurred to her was that even though her great desire now was not to *dance* again, which at her age would be an absurd ambition, but to create dances *others* could perform, and to see those dances into production, this did not mean she had to disavow writing stories.

There was no reason, she reasoned, why she could not in the coming months and years, do both: set down her stories on the page at the same time that she created ballets more or less modeled on stories she had written. She might also, it occurred to her, as with the story of her meeting with Camus and their visit to Montparnasse Cemetery, write both an embellished account of an actual experience—a true event deliberately transformed into fiction—as well as a non-fictional account of an actual experience, knowing full well it was literally impossible to write a *completely* true account of an actual experience since—as she'd said to Camus in a sentence he'd promised to steal and make his own—imagination was forever messing with memory.

When she was still a good twenty minutes' walk from Fiona's

hospice, she checked her watch, saw that it was already a half hour later than the time—four o'clock—she had said she would be arriving, and she stopped, and telephoned the hospice. When a receptionist answered, Tolle identified herself and explained that she had an appointment to visit with Fiona Casey at four o'clock but was running late. Might she speak with someone at the nurses' station on Fiona's floor.

The receptionist asked her to wait, and a moment later a woman came on, and as soon as Tolle began to apologize for her lateness, the woman, who identified herself as Sister Margaret, interrupted and said that she had some very sad news: Fiona had passed away quietly at about three o'clock that afternoon. A nurse had checked in on her at one-thirty, had found Fiona sleeping peacefully, and when the nurse checked in again at three o'clock, Fiona was gone.

Tolle asked if they had informed Fiona's family, and Sister Margaret said they had spoken with one of Fiona's sisters. Had they informed Fiona's friend Julia? Sister Margaret said they had not.

Tolle imagined Fiona asleep and, thanks to the fact of dying in a hospice and not in a hospital—Saul had, through Julia, persuaded Fiona's family that this was the *merciful* course of action—she would not have had drains, wires, and tubes going in and out of body and face. There would have been, she hoped, only oxygen and a single morphine drip, and for this, Tolle assumed, everyone, Fiona included, was grateful.

On the train from New York to Boston, Tolle had fantasized a deathbed scene wherein Fiona, her eyes closing, had said that it was time to go—to sleep what they told her would be the sleep of angels, though she remained skeptical of the metaphor's aptness—and Tolle, taking her hand, would have asked if Fiona wanted company on her journey. If so—it would depend for Tolle on the day, hour, or moment, she would say—she might find herself prepared to join her.

She imagined Fiona smiling at the offer, saying no thanks—she would be fine on her own—and then changing the subject and saying that the proof there was no *true* justice in the world was not that she was dying before her forty-third birthday, but that she was *not* dying of the demon virus that had infected and destroyed the many men, women, and children whose deaths, early and late, she had been helpless to prevent. Instead…

Tolle put her cell phone back in her purse, turned around, and began to walk back towards the center of Cambridge, and Julia's apartment. That Fiona was not yet forty-three had reminded her that Camus had been only forty-six when he had been taken from the world. She wished, a familiar impulse, not to have to think about anyone or anything, but taking her cell phone in hand again and thinking of calling someone—*anyone!*—she recalled the time her father had collapsed at the Harvard Faculty Club. He had been standing upright one minute, laughing and braying, and the next minute he was flat on his face and could not be awakened. She had walked away, wandered around the Club until she found a telephone booth, had entered the booth, pulled the booth's doors closed behind her, dialed the operator, and said she wanted to make a collect call from Tolle Riordan to her mother—"It's to my *mother!*" she recalled saying to the operator's demand that she give her the name of the person to whom she was calling—and had given the operator her home phone number.

When her mother came on the line, Tolle told her that her father had been drinking *a lot,* and had fallen asleep on the floor. Her mother told her to ask someone at the Club to find a taxi or car service, and to get in the car and take her father home—that she would pay the driver when they arrived. Tolle did what her mother said—she could recall watching two men hoist her father into the car's back seat—but her mother had not, when she and her father arrived home, thanked her for what she'd done. And yet on that day she'd felt as triumphant and *in control* as she could ever remember feeling. "I'm eight years old but everyone says I'm terribly grown-up," she said to the driver when he asked her age, and years later, when returning again and again to this day from her analyst's couch, she had also, as if to a recurring dream, come to understand that she had felt many other things…

She wished she'd been able to tell Camus the story, and to have a

319

conversation with him about it—about what she thought and felt now, and had thought and felt once upon a time. And she also wished she could tell him that while she was talking with Sister Margaret about Fiona, she had found herself thinking about something he had once said to her very directly, without qualifications—what he had written about often, if more *in*directly: that it was precisely *because* life was absurd, that it had meaning.

She had told him that she agreed with what she called his 'sentiment,' and he had professed mock-fury that she would call his belief a *sentiment*, and then…

I miss you, she wanted to tell him. I truly miss you.

She had never told Saul the story about the day she brought her father home from Cambridge. After she arrived at Julia's apartment and gave her the news, and in the evening, when Julia and Sam were asleep and she was in her room at the Hotel Charles, she would telephone Saul—by then, past midnight her time, it would be early morning in Cape Town—and she would talk with him about Julia and Sam. Although she knew it would be better to wait until they were together, she just *might* tell him about what had happened at the Harvard Faculty Club, and of how it had led to her remembering the time, as a girl, she had been in charge of bringing her father home.

But before that—now!—she would call and tell him that Fiona had died, and she was, she realized, eager to do so—to be the messenger of what would surely be wounding news. And later, after her visit with Sam and Julia, she might ask him about *his* plans, and if he would be returning to New York soon. She expected he would ask her what she meant by her question, and she would be evasive. Certainly she would not, by telephone, tell him what she had been thinking: that perhaps, given all they had lived through together, they could become to each other what young people these days often claimed they were to each other: friends with benefits.

Despite all, she reasoned, for the most part, she and Saul did still respect one another and, when together, they did get along reasonably well—had rarely fought the way other couples of their acquaintance

320

did—and their sex life, remarkably, remained pleasurable and, at times, adventurous. Saul's recent physical setbacks notwithstanding, she believed they could have more than a few good years together, although—she imagined Saul smiling in agreement—she would admit there were probably fewer years ahead than those that lay behind.

There was of course the ever-present possibility, as she had said to Fiona, that she could be seduced to exit this world by the promise of those things one rarely if ever experienced in a single moment if at all: peace of mind, relief from pain, an end to loneliness and despair, the expectation of a future that held no disappointments, the sweetness of wreaking guilt and vengeance upon the living, the thrill of commiting a crime without a punishment and, what one imagined, in prospect, would be absolute control of the moment and manner of passing from this life. And when she talked with Saul about his plans and, possibly, about *their* plans, the question she could hear him ask, if teasingly, and in order to retaliate for the words she had used to tell him about why their separation had been necessary, was whether or not whatever they did would—fortunately—always be too late.

JAY NEUGEBOREN is the author of 22 books, including five prize-winning novels, four collections of award-winning stories, and two prize-winning books of non-fiction. His stories and essays have appeared widely in *The New York Review of Books*, *The Atlantic Monthly*, *The American Scholar*, *The New York Times*, *The Wall Street Journal*, *Ploughshares*, *Tablet*, and *Commonweal*, among others, and have been reprinted in more than 50 anthologies, including *Best American Short Stories*, and *The O. Henry Prize Stories*. He is the recipient of fellowships from the Guggenheim Foundation, the National Endowment for the Arts, and the Massachusetts Council on the Arts, and is the only author to have won six consecutive Syndicated Fiction Prizes. His archive is housed at the Harry Ransom Humanities Center in Austin, Texas.